DEATH BY ASSOCIATION

R. Z. CROMPTON

Zoller Publishing, Inc.
P. O. Box 461661
Aurora, CO 80046

Book cover design by:
Horsley Enterprises
Rapid City, South Dakota

Library of Congress Cataloging-in-Publication Data

R. Z. Crompton

CIP 95-71134

ISBN 0-9649438-0-8

This book is dedicated to:

my two darling daughters, whose faith in my abilities never wavered,

my cynical husband, who spurred my tenacity for success,

Michael, my most valued reader, and

my sister, who gave me so much more than verbal support.

Death by Association

"Once in a Blue Moon a person has the opportunity to answer a new challenge. I thank God for helping me hear mine."

by R. Z. Crompton

Death
by
Association

Death by Association

CHAPTER ONE

"Mrs. Carson? Mrs. Rachael Carson?" As the uniformed police officer at the front door loomed over her, uncontrollable fear swept through Rachael's body. The evil red glow of his eyes raised the hair on the back of her neck nearly choking off her ability to breathe. The man was surrounded by thick gray fog that slithered in around her feet slowly twisting its way up her body until it seemed to be engulfing her entire world. Rachael didn't want to hear the words: the same words she heard every time she opened the door to the fog and the giant man who forced her to hear his pronouncement of death again and again.

"Mrs. Rachael Carson, your husband is . . . "

"No!" Rachael screamed. She could feel herself falling slowly backward, back into the fog that swallowed her up and sent her spiraling down into the dark endless tunnel. She fell, swirling downward, grasping for something to stop the descent; but her fingers could find nothing for support. At the top of the dark abyss, the face of the police officer was clearly visible through the fog. His fiery eyes seared her soul as she heard him repeat the haunting word: "DEAD DEAD DEAD"

"Help me! Helllllpppp . . . meeeeeeeeee," the desperate cries echoed around her as she fell endlessly through the darkness.

Rachael sprang up in her bed with her arms folded around her body. Tears of fear mixed with perspiration rolled down her face, and she rocked slowly back and forth. As reality gradually pushed back the subconscious fear, Rachael realized the nightmare; it was the nightmare that was trying to suck the breath of life from her again.

Death by Association

Jack's tragic death two years ago was the reason for the nightmare; even though the dreaming had not started right away, it now seemed to be a regular part of her life, and it was always the same. Rachael would be standing at the front door watching the eerie gray fog creep in around her feet. The policeman seemed to grow larger right before her eyes until he was towering over her forcing her backward, and then she was falling. His wicked laughter mixed with her own cries for help created a haunting vibration that shook her very soul. She continued spiraling downward endlessly until her involuntary screams woke her and, probably, the whole neighborhood out of a deep sleep.

Why was she so afraid? It hadn't really been that way. Why did the dream terrify her so? Each time Rachael woke up trembling with fear, she reminded herself that the policeman had really been very considerate and soft spoken. He was truly sorry he was telling her that her husband had been killed when a car struck him throwing him off his bike. So why the ominous feelings of doom? Was it a warning of some kind? Rachael was sure the nightmare was more than just grieving thoughts about Jack because the fear it sparked in her was stronger than the feelings of loneliness. As the fear subsided, the warm loving memories of their relationship began to soothe her raw nerves.

Rachael had always felt her life had not had much meaning until she had married Jack. The two of them had dated for only six weeks before deciding to marry. They enjoyed each other's company, but more importantly they could make each other laugh. There was no doubt in her mind that he was the man of her dreams; and now, it seemed, everything brought back images of him.

"Mom, Mom! Are you all right?" the girls questioned as they ran into the room. Aurora and Allison, her two teenage daughters, didn't always wake up when she had the nightmare; but as the episodes became more intense so did her screams. The girls slept upstairs in the two story brick house, so there was always a delay in their arrival; but the thunder of their running had told Rachael her daughters were on their way.

"Yes, I'm fine. Thanks for getting up." Rachael gave each of the girls a hug and then reached out to caress Chance, the big yellow dog on the bed next to her. He always wanted his fair share of the attention. Allie sat on the bed next to him.

The girls looked at each other. They were worried about their mother, but she made it difficult for them to help her. As the older sister, Aurora, or Rorie among friends and family, decided it was time to push the issue again. "Mom, we think you need to talk to someone about this nightmare you keep having."

"I know what you think, and I'll tell you the same thing I always do. I won't see any therapist."

"Mom, this is crazy." Rorie hadn't meant to imply her mother was nuts, but Rachael didn't appreciate her choice of words.

Rorie quickly tried to retract her words when she noticed her mother's stiffening reaction. "Sorry. I didn't mean that *You* are crazy, but not wanting to find someone who can help you is crazy."

"Rorie!" Allison tried to get her sister to close her mouth. "Are you finished choking on your big feet yet? You're not helping." After silencing her older sister, Allison turned her attention to her mother. "Mom?"

"Yes, dear? Give me your best shot, but I still won't see a therapist."

"Fine, don't see anyone, but at least do something that will get you out of this house. You've got to start living again, or this dreaming will just continue to get worse. Why don't you find one of your old friends to play tennis with?"

"Yeah, Mom. That's a great idea, Allie."

"I can't even look at my racquet without seeing your dad's face across the net giving me that 'Howard Cosell' commentary he was so good at."

"He certainly could make us laugh, couldn't he? Remember how he used to run across the floor to be the first one to put foot prints on your freshly vacuumed carpet?"

"I remember; it used to make me so angry at him when he did it just to be cute."

"Yeah, he used to think you were nuts for vacuuming every day."

"I still do, but at least you girls don't run across the rug as soon as I leave the room."

The girls smiled at each other, "No, but the thought does cross our minds. We just can't do it as funny as he did and get away with it."

"I can still see you girls jumping on the trampoline with him."

"Yeah, until we all fell over each others legs."

"I could never tell if we were laughing because we fell or fell because we were laughing."

"Your dad loved you girls so much. You were his whole life. I never knew any man who was so devoted to his girls."

"That included you too, Mom. You never saw Dad look at you the way we did. His whole world revolved around you." Allie and Rorie both tried to control the tears filling their eyes. This reminiscing did not help get their mother out of the house.

"Mom, we miss Dad too; but he wouldn't want you to stay cooped up in the house this way. It wasn't his style. You know that. He had a zest for life that filled all of us."

"I know, honey. It just hurts me so much to think of him dying alone the way he did. I wish I could've been there for him. He hated being alone."

"Mom, you have to stop reliving that day. I know you can't forget and it's okay, but it's time to put his death behind you."

"Can I bring you a cup of tea to help you relax?"

"I'd like that, Allie. Let Rorie go make the tea so she'll stop badgering me about getting out of the house."

Allie was quick to defend her sister because she shared the same concern about her mother's welfare. "I'll get the tea because Rorie is tougher than I am, and we agree about your future. If you don't get out of this house, Mom, you won't have a future."

"C'mon, girls. I appreciate your concern, but you really are exaggerating. I do get out of the house almost every day."

Allie shook her head as she left the room, but Rorie wouldn't stay quiet. "You go to the grocery store or to the cleaners. You used to play tennis three or four times a week. You loved working with your flowers, walking the dog and going to the mall. We used to travel three or four times a year. You haven't left town since Daddy died. Remember all those fancy dresses you used to wear when you went on business trips with him? Allie and I found most of them packed away in the attic. We went through them remembering each occasion and Dad's reaction. He loved seeing you all dressed up. Mom, it was like looking at your life all packed away."

Rachael knew her daughters were right. Jack wouldn't like the way she had curled up inside of the past. It was time for her to focus on the outside and the living. Living in memories fueled the nightmare that was draining the little vitality she had left.

Rachael was a beautiful woman in her early 40's. Before Jack's death, she had always exercised and watched her diet. Her long legs and slim waist were the perfect host to most fashions. It was not unusual for strangers to assume Rachael was the girls' older sister rather than their mother. They all had a good laugh at that mistake, especially Jack since Rachael was even older than he. Now, however, she was too thin. There was no sparkle to her eyes, and the gray circles under them emphasized the ghostly pallor of her skin.

Allie came back into the room walking around the corner of the bed to hand her mother the hot cup of tea. "So has Rorie convinced you it's time to change the routine around here?"

"Maybe. Now you two get to bed. Your alarms will be ringing before you know it. We'll talk about this more when you get home from school."

The girls left their mother lying on her bed sipping tea with Chance at her side. "Old Chancy will keep her company tonight, Allie. We'll break her down eventually if we keep working on her. Did you add some honey to her tea?"

"Yeah, but a few teaspoons of honey won't help her to put some weight on."

"I know, but it won't hurt her either."

"Chance keeps her company every night, but that's not the type of male company she needs."

"Would you like to hog tie some man, put a ribbon around his neck, and have him delivered?"

"Creates an interesting possibility, but she'd just scribble 'return to sender' on his forehead and stuff him in the mailbox. You know how stubborn she can be."

"She also has a tenacious spirit, so eventually we'll get her to open the doors and let the sun back in. Will you be home to make supper? We have to make sure she eats every night because if she cooks, it's only enough for us."

"I know. I started watching her after you told me that. You were right. She'll make us something and go tutor a student, but she never comes back out to eat. Do you think she's not eating on purpose?"

"Of course not. Don't be silly. Besides, I already thought about that. When Daddy was alive, Mom always got up early with us and had breakfast; and she still does. For lunch she always drank that high protein, no fat, no sodium stuff; and she still does because there are always more cans in the cupboard after she goes shopping. The only thing that has changed is we would eat while she was tutoring, and she would eat with Daddy later. Now she'd have to eat alone. All we've got to do is make sure one of us is eating about the time she gets done with her last student."

"Rorie, supper time was never a major family event around here. We were always so busy, and Dad would get home anytime between noon and midnight. Mom never planned big meals during the week."

"I know, but they always went out two or three times a week; so that made up for the nights she didn't eat. Now she never goes out."

"You're right. I'm just so worried about her. Let's see, tomorrow I think her last student is done by seven o'clock. I'll get something ready for us. What time will you be home?"

"About six. We better get to bed. Good night."

"Good night."

Rachael rubbed Chance's soft yellow ears. He didn't like having his nightly slumber interrupted and had barely moved during all of the commotion. Only a strange sound from outside could raise him off his part of the bed.

The picture on the night stand stared back at Rachel as she set the cup down. The empty spot in her heart ached as if a giant log was slowly squashing all of the life out of her. The day Jack died she had fallen into a deep black pit. She looked into the hazel eyes that had caught her attention. To the critical eye, Jack was not necessarily handsome; however, he was attractive in a healthy athletic sort of way. His thick mahogany colored hair with flecks of gray framed a round face that was tan most of the year. Rachael especially enjoyed Jack's broad shoulders and thick muscular chest covered with soft hair. He was thoughtful and kind; and her years with him were all a woman could have hoped for. He had become her hero, and now she was alone.

Rachael turned off the lights and put her arm around Jack's pillow. She closed her eyes seeing images of Jack and the girls playing in the yard. The girls. *You aren't alone. You have to take care of the girls. They need you now that their father is gone. They need you!* Rachael's conscience finally broke through some of the grief making her realize that for the sake of her daughters, she had to move on, past the grief.

Rachael sat up in bed turning the light back on. She reached over and took the picture of Jack off the night stand. *My dearest Jack, I have to put your picture away for just a little while. It's just not healthy for me to go to sleep thinking only of you. I have to think of your girls - our daughters. They have to stop worrying about me and live a full happy life like we had. I'll do a good job for you. I promise.* The final tears of good-bye ran down her face as she opened the drawer putting the picture safely inside. Tomorrow she'd get out some pictures of the girls to put in that spot. This time when she turned off the lights, she deluged her mind with thoughts of the girls and their futures.

At seventeen, Rorie looked like her mother with long naturally curly brown hair. Her tall, lean well-proportioned body had been attracting looks from admirers for a long time. Intellectually, she resembled her father with a quick logical mind. She was the organized child always making lists for herself and setting schedules to follow.

Rorie was headed for a career in the life sciences. Her love for dolphins and the sea would probably take her on to Texas A & M for an education in marine biology. When she was not studying, Rorie found great pleasure in playing her saxophone. She had become an excellent musician and band member, traveling all over the country with the high school marching band and jazz band.

Allison was eighteen months younger than her sister. About four inches shorter than Rorie, Allie was just a little jealous. She didn't appreciate the fact that Rorie had gotten the height, the curly hair, and the bust line she had wanted. However, Allison was a beauty in her own right. Her hair was a softer brown with relaxed curls. She had an easy smile and warm laughter that made everyone want to be her friend. Her special devotion to animals was leading her into the field of veterinary medicine. When she had the opportunity, she worked for Dr. Carely, the family vet.

Allison's imagination inspired her to write mysteries. She had one teenage mystery published and was working on her second. Rorie helped Allie with some of the plot outlines and the computer work. Allie felt that sitting at the computer hampered her creativity, so Rorie had become her technical partner and resource person. It was a great way for the girls to make some money and keep them at home.

Rachael knew they had given up a lot of their time to stay home with her. Thinking back over the months made it obvious to her now that they stayed home because they were worried about her. She was grateful, and now it was time for her to give them back their lives. Tears filled her eyes and washed down her face until, somehow, the darkness of the room faded into sleep.

CHAPTER TWO

As a gust of wind played with the car, Alex Zamora's strong lean fingers gripped the steering wheel. Alex caught a glimpse of himself in the rear view mirror; his ebony black hair was definitely graying and not just at the temples thanks to the stress of the last couple of years. The monotony of the highway was a welcome escape from the turbulent months that had just passed. His successful life as a surgeon had been shattered when Heather, his wife, had been arrested for conspiracy to commit murder.

The investigation and trial dragged on day after day until Alex felt comatose. At first he was angry at the police and prosecutor for disturbing his happy and stable life, or what he had thought was a happy and stable life. Eventually, he directed his anger toward his wife where it belonged, and finally at himself for being so naive as to have been duped by her display of wifely devotion. By the time the long days and seemingly endless courtroom hours had sucked all of the anger out of him, he felt numb inside.

Alex had worked what was considered normal doctor hours: long and erratic, but he had thrived on his life at the hospital. Energy begat energy, and he felt fulfilled. However when fatigue set in, Alex was glad to retreat to his sanctuary where he assumed Heather, soft and beautiful, would always be waiting for him. She had given him the peace and tenderness he needed after the long hours of surgery. Surprise! Surprise! Her love, their life together, had been an illusion. He had been living his fantasy, and she had been living hers.

Now, every waking moment was haunted by the mental replay of the scene that had changed his life. The police were reading Heather her rights; she just stood at the front door staring into space as if she could will her soul to leave her body. Alex assumed she was in shock. The words of the officer grew faint as Alex realized the life he had known was dying, and no medicine or surgery could save it. In spite of all his education and experience, Alex's gut feeling was that he couldn't stop the passage of the life he had shared with Heather and their son Mark.

Alex had called John Malcomb, a good friend and attorney, as soon as he regained some composure. John had arranged for the three of them to meet at the police station. Heather, unable to control her crying, sat at the head of the table with Alex on one side and John on the other.

"Heather, how did you get tied up with the guy? Did you even know him? How could they possibly believe you helped him kill his wife?" It never dawned on Alex that his wife could have been having an affair. It just wasn't possible.

Alex was almost yelling at Heather, "Stop crying! You have to help us figure this out. Tears won't solve the problem." Alex noticed the tears streaming down her tanned face. Her sun bleached hair was disheveled but still shimmering with all of its soft alluring beauty. Touched when he saw the tears falling onto her wedding ring, Alex reached out and took her hand - it was cold and trembling. He softened his tone. His shouting had been a mask for his own emotions; and as his tone fell, so did his mask. The tears welled up in his eyes, and his voice began to crack, "Heather, tell us . . . "

John motioned for Alex to leave the room. Alex felt relieved to have the opportunity to get some fresh air. He had to concentrate on taking long breaths in order to get some control of his emotions. He felt helpless and at the mercy of a system he didn't understand. Now, desperate for help, he needed a friend.

Alex had always respected John. His reputation as a lawyer was impeccable and his ethics above reproach. John had talked often about the law, and his dedication to his clients was just as strong as Alex's was to his patients. Now Alex knew how desperate the relatives of his patients felt. Alex didn't understand the law any better than John had understood medicine when his daughter had to have a minor tumor removed from her left lung. Even though Alex knew the tumor was not really life threatening, the word *tumor* sparks fear in every parent. John had trusted Alex to do the very best for his daughter; now Alex had to trust John to do the very best for Heather. Alex, at that moment, believed what was best for Heather was best for him; and that was for her to get out of this mess. John would set the record straight: straight and sharp like a scalpel through Alex's heart.

John opened the conference room door looking for Alex. Heather had already been escorted back to her cell. "Alex, we have to talk privately. You're not going to want to hear this. I'm sorry."

"John, tell me what to expect. I want to know the bottom line."

"Let's go back to my office, Alex, where we can have more privacy and a drink. You need a chance to catch your breath and absorb what's happening."

John was right. Alex was anxious to get out of the station and onto more friendly ground. He felt everyone at the station was the enemy and he was their prey. He was sure all eyes were staring at them as they walked through the lobby of the police station. As John and Alex escaped the building, several people did glance at them. The sight of two tall, handsome, well-dressed men always caught the attention of the women in the area.

John was definitely the better dresser of the two. He felt his appearance was important to his career, so all of his suits were tailored by the finest shops in Chicago and New York. John was not actually arrogant about his looks; however, he had the money and enjoyed looking his very best. Without the fine clothes and expensive haircuts, John was good looking but not breathtaking.

Alex, on the other hand, was breathtaking. His six-foot four inch frame was contoured with hard lean muscles. Being a doctor had made him conscious of his own body, but Alex had never given much stock to being good looking. His looks didn't serve him in the operating room; however, being in good health did. His thick coal black hair was just starting to gray at the temples, and his square chin was softened by the broad smile that normally adorned his face.

Alex and John returned to John's office on Michigan Avenue in downtown Chicago. John came to stand by Alex at the window after he made a couple of phone calls to collect some information. Both men, savoring the aroma and taste of the fine French Cognac, stood staring out the windows of John's huge corner office. The lights of Chicago glittered below them as they stared down the Magnificent Mile. The skyline of Chicago had no equal.

John took a deep breath and softly said, "She's guilty, Alex. The evidence that will be found, if not already on the prosecutor's desk, will be staggering. Heather and Masterson planned it together. Their affair had been going on for several months, and they were seen together several times at various restaurants and hotels. In the beginning, they just didn't pay much attention to who might see them together or where. The prosecution will be able to place them at the Drake Hotel and the Stopher Riviera, where they've signed in together several times over the last six months. They were seen at the restaurants together and even had room service, each signing their real name."

"Just because they were having an affair doesn't mean Heather helped Masterson plan to murder his wife."

"You're right, and it would be easy to get her off if that's all I had to worry about. Unfortunately, the cause of death was an overdose of Valium. It was supposed to look like a suicide, but Masterson's wife was never given a prescription for Valium. It was

Heather's doctor who had written a prescription obviously for Heather. Both doctors will be asked to testify for the prosecution. That alone will tie Heather to the plan. In addition, Heather told me she handled all of the medicine vials when the pharmacists handed them to her. She never thought to wipe her finger prints off. If Masterson did, then he wiped off the pharmacist's prints also. Either way, prints or no prints, it will look bad for the defense.

Still not wanting to believe, Alex questioned, "Why didn't she just ask for a divorce?"

"Divorce wasn't an option they even considered. You have to realize they either weren't thinking rationally or intelligently, or they wouldn't have left such an easy trail. Between the two of them, there wasn't enough money to last a year, at least not in the style they enjoyed. As far as they were concerned, they had to have money; and that meant murder."

"I can't believe you make it sound so matter-of-fact. She's guilty! That's it? No trying to save her? No plea bargaining? Nothing!"

"Alex, you can get another lawyer. In fact, that may be a good idea. I think I may be too close to this. She told me things she probably wouldn't have told a stranger. With what she said and the additional information I picked up from my friend in the District Attorney's office, I pieced together this story. If I could do it in a matter of minutes, I know the prosecution won't have any trouble doing it in a matter of days. I can represent her; but now that I know what she did, it's difficult for me to have her plead 'not guilty.' She didn't come right out and say, 'yes, I committed murder.' She did, however, answer all of my question without raising her voice or shedding a tear. I'm sorry, really sorry. I had a feeling, a gut feeling, that she was involved. Maybe, I shouldn't have asked the questions so bluntly. The first thing I always ask a potential client is if he committed the crime. I like to believe my client is innocent before I take a case."

"Why, John? Do you always have to win? What kind of doctor would I be if I only took the patients I knew I could heal?"

"Not a very good one, but this is different, Alex. Just knowing the law isn't enough to get someone acquitted. I know it sounds terrible, but a lot of acting goes into being a good lawyer. It's part of the job because when I get in front of a jury, I have to convince each person in that jury box my client is innocent. It's much easier when the client hasn't admitted to having committed the crime. You know if your patient has cancer or not. You don't have to convince twelve people that the disease is really there."

"I'm sorry. This mess isn't your fault. It's hers . . . and mine. I had hoped you could make it go away. Kinda like removing a tumor. You know what I mean?"

"I wish I could, Alex. I'll give you the best legal counsel I can and give you the name of an excellent criminal attorney. I'll also give you the support a friend needs. You said you wanted the bottom line? Are you sure? Before you exhaust your financial and emotional resources on Heather, you should know it could have been worse."

Alex wasn't ready for John's gut wrenching revelation. "How can it get worse, John? There's nothing worse than murder."

"There could've been two, Alex."

"Two what?"

"Come on, Alex. Haven't I told you enough to make you realize, as sloppy as they were, they did have a plan? You were the second part of the plan."

It took a moment or two for John's meaning to sink into Alex's unbelieving mind; but he knew it was true. Heather and her lover had not only intended to commit one murder; they had intended to kill him also.

Death by Association

The rest of the trial sequence was just routine. John did handle Heather's case for the benefit of Alex. Alex hadn't wanted a stranger getting into his life at this point. John had been right: the evidence was staggering. Alex couldn't believe the two of them had been so stupid.

Finally, the day Alex had feared and yet longed for arrived. Heather and John were waiting for the jury to return to the courtroom. Alex was seated right behind them feeling nauseated from the anxiety. Heather had never talked about the affair or the murder. After her first session with John, she never admitted to anything again. She wouldn't even see Alex. Even though he sat right behind her every day in the courtroom, she never acknowledged his presence. Alex didn't know if she was really so ashamed of what she'd done that she couldn't face him, or did she just hate him that much? Eventually, Alex realized it didn't really matter anymore because their marriage was over whatever the outcome of the trial. Alex wanted a divorce as soon as it could be arranged. He was lucky to be alive, and he wanted no attachment to the woman who'd wanted to kill him.

John motioned for Alex to exit with him to the hallway. After the two of them left the courtroom, John turned to Alex with a frown creasing his forehead and ran the length of his face. "I'm really concerned about Heather, Alex."

"Why? We know what the verdict will be. We just don't know if she'll get the death penalty. What else is there to worry about? Isn't that enough?"

"It's Heather I'm concerned about. She has said nothing at all to anyone. The guard told me this morning that she paces her cell all night, like a she-cat waiting for a kill, stalking its prey. The guard said he has never seen anything like it before. She never bothers anyone or talks to anyone, and what's even more strange is that no one bothers her."

"Why's that so odd? She isn't at a social gathering."

"You don't understand, Alex, what it's like in jail, even the rather mild county jail where she's being held during the trial. It's an animalistic way of life where the strong and mean prey on the weak and timid. The inmates always let the newcomer know the rules, and who has the power. Come on, Alex, think about it. You're no fool. The significance of what the guard told me yesterday is still escaping you. It was enough to make the hair on the back of my neck stand up. When her anger is released, I wouldn't want to be in the way. Obviously, most of the inmates feel the same way, and that's what's so odd. Somebody, there's always somebody, who ultimately challenges the newcomer."

"She's in prison, John. How dangerous can she be?"

With a simple shake of his head, John stated emphatically, "You have no idea, Alex. No idea at all. Just watch yourself, my friend," and the two men walked back into the courtroom.

Alex watched Heather with new intensity now. He really hadn't been able to see her face or how severe her glare was on the jury. He remembered wondering why so many of them fidgeted when her head turned their direction. For the first time, Alex started to pay heed to what John had said, and he watched her.

The door opened and the jury started to file in. Heather's eyes must have been prying into each of them as they crossed the threshold of the courtroom, for each one came into the room looking at Heather and then quickly turning away. Only one juror held his eye contact with her as if he was daring her to do anything to challenge him. Only when the man took his seat did he look away from Heather. She had never wavered in her hateful glare.

Eventually the jury was seated and the judge was asking for Heather to rise. Alex knew what the verdict would be. John had been able to do little to give the jury any doubt as to whether or not

Heather had been involved. He had asked all the questions he could, but Heather hadn't given him much help. Masterson had been found guilty of murder in the first degree and was sentenced to death. All of the evidence that had been used against him was also used in this case. Masterson had thrown all the vials away except the one that was found under the bed. Both his and Heather's and the pharmacist's prints were on it. The pharmacist, of course, testified that Heather was the one to pick up the prescription every month. He said he remembered how pretty she looked.

Even as Alex heard the words he was expecting, he felt his breath rush out of him. Heather was guilty. There had been no doubt in his mind; and obviously, no doubt in the jury's mind. Heather would spend the rest of her life behind bars.

Everyone in the court room rose as the judge prepared to leave for his chambers. Heather slowly turned to face Alex. The deep hatred seethed through her body and rose to her mouth. As John reached out to take her by the arm hoping to gain some control over her, she clasped onto the rail that separated the attorney and his client from the gallery.

Alex couldn't back away from her before she grabbed him by the tie. No one but John heard what she said to Alex, "You arrogant son-of-a-bitch. You deserved to die. How dare you pass judgment on me. Most of what has happened is your fault. You lived your life in that fucking hospital of yours. All you wanted from me was a quick piece of ass when you were horny. You assumed your money was all I needed or wanted from you. Watch your back, baby, because someday you'll get what you deserve. I promise."

Alex nearly severed her fingers to get them off of him. The guards finally dragged her away. Now Alex understood what John had tried to tell him, and he was afraid, truly afraid as the two of them left the courtroom.

****

Alex was relieved that the trial was finally over. He hoped now he could go back to work and try to forget what had happened by hiding in surgery. Fat chance! He realized not only had Heather been on trial; but his life had been on trial also. People actually blamed him for her *fall from grace* because he had obviously not been there when she needed the love and support of a husband. Doctors who stood by him in surgery made their gutter jokes about him in the doctor's lounge, and the nurses who used to flock around him acted like he was a contagious disease they might catch. He remembered a time when, ironically enough, most of those horny nurses had wanted to get *more* than just close to him.

Alex refused to let any one make him feel guilty for what Heather had done. She knew the rules when she said those two little words: "I do." Alex had not lied to her during their dating years when he was in medical school. Heather knew the long hours a doctor would keep. Alex's father had been a doctor before he died and her father was a doctor. She knew the reward for putting up with the long hours was an expensive house, country club membership, and a reasonable amount of money at her disposal. Heather had seemed to accept the rules of the game without complaint. Now Alex wondered if she had planned all along that his long hours would allow her the freedom to play as she wanted. Alex questioned his own ability to assess their relationship. He now wondered if there had ever been any truth to their marriage or had it always been a sham.

Mark took the worst of the trial aftermath in school. The poor kid was constantly teased, harassed and ridiculed about his parents. He needed his father now for love and support; but Alex had never been a father. He didn't even know how to talk to his son let alone be a father. Heather had always done the parenting. At least that's what Alex had thought. What he found out was the other mothers and fathers in the neighborhood had done most of Mark's rearing because Heather was out *playing* with her *friends.*

During the trial, Mark's life was actually more routine because John had suggested taking Mark out of school and hiring a private tutor and nanny for him. John knew how bad it could be for a child in school when a parent was on trial. This was welcomed advice, for Alex had no idea what to do with the boy. In fact, because of Alex's difficulty in dealing with Heather's trial and the reality of her intentions, he rarely even thought of Mark's needs.

Mark was confused and afraid; and, of course, this was reflected in his attitude. Between the tutor and the nanny, the eight year old was kept under control, but he was a challenge for them. The two women, feeling sorry for the family, did their best to give Mark the attention he was craving; but Mark didn't like being kept from school. The only good times he really remembered were being with his friends and their families. The poor boy didn't have any comprehension of what would happen to him now that his mother and father were the topic of local news and gossip.

Mark blamed his father for what was happening because his mother had always blamed Alex. He had spent years believing Alex was the reason everything bad happened. She used a variety of excuses, but the final blame always went to the man who was absent. Mark knew his mother was in trouble, but the severity was beyond his comprehension. The isolation at home protected him from the reality of the situation, but his innocence made him resentful. He felt like he was in prison. No one told him what was really going on, and that was also his father's fault.

In addition, Mark hated having a tutor every day. School had never been Mark's favorite pastime; however, with his friends there, at least he did do some learning and generally stayed out of trouble. This one-on-one stuff with a tutor was too intense for him. Thinking so hard gave him a headache; or, at least, that's what he claimed. The tutor was too serious: she never laughed and had fun with him. She was more focused on English grammar than she was on her student. At the moment, he needed a friend, a smile, and a soft hand.

Shortly after the trial, Alex had put Mark back in school believing that returning to the old routine as much as possible was best. Unfortunately, Mark was not ready for the rude reception he got. Generally, if he didn't come home bleeding from a fight, he came home crying. The kids who had been his good friends, wouldn't play with him anymore because the other kids would pick on them, too. Old friends felt it was just easier to leave Mark alone. The worst part of the situation was that he felt more isolated than ever. The classmates whom he had longed to be with were now some of his harshest persecutors. Now he understood why his father had pulled him out of school, and he wished he'd never gone back.

How could Mark explain his frustration to Alex? He didn't even know the man who claimed to be his father. Oh, he knew Alex was truly his father, but it was a relationship in name only. Mark didn't feel like a son, at least, not to this man. He envied the special connection he noticed between other boys and their fathers. It caused Mark to wonder what he had done to make his father dislike him so much that he never wanted them to be together. Now with his mother gone, Mark was really confused. Would his father try to get rid of him too?

After the tutor had gone, the nanny hadn't been able to help much. She had never been a companion for the boy and certainly not a confidant. She had known she could never be what the boy really needed; so when Alex came home one night, she informed him she could no longer be of service. Alex could easily recall her words . . . "Doctor your son is crying inside for you. He has lost his part time mother, but at least she was better than nothing. He has lost the few friends he had and their families. Now, he's looking for you, and he cannot reach you. He's grieving for everyone who has given him any stability at all. Must he also grieve for you? You're his only hope. I have to leave because it's the only way you'll learn to love your son. Together you can save each other - alone you will both be lost."

Alex knew she was right. He had to get in touch with his son, the boy he had simply patted on the head from time to time. Alex had never had to prepare a meal, set rules, clean up or invoke discipline; but everything had changed. He promised himself he was not going to let Heather ruin their son's life this way. Alex swore to himself he'd learn how to be a good parent. They'd start over. A new town, a new job, a new school---a new future.

The first step in starting over would be talking to Mark. Honesty would work best. Heather had never used it, and Alex hoped Mark would react favorably to this maneuvering tactic. After the nanny left, Alex took a deep breath and called Mark into the room.

"Mark, Mrs. Childers has left us. She believes we need each other not her."

"Well, I don't know about you; but I don't need her," Mark huffed throwing his head up and shoulders back. "I don't need anybody, especially you."

Alex was uncomfortable with the animosity coming from Mark. He'd hoped for the best, but that would've been too easy. He had to earn the love and respect of this boy who was a stranger to him. *Be honest,* he reminded himself.

"Mark, please just sit and listen to me. I know I haven't been a good father to you. I was a fool to believe that all I needed to do was to give you and your mother a house and money. It was time you both needed, and I gave that to the hospital." Mark turned away from him staring out the window.

Alex continued, "I'm so sorry, Mark, that your mother and I have screwed your life up so badly." His voice began to crack causing Alex to stop and take a long slow breath to help control his emotions.

Now he had Mark's attention. Even though Mark wouldn't give his father any satisfaction by turning to look at him, he did wait to hear the next words.

"Please, Mark. I want to make it up to you. I do want to be your father, but I need your help. It takes more than one to be a family. We can start over in a new place; everything new, including us. What do you say?"

"Did she do it?"

"What are you talking about?"

"Mom, did she do it? Nobody will tell me the truth. I hear all the kids talking bad about her; all the adults just brush me off. They treat me like a baby. I have a right to know." Mark was pretty sure about the answer. If his mother wasn't guilty, she would've come home not gone to prison. This was a test for his dad. Mark wanted to know if he was strong enough to tell the truth. If he did, then Mark could believe him about wanting to be a good father.

Be honest, the words vibrated through Alex's mind like timpani drums. He adjusted himself uncomfortably in his chair and said. "Yes, Mark. I'm sorry. She did help to kill that woman."

Surprised that this man was capable of being so frank with him, Mark now turned to face his father. Maybe there was hope for them. Maybe he would have a father he could love and count on.

"Some of the kids said she was going to kill you. Is that true?" Mark was sure that this would get him. The kids in school had heard their parents talk, and they held nothing back when it came to taunting him.

"Your mother never admitted to that."

Mark prepared himself mentally to hear the evasive answer.

"However," Alex continued, "Mr. Malcomb, her attorney and my friend, believes it was part of their plan. He figures if they killed that man's wife then they were probably going to try to kill me. I guess we were lucky I was the second target rather than the first." Alex was surprised by the amount of information that came spilling out of his mouth, but he did not drop his hold on Mark's eyes.

Alex's honesty with the difficult questions caught Mark off guard. He stared at his father's face. The eyes told it all: they were the polygraph test that told Mark he could trust this man. For the first time in his life, he knew he had a real father and there was hope.

"Where will we go, Dad?"

The question was an affirmative answer to Alex's hope. It was Mark's way of saying "Yes." With a smile on his face, Alex answered, "I'm not sure yet. Do you have any ideas?"

CHAPTER THREE

Traveling south on I-55 through St. Louis, Alex and Mark were on their way to Tulsa, Oklahoma. They were giving up the small Chicago suburb, where everyone, it seemed, knew their life story, for the larger arena of Tulsa proper. Alex had accepted a staff position at St. Thomas Hospital. No more Head of Surgery - Alex had insisted on shorter more flexible hours. Knowing the Chief of Staff had been a great help when Alex had to negotiate the terms of employment.

As Chief of Staff, Dr. Debra Gilman was thrilled to add a surgeon like Alex to her staff. Rarely did a world-famous doctor like Alex fall into one's lap, so agreeing to his requests was easy. She appreciated the difficult position Alex was in; and to have his expertise in the operating room, she would have agreed to almost anything.

Dr. Gilman had known Alex for years. They had gone to med-school together and had stayed in touch over the years. She had even gone to Alex and Heather's wedding. Heather hadn't liked Debbie, but Debbie didn't lose any sleep over it. She was Alex's friend not Heather's. In fact, Debbie remembered feeling this was one match that'd never last. She had brushed the feeling away assuming it was just her dislike for the bride. Well, Debbie liked Alex, and she would do anything she could to help him and his son, especially since it helped the hospital also. She knew Alex was grateful for the job and the friendship.

Alex and Debbie had been friends for as long as he could remember. His true blue friends could be counted on one hand these days; and he knew he'd need at least one ally wherever he went. Since Debbie was the best friend he had in a position to hire him, he had chosen Tulsa. He knew she would never talk about his background with other people, but he also knew that wouldn't stop others from asking questions. It was normal to be curious when a new guy came to town, especially when the new doctor had been the Head of Surgery at the University of Chicago, Medical Center. Alex needed a short, sweet explanation that would satisfy the curious and maintain his privacy. Eventually people would find out about Heather, but he wanted to put it off as long as possible.

Driving along, Alex played various conversations over in his head. "What brings you to Tulsa, Doctor?" This was the main question for which he practiced several answers.

"My son was having trouble adjusting to the loss of his mother."

"I was sued for malpractice." *Not a good idea.*

"I wanted to wring my wife's neck, but she was already behind bars." *Wouldn't do much for privacy.* Mentally, it sounded better when he blamed it on Mark. At least it would make him seem like the gallant father rather than someone running away.

Alex knew he was not leaving Chicago just for the good of his son; he was leaving to save himself. He no longer liked or even respected the life he had been living the past ten years. This tragedy had shown him there was more to life than what he did in the operating room. He needed to build a future with his family, with his son; and that would take time - the time he had given to the operating room. He could no longer afford to assume someone else was doing his fathering for him. Alex wanted his son, needed his son. If he expected the feelings to be mutual, then he would have to be there to make sure it happened.

"So, Doctor, why on earth would you leave the University of Chicago for Oklahoma?"

"The weather is better here. We were getting tired of all the snow and ice." *That's easy. I wonder how long I could use that one? .*

"Dad, what are you mumbling about?"

"Sorry, Mark. I didn't know you were awake."

"I was and I wasn't, if you know what I mean. I was kind of drifting."

"So was I. You want to talk for a while? There's something on my mind."

"Sure, Dad. What's up?"

"Well, Mark, people are going to be curious as to why we moved to Tulsa. It's normal to ask. We have to come up with a story that's simple and sounds true. How about saying we were tired of the cold weather?"

"That's fine for openers, but what about when they ask, 'Where's your mother?'"

"You're right. That's bound to be the next question. How about, 'We lost her.'?"

"That sounds better than saying she's behind bars, but doesn't it sound a little fishy? It isn't like we can't find her. You don't just misplace a mother and wife."

Alex let out a chuckle, "I mean lost like in die; not lost and can't find. In a way, we did lose her. We lost the person we loved to something evil."

"Dad, let me fiH you in on reality. She was never the person you keep pretending she was. I don't ever remember her being the wonderful *mother* you keep referring to. You believed she was a good wife and mom because you wanted to. Honest, Dad, she was never like that. She'd put on a great act whenever you were around, but it was a lie."

"Mark, why didn't you ever say anything to me?"

"Come on, Dad, would you have believed me? Besides, she was my mother. Until the last couple of years I really didn't realize my life was any different from any of my friends. Mom was always good to me when we were home together. I enjoyed playing with her. She could really hit a wild ping pong ball, and she'd watch cartoons with me. She wasn't around much, but she was still around more than you were. We've been together more in the last three months, Dad, than we have in the last three years. I know Bobby's dad better than I know you."

"Are you being honest now, or are you exaggerating?"

"Honest, Dad. Bobby's dad taught me how to play soccer and basketball. He made sure I got signed up and had a ride to practice. He helped me with fractions and my science project. You were never home when I needed you. You always assumed Mom was able to do everything for me. At first that was okay; but as I got older, she wasn't around as much; and when she was, she couldn't give me the help I needed. The housekeeper said it was like I was growing up but Mom wasn't. Do you think she was right?"

"I'm sorry, Mark." The guilt turned like a knife in his chest.

"That's okay, Dad, it wasn't all that bad. The housekeeper kept an eye on me when Mom wasn't around. Like I said, Mom and I had some good times together. She wasn't all bad. Ya wanna know something funny, Dad?"

"What, Mark?"

"I kinda miss her, and then again I kinda don't. Things are better now. Aren't they? I don't feel so sad all the time. Will I ever see her again?"

"I honestly don't know what will happen. I think things are better now, too. We're going to start over, taking it one day at a time. From now on you're the most important thing in my life. Do you understand? I'm counting on you to let me know if I start screwing things up. Deal?"

"It's a deal, Dad. By the way, thanks for firing the nanny. I really didn't like her. She was too bossy. Will I have to have another one? Ya know, I'm nine now. I don't think having a nanny is cool at all."

"Mark, I didn't fire her. She quit, remember? She walked out on us."

"Gosh, I never thought she was smart enough to do that. I don't want another one."

"All right, no nanny, but how about a housekeeper and maybe a tutor to get you going on the right foot in school?"

"I'll agree on two conditions. One, I get to go to the public school and not a snobby private one. I've had enough of that. Second, you have to learn how to cook something besides microwaved hotdogs. I don't think hotdogs are supposed to explode to show they're done."

"Agreed. No private school as long as you're getting a good education, and maybe I'll make sure the housekeeper can cook. I'm getting tired of hotdogs too."

Mark drifted off to sleep with a rare smile on his face. The two of them were getting closer, starting to enjoy each other's company, depending on each other; and Alex realized he was smiling too. Things were starting to fall together for them, and that fact filled him with a hope which had not been part of his life for a long time.

The sun was just rising as Alex turned off the Will Rogers Turnpike heading toward Tulsa. He was supposed to go south on Yale Avenue toward the hospital. The directions were easy to follow; and within minutes he found what he was looking for. Adorning the hospital property was the statue of St. Thomas welcoming Alex to Tulsa. The white statue graced the green rolling hills while the morning dew glistened like a sea of diamonds around the ethereal pink edifice of the hospital. The pear trees, rising out of the diamond sea, were haloed in fragrant blossoms. This place symbolized their new home - their new beginning. The holy image reminded Alex it was the Easter season, and it seemed appropriate their new life should be starting now. Alex had been a Christian in name only since med school, and it was time to put God and the Church back in his life especially for Mark. Sunday was four days away, and Alex vowed to make sure he and Mark were sitting in a church pew.

Alex turned onto the long drive leading up to the entrance of the luxury DoubleTree Hotel at Warren Place. Dozens of bartlet pear trees, lining both sides of the drive, were elegantly groomed in white foliage. The hotel was conveniently located just across from the hospital and north of where they would be living. Alex had a week to get Mark settled in before starting to work. He planned on staying at the DoubleTree for at least two weeks while he waited to close on their new house and move in.

"Gee, Dad, nice place. You can walk to work. Ya know, I've never seen a pink hospital before."

"It's impressive, isn't it?"

"Yeah, I guess so. Does this place have a pool?"

"I think so." Alex answered smiling at his son. Having a swimming pool was important to an eight year old. *Nine year old. There was a birthday about the time the trial ended. That's another one I owe you, Mark. Just add it to the list.*

The list with 'I owe you's' was long, but Alex was working on it. He had told Mark they'd work together one day at a time. Once the two of them had decided to leave their small suburb, things moved along quickly. Alex gave two weeks notice at the hospital and was glad to be finished there. The days had not gotten any easier for him; however, the good side to that was his ability to relate to Mark when he came home from school had improved. Alex knew if it was hard on him, it was harder on Mark. The hours they spent together talking about what Heather had done and why people persecuted the innocent simply because of association went a long way in fusing their relationship.

Bob, the bell man, quickly started unloading the baggage onto a cart. Alex took an instant liking to the small man. The spry old guy was the youngest old man Alex had ever known. *I hope I can move with such zest in thirty more years.*

"Welcome, Sir. Please let me do that." Bob reached to take the bag from Alex's hand. "I have perfected a great system for precision loading. It works every time."

Alex smiled at the man appreciating his professionalism. Rarely did someone take such care and pride in doing a job well.

The lobby of the hotel was quiet elegance and it was professional. This was a businessman's hotel. The only extravagance was the baby grand piano. No frills for kids. Alex had chosen the hotel for convenience not for accommodating Mark's interests. Now Alex felt selfish and unsure of himself because he hadn't considered his son's needs. He silently prayed that there was a swimming pool.

Check-in at 6:00 a.m. was easy, and Bob was waiting to escort the tired men to the two bedroom suite on the top floor. Mark headed straight for a bed when Bob opened the door. Desperate for some sleep of his own, Alex helped Bob unload the luggage cart and then generously tipped him. Mark was face down and stretched out diagonally across the bed. The gentle rise and fall of his back and soft breathing told Alex his son had the right idea. Quickly covering Mark, Alex planned on joining him as soon as he could get his head on a pillow.

****

"Dad. Yo, Dad. Wake up."
"What's wrong, Mark."
"I'm starving and there's absolutely nothing to eat in this place."

"Order room service and call me in two hours."

"Really, Dad? Can I order something?"

"Sure, why not? Just try to be quiet."

"You got it, Dad. See ya later."

Several hours later Alex rolled over to notice the time on the clock read 2:00 p.m. He stretched and moaned; stiffness consumed his body. He couldn't even remember the last time he had driven all night to get somewhere, and now he knew why he didn't do it. The next day was a waste. Mark had certainly honored his request for silence, for Alex couldn't hear a sound.

"Mark, Mark? Where are you?"

Getting out of bed and upright, Alex thought, would be the major accomplishment of the day. He hadn't even noticed the room when they arrived several hours ago, but now he realized there would be plenty of space for the two of them to stay comfortably. The living area was tastefully done in light greens and mauve. A sofa and easy chair occupied one side of the room, while a rich round walnut dinner table on the other side added a sober sophistication to the ambiance.

Alex's main concern right now was not the decorating; he wanted to know where his silent son was hiding. Alex took a quick glance into the room Mark had instantly claimed as his own, only because last night it offered the nearest bed, but the overall quietness of the suite told Alex his son was not present. He did notice the empty tray sitting on the bed. Mark had obviously taken his father's advice and ordered room service. As Alex approached the bed, he saw a quickly scrawled note. *Dad, I've gone to check the place out. I'll be back later. If you wake up before I get back, the Eggs Benedict is great. Just call room service.* Alex, glad that Mark showed the assertiveness to check things out for himself, smiled at the note and headed for the shower.

"Hey, Dad! Dad, where are you?" Mark yelled as he ran through the suite toward his father's room. Bursting through the bedroom door he blared, "Are you up yet?"

"Thanks, Mark. If I wasn't already up, that crowing would've done it. Where have you been?"

"Well, the place is pretty neat, but it certainly isn't for kids. Bob showed me around the whole place. He's the coolest old guy I've ever met. Come'ere. Ya gotta look at this view." Mark pulled his dad toward the window and threw open the curtain.

Mother Nature in her most heavenly glory was dancing below their window. Angelic pear trees waltzed among rainbows of pink, red and white azaleas. Yards of green satin glided over the rolling hills to encircle the biggest white church Alex had ever seen, and the golden rays of sun were like a wedding veil adorning the ivory steeple. The masterpiece was painted on the sapphire blue background of the sky.

Alex had forgotten such natural beauty even existed. People spent hours locked in offices and even operating rooms in order to buy beautiful things. At this moment, Alex realized the irony to the whole concept of working hard for something better. Like others, he always assumed that better meant more. But the greatest beauty was free for those who took the time out of their square boxes of ugliness just to soak in the gracious offerings of Mother Nature.

Alex reflected on what Heather had said to him before she was dragged out of the court room. *Maybe she was right. My life has always centered around the operating room: my ecstasy was saving lives. I had an emotional and physical high every time I came out of a successful surgery, but now I understand I've missed so much of what life is really all about.*

Thank you, God, for opening my eyes. Alex prayed the silent thoughts.

"Dad, what's that big white building?"

"It's a church, Mark." Putting his arm around Mark's shoulders, he added, "Maybe it will be our church."

"It's gorgeous, Dad. I mean the picture is really beautiful. I can't remember ever seeing such a blue sky. I'm glad we came to Tulsa. Any place so beautiful has to be good. I think I'd like to go to that church."

"We'll go on Sunday, okay?"

"Ya, sure. Bob told me that thousands of purple martins nest in those trees every spring. Dad, what's 'a barrel of monkeys'?"

"What are you talking about?"

"Bob keeps saying that he has more fun than a barrel of monkeys, but I have no idea what he's talking about."

"It's just an expression people use. I guess that a barrel of monkeys really have a lot of fun."

"Bob sure thinks they do."

"Sounds like Bob has become a friend."

"Ya, he's old but at least he's my size." Both of them laughed at Mark's comparison. "He took me for a walk through the trees and flowers. The birds were singing like a... a... big choir. Ya know, I bet it's just like a church choir. They didn't even fly away when we got close. The path around is a half a mile. See it? We could go for a walk together for exercise. It'd be good for you."

Alex smirked at his son's reference to health. Maybe he was a doctor in the making. "That'd be great, Mark. I need some exercise, but let's find a grocery store first and buy some food and drinks to keep in here."

"That's no big deal. I kinda like ordering room service."

"You can't have room service every time you want a can of pop or a quick snack. Let's see if the hotel can bring a small microwave." Holding his hand over his heart, Alex added, "I promise: no hotdogs.

We'll get a few things to keep in the fridge, so that you have stuff handy."

"No more room service?" Mark asked, allowing the disappointment in his voice to overflow.

"Only for breakfast, deal?"

"Deal!"

"Let's go check this town out."

CHAPTER
FOUR

Rachael's eyelids fluttered open in response to the large wet tongue licking her hand. The dog needed to go outside. She could tell by the amount of sun piercing through the blinds it was late in the morning. Generally, Rachael heard the shower running or Chance's yiping at the girls; but the deep sleep that had finally engulfed her hadn't loosened its grip for several hours. Now the house was silent, and the girls were gone to school.

"Come on, boy. Let me start my coffee, then we'll go outside." The fresh air and warm sun caressed Rachael's face as she walked out the door with the impatient dog tugging on his leash. The light fragrance of early spring blossoms drifting in the air testified to the arrival of a new season. Even though the morning glories and trumpet vines were the full height of the eight-foot fence already, they wouldn't be in full bloom for a few more weeks. Even the beautiful southern magnolia was showing the early signs of its summer flowers.

Springtime in Tulsa was magnificent, and Rachael realized she was actually glad to be alive for the first time in months. The winter hadn't actually been so gloomy as to make spring such a contrast; however, her mood had been dark: mentally she had been in a dark dreary winter for as long as she could remember.

It was time to live again. Rachael remembered the promise she had made to herself the night before: she had to live and enjoy herself again for the girls and for Jack. Springtime was the perfect opportunity for her to renew her life.

Unfortunately, Rachael's nightmare kept the recent past a close companion. *Companion? Enemy? Warning?* Maybe, Rachael considered, it was time to see the nightmare in a new context. Just maybe it meant more than grieving for a past way of life. She had a feeling there may be a deeper meaning to the nightmare than just her subconscious haunting her. Seeing the dream from a different perspective might just help her to understand it. In fact, she wondered if her fear of going to sleep at night might be the reason for the increased intensity of the episodes in the recent weeks. For the first time Rachael admitted she might need the help of a professional to truly put the nightmare behind her.

Enough thinking about that. It was a glorious day, and Rachael had only a short time to enjoy it. She leaned back in the patio chair letting the sun's rays massage her aching soul. Gradually the warmth filled her body allowing her mind to wander.

This afternoon Rachael had a meeting with a man about his son. He needed someone to tutor the boy when they moved to Tulsa. Rachael hadn't taken a new student for over a year, but this man sounded uneasy for some reason. The school the boy would be attending had told the father that Mrs. Carson was the best tutor in the district for his son. Rachael was pleased to hear the compliment, but she knew there were other good tutors in the area. Maybe it was the sound of his voice that led her to believe there was more to the situation than just a simple relocation. Whatever it was, the man piqued her interest and convinced Rachael to meet with him; and now she was glad she had agreed. She wanted to be involved again. It would help her to help this boy.

Rachael had been a tutor for over fifteen years now. She had started the year Allison was born. It was a small at-home job with just enough income to help with gas and a meal out now and then, but it made Rachael feel good to help her students. Eventually, however, the job grew into a thriving business: it became her career. Everyone wanted Mrs. Carson, and she always had a waiting list. She was good

-- very good, and she enjoyed her work. In fact, the whole family took part in the tutoring. Jack taught the more advanced math classes after he got home from work, Rorie did computer work for her on the weekends. Both of the girls had even tutored younger children in math when Rachael had too many students to handle on her own.

One of the benefits of the tutoring business was that Rachael worked when she wanted and with whom she wanted. She set the rules and the students played her game, or they didn't play at all. That was one of the biggest reasons why she was so successful. Rachael also knew from years of experience that poor grades were often the symptom of a greater problem in a child's life. If she could help the student and the parents identify the problem, the grades would usually improve. Some students knew what the trouble was and just needed an objective person to talk to. Over the years, she had dealt with students harboring a variety of problems. Rachael knew a good tutor was a blessing to the parents and the child, but a bad tutor was a disaster.

Rachael was not surprised that Dr. Zamora was arranging the tutoring for his son. A lot of fathers had called her in the past. He had not given her much information about the boy, but she would ask her questions this afternoon. The doctor, in fact, seemed to be very vague, which was unusual. Parents liked to talk about their children. Generally, Rachael had to cut them off in the first conversation. Oh well, he wanted to interview her, and that was a good sign. Rachael had a file with her résumé and references for any parents who wanted to check her out. She was always surprised by how many parents never asked about her experience before turning their child over to her.

Rachael's absent minded stroking of the dog's neck was interrupted by Chance's persistent scratching at his ears. "Let's go in boy. It's time to get cleaned up. A new father will be here shortly to discuss my tutoring his son. Be nice this time. Your fierce growl always makes new clients uncomfortable."

Rachael smiled at Chance. He was her best friend and constant companion. Taking his position as *the man* of the family very serious, Chance carefully scrutinized everyone who came through the door. He had never been particularly fond of males, and he made that very clear. Rachael considered this a positive trait; however, the girls didn't particularly enjoy having their dates screened by a dog. When strangers came to the house, especially those of the male gender, Chance's hair stood straight up on his back. He resembled a porcupine. His top lip curled up enough to show off the large white canines, and his normally high pitched bark dropped about ten octaves. In fact, he reminded her of Jack's reaction every time a new boyfriend showed up at the front door. Chance, cocking his head slightly, looked up at Rachael when he heard her laugh and then followed her into the house.

CHAPTER FIVE

Rachael opened the front door to a tall handsome man, "Dr. Zamora, I presume?"

Smiling at the way her tone made reference to the famous Dr. Livingstone Alex asked, "Are you Mrs. Carson?"

As he spoke the words, the deep angry bark of a very large dog made the man take two steps back. Rachael was afraid the poor guy was going to run. *Good boy,* thought Rachael smiling to herself. Chance did earn his warm bed by keeping strangers at a distance. She had no doubt in her mind if she needed him, Chance would be at her side in an instant; and the poor Dr. Zamora would be running down the street.

"It's okay. Chance won't come unless I call him. Please come in." She gave the doctor her warmest smile and tried not to laugh, but the look on his very attractive face made her think of a frightened little boy. *He was certainly good looking. To bad 'Prince Charming' looks rarely went with a 'Prince Charming' personality* Rachael thought to herself. Then she chastised herself for stereotyping the man. *Give him a chance. Besides you won't be tutoring him.* Then her cynical side added, *Yes, but shallow fathers often have shallow sons.*

Tentatively Alex started through the door, waiting for the monster dog from hell to run him down. Alex had never spent any time around dogs. His only experience with them was treating the dog-bitten patients in the emergency room during his residency years. That alone was enough to make him afraid of dogs, for he saw no positive side in owning one. *This is not a good start,* Alex told himself. Alex's first impressions of Rachael were not much better than hers had been of him. His first instinct these days was never to trust a beautiful woman. Now as far as he was concerned, Mrs. Carson had two strikes against her: she was beautiful and she had a big bad dog.

"Please, Dr. Zamora, don't worry about the dog. He won't come through that door unless I call him, and he's not nearly as big as he sounds." Rachael didn't usually admit Chance was so well trained, but she was really afraid the doctor's fear of Chance would keep him from sending his son to her for help.

The sound of Rachael's voice was reassuring, and Alex found himself relaxing as she led him toward the living room. He forgot about the dog momentarily as he took his first look around the inside of the house. Alex had never seen cherry stained hardwood floors before. He could almost see his reflection in the high gloss finish that was on them. They walked past the circular cherry wood staircase which led up to an open sitting area. Alex assumed by the amount of sunlight coming into the room there must be a large window on the far wall. The first thing to catch his eye when he entered the living room was the magnificent floor to ceiling mantel, also cherry wood, around the fireplace. The cream and mauve colors of the room blended with the cherry woodwork making the room feel warm and elegant at the same time. She hadn't overly decorated as Heather had. He liked it; maybe he'd have the woodwork in his new home redone.

Rachael caught his attention again, "I'm sorry my dog gave you such a start. It's his job to bark when he hears a strange voice."

"Well, he's very, very good at it." Alex tried to sound indignant and then broke out laughing at how silly he sounded. The two of them smiled and then giggled for several seconds before Alex could clear his mind of how ridiculous he must have looked. "After today, I think your dog deserves a raise."

The two of them smiled at each other for an instant, but they were both uncomfortable with the intimacy and glanced away. Rachael broke the rather awkward silence with business. "Please, tell me about your son, Dr. Zamora."

"Mark's starting a new school next Monday. He's anxious about meeting new kids and teachers, so I was hoping that having a tutor who knew the system would help him to adjust more easily."

"I understand your concern. It's difficult to move into a new school system. What can you tell me about his educational background. The more I know about Mark the more I'll be able to help him. How were his grades? What are his favorite subjects? That type of thing."

Alex felt uncomfortable with the questions because he didn't know the answers. He tried to remember the last report the Illinois school principal had given him. He had planned to study the report before enrolling Mark in school, but the time passed before he had taken care of this fatherly responsibility. He silently admonished himself for getting into this situation. Fumbling for answers, Alex tried to remember what he had seen in the report. He knew it hadn't been a *bad* report gradewise, but there definitely were behavior problems that had to be dealt with. The report had focused more on Mark's recent fighting episodes than on his grades. *How much should I tell her?* Mark needed her help, but Alex didn't want to tell this stranger everything.

"I'm sorry," answered Alex. "I left his school transcript file at the hotel."

"That's okay," Rachael was quick to answer. She had assumed he hadn't brought it because he wasn't carrying anything. Rachael was concentrating on the man's anxiety over her questions about his son. Something wasn't right. She had to be careful. *Don't pry - or you'll lose him and, more importantly, the boy who needs the help.*

"Just tell me what you know about him," Rachael encouraged.

Alex felt slightly relieved, but he wasn't off the hook yet. He tried to think of something positive to say that sounded honest. "His grades are about average." *Oh, that was great! Be generic with your answers, and she won't suspect anything. If this woman is as good a tutor as the school said she was, she'll see through my answers in a heartbeat.*

Rachael was beginning to wonder about Dr. Zamora and his son. The man must have lived at the hospital. It wasn't unusual for a father to be unfamiliar with school records, but most fathers would know something specific about a son no matter how trivial it was.

"This adjustment must be as difficult for you as it is for your son."

"What do you mean?" Alex asked defensively.

"Apparently, you don't know your son very well; and if you don't know him very well, then he probably doesn't know you either. It must be hard for two near strangers to be forced into companionship when their common bond, the boy's mother, has been taken away."

Alex was startled by her choice of words. *Did she really know what had happened to them? Could she be playing him for the fool by letting him talk this way? No, that's impossible. She doesn't know anything about us.* Alex tried to convince himself. He had carefully implied that his wife was dead. That was the plan. Frustrated, Alex stood up shoving his hands into his pockets. As he walked toward the old upright grand piano, he wondered if it was in tune. His life certainly had not been. The metaphoric reflection surprised Alex because he was not the poetic type. Alex turned to face Rachael surprising her with sadness flowing from his eyes.

"Mrs. Carson, you're right about the relationship between my son and me. We don't know each other very well at all. However, we, at least I'm finding parenting very challenging and enjoyable. My greatest sorrow is that it took a tragedy to bring us together." Alex felt he could let the explanation go with that. Nobody with an ounce of sympathy would push for more details, but the deluge of words kept pouring from his mouth.

"It's amazing the perspective children have about the different events in their lives. I think Mark believes he had only his mother for the first nine years of his life, and now he has his father. He hasn't really lost a parent only traded one for the other."

"Doctor, obviously your son feels good and safe with you; but his mother was his first bond, he must've grieved for her. Children don't make an even swap of parents: it's too emotional."

"Oh, he did grieve for his mother, but the circumstances allowed him time to accept her absence gradually. She was gone, but not necessarily gone forever. He had time to get used to the change without having to face the final reality until later. Once it was final, he'd been without her for over twelve months."

Emotionally, Alex added, "I don't mean to trivialize my son's feelings. Honestly, I was so wrapped up in my own fears and emotions I missed most of what Mark went through. I guess that's why the other tutor didn't ...a...work out," Alex stumbled over his words. He was afraid he'd offered too much information; it was certain to pique her curiosity.

Rachael knew better than to ask too many questions. Parents didn't like her knowing so much about their private lives, especially in the beginning. That was understandable, after all she was a stranger, so she tried not to cross the line. "Dr. Zamora, please relax. I'm not here to drill you about your parenting skills. I've dealt with a lot of students and parents with very unusual situations. Just tell me what you want to."

Alex was irritated by her comment insinuating that he was an inadequate father and even more frustrated because she was right.

"Mark's a nice kid, but I don't think school work ranks high on his list of pleasurable activities. He does what he has to in order to be with his friends." Again, Alex felt like he was fudging about the truth. By the time the two of them had left the Chicago area, Mark didn't have a friend left. They had all turned against him because his mother had been sent to prison for murder. Having a mom in prison just wasn't cool in their upper class neighborhood. No wonder Mark had insisted on going to a public school instead of what he referred to as a "snobsville" private school. Mark assumed the kids in the public school would be a little more tolerant of his situation if they found out about his mother, and both Mark and Alex hoped to put that off as long as possible.

If it was difficult for Alex to talk about their background, it was going to be especially hard on Mark when someone asked him about the past. Maybe he should tell her the truth so she could understand the anxiety he shared with his son about starting a new school. Alex's protective parenting instinct told him "no." If Mark felt comfortable enough with the woman, then he could tell her what he wanted to. That would be up to Mark since he was the one who would be spending the time with her. With that decision made, Alex tried to continue the discussion at hand which was giving the information he felt was important.

"Mark's had some trouble adjusting. That's one of the reasons why we decided to move to a new place and start over. He started getting into fights at school and became very introverted. The teachers said he often stared into space rather than doing any work. There are times when he sounds more like an adult than a kid. We needed a new life together; and if I was going to spend more time with him, I had to change hospitals."

Rachael could tell by all of the hesitation in his voice he was struggling with what to tell her. He had reached his limit. Eventually the truth would come out; it always did, so there was no reason to push now.

"It really isn't so unusual for a child to sound older than his years when he has gone through some tough times. Kids listen to what is going on around them, picking up the comments and attitudes more than adults and parents realize. It's possible Mark wasn't as introverted as his teachers thought. The way a child acts reflects what he has been through. I won't mention to Mark what you've told me because I don't want him to feel like I know things about him that might make him uncomfortable. If he decides to tell me anything, I'll take the information as he gives it. I'll try to get him to talk about what bothers him rather than taking it out on the teachers and other kids at school. Hopefully, he'll see me as his partner and ally rather than just a tutor."

With a desperate sigh Alex responded, "So do I. So do I."

Rachael was slightly surprised by the Doctor's show of emotion. It seemed as though he was relieved to think he would have some help dealing with his son. Maybe becoming a full time father has been a little more overwhelming for him than he wants to admit, and just maybe this man needs help as much as his son.

"When do you want him to come over and how often?"

Alex felt a little more at ease now that she had changed the subject. "I hadn't thought about that yet. How about everyday?"

Rachael wasn't sure if he was kidding or not. It wouldn't be the first time a student checked in with her everyday, but it was a little extreme. "How about if you ask Mark first before you make the commitment? It'll make him feel better if he has some input to the relationship. After he starts school, we can get a better idea of how often he should come over."

Alex appreciated her concern for his son's feelings. "That sounds like a good idea. Mark starts school on Monday. We have to go over and register him tomorrow. Could we stop by afterward so the two of you can meet?"

"That'll be fine. I assume you'll want Mark's appointments after the supper hour since you'll be bringing him over."

"Actually, I was hoping he could walk over after school."

Rachael raised her eyebrows trying to calculate where the Doctor and his son would be living to allow the boy to be within walking distance.

Alex read the question on her face. "We'll be living in the subdivision on the other side of Yale, which is about a four block walk or so."

Now Rachael really did have some questions. It seemed to her there may have been some premeditation here. It was too much of a coincidence that the Doctor and his son just happened to be buying a house four blocks away from her without having decided ahead of time which tutor he was going to use. It did make things convenient; but Rachael didn't like the fact he had assumed she would do the tutoring. She didn't like the feeling he had manipulated the whole situation.

Alex was no novice at reading people's feelings, and he could tell by the look on her face she was getting angrier by the second as she realized the implications of where he was living. He had made a tactical error in telling her so early. Actually, he didn't think she would grasp his manipulation so quickly. He was wrong; she was good; and now they were even: she felt as uncomfortable with him as he was with her. The question was how far would she push him now. Would she confront him or wait for a second move?

"How convenient for all of us. It'll be better for me if Mark does come after school rather than later in the evening since my older students come after supper. It's easier for the older ones to come late because most of them have after school obligations."

Smart, thought Alex. *She's going to play it out rather than confront me now. I don't know whether to admire her or be afraid of her or both.*

Rachael tried to control her desire to ring the handsome man's neck. *He deserves it. On the other hand, I think it'll be interesting to find out what's behind the scheming. It may be simply out of the desperation to help his son, and then there is really no harm done. I'll wait and watch.*

"What time will you be seeing the principal tomorrow? I'll be gone in the morning, but anytime after 1:00 p.m. is fine."

"Let's plan on that. We'll be done at the school by then and can get a little lunch before coming over."

"Fine," Rachael stated bluntly. There'd be no small talk with this man. She didn't want him to know any more about her and the girls than he already did. Rachael stood up and walked toward the door.

Alex could tell the conversation was over, and she was graciously throwing him out. "Thank you for your time, Mrs. Carson. We'll see you tomorrow."

As Rachael opened the door, she saw the bright red Mustang convertible pull up in the driveway. A smile of relief came over her face as she waved realizing Mathew would give her an easy way to say good-bye to Dr. Zamora without having to awkwardly linger with him in conversation. What Rachael couldn't see was the deep questioning frown on Mathew's face.

"Hello, Mathew," Rachael called to him as he opened the car door stepping out onto the driveway. "Dr. Zamora, please excuse me."

"Of course," he answered as he watched her walk to the new arrival. A tall young man with broad muscular shoulders, broad bare shoulders and bronze chest, towered over Rachael. *Touché, Mrs. Carson. You made a graceful exit which also served as a slight affront to me. You won this round. I deserved the verbal slap.* Alex walked away with a smile on his face and a strange mix of feelings.

****

"Mrs. C. how ya doin today?"

"Mathew, I wasn't expecting you today, but I'm glad you came over." Rachael stumbled over her last couple of words not wanting to sound too eager for Mathew to be there. She didn't want to give him the wrong idea, but she had enjoyed the opportunity to give a slight jab to the manipulating doctor.

Mathew had been a student of Rachael's a couple of years ago. He'd had a harmless schoolboy crush on her all the years she tutored him, so she had learned to be careful of his feelings. Feeling sorry for Rachael and the girls when Jack died, Mathew started coming over on a regular basis to check on them. Often Rachael didn't feel up to seeing him when he came by, but it didn't seem to bother him. Mathew understood her need to grieve and be alone. Once-in-a-while, seeing something that needed to be done around the yard, he had just done it.

Eventually, Rachael became more aware of his presence and what he was doing around the house for her and the girls. Mathew gradually became a regular fixture: taking care of the outside of the house and the yard. He needed the handy man pay she gave him, and Rachael needed help keeping up the house. The yard took hours to mow and clean on a weekly bases. In addition to the basic gardening and repairs to the house, Mathew had also kept up the routine maintenance on her car.

Rachael knew she and the girls could have taken care of everything themselves, but for the last two years it had been hard enough just keeping herself pulled together. The girls had taken over most of the housework, cooking, and laundry; but then Rachael had never been much of a cook, and tutoring during the supper hour had encouraged everyone to fend for himself or starve. As Rachael progressed through the grieving process, she became more aware of how much Rorie, Allison, and Mathew had been doing for her. She was grateful and tried to show it by doing more things for herself and for them. Even though the yard work would have been good exercise for her now, she felt obligated to keep Mathew around a little longer to show her appreciation. Rachael knew the odd jobs he did for her gave him a little spending money while he was still in school. Mathew had to study hard to get decent grades, and being on the football team sucked up any extra time that might have been available for a part time job.

Rachael had tried to have Mathew do a couple of repair jobs in the house, but Chance went nuts every time Mathew crossed the threshold. The dog barked and paced the entire time Mathew was on the property; but as long as one was outside and one inside, Rachael could tolerate the situation. It wasn't normal for Chance to show so much hostility to someone. He had never liked men, but he usually calmed down with a caress from Rachael's hand.

The whole situation was rather odd, but Rachael hadn't actually been an astute observer the last couple of years. While she had been tutoring Mathew, Chance was fine with him. The dog never bothered her students after he got a good smell of them and a kind hand on the head or a rub behind the ears. At some point after Jack's death, Mathew grew into a young man's shoes and the dog's disfavor. Anyway, that's how Rachael explained it to herself and the girls. She never talked about it with Mathew; he just accepted the fact that he was much better off outside.

In truth, Mathew was terrified of the dog. The farther away he stayed the better. The first couple of times he'd come to the house, he tried to win the dog over, but Chance never wavered in his hatred. Then Mathew had tried to intimidate the dog by shaking his fist or a newspaper at him, but that didn't stop the threatening show of teeth. Mathew couldn't yell at the dog because he didn't want to draw Rachael's attention to the situation, so he backed down knowing that without a weapon for protection he didn't stand a chance against the dog. Rachael loved that damn dog, and she had suffered enough.

"What's up Mrs. C? Do you have something that needs to be fixed? I finished up my exam early, so I thought I'd stop by and get a start on the lawn. The weather's great today, but it's supposed to rain later in the week."

Rachael needed a gracious way to explain her eagerness to see him. "I heard the report this morning too; and I was afraid if you waited until the end of the week, the yard wouldn't get finished for the weekend. Thank's for being so thoughtful."

Mathew enjoyed the compliment and a big smile filled his attractive face. His blond hair glistened in the sun, and beads of sweat were beginning to show on his muscles. *I'll bet he turns a lot of heads on campus.* Rachael had not noticed his masculinity before, and it made her feel uncomfortable. Embarrassed by her thoughts and surprised by her surfacing latent desires, Rachael excused herself.

"Mathew, I have some work I need to get done. I'll be out before you leave."

"Sure, Mrs. C. By the way, who's the new guy? I haven't seen him around before." Mathew didn't want to sound too nosey, but he was wary of strangers around the house.

Rachael was surprised by his question. She didn't owe him any explanations. *He's just curious. Don't let your hostility for the doctor reflect on your relationship with other people.*

"He's the father of my new student. I'll meet the student tomorrow."

Mathew acknowledged her answer with a nod and went to work.

Rachael went into the house to quiet the barking Chance and to collect her thoughts. She couldn't even remember the last time she had so many different emotions going through her: emotions that had nothing to do with Jack. It was good to feel alive with the present even if the feelings were strange and confusing.

Rachael walked through the house heading for the sun room off the master suite. Jack had built this room especially to satisfy her long time desire to have a palm tree in the yard. Because the winters were too cold to accommodate a palm tree, Jack had taken the next best option which was to put Rachael's tree in a sun room. The tropical paradise opened onto the deck at the back of the house, allowing easy access to the jacuzzi beside the pool. Rachael had carefully planned the landscaping around the patio and jacuzzi so the sun room and the patio gave an illusion of being an open space: one area easily flowing into the other. Tropical plants were carefully arranged taking full advantage of the sun and giving maximum privacy on the southwest end. An eight foot high rock garden had been built up around the outside edge of the jacuzzi to isolate it from the rest of the back yard. The water delicately cascaded over the rocks and into the hot tub. From the sun room, Rachael could enjoy the view of her palm tree, hibiscus and other tropicals that she never remembered the names of in addition to the waterfall and hot tub. It was quite a sight on chilly winter days when the steam rising off the hot water gave the illusion of a misty rain forest.

Rachael loved her beautiful backyard paradise. The patio stretched from the breakfast nook on the northeast side of the house, where Rachael often enjoyed the rising sun with her first cup of coffee, around the back of the house to the pool. The wood deck, which was two steps up from the pool level, ended at the southwest corner of the master suite. Trees and shrubs provided the backdrop for the efflorescence.

Rachael sat reminiscing about long walks on the beach with the water lapping at her toes and the sea breeze caressing her skin. Chance sat attentively beside her moving his head with the motion of Mathew's track across the yard. All that was visible above the greenery was the top of Mathew's head, but it was enough to satisfy the suspicious dog.

Rachael decided it was time for her and the girls to get away for a vacation. They had not been away for over two years. Before Jack had died, they had traveled several times a year. It was tradition to ski over spring break and go to the beach right after school finished in the spring. Sometimes Jack was able to get away with them, but those two trips were usually just for the girls. The planning this year would be tight since spring was here and the beach front condos would be hard to come by, but Rachael felt getting away would be good for all of them. Just then the door chimes sounded, and within moments both of the girls walked into the room filling it with their warm smiles.

Chance immediately started the ritual greeting dance he displayed only for those he loved. It was a boost to the morale to know no matter what had happened during the day, someone was glad to see you; and the dog certainly did lift the hearts of all three of them. The girls both had to acknowledge him before the dancing stopped, and they could move to give their mother a hug.

"Hi, Mom. How was your day? I noticed Mathew has most of the back yard finished. I'm really glad he does it; I hate mowing. Now, if you'd get a riding mower, I'd be happy to cruise along in a bikini and my walkman."

"Yes, dear. I know; you've told me that many times. And may I remind you, your bikini would look better if you pushed the mower more often." They all laughed walking toward the kitchen.

"Did that new guy come over today?" Rorie questioned. "What was he like?"

"He was here; he is strange, arrogant, and manipulating..."

"Yes, but is he good-looking?" Allison jumped in.

"Allison, really! Is that all that's important to you?"

"No, is he married? How about rich?"

"It really doesn't matter as long as he pays me. I rarely see the parents of my students anyway. As long as I can get him by phone, I don't care if he is handsome, married, or rich."

"Well?"

"Well--what?"

"Is he handsome, married and rich?" Allie questioned with a smirk on her face.

"Really, Allison," Rachael recognized the impish sparkle in her daughter's eyes and tried to sound very disgusted when she answered "Yes, no, and maybe. Okay?"

"Yes, thank you for the information." Allison flung her long brown curls haughtily over her shoulder making the three of them laugh.

Rachael told the girls about her experience with the "handsome" Dr. Zamora. The more she discussed the afternoon with them the more she realized how annoyed she was at his manipulation.

Dr. Zamora had decided before he'd ever called her the first time that she was going to tutor his son. He hadn't come to interview her as he had insinuated when the appointment was made.

"The arrogant jerk just assumed that if he wanted it - I'd do it."

"Mom, maybe you're taking it the wrong way. It's possible he was desperate, and the school did say you were his best option."

"He could've had the decency to ask before he bought a house four blocks away."

"Wow," commented Rorie, "he really was desperate."

"No, he was really sure of himself."

"Give him a chance, Mom. After all, "Allie was adding with the familiar gleam in her eyes, "he's handsome, not married, and probably rich. He can't be all bad."

"Yes he can!" Rachael answered emphatically trying to keep the fading anger in her voice.

Now Rorie joined forces with Allison, "Just think of the poor boy: he's lost his mother, and his father's a jerk. It's a desperate situation. The boy could be doomed forever to live his life as a jerk." Rorie placed extra emphasis on "doomed."

"Mom, you're just the person to save him." Allison poured all of her theatrical emotions into the word "save" and crossed her arms over her chest in a pious gesture.

"By the way, Mom, if my memory serves me correctly, I remember Dad accusing you of being arrogant and manipulative at least a couple of times." Rorie tried to look thoughtful, but she had trouble hiding the teasing smile that was trying to escape from her heart. Both of the girls had infectious senses of humor, and Rachael had a hard time keeping her anger fired when the two of them started poking holes in her armor.

Hands on hips and a tapping foot, Rachael made a futile attempt to defend herself. "Only once or twice, and he was always wrong. Wasn't he?"

"Oh, yes. Absolutely." Allison agreed and Rorie nodded her head affirmatively causing them all to laugh. The girls didn't miss the new life that was in Rachael's humor. It had been a long time since they'd been able to tease her about Jack without noticing the sadness return to her face. It was refreshing to have some of their mother's old joyfulness back.

Rachael noticed the girls glancing at each other and appreciated their concern for her well-being. "Girls, I was thinking it's time for us to take a little vacation. You know, school will be out in about six weeks and the beach is calling us."

"Are you sure, Mom? That sounds great."

Rorie was skeptical. "Why?"

Rachael understood why her daughter was asking. Rachael hadn't thought about anything into the future for a long time. She had been living day to day, and Rorie knew this. The change was a big one for Rachael, and she simply answered her oldest daughter, "Because it's time."

With tears in their eyes, Allison and Aurora walked over to embrace their mother.

CHAPTER SIX

Alex was bothered by his reaction to Mrs. Carson. He was sure she was aware of how he had just assumed she would gladly be his son's tutor. The honest truth was he had not even considered the possibility she might decline, but he could tell by the tone of her voice she had been irritated by his presumption.

The possibility that Mrs. Carson might hold a grudge against Mark for his father's errors was quickly put to rest. Her true concern for her students would keep her feelings for them and their parents separate. She was a professional in the true sense of the word; and he respected her for it, even if he didn't like her. The woman had made him feel uncomfortable and unsure of himself. He felt vulnerable with her because she could read his feelings and thoughts more than anyone else could. Heather had never been in touch with him mentally, so he had never felt emotionally naked as he had this afternoon. This ability of Mrs. Carson's was probably an asset when dealing with students, but it must be a little disconcerting to the parents; at least it was to this parent.

"Come on, Dad, tell me again what she's like," Mark pressed his father for more information.

Alex appreciated his son's nervousness over meeting the woman. They were almost at her front door, and he was having his own anxiety attack. Sweaty palms and butterflies in the stomach were the common symptoms, and his was a classic case. He and Mrs. Carson definitely had a personality conflict. They each wanted to control a situation. *Control is too strong. Maybe, dominate is a better choice,* he thought to himself. Alex had never thought of himself in this way before: never considered himself the controlling or domineering type. However, he certainly felt that the two of them had had a verbal tug-of-war yesterday; but he wasn't sure if either one could be considered a winner.

"Mark, I told you she seemed very nice and very qualified to do the job. I think you need to help make this decision. You know the school told me Mrs. Carson was the best tutor in the system for students your age; however, it doesn't matter how good she is if you don't like her. Do you understand?"

"Yeah, Dad. I understand. Thanks."

"For what?"

"For letting me have some say in this. It makes me feel more responsible. Ya know what I mean?"

"You're welcome. I want to give you a little advice first. It'll be hard to tell if she's a good tutor at your first meeting. Try to give her a little time, okay? After all, you aren't looking for a best friend, only someone to help you with your homework."

"Is this the house? Wow! It's nice."

"Come on, Mark."

Rachael had been waiting for the two "gentlemen" to show up. No one had piqued her curiosity or anger as the doctor had in a long time. When the door bell rang, Chance instantly started his battle cry; but Rachael took her time getting to the door. She couldn't explain why she had the desire to play mental war games with this man, but she could feel the adrenalin racing through her system. Rachael was ready for the next battle.

"Dad, you didn't tell me she had a dog. How could you forget that? A dog! I love dogs! Wow, a dog! He sounds like a big dog."

Alex was stunned. The woman was exasperating. She'd won his son over without even opening the door. He was irritated with himself because he didn't even know his own son liked dogs. He had been sure Mark wouldn't like any tutor; and by giving him some choice in the matter, Alex had hoped to minimize his son's discontent.

"Yes, Mark, she has a dog." *The dog from hell,* he added to himself.

Just then Mrs. Carson opened the door. "Hello, Dr. Zamora, Mark. Please come in."

Mark looked around the entry for the dog but didn't see him. Finally, he caught sight of the big yellow dog in the kitchen. He could hardly contain the desire to run up to it.

"Mark!" His father said a second time. Obviously Mark wasn't interested in anything but the dog.

"Yeah, Dad. Sorry, I was looking for the dog."

"That's okay. Hi, Mark. I'm Mrs. Carson. " Rachael held out her hand waiting for Mark to respond with a handshake. That got his attention and his respect. He was surprised an adult would want to shake his hand. Looking Rachael right in the eyes, Mark responded to her welcome. The eyes had a warm comforting gleam to them, and she had a pretty face. Her long soft fingers wrapped around his hand and her light fragrance appealed to him. This was much better than his last tutor. The dog moved his head, and Mark's peripheral vision caught the slight motion.

"Would you like to meet him?"

"Huh?" Mark's gaze returned to Rachael.

"The dog. Would you like to meet the dog?"

"That'd be great! Can I, Dad? Please?"

Alex didn't want to pass his fear of dogs on to his son, but he really wanted to say no. Instead, he heard the words, "I don't care." He knew he would lose the battle over the dog, and he might as well give in without making his feelings obvious. Mark certainly didn't share his fear.

"Come, Chance," was the command. The dog obeyed instantly and was sitting at her feet. "This is Mark," she said. The dog wiggled his body and licked Mark's hand. Mark dropped to his knees so Chance could lick his face and nuzzle his upper body. The friendship was bonded that fast.

Chance looked at Alex and backed toward Rachael. As his hair started to rise up on his back, the long white canines appeared under the upper lip. "It's okay, Boy." Rachael soothed him by stroking his head. "Hold out your hand so he can get your scent."

Alex backed up. "You've got to be joking."

"Stop backing up," she said. "He won't hurt you unless I tell him to or he feels I'm in danger, so stop backing up. Just hold your hand out. If you don't make friends with him now, you'll go through this every time you come over."

"I just won't come over," he said defensively. "You aren't my tutor."

Rachael had the strong urge to laugh, but knew it wouldn't be wise to belittle the father in front of his son. She felt sorry for him in a way, but fear wasn't a funny thing, and she wondered at the cause.

"Come on, Dad. He really is a nice dog."

For the sake of his son, Alex felt cornered into holding out his hand. He didn't want to admit his fear, but he was sure the dog could sense it. Slowly, Alex uncurled his hand extending it to the dog, realizing his future could be in jeopardy if this monster dog decided to bite off any of his fingers or his whole arm for that matter; he held his breath.

"It's all right, Chance," Rachael's soothing voice stroked the dog's temperament while he hesitantly approached the outstretched hand.

Alex actually felt jealous that this exasperating woman took more care in comforting a goofy dog than she did in helping a fellow human being. The dog sniffed at his hand; and gradually as the hair on his back went down, so did the lip exposing the vicious white teeth. Chance licked the soft fingers and mentally logged the scent.

Now the dog seemed harmless, and Alex found himself rubbing Chance's left ear and relaxed a little with the dog's acceptance of him. Alex wasn't looking for a lifelong friend here; but, on the other hand, he didn't want the dog ready to bite his leg off every time he had cause to step through the door.

"Just a word of warning, doctor, as long as you don't do anything to endanger me or my girls, or cause Chance to think you are, he'll be your friend. We don't know why he's always been wary of men, but I like him that way."

Mark was on the floor talking to Chance and rubbing his belly. Rachael was glad to see him relax and enjoy the new friendship. Chance had this effect on students, especially the boys. It had always seemed odd that Chance liked girls best, but boys sought his attention and friendship the most. Only a few students, generally girls, had ever been afraid of him, and eventually he even won them over.

"Mark, I'm glad you like Chance. He certainly likes you. Have you ever had a dog of your own?"

"No, Mrs. Carson. I used to ask all the time, but everyone kept saying 'no', so I stopped asking. Chance is just the right size; not too big and not too small."

"Whenever you come over to study, you can take some time before you leave to play with him if you want, and if it's fine with your dad."

Well, she had certainly sealed the relationship. It didn't matter now if she could teach Mark anything or not, he'd come over as often as she would let him just to see the dog. Alex didn't know if he had won or lost. At first, he was afraid Mark wouldn't like his new tutor and refuse to go for lessons. Now he was concerned Mark would like her and her dog too much.

"If the studies get done and Mark isn't bothering you, I don't mind if he visits Chance once-in-a-while."

"Did you go to your new school today?" Rachael asked returning her attention to Mark.

"Yes. I met two of my new teachers. I had different teachers for the different subjects in my old school, too.

"So what do you think of Tulsa so far?"

"It's not bad, so far that is. I hope I can make a new friend soon. The hotel is boring without somebody to play with."

"I'm sure it is. You start school on Monday right? Maybe you'll meet a new friend then."

"Yeah, maybe, but we have to live in the hotel until the house is ready."

Mark missed the quick glance Rachael shot to Alex, but Alex didn't miss it. Her eyes shot arrows of accusation at him, and his flinch admitted guilt.

"Your dad told me you'll be living just a few blocks from here. Have you seen the house yet?"

"Yeah. We saw it this morning after we went to the school. It's neat, but really bare. It doesn't look like your house, full of color."

"I'm sure it'll be beautiful after you get all of your furniture and stuff moved in. When does your dad start work at the hospital?"

"He starts the same day I start school."

Alex liked the way Rachael dealt with Mark. He was going to be her student, and she gave him all her attention. Now, however, she was going a little too far. He didn't like being talked about as if he wasn't even in the room.

Alex jumped into the conversation, "I felt it was important for Mark and me to have some time together. Besides, I didn't want to run off and leave him alone in the hotel. We both needed some time to explore Tulsa." Before he was done with the sentence, Alex knew he had exposed his insecurity by jumping into their conversation. Damn! She brought out all of his weaknesses.

Giving Alex a belittling glance, Rachael focused her attention back to Mark. "Mark, would you like to wait and come over Monday after school, or do you want to come over tomorrow for awhile? You can tell me what you were learning in your old school, and we'll take some time to play with the dog."

"Yeah, that'd be fine. Can I come over tomorrow, Dad?"

No wonder the school said all of her students really liked her. Of course, she can get along with them. The woman has a way of pushing the parents out of the conversation in front of our own kids. She puts our kids right up on a pedestal and ignores us. I'm sure it makes the kids feel great to see their own parents out of control. Alex watched the two of them talk as if he were absent. *You're being a fool. She's just doing her job, and doing it very, very well.* Alex admonished himself. He realized that if Mrs. Carson was going to work one on one with a student, she had to establish a good rapport as soon as possible. He just didn't think it would have been so easy with Mark. They both had put up walls to keep strangers at bay. Mrs. Carson had asked non-threatening questions to get Mark talking and gradually, Alex was certain, Mark would tell her everything. Feeling guilty and ashamed, Alex finally understood Mark was just hungry for some love and attention, even if it was from a stranger and her dog.

"Mark, Chance's leash is on the counter. Why don't you take him out for a little walk so you can get to know him. I need to talk to your father for a few minutes."

"Okay, Mrs. Carson. I'll see you tomorrow. C'mon, Boy."

The two of them were gone before Alex could say anything, and what would he have said? *I don't want to be alone with this woman because......because. Why? I don't know.*

"Doctor, do you mind bringing Mark over for about an hour tomorrow?"

Alex was still lost in his own thoughts, and she'd caught him off guard. "What?"

"Do you mind if I see Mark tomorrow? I'd like to find out how far along he is with his math and English grammar. The other classes won't matter so much, but he'll have to make up work if he is too far behind in these two subjects. If he isn't up to par with the rest of the class, I can help prepare him so he won't feel so frustrated on Monday."

"That'll be fine, Mrs. Carson. I do appreciate the way you've treated Mark. He hasn't had many people treat him with respect lately."

Rachael was surprised by his thanks. She was sure she had detected some hostile feelings earlier. "You're welcome. It's important a student feels like a partner in this relationship because he has to do his share of the work. I can't and won't do it all for him."

"What time would be good for you?"

"It really doesn't matter. If there's anything you need to take care of, I can arrange my day around your schedule. I remember there are lots of details to tend to when setting up residence in a new place."

"I'm supposed to stop by the hospital about 11:00. It would be nice for Mark if I could drop him off here rather than leave him alone in the hotel."

"That'd be fine. Mark seems like a nice young man; by visiting with him for a while, I'll be able tell how far along he is in his skills. It's very likely he'll be fine, but I know from experience that being behind can be a major cause of frustration for a new student."

Alex and Mark drove away with Rachael watching them from the driveway. Having walked Mark to his side of the car, Rachael finished their conversation by telling him she was looking forward to seeing him tomorrow. *God, she's a tough woman to figure.* Alex felt uneasy with her. She could be so nice and comforting, which was harder to deal with because Alex tended to lower his guard. He liked it better when she was manipulating, then his natural response was to keep the walls of protection up.

CHAPTER SEVEN

Alex parked his midnight blue Lincoln in the employee parking lot and proceeded to walk through the front doors of St. Thomas Hospital. He wasn't familiar enough with the layout of the hospital to enter through the staff entrance, so he approached the information desk asking the volunteer to contact Dr. Gilman.

Dr. Gilman had been waiting for Alex to arrive at the hospital. She was excited about seeing a good old friend, but the professional part of her still couldn't believe Dr. Alex Zamora was becoming part of her staff. The Board of Directors and veteran doctors had been buzzing with anticipation for weeks. Some of the old buzzards felt it was their main purpose in life to give her a hard time because she, a woman, was Chief of Staff and not one of them. Bringing Alex on board was going to change the political structure in this hospital, and every doctor and nurse at the hospital was aware of it. For the first time since she had taken the reins, Dr. Gilman felt the balance of power was finally in her favor. It only took one strongly respected doctor to influence others, and now she was sure she had one in her pocket.

"Alex," Debbie addressed him with a big smile on her face and an outstretched hand. "It's wonderful to finally have you down here. I kept telling myself it wasn't my imagination, but I knew I wouldn't believe you were coming until I had you in the building."

"Debbie, it's good to see you, too. I feel just like Mark; you know, the new kid in class. I'm counting on you to help me get settled in."

"It'll be my pleasure to show you around the hospital and Tulsa as well. It really is a great city. Where's Mark today? I expected him to be with you."

"He's with his tutor this morning. She invited him over."

"And he wanted to go? I thought kids hated going to a tutor."

"This woman's different, Debbie. She makes him feel important when he's with her. The two of them talked yesterday like old friends; and, as far as Mark is concerned, her greatest asset is not necessarily her teaching ability but her dog."

"I see. She has a secret weapon, huh? Kids are suckers for a friendly dog."

"I thought it was more like the dog from hell, but I guess he isn't so bad. At least with the dog I know where I stand. The dog doesn't like me, and I don't like it."

That remark caught Debbie's attention. "So tell me about the tutor. If she's good with Mark, why do I get the feeling you don't like her?"

"I really don't know. I just feel uncomfortable with her. She's so different from - from...."

"Different from Heather, maybe?"

"No! I mean yes. They aren't alike at all."

"I see."

"I really don't care as long as she's a good tutor for Mark, I don't have to like her."

Debbie didn't want to distance Alex on his first day at the hospital. She needed him as an ally, so she casually changed the subject moving the two of them back to neutral ground.

"Come on, I'll show you the doctor's lounge and the surgical unit."

****

Mark enjoyed his time with Mrs. Carson; and she liked having him around. They didn't do much the first week because he wasn't in school yet, but Mark became more comfortable with her and Chance. She never asked him personal questions about the past. They talked about his opinion on school and people and movies they had both seen. She told Mark about the funny things Rorie and Allison had done when they were his age, but she never talked about Jack. Rachael didn't believe the boy should hear any negatives right now. She intuitively felt he had too many of his own. He needed good thoughts; he needed to laugh, and she tried to provide him with a reason. Maybe someday they would feel comfortable enough to tell each other their bad memories.

Besides Bob the bellman, Mrs. Carson was Mark's only friend; and playing with the dog was the best time he'd had in a long time. Mark could say anything he wanted, and the dog just listened, cocking his head from side to side. Chance never offered advice or judged him; he just licked Mark on the nose from time to time to show he cared.

Mark liked Mrs. Carson as a teacher too. He could tell when she was quizzing him about how much he knew, but he didn't mind. In fact, he rather enjoyed learning with her. Instead of just sitting in front of a book, she asked him about measurements when they took the dog for a walk or about fractions when he ate a cookie. He knew they'd eventually have to use his school books, but he didn't think it would be too bad.

Rachael could see the two of them sitting on the trampoline nose to nose deep in conversation. Chance was the best listener she had ever known. He'd never thrown any of those old clichés at her when she had talked about missing Jack. He kept loneliness at bay, and she loved the tailless, old yellow dog with the turned down ears. Watching the two of them together helped her to understand Mark better. He needed a friend desperately; and without realizing it, so did she.

Rachael spent a lot of time during the past week talking with Rorie and Allison about Mark. She went to bed thinking about the best way to teach him what he needed to know. He wasn't seriously behind in school, but the first few weeks would be hard. Just the social part of being a new kid in school was hard without being scholastically behind. She had met with his fourth grade teachers, so she knew what was going to be expected of him. Rachael also tried to give the teachers some insight to the boy's personality. With regular help, he would catch up quickly if he wanted to. The child's desire was always an important key to the equation.

"Hey, Mark. I have time for a walk before my first student shows up. Do you want to come with me?"

"Can we take Chance?"

"Of course. I already have his leash. Here, you can walk him."

"He really likes to walk, doesn't he?"

"I've taken him walking and running with me since he was a puppy. We try to go everyday. In fact, if I come out of the bedroom with my running shoes on, he goes to get his leash."

"He's a smart dog, Mrs. Carson. I really like him."

"I know you do. He likes you too. Sometimes he's the only one I can talk to. You know what I mean? He doesn't tell me what to do; he just listens."

"Ya, he's great to talk to. My dad doesn't understand that. He never had a dog."

"I would never have guessed that." She smiled and Mark laughed at the joke.

"Sometimes my dad has a hard time understanding what I'm feeling, but he's getting better. It's nice to spend so much time with him. We never got to do that before when my mom was...was still with us.

"Mark, I know sometimes life can be really difficult. If you ever need a place to go where nobody will ask nosy questions, you can come here. You'll be living close enough to walk over, or one of us will come to get you. Deal?"

"Deal. Thanks." Mark knew she was being sincere with him, and he liked her for it. He hadn't met her two daughters yet, but he had a good feeling he'd like them, too. "I really wanted to ask you for a favor."

"Sure. What's up?"

"Well, I have to start school next Monday, and my dad starts work at the hospital. The bus can't take me to the hotel, and I was, ah, wondering if maybe I could get off the bus here. I promise I'll be really quiet and stay out of your way."

"Mark, of course you can come over here after school, and you don't even have to be really quiet and stay out of the way."

"Really! You mean it? I'll ask my dad. Boy, I sure hope he says yes."

Rachael was surprised Mark hadn't already asked the doctor. In fact, she had suspected it was the doctor's attempt to set her up. Well if it was, she wasn't going to be the one to tell Mark "no". Irritation seethed through her at the idea of a father putting his own son in the middle of his personal games. On the other hand, she was glad Mark felt comfortable coming over. The truth was, during the day, his company kept her mind off the past.

"Tell your dad I'll do a tutoring session for you after school, then you can do some homework and wait for him to come and get you. Okay?"

"Okay!" Mark smiled and rubbed Chance's neck as the three walkers climbed up one of the steep hills in the subdivision heading towards the house.

Shortly after their walk ended, Mark went outside to wait for his father. The warm April sun felt good on his skin, and he enjoyed looking at the blue sky remembering the Chicago sky had always seemed hazy. Noticing his father's car coming down the street toward the cul-de-sac, Mark stood up. The car stopped in front of him, and he opened the heavy blue door to see his father's smiling face.

"Hey, Dad. How was the meeting at the hospital? Are we going to see the realtor? Will we be able to move in soon?"

"Hi, Mark. You're certainly full of questions. Hopefully, by the end of next week we'll finish everything up and have the moving van deliver our stuff."

"When will we have a cook?"

"Why? Are you worried about starving to death if I do the cooking?" Alex asked his son with a smile on his face. Everything seemed to be going along so smoothly, too smoothly.

"Not really. It's just that after the great cooking at the hotel I'm used to some pretty good stuff. You're not exactly equal to the chef at the hotel restaurant."

"You don't think they should feature exploding hotdogs at the Duck Club?" Both of them burst out laughing.

"Dad, have you thought about how I'm going to get home from school next week?"

"Yes, I'll get off work everyday to come and get you."

"Oh."

"You sound disappointed. Did you have something else in mind?"

"I didn't realize you'd be willing to do that, so I asked Mrs. Carson if I could get off the bus at her house."

"You did what?" Alex shouted. "Why'd you do that?" Alex felt the green wave wash over him like a giant wave overtakes a surfer. *I can't believe I'm so jealous of this woman. I didn't even feel like this when I found out Heather was having an affair. She's going to worm her way into his life and find out everything.* Alex suspected Rachael must have planted this idea in Mark's head. He certainly wouldn't have thought of going over there every day by himself. Alex remembered suggesting to Rachael that Mark come over after school every day, but he had only been jesting. *Isn't that why you made sure you bought a house that was close? She's beating me at my own game. Shit! I don't even go into the house, and I still feel like she's manipulating me.*

"I'm sorry, Dad. I thought it'd be helping you out if you didn't have to worry about me after school. Besides, I need to have a tutoring lesson anyway. I might as well go after school and finish my homework before you get home."

Alex knew this all made sense, but he still didn't like the idea of Mark going over there every afternoon. She'd be the first one to see him after school and hear what had happened during the day.

"Mark, has Mrs. Carson asked you any questions about our background? You know, anything about your mom or why we moved."

"No, not a single one. Maybe that's why I like going over there. She doesn't pry."

"Hum." *I wonder what her next move will be.* Alex formed the thoughts as he heard Mark plead.

"Please, Dad. I really like being there. It's hard to explain, but she makes me feel good, comfortable, not on guard like I had to be during the trial with the nanny and other tutor."

"Let me think about it." When that line came out, Mark knew the topic was closed for the present, but he was determined to bring it up again. He really didn't understand why his father didn't like Mrs.

Carson. Sometimes he just couldn't understand adults, but Mark felt his dad was wrong about Mrs. Carson. He was sure.

CHAPTER EIGHT

On Easter Sunday, Alex and Mark walked a little uncomfortably through the large front doors of the white church they had admired all week. Even though they were unfamiliar with the setting, they had looked forward to becoming part of the picture they had been enjoying from their hotel window. A throng of members were in the narthex waiting for the earlier service to end so they could enter the sanctuary. Alex and Mark looked around at the people not expecting to see anyone they knew but still interested in who was present. Within moments the masses filed out past those who were waiting for their turn to worship God.

Several dozen people entered the sanctuary before Alex and Mark. The massive white room was simplistic holy elegance. A single grand cross hung behind the pulpit against a dark blue background. There were no ostentatious stained glass windows or gold ornamentation. Alex had grown up going to churches which were covered with decorations in the name of God. He had often found himself sitting in the pew wondering if the collection was spent on the church building or on the benevolent missions.

As Alex glanced around the room, he didn't realize Mark was leading him toward a specific pew. "C'mom, Dad. Hurry up before somebody else takes the seat."

"What seat? Where are we going?" Alex queried being pulled along by his arm.

"Here, Dad. Right here."

Before Alex could object, he was pulled into a pew and was staring into the face of Mrs. Carson. Dragging Mark forcibly back out of the pew would have been just a little obvious, but he thought about it. Then it was too late; the greeting had started, and he was stuck like a mouse in a trap.

"Mark, it's wonderful to see you. Happy Easter."

"Good Morning, Mrs. Carson. We really didn't expect to see anybody we knew in this big church. I'm glad we found you."

Rachael didn't think Mark's father was in agreement with the situation; however, there wasn't much he could graciously do about it. Rachael, on the other hand, was glad to see Mark. "Mark, I'd like to introduce you to my daughters: Allison and Aurora; we call her Rorie."

"Hi, Mark. We've heard a lot about you." Allison addressed him with a warm smile on her face.

"Hi," Mark replied, "This is my dad."

The gentlemanly instincts kicked in causing Alex to offer his hand to each of the girls saying, "Hello, it's nice to meet you.

"The pleasure is ours, Dr. Zamora."

"It really is," Allison added in a voice dripping with honey.

Rachael knew if she looked at her daughter now, she'd see dreamy eyes and a seemingly shy smile. She had to admit that in the double breasted navy blue suit with the red and navy geometric tie, the man could take a woman's breath away. He was definitely "prince charming" handsome.

Before Rachael knew what had happened, the girls had whisked Mark off to show him some of the church. "We'll be back in a few minutes, Mom. Save our places."

"Happy Easter, Dr. Zamora. I hope you enjoy the service." Rachael added to herself, *even though, I'm sure you won't like where you're sitting.*

Alex had no choice but to converse with her. "We could see the church from our hotel room. The whole picture was so breathtaking, we decided we should try it."

"I'm glad you did. Reverend Gordon is an excellent speaker, and the student program is a fun learning experience for the kids."

"Have you been members here for a long time?" Alex found the conversation coming easy as they sat down beside each other.

"Ever since we moved to Tulsa about six years ago."

"I thought, for some reason, you had been here longer than that. Where did you move from?"

Rachael hadn't realized the coincidence of her living in the Chicago area for sixteen years before leaving for the warmer climate of Tulsa. "Well, Doctor, we spent several years living in a suburb south of Chicago."

The look on his face told her that he'd had no idea she was also from Chicago; however, he had not missed the connection either. "Really? I didn't know." The words were out of his mouth before he could stop them. "I swear."

Rachael smiled and then laughed, "I know. I could tell immediately by the look of shock on your face. Honestly, I hadn't even made the connection about us both being from Chicago until now."

People were pouring into the sanctuary at this point. Rachael hoped the girls and Mark would return quickly. Seating was always tight on Easter that was why they had come so early. Suspecting the three might be up to something, she turned around to look for them. They all came through the door wearing big smiles and whispering among themselves. Rachael recognized the gleam in her daughters' eyes.

"Doctor."

"Alex, please call me Alex rather than doctor."

"Alex, the kids are up to something."

Alex saw the three coming toward them displaying big smiles. "What makes you think so?" He whispered.

"Trust me. You know your patients; I know kids. These three are conniving something. They are weaving the web; and, I have a funny feeling, we are the prey. By the way, please call me Rachael." At that moment, the three partners wiggled past the seated worshippers and sat down forcing Rachael to move so close to Alex she couldn't avoid brushing against his leg. She felt him flinch and tried to pull away, but Rorie was pushed up tight beside her.

Alex leaned forward seeing Mark's smiling face and a quick wink. "I think we've been caught." He softly admitted to Rachael.

The music started, and Rachael felt Alex begin to relax. This was certainly not the type of Easter service each had expected. Rather than sitting alone to contemplate private feelings, neither could stop thinking about the person sitting a heartbeat away.

Everyone stood to sing the first hymn, and Rachael found herself without a hymnal. The girls were sharing so Mark could have his own book; and even though it was possible for three to share, it was hard for Rachael to see the words. To Alex's disbelief, he found himself offering to share with her. Rachael moved closer to accept the overture. For the first time, she was aware of his height; coming only to his chin, she had to look up to thank him.

Alex had decided to stop fighting the inevitable: if he was going to have to be so close to her, he might as well enjoy the sermon. In spite of the close proximity to the one person who made him feel uneasy about himself, Alex found himself partaking fully in the pleasure of her fragrance. There was no doubt about it: in addition to the pleasant scent, Alex enjoyed the way she looked.

It was a moving service that made Alex and Rachael reflect about how they had judged each other; however, neither would have admitted it. All three kids smiled and giggled to each other sneaking glances at their respective parent. Rachael wondered if any of them heard a word Reverend Dan said. Every time she tried to move closer to Rorie, Rorie pushed back not giving her an inch of space. Rachael wasn't angry at any of them. The whole situation was rather funny, and she hoped Alex would see the humorous side of the predicament and not condemn her daughters and her. After all, it was Easter.

When the service ended, all five of them stood up. A petite white haired woman behind Rachael and Alex tapped him on the shoulder. "Sir, I just wanted to tell you that I think you two have a beautiful family." Before either of them could deny the relationship, she added in a wispy fragile voice, "it's so nice to see family members being kind to each other."

Rachael was totally taken off guard by Alex's gallant answer, "Thank you, madam. They do have their moments," he finished with a warm handsome smile.

Rachael looked up at him with a question in her eyes, and he answered, "What else could I say? It's Easter, and I didn't want to destroy her illusion. Besides they don't look too bad together."

"The three of them can certainly lay a plan together. I think the rest of the trap is about to spring. Are you ready?"

"How do you know?"

"Look at the mischievous gleam in the eyes and the smirk on the faces. They haven't stopped whispering since the music ended."

"Dad, the girls invited us over for Easter dinner. Can we go? We aren't doing anything." The trap was sprung. The invitation was issued by the darling daughters and could not graciously be retracted. The son had made it clear there were no other plans. The parents were caught in the web, and if either one turned down the offer now, it would have been an affront to all.

Rachael turned around to face Alex. She met his dancing eyes and realized he had a softer side that she liked. "It would be nice to have company for dinner. Will you come?"

"Thank you, I think we'd both enjoy it."

The three scheming culprits responded together with an over loud, "Yes!"

Everyone laughed, and silently each parent vowed to have a serious talk about the penalties of manipulating parents by putting them in awkward situations.

"What time can we come over?" The eagerness flowing from Mark's body was unmistakable.

"Mark, you can come over any time you want. You should probably change clothes first and bring your swimming suit. We always open the pool for Easter Sunday. It's tradition."

"Really?"

"Really. Dinner will be about 2:00, so don't eat anything."

The girls walked out ahead of the others. They both knew they had tampered with fate, although they saw it more as just giving fate a helping hand. However, Mom would have some words of admonishment they might as well face in the car in order to get the scolding over with.

Mark took his father's hand as they walked from the building. He didn't realize the significance of what he had participated in; but feeling just a little guilty, he looked up at his father and said, "Thanks, Dad."

All of the words Alex had considered saying to his son melted away. Mark didn't want to spend the holiday stuck in a stuffy hotel no matter how grand it was; and in reality, Alex didn't either. "You're welcome, son. I love you."

"I love you, too," Mark added as he took a firmer grasp of his father's hand.

As the car doors closed beyond outside ears, the girls braced themselves. They gave each other a "here it comes" smile and waited, not feeling even a little sorry, for Rachael's scolding remarks.

"Well girls, are you feeling happy with your morning's accomplishment?" Rachael asked trying to sound very motherly and very angry.

"Actually, Mom, we are. We like Mark and felt bad that he and his father would have to spend the day alone. After all, they really haven't had time to make many friends yet."

"Yeah," Allie added, "You might say: it was the Easterly thing to do."

"You can't justify putting me in a very uncomfortable position. You know how I feel about the man."

"You could've fooled us. We didn't notice any animosity between you two."

Now it was Rorie's turn to do the follow up, "Actually, you looked quite friendly."

"Thanks to the three of you and especially you, Rorie, I had to almost sit on his lap."

"We were pretty slick about that one. Honestly, we didn't plan the move; it just happened."

"Oh sure." Rachael responded with skepticism.

"Really, Mom. We took Mark on a quick tour through the education wing and then plotted lunch." Allison finished up with pride in her voice that made all of them laugh until the tears rolled down their faces.

It was time for Rachael to admit they had done what she couldn't. "Actually, I'm glad you did invite them over. I don't think Alex..."

"So it's 'Alex' now?"

"Yes, I don't think ALEX would've agreed if I had just invited them myself without your help, as scheming as it was."

"You're welcome," was the uniform response.

Allison still had to add her romantic remarks, "Mom, he is so handsome. No, I mean really gorgeous." Again the laughter vibrated the car.

****

Rachael and the girls had a delicious Easter dinner planned. A beautiful smoked ham was baking slowly to perfection. The sweet potatoes and augratin potatoes were ready to put in the oven. Each of them had picked her favorite part of the Easter meal to make, so there would be plenty for two hungry men. The traditional Easter lamb cake with his jelly bean eyes and nose was sitting in a garden of green coconut. Rachael was especially glad now that at the last minute she had pulled out a few of her old Easter decorations when she unpacked the girl's Easter baskets.

"Rorie, quick run upstairs to the attic and find me one of the old baskets. Let's make one up for Mark. I doubt if Alex thought about it."

Quickly Rachael dialed the phone. Not wanting to make Alex look bad, she decided to call and see if he had anything to put in the basket. "Hello, Alex?"

"Yes," was the response. He knew it was her voice, and he wondered if she would really call to cancel the dinner invitation. Alex wanted to kick himself for thinking such a horrible thought. It was the cynical side of him reacting to what he suspected could be the cynical side of her.

"Alex, do you mind if the girls and I make an Easter basket for Mark? I didn't want you to think we were trying to a .." Rachael didn't know how to put her doubts into words without making them sound patronizing. "Well, I didn't want to do it without your having the opportunity to add something."

"Thank you for thinking about Mark and for calling, I hadn't even thought about an Easter basket. I don't have anything, but let me think about it."

"Okay, we'll see what we have handy and keep the basket hidden until after you have a chance to add something if you want. Alex, I don't want to put you in a bad position with this. We didn't think about it until we walked in the door."

"Stop worrying. I'll see if I can come up with something. We'll be there in about half an hour." With a warm humorous tone, Alex added, "I don't think I can keep Mark here any longer than that."

"We'll be waiting for you."

Everyone enjoyed the fine Easter meal and especially the company. Discussion about school and feelings were plentiful. The girls wanted to tell Mark about everything he could enjoy during the summer. They compared the cold frigid winters of Chicago with the mild affable winters of Tulsa.

"I hated that cold north wind. It would last forever."

"I know," agreed Mark. "I couldn't go outside for weeks without freezing my.... ah, body parts off." Mark blushed from the tip of his nose to the tips of his fingers and probably other parts as well. Everyone laughed at his innocent slip.

"You'll be able to wear shorts to school in January," Allison tried to help Mark save face by changing the subject."

"Now don't exaggerate," Rachael warned, "Or the poor boy will assume every morning this next winter will be warm. It still gets cold here, Mark. Don't be fooled by what these two say."

"It's a lot nicer than those cold north winters, Mom. You have to admit that."

"I do admit it; however, I think most of the country has better winters than Chicago does. I had to wear long underwear and gloves to bed."

"Where's Chance? He hasn't come to see me yet." Mark's question was full of concern.

"He usually stays in my room when we eat. And, I didn't want your father to be uncomfortable all afternoon."

The smiles were warm and genuine. Rachael's eyes locked onto Alex's, and she marveled at the dancing blue pools of light. When he was happy, his eyes didn't simply twinkle like other peoples'; they did the jitterbug. His smile and laughter were pleasant, but the eyes were stunning, and Rachael felt her breath catch in her throat when she realized he was returning the eye contact with equal emotion. Only Mark missed the exchange between the two parents; however, the two daughters had been watching every move with hopeful anticipation.

Rachael was the one to break the moment, "Mark, I think there was something left here for you."

"What? I haven't lost anything."

"Mark, what do you get on Easter?"

"An Easter basket?" It was more of a question than an answer. "Really? You mean it? Where? I haven't had an Easter basket for a long time."

The girls were quick to give instructions. "You have to find it. The Easter Bunny always hides the baskets that get delivered here. We found yours this morning while we looked for ours."

"No way. You guys are too big to get Easter baskets."

Rachael looked him straight in the eye and said with the love only a mother has to give, "In this house, everybody gets an Easter basket. Now go find yours."

Mark was off in an instant with the girls going after him to give the clues of "warmer or colder."

"Would you like some more champagne while we wait, Alex?" Rachael offered getting up to reach for the bottle.

"Thank you, it's excellent. What is it?"

"I have some friends in France who come and stay with us for a few weeks during the summers. Sometimes they send a case of champagne for Christmas, and I savor each bottle until the last drop is gone."

"I feel special you shared some with me." They smiled, but this time Rachael specifically avoided the eyes. She wasn't ready for the intimacy that went with the contact. At least, she didn't think she was ready for it yet.

"By the way, does everybody in this house really get an Easter basket?"

Now she looked up at him, "Absolutely, it's tradition. Christmas stockings, too."

"Traditions are nice. We don't really have any yet, but we will."

"Here's to tradition, then." Rachael said as they moved to tap their bubbling champagne glasses together. This time there was no escaping his eyes as they locked onto hers not letting go. She knew her cheeks were raging flames of red; and she blamed the champagne rather than her desires. After all, those feelings were dead; weren't they? Rachael had believed her romantic feelings had been buried with Jack. True love was a once in a lifetime experience.

Alex had noticed her reaction when their eyes locked and was as startled as Rachael about the feelings they were both trying to deny. He had felt like a teenager when he noticed more than just his body temperature rising. He didn't know why they had gotten off to such a bad start, but this was certainly more enjoyable than fighting. In fact, Alex couldn't even remember the last holiday meal he'd had with a family. Most of his holidays had been at the hospital with big dinner leftovers when he got home. Even as a child, he and his mother usually ate without his father because he was in surgery or seeing a dying patient. Like father like son. The lyrics of the song "Cats in the Cradle" suddenly seemed heavy on his mind. He didn't want the same destiny for his son. This was what Alex had missed all of his life; and if he was going to start over with his son, then this is what he was going to fight for: a family for him and Mark. As Alex relished in the idea of what a family could mean for him and Mark, the word "family" hit him in the gut. There was a family here. Just because there was no man present now didn't mean there wasn't one. A Mr. Carson had to be around somewhere. Alex was ashamed of what he had been considering. A few hours ago he had still disliked, or a least thought he disliked this woman; and now he was just a little jealous thinking she must have a husband somewhere.

The moment was saved by Mark's running into the room, "I found it! I found it!"

"What did you get from the Easter Bunny, Mark?" His father asked with interest.

"Well, I got lots of jelly beans, a big chocolate bunny, and a pass to Big Splash? What's Big Splash?"

"It's the best water park in town. We have a ton of fun, Mark, and we'd love to take you."

"Wow! Dad can I go? When does it open?"

They all laughed at his enjoyment. Mark picked up an envelope and opened it. As he read the words, his eyes grew large and filled with tears. "Really, Dad? I know this is your writing. I can get a puppy as soon as we move into our house?"

"Yes, Mark. I promise. The first Saturday we are in our house we'll go get you a puppy."

Mark was in his father's arms instantly. "Thank's, Dad. This is the best Easter I've ever had."

"It's the best Easter for me, too, son."

"Wow! My own dog. I can't believe it. Can we go swimming now?"

"Kids!" Alex said with disbelief hanging on his tongue. "It's amazing how quickly their thoughts can change."

"The change can be swift. Girls, why don't you go out and play with Mark while I clean up."

"I'll help," Alex offered, which caused everyone to stare at him. "I promise, I'll try not to drop anything. By the way, please let Chance out. I'd better get used to having a dog around."

Mark couldn't wait for the dog to come around the corner and went to meet him. Chance didn't need a tail to show his excitement: his whole body shook from the nose to the tuft of hair where a tail would have been. The two friends greeted each other by rolling around on the floor exchanging kisses and licks. The scene caused Alex's heart to swell. He had wondered whether or not he was doing the right thing by promising to get Mark a dog, but his concerns were quickly put to rest.

Chance was glad to be set free and had to greet all of those in the room. Alex was the last one to be approached, but he was part of the group and deserved a greeting. Chance walked with reservation up to the man who didn't like him.

"Hold your hand out to him. Let him get your scent, Dad."

"Come here, Boy. I've heard a lot about you." At the kind words of greeting, the dog started his ritual sniff and wiggle. Within seconds, the licking stage was finished, and the two of them were friends, at least from the dog's point of view.

"See, Dad. He's a great dog. C'mon, Chance, let's go outside." The dog and Mark were gone before anybody could stop them.

Alex was grateful to Rachael for making the day a memorable one for his son and for him as well. "Thank you for giving him the Easter basket. I didn't realize such a small gesture would mean so much to him. As a child, he has missed a lot." The regret was heavy in his voice.

Rachael wanted to reach out verbally but hesitated for a second. Then as she started placing the dirty plates into the dishwasher the words comfortably came from her mouth, "Alex, we both have a past. I assume that yours is like mine: some of it's happy and some of it's not." As long as she didn't look at him, the words were not so difficult to say. "I haven't told Mark anything about my past, and I haven't asked him anything about yours."

"I appreciate it, but..."

Rachael stood up and looked into his eyes. The shadowy glance she had noticed the first time she had met him had replaced the dancing eyes, "I don't want to ruin the afternoon, so please let me finish before I lose my nerve. I just wanted to say, if you or Mark ever need or want to talk, I'm a good listener."

"We're just pulling ourselves together as a family if you can consider two males a family. It's been hard. You're helping Mark make an easier transition. Thank's."

There was more to say. It was hanging on the tip of her tongue, but the words stopped as she stared into the deep pools of blue: the dancing had ceased, but the shadows were also gone.

"As long as we are talking, I have a question I've wanted to ask you all afternoon; but I felt awkward asking something that was really none of my business."

Rachael had wondered how long it would be before one of them noticed there was no man around the house. Mark hadn't really been around when Jack would have been home, but the absence of a father on a holiday would be enough to raise the question.

"I would imagine you want to know if there's a Mr. Carson?"

"I didn't think I was so shallow that you could read my mind this easily, but then you have been good at reading me since the day we met."

Rachael remembered their first meeting and how they had gotten off on the wrong foot. "I'm sorry about that first meeting. I shouldn't have jumped to conclusions about your relationship with Mark."

"Your guessing was pretty much on target. I didn't know my son at all, but we're making progress. We did - do have a background we try not to talk about. It causes people to give us both a hard time. I don't know if I'm ready to tell anyone here."

"Maybe, someday, you'll be ready to tell me. You wanted to know where my husband is." With a deep breath, she continued, "He was killed in a hit and run accident two years ago. There, I've said it. You see, I've had a hard time talking about my past also. The girls were faster to move on with their lives than I have been." Even though she had said the words without falling into tears, the stress was in her voice, and Alex could feel the pain with her. He understood loss and grief and pain so well.

"Did the police ever find out who hit him?"

"They never really had any clues to go on. They could tell me the car which hit Jack was blue because of the paint marks on his mangled mountain bike. However, since there were no skid marks, they just assumed the driver hadn't seen him. After a short investigation, the accident was classified as 'hit and run: unsolved.'"

"I'm sorry to hear that. It's hard to put closure on a part of your life when the questions go unanswered."

"At the time, it didn't really matter. Having the accident solved or unsolved wouldn't bring Jack back to me."

"That's true."

"The hardest part for me is knowing he died alone. Jack hated being alone. You see, he didn't die instantly, but several minutes after being struck. The police said the marks on the ground led them to believe Jack pulled himself out of the way of on-coming traffic. They said the head injury was fatal; and even if there had been immediate help, death was imminent. I just hate thinking of him being alone for those last few minutes."

There was a lot more to be said, but now was not the time. A friendship was building; but, like anything else, rushing could ruin it. Rachael liked the man who was sharing the day with her, but....the slightest ring of a door bell registered with her senses.

"I'd better get the door." Her remark broke the bond and regretfully, she pulled herself away to see who was interrupting them. "Mathew, this is a surprise. What're you doing here?"

Indignantly he snapped, "I came over to wish you and the girls Happy Easter and to share this bottle of wine with you."

Rachael was surprised not only by his appearance but by his attitude. She tried to comment without showing the irritation she felt. "Thank you, Mathew, we've had a wonderful Easter."

"I can see that." Mathew snapped the words at Rachael but was glaring at Alex. "When did you start tutoring on holidays?"

"I beg your pardon?" She responded with her own sarcasm.

Mathew knew he had over stepped the bounds of his relationship. "I'm sorry. I just didn't expect to a ....find....a anyone here."

That was obvious to everyone. To cover up his frustration, Mathew thrust the bottle of wine out to Rachael. "Here, we'll drink it some other time."

Rachael didn't want a rain check with Mathew. The two of them had casual conversation from time to time but never with a glass of wine. How could she affably get out of this? "I appreciate your offer; however, you should really share this with one of your friends."

"Fine," he snapped yanking his hand back as if he'd been slapped. Without another word, the angry young man turned from them and stomped away from the house.

"That was the boy who came over the afternoon I met you, right?"

"Yes, he used to be a student of mine when he was in high school. After Jack died, he started coming over to take care of the yard and the pool for us. I've never seen him act this way. We've never shared a bottle of wine or anything else." Rachael was baffled by the whole scene, shaking her head in disbelief as she backed away from the door to close it. They didn't see Mathew turn and look just before he drove away.

"Rachael, I honestly think he believes there's more to the relationship than you do," Alex said offering her an explanation.

"That's impossible. I've tried to be especially careful not to give him any indication that there was anything more than just a casual friendship. He's the handyman. That's all!"

"I may not be able to see people close to me very objectively, but I do understand something about human nature. After all, I'm a doctor; and that young man has a mountain size crush on you."

"I hope you're wrong, Alex. Mathew's a nice young man, and I don't want to hurt him."

Both of them brushed off the incident as harmless and walked back through the kitchen toward the patio and pool. The sun was shooting its bright spring rays toward them warming their hearts as well as their bodies.

"Hey, Mark, is the water warm?"

Mark didn't even notice his father until he heard the question, "Yeah, I guess so. I like it. C'mon in."

"I don't think so. I really prefer warm water."

Rachael laughed at his remark, "Me, too. I prefer the jacuzzi to the pool until about the middle of June. Then the pool water is great."

"This yard is beautiful. No wonder you need help taking care of it. It must take hours just to mow the lawn."

"I used to do most of the work myself except the pool. That job belonged to the girls. They wanted the pool - they got the job of taking care of it."

"Great philosophy. I'll have to remember that with a new puppy on its way."

"Mark was so surprised. I don't think anything else could've made him happier."

"I'm sure he'll enjoy it, but having a dog around will be a challenge for me. In case you haven't noticed, I'm not real good with dogs."

"I assume you never had a pet when you were a child?"

"How could you tell?" A smirk accompanied the friendly sarcasm. "What's the pleasure? I don't understand. Animals are dirty, noisy, and often dangerous."

"The bond that can form between an owner and his pet is an unconditional love most people never understand. Unconditional love and devotion are rare gifts one person can give to another, and very few people are capable of giving them; however pets give the gifts easily. All they want in return for their love and devotion is time and love from their owner. In a way a pet is a lot like a child."

"What do you mean?"

"Kids need food, shelter, love, and consistent discipline. So does a pet."

"I have trouble with the discipline part and the love, for that matter. Food and shelter are easy."

"You seem to be doing all right. Your time is the most important part of love. If you spend time with Mark the love will come naturally, and you'll need less discipline. Consistent discipline is important."

"Why?"

"I don't mean punishment. I mean rules. The rules Mark has to live by in your household. That discipline is his safe boundary marker, his security."

"Actually, I've never thought about it. My wife had always handled everything."

"Consistent discipline means that if Mark breaks the rules there is reasonable punishment for the infraction. Discipline for a child is like the sides of a crib for a baby. He stands at the side bars shaking the bed till it rattles. Those side bars are his boundary, his security. Without those boundaries, he'd fall and get hurt. It's the same with rules and consistent discipline. Without them a child feels insecure, but he continues to test the rules just like the baby rattles the sides of his crib."

"Interesting analogy. Mark and I will have to establish our rules when we move into our house and get on a regular schedule."

"He won't really start to test you as his parent until he begins school and has to deal with peer influence."

"He hasn't spent much time with anyone but you and me for the last month or so. Actually, I haven't experienced any of the emotional problems his teacher and principal alluded to in their report. Of course, he isn't around other kids to fight, and he really didn't have any friends by the time we left Chicago. He has seemed like a normal happy kid ever since we moved to Tulsa."

"I haven't noticed anything unusual about his personality either. In fact, he really has been a pleasure to have around. Just take it one day at a time. Maybe the change of scenery was just what he needed."

"He's been fine around us; however, the challenge for him and for us will start tomorrow. He wants to make friends so badly that I'm afraid he might get mixed up with the wrong type of kids."

"We'll just have to talk to him about what happens everyday. It'll be better for him to stop over here after school rather than go home to an empty house. Kids always want to talk as soon as they walk in the door. If you put them off, the excitement of the day is gone. This way if anything has happened, I can let you know right away."

"I'm going to hire a housekeeper as soon as I can. Hopefully, she'll be willing to keep an eye on him for a couple of hours until I get home from the hospital. Besides, we need a cook."

"Mark tells me you have an interesting way of preparing hotdogs."

The remark caused both of them to laugh, "If I eat another hotdog in this century, I'm sure I'll grow big droopy ears and my nose will be forever wet." The laughter caught the attention of all three kids in the pool, and they smiled at each other sharing the hope that the plan was working.

CHAPTER NINE

Rachael knew before she opened the door who was standing there because of the mist creeping around the threshold. In spite of her desire to not answer the constant ringing of the bell, she could not stop her hand from reaching out to turn the knob. Gray mesmerizing mist flooded in around her as the door opened. The man was so much taller than before, Rachael couldn't see his face. In fact, she couldn't even tell if he was wearing a police uniform. Only the words he said registered in her mind, "Dead Dead Dead."

"Noooooo!" The word echoed around her as she fell into the endless black pit of fear. Her arms thrashed through the emptiness trying desperately to grab anything that would stop the descent.

Suddenly, Rachael was awake in the darkness of her room panting with desperate fear. She listened but there was no sound of running feet, so she must have been able to pull herself out of the dream before any audible screams had disturbed the girls. Even Chance had not gotten up yet. He was always the first to show some reaction to having his cherished slumber interrupted.

"Hey, Boy, this one wasn't so bad. It was different too. Let's go get something to drink." The two friends quietly moved through the house toward the kitchen.

Rachael put on the tea kettle and gave Chance some fresh water. His look told her he would rather be asleep, but he patiently followed her to his water bowl. Rachael sat in the breakfast nook and sipped a cup of herbal tea contemplating the new twist to her dreams. When the kitchen ceiling light came on, it caused her to jump spilling some of the steamy liquid onto her lap.

"Honey, what are you doing up?" Getting up to get a towel, Rachael softly asked the sleepy eyed Rorie.

"I'm getting ready for school. What are you doing up?" But she knew the answer before she had asked it. "You were dreaming again, weren't you?"

"Yes, but it was different this time."

"Tell me while I eat breakfast. I'm starving, and I have to get to school early."

"First, the guy was different: he was much taller, and it wasn't the same face I usually see in the dream. Second, it didn't last as long; I was able to wake myself up before I started screaming."

"Yeah, I didn't hear anything until my alarm went off. What do you think caused the change?"

"I don't really know. I've been trying to think about what was different yesterday, and the only thing I can think of is that the Zamoras spent the afternoon with us. Mathew came over, but his being here wasn't new."

"No, but his attitude was different. Right?"

"True. His attitude was very different."

"Mom, my suggestion is to approach this scientifically. Write down everything you can remember about the past nightmares and any approximate dates. Then write down dates and events from now on. See if any patterns come up. Maybe that'll help. Now, I've got to go get ready."

"Thanks, Dear. Spoken like a true scientist." Rachael drew a warm smile from her daughter as she walked out of the kitchen to get ready for a long day at school. Rachael liked the idea of logging her dreams and the events that occurred on the given day, so she got up for a pad of paper and returned to the table to write and watch the sun come up.

****

"So, Alex, what did you think of your first staff meeting?"

"Actually, Debbie, it wasn't much different than any other staff meeting. Every hospital has it's politics, and St. Thomas isn't any different. You do have your hands full, don't you?"

"Yes, a few of the older doctors don't like working for a woman."

"I can tell. Their body language started yelling as soon as they walked into the room."

With a light chuckle, Debbie answered, "I know; they walk into every meeting with their hands shoved in their pockets and frowns on their faces. Then they sit through the whole meeting with their arms crossed and grunt when asked a question. I have to give them credit though because no matter how they feel about working for a woman, their vote always seems to reflect what's best for the hospital and patients. You know what I mean? They never disagree with me just to disagree. It's funny how things change. Before I became Chief of Staff, I got along fine with them."

"I know what you mean about change. Our human nature is to fight it; but no matter how hard we resist, it happens anyway. Boy, does it happen." Alex finished with a sigh.

"You're right. People always say the only guarantees in life are death and taxes, but I think change should be added to the list.

"I agree. Now what's on the agenda for me?"

"Right now it's mostly consultation with several of the doctors who want to pick your brain for information. Dr. Paterson wants your help with a tough case in pediatrics. He has a fifteen year old boy with a tumor in his lower spinal cord. He'll meet you there right away if you have time. I've put a half a dozen or so additional cases on your desk. The name of the doctor requesting your help is on the cover of each case file. I suspect within a week or so you'll have more cases than you want. Your reputation has preceded you, doctor, and patients naturally want the best."

"Thanks, I think."

"I know you want to limit your time at the hospital. The number of cases you agree to take is up to you."

"I appreciate your letting me start at my own pace. I really need to make sure Mark is settled in before I take on too much."

"As a mother, I certainly understand. You're all he has. Come on, I'll take you down to meet Paterson, then you're on your own for the rest of the day."

As they stepped out of the elevator into the sterile white hallway, the din resembled a school cafeteria not a hospital ward. Every room pulsated with noise and motion.

Dr. Gilman and Alex approached the nurses station where everyone was moving as fast as she or he could. They waited at the counter for one of the nurses at the desk to look up.

"Excuse me," Dr. Gilman said a little irritated that it was taking so long for one of the nurses to acknowledge the two doctors standing right in front of the counter.

Looking up and seeing the handsome eyes, a very pretty young nurse answered, "Yes, Doctor. I'm sorry. We're really swamped today. What can I help you with?"

Debbie knew Alex would attract the attention of most of the nurses, married and single alike. She was glad that their friendship was firmly established because she would enjoy watching the chickens chase the fox, or maybe in this case, Alex was the chicken. *Poor guy, he is going to have his hands full trying to stay out of the traps that will be set to catch him.*

"We need to know which room the Broadmore boy is in."

Without taking her eyes off of Alex, the nurse answered Debbie with a honey dipped voice, "He's in room 428, and Dr. Paterson is waiting for you, Dr. Gilman."

The two of them walked into the room where Tony Broadmore was waiting to be examined by another doctor. The tumor had gone undetected until the pain forced the boy to tell his parents something was wrong. By then the tumor was the size of an orange and had grown around the nerve endings of his spine. Successful surgery would be nearly impossible. Dr. Paterson had used every source available up to this point; and, for the first time since he had found the tumor, he felt there was hope for the boy. If he had to recommend any doctor in the country, it would've been Dr. Alexander Zamora.

"Dr. Zamora, I'm so glad to meet you. We didn't really have a chance to talk this morning." Dr. Paterson reached past Dr. Gilman to shake Alex's hand. "We were all pleased when Dr. Gilman told us you'd be joining the staff. It's certainly our good fortune."

"Thank you, I look forward to working with all of you. Please introduce me to this young man."

Alex looked directly at Tony and introduced himself. Tony was used to the doctors treating him like a piece of meat rather than a person in pain. He was surprised by the bed side manner of this new doctor.

With reservation he answered, "Hi, my name is Tony." Alex responded by holding out his hand, and the sick young man smiled returning the gesture. The hand shake was a new tactic for Alex. He had been impressed by how it had worked on Mark when Rachael did it, so he thought he'd try it himself. It was amazing how much the kids responded to the simple sign of respect.

"Dr. Zamora, will you be able to remove this thing from my back?"

"Let me take a look at all of the information then I'll let you know."

"Will you tell me honestly?"

"Yes, I'll tell you honestly, Tony. Now I need to take a look at your back."

After Alex had a look at his first patient, he and Dr. Paterson went to Paterson's office to look at the X-rays and other test results. The two doctors spent a couple of hours discussing the necessary surgery.

"How did the tumor get so big without the boy noticing?"

"He was playing basketball and hoped the pain was caused by a pulled muscle or something equally harmless. I think he was scared to death it was serious and would take him out of the game."

"Who knows what goes through a kid's head. It's even possible he mentioned it to his coach or parents, and they told him it was nothing."

"We were all relieved when the biopsy showed the tumor was benign. I would've bet a month's pay that it was going to be malignant, and I think his parents would've made the same wager."

"He isn't out of the woods yet, but at least he won't have to go through chemo. That's the worst treatment there is."

"Man, I agree. What do you anticipate for Tony?"

"The operation is going to be risky, but not impossible. Some of the nerve endings will probably be damaged, but it'll be hard to predict how severe it will be until we get in there. I can tell by the two different X-rays the tumor has increased in size slightly since Tony was admitted."

"Yes, I noticed the growth right here at the bottom," Dr. Paterson pointed to the screen.

"The sooner we operate and get that thing out of there, the better his chances are of walking again."

"I agree. Will you do the operation? I'll assist."

"If that's what you want, I'd be happy to do it."

"It's what's best for the boy. You've had more experience with this than I have."

****

Later that afternoon, Alex caught up with Debbie again. "Is the noise in pediatrics always that bad?"

"It's kids."

"Aren't they too sick to cause so much commotion?"

Debbie laughed at him. "Not all of them are at death's door, ya know. They're kids. They get bored and they make noise. They play games and sometimes they even fight."

"Aren't most of them missing school? Shouldn't they be studying?"

"A lot of them could be, probably should be. Some of them even have their school books. However, parents are generally more stressed about the illness or injury; consequently, school work is easy to put off."

"Wouldn't everybody be better off if the students did do something constructive with their time rather than just wait. The kids would be better prepared to return to school which, I assume, is the ultimate goal for most of them. The nurses wouldn't have to be 'nursemaids'; they could be the nurses they're trained to be. In addition, the patients who need to be quiet wouldn't be disturbed by the pent up frustration and boredom of the others."

"It's a good idea, but none of the nurses have time to play teacher even if they knew what to do."

"I know. I was thinking about a professional who's in touch with the school system and well respected by the teachers and the kids."

"I see. Do you have someone particular in mind? Anyone you know perhaps?" Debbie asked him with a smirk on her face and a raised eyebrow.

"Just talk to her about the kids and see what you think. Consider what's best for the kids. She has a way with them."

"It wouldn't be bad for the hospital either. Just think: the only pediatric ward in the city with a tutor on staff."

"Don't get on your hospital political horse yet. We have to talk to her first. I know only one thing for sure about Mrs. Carson, and that is she doesn't like being taken for granted."

"I thought you didn't like her. What happened?"

"Mark and I met Rachael and her daughters at church yesterday and were invited to spend the afternoon with the family."

"And you enjoyed yourself? I'm surprised you even went!"

"Well, we were kind of set up by the three kids; but now I can see why Mark likes going over there. It was nice; I, we both relaxed and enjoyed the day."

"You were set up, huh? May I ask if there's a Mr. Carson?"

"No there's not, but I don't see what that has to do with anything."

"Yes you do. I know you aren't that naïve," she finished with a smile.

"We may become friends, okay. Friends." Alex added extra emphasis to the last "friends" just to get his point across.

"Sure, friends. That's nice. We'll see. So, was Mark ready to start school today?"

"He really was excited. I hope everything goes well for him."

"When does he get out for the day?"

"He'll be done at 3:15 and will go over to Rachael's until I get done here."

"Oh, that worked out nicely." The smiled covered her entire face, and she tried to look away from Alex.

Alex tried to sound indignant but he was smiling too, "Yes, it did. Just like I planned it."

"So when will you be able to talk to her about coming to work for us?"

"If you can clear it with the Board by Saturday, I'll talk to her when we go get Mark's new puppy."

"New puppy? WOW! That's a major step for you. You hate dogs."

"I think it'll be good for Mark. The moving van will deliver our stuff on Thursday, and I promised Mark that on the first Saturday in our new house we'd go get him a puppy."

"You're right. Having a puppy waiting for him when he gets home will make his adjustment easier. It takes time to make friends, but it doesn't take long for a boy to bond with his dog."

"You sound just like her."

"Who? Rachael?"

"Yes, she loves her dog; and it was seeing her with him that convinced me maybe I had missed something as a kid. I don't want to deprive Mark of some special relationship especially after watching him play with her dog."

With a touch of sadness in her voice, Debbie looked at him, "You've missed a lot over the years, Alex. I hope someday you find someone who will help you get some of it back, maybe you already have. She's having quite an impact on your lives already."

"Actually, all I hope for is that I can give Mark what he needs so the things I missed as a child will not be missing from his life."

"Alex, you didn't only miss things as a child. Keep your focus on Mark not on the operating room, and you'll start to fill in the gaps for yourself as well as him and please, don't tell another doctor what I just said. A new puppy will be good for both of you. Just remember to keep a sense of humor."

"Why does that sound more like a warning rather than advice?" Alex raised an eyebrow at Debbie's smile and walked toward his own walnut paneled office to return the call from John Malcomb.

"John, how're you doing? Your message sounded urgent. What's up?"

"Hey, good afternoon, Alex. You sound great. Life down south must be agreeing with you. Maybe I should consider moving my practice."

"Why? The stress of the big city getting to you?"

"Must be. I was at the prison today."

"Ya, what's happening with my dear beloved wife?" The sarcasm in Alex's voice was as sharp as the ax he wanted to use to sever their legal ties.

"She's a loner. No one will work with her. It's just like when she was in the local jail. The warden has assigned her clean up duty. She gets to clean sinks, toilets and showers all night when everybody else is locked up."

"I'm sure that puts her in a lovely mood every morning. She hated housework. The housekeeper did everything for her."

"Your right about that; she was brimming over with laughter and good cheer when I talked to her. It was a real experience."

"Ya, sure John. What'd you really talk about?"

"I tried to serve Heather with the divorce papers you had signed."

The announcement erased the good feeling that had been evident in Alex's tone of voice and replaced it with sobriety. "So? What happened?"

"Alex, she refused to sign them."

"So what's our next step? I want this to be finished."

"I know. Let's give her some time to think about it and cool off, then I'll try again."

"How did she react?"

"She certainly wasn't happy about it. In fact, I could see the rage working its way through her body until it poured out of her eyes. She jumped over the table and grabbed me by the tie before I could get out of the way."

"You're kidding, right?"

"I wish I was, Alex. It was just like in the court room when she attacked you. She really has something for ties. I'm not going to wear one the next time I have to see her. I could barely scream for the guard to help me. My God, she's strong! I think she has been taking steroids or something."

"Don't joke, John."

"I'm not. She's crazy, Alex. Her brain is going to explode with rage, and I sure as hell hope I'm not in the same building when it happens. Shit, I hope I'm not even in the same state when it happens."

"Did she ask where we were?"

"No, I don't think she's even considered the possibility that you might have moved."

"Good. Thanks, John, for taking care of this. I owe you big time."

"Just keep a room ready for me so when I need to escape the city I have a place to go."

"Sure, anytime, John. Keep in touch."

CHAPTER TEN

Rachael had been nervous about starting work at the hospital, but everyone agreed it was worth a try. When Alex had presented it to her, the parents, and other doctors, he made it sound as if everyone would be a winner. The hospital had offered Rachael a nice salary and more importantly benefits she and the girls had been lacking since Jack's death; so off she went for about five hours everyday to see students, visit with parents, and check in with teachers.

So far it seemed Alex had been right. After a few weeks everyone could see a pleasant difference in the pediatric ward. There were fewer televisions blaring which helped immensely to keep the noise down. Rachael was meeting with only a few students on a trial bases, and the parents seemed genuinely grateful that someone else was worrying about school work and talking to teachers. Most of the kids accepted the studying without any hassle. They knew when they went back to class it would be much easier if some work had been done. Besides, the kids didn't have to be rocket scientists to realize that time moved faster when they were busy, and studying made most of them excited about getting back to school and their friends.

The semester would be ending in a couple of weeks, and Rachael had been asked to work during the summer with a few of the long term patients who had missed the end of the school term because of injury or illness. Once the patient was in the recovery zone, studying helped keep them motivated and actually seemed to speed up their healing process.

"Good morning, Tony. My name is Mrs. Carson."

"Yeah, so what. I've heard about you. I can't walk, and you want me to do school work? Shit, I don't even care about school."

"I see. Dr. Zamora tells me you will walk again if you want to. But whether you walk again or not, you will go back to school in the fall. After talking to your counselor at school, I believe you have to make a decision. You can do some studying with me and be prepared to return to class, you can go to summer school in a wheel chair to make up what you've missed, or you can take this year over while all of your friends go on. The choice is yours. When you make your decision and clean up your language, let me know." Rachael turned around and walked out of the door.

"I don't care! Do you hear me? I don't care." The sound of his voice faded, and she knew that he did care.

Alex was waiting outside the door for her. "I was afraid he might give you some trouble. He's had a negative attitude ever since he woke up from the surgery and realized he couldn't walk. The paralysis is not permanent as long as he stops feeling sorry for himself and gets to physical therapy."

"He's no trouble yet. I just want him to think about his options. I'll give him a day or so to mull things over while I talk to his parents. Maybe he needs to see some of his friends."

"He's refused to see anyone but his parents and me."

"Well, maybe it's time to take that choice away from him. He's not the adult here. Kids are kids that's why they need parents and other adults to help them make decisions and guide them. Let's give him some time to digest what I told him. It's possible that if he knows going back to school isn't an option but a reality, he'll come around. Having a few of his friends drop in on him will get him motivated, too."

Rachael turned around and looked behind her. The hair on the back of her neck was standing on end and she shuddered. When Alex reached out putting his hand on her shoulder, she jumped to face him.

"What's wrong?"

"I don't know. I just had the strangest feeling someone was watching me. Silly, huh?"

"Do you want me to go look?"

"No, I'm sure it was just my imagination. I've got to go see a couple more students, but I'll see you when you come to get Mark. Since it's Friday night, I'll finish tutoring my other students at 6:00; why don't you and Mark stay for dinner? You still haven't hired a cook yet, have you?"

"Thanks, that'd be great. No, I haven't hired a cook yet, but I've stopped making hotdogs. Every once-in-a-while I even read a cookbook. By the way, thanks for teaching Mark how to make macaroni and cheese. He claimed mine was too lumpy."

"He told me," Rachael smiled at him. "He also likes playing fort with all the big moving boxes that are still stacked in the family room."

"I know. We're still living out of boxes in most of the house. I hate to hire a housekeeper until I get some of the rooms cleared out. Frankly, I don't think anyone will take the job if all she sees is boxes. Mark and the puppy enjoy them though. Mark builds new obstacle courses every night, and the two of them follow each other in and out of the maze for hours. It's the best entertainment I've had in years. See you tonight." With a vision of his son and the new puppy chasing each other around strange configurations, Alex smiled as he left Rachael and headed for his office. The phone started ringing as he opened the door.

"Hello, Dr. Zamora speaking."

"Alex, John here." The panic in John's tone reached through the phone to grab Alex's attention instantly.

"What's wrong, John? You're making me worry, and you haven't even said anything yet."

"I'm sorry, Alex, but I'm worried for you. Heather escaped from prison last night."

"Jesus Christ, John! What happened? Did anyone get hurt?"

"She killed a guard and took a new born baby and its mother as hostages in order to get out of the prison."

"My God! Please, tell me she didn't kill the baby."

"We don't know. No one has found either of the hostages yet."

"What was a baby doing at the prison anyway?"

"The mother was pregnant when she was convicted. She gave birth in the prison infirmary yesterday. The warden guesses that when Heather went in to do her janitorial work, she saw the opportunity she'd been waiting for. She must've grabbed the baby and forced the mother to go along. Nobody can tell us exactly what happened because no other inmates or guards were in the area at the time. She forced the driver of a delivery truck to take them out of the prison before anyone else knew what was going on. The attending physician said the mother was very weak and probably couldn't offer much resistance."

"John, does she know where we are?"

"I honestly don't know, but don't take any chances. The truck driver told the prison guards where he dropped her. He's really lucky to be alive. The police are doing everything they can to find her. They've notified the State Police and also the Tulsa Police Department, so don't be surprised if they contact you."

"Shit, John, Mark and I were just starting to feel like we're home."

"They'll catch her."

"What do I tell Mark?"

"I don't know, Alex; but I would tell him something because he is going to have to be awfully careful. You be careful, too."

"Thank's John. Maybe you should think about leaving town for awhile."

"No, I'll be okay. They'll get her. I've got to get to court, but I'll keep you posted."

Alex felt like someone had kicked him in the stomach. He'd have to tell Rachael now what was going on because he might need her help with Mark. On the other hand, maybe it wasn't fair to involve her at all. This wasn't going to be easy. *Damn her! Damn her! She had promised to get even.* Alex felt sure that somehow she'd found out where they were and was on her way to Tulsa if she wasn't already here.

****

Rachael closed the front door after watching her last student walk down the driveway to meet his mother. Friday afternoon students were common at the end of the year. Most of the year Friday afternoon was a sacred opportunity for students to just do nothing; however, by the end of the year desperate kids would take any time she had available. Rachael was pooped. She wasn't used to tutoring ten hours a day, and the emotional drain of the one-on-one work left her exhausted. Even her hair looked droopy which matched her eyes. It was a good thing nobody would see her like this, she thought as she leaned against the door.

"Hey, Mom, Mark wants to know when his dad's going to get here."

"Alex? Oh, no! I forgot. Rorie what can we have for dinner? Quick, honey, help me. I look terrible. Maybe a shower would help. I need about fifteen minutes to get myself pulled together."

"Mom, what's with you. It's just Alex. He won't care if you shower or not."

"Rorie, just go see if you can find something to go with the steaks I bought."

"Steak? What's the occasion? Did you get paid today?"

Rachael was headed for her bathroom stripping off her clothes with Rorie on her heals. "Stop with the questions, honey, and help me get ready."

Rorie's face was bright with anticipation, "Mom, is there anything going on?" The inflection of her eye brows matched the rise in her voice.

"No, I've been working all day, but I don't want to look like I've been. Do you understand? There's nothing going on. It's just that when Alex comes over, I want him to a ... enjoy himself. Now go start something to eat. Please."

"Okay, Mom, but I want you to know that if anything does happen between the two of you, I think it'd be wonderful."

"Rorie." This time Rachael did snap at her daughter. "Don't be ridiculous! He's a friend. I hope he becomes a good friend, and I believe he needs a friend too. That's all." Then she looked at her daughter and softly added, "I had my love, my true love. A person is lucky to have one good marriage, so I have to count my blessings and move on. Do you understand?

"Yes, I guess so," but she really didn't. Rorie thought her mother was being melodramatic.

"Good. Now go, so I can get cleaned up."

Alex arrived shortly after six o'clock. Even though there was an emotional thunderstorm brewing, he was looking forward to seeing the family again. The five of them usually had at least one meal together on the weekend and sometimes more when there was time. They went to watch Rorie play soccer and then out to eat on Saturday mornings and always sat together in church. The five of them together had become more of a family than Mark had ever known. Alex didn't take the relationship for granted, but he didn't want to push it either.

"Hi, Alex," Rorie greeted him with a big smile when he arrived. She did agree with her sister that this man was so incredibly handsome she couldn't resist letting her eyes linger on his face. She was surprised to see him with the pup on a leash.

"Hi, I hope you don't mind my bringing Snickers over. He was so glad to see me when I got home that I just didn't have the heart to leave him alone again."

"Alex, you're a softy. Of course you can bring him over. He's so cute; and he's part of the family. Come on, Snickers, your best boy is outside with your friend Chance. Mom wanted to freshen up a little after her last student. She'll be done any minute. The rest of us are out back. I'll put the steaks on as soon as Mom comes out." So he had gone home to clean up too. No man was so clean shaven after working all day, and the cologne was fresh and Wow! Nice. Just friends? She took another whiff of the masculine essence as she walked away, wondering how her mother could not notice.

Rachael put on neatly starched navy shorts and a cropped taupe shirt. It didn't actually reveal anything, but then it didn't actually cover everything. Her long shapely legs had started to tan, and they made the short shorts look even shorter. Alex's first thought when she walked onto the patio was that she certainly didn't look like she had worked all day. Rachael carried a glass of red wine for each of them and sat down beside him to watch Mark and Allison play with Snickers. As she offered the glass of wine to Alex, she noticed the shadows in his eyes. They hadn't been there for a while. Something had happened this afternoon.

"Thank you. You look refreshed."

"I feel much better," Rachael admitted. "So how are you and Snickers getting along?"

"Better than I thought. It's wonderful to watch the two of them playing together."

"Do you let him sleep with Mark yet?"

"No!" The sound of his voice was absolute. "I hadn't even considered it."

"Oh." Rachael's inflection told Alex that it was just a matter of time until that arrangement changed.

"Where does Chance sleep?"

"On my bed."

"I shouldn't have asked. Please don't tell Mark."

"Sorry, he already asked. That's why I thought I'd let you know, so you could be prepared."

"Thanks, I think. Did my conniving son tell you about his day at school? Does he have a lot of homework for the weekend?"

"He had a great time, but I'll let Mark tell you about it. We started his homework this afternoon and Allison helped him finish it."

"Rorie and Allison have become like big sisters to him. I think when he says he's going home he means here. We sleep at one house, but this is more like home."

"Maybe it's the boxes." Both of them smiled, but there was a slightly serious tone to Alex's voice.

"No, I think there's a lot more to it than that."

"Well, we think he is pretty special too. I hate to admit it, but he really doesn't need a tutor anymore. He's doing very well, and his teachers and I believe he has adjusted to his new school nicely."

"I never thought moving him would be so successful."

"If the stress is gone, it is amazing how much easier life can be even for kids. Too many parents believe stress is only for adults."

"Unfortunately, stress can creep back into your life when you least expect it or want it."

For the first time Rachael felt she was seeing into the darkness that plagued Alex's life. She didn't say anything, only looked into his sad eyes.

"I'll never be able to put my guard down. Never totally relax because the past will always be there ready to strike. Since she's part of my past, my memory, she'll always be able to cause pain."

Rachael assumed he was speaking about the pain caused from losing someone you love and she responded, "I understand, Alex."

Alex raised his eyes again to look into her soul to watch the reaction to his confession. "No you don't, Rachael. You don't understand because you don't know the truth."

Rachael took a breath to say something, but he raised his hand to stop her.

"My wife, hopefully, soon to be ex-wife, isn't dead. I know I implied that she was. It just seemed so much easier that way."

Rachael never broke her eye contact with him. He was reaching out to her emotionally, and she didn't want to threaten his trust by looking away.

Alex continued, "I never wanted to have to admit this; but if I'm ever going to have a true friendship with anyone, I have to face the past. Something happened today that made me realize my past is part of who I am and I can't ignore it."

Rachael reached across the table and touched his hand. "Alex, you don't have to tell me anything. You owe me no explanation. I like you and Mark, so do the girls. Whatever happened won't change that."

The tenderness in her voice caressed his mind and heart the way her touch did his hand. The anger and pain that had imprisoned his emotions were melting away; and for the first time since the police came to arrest Heather, his eyes filled with tears.

Vulnerability caused Alex to pause and clear his throat; and as he looked away, he remembered they were not alone. Allison looked up at him from the far side of the pool, and he realized this was not the best place for a confession.

Rorie broke the intensity of the moment when she closed the kitchen door behind her and yelled to Rachael. "Dinner will be ready in about fifteen minutes, Mom. Do you want to put the steaks on now or should I?" As soon as Rorie looked at Alex, she knew there had been something special passing between them; but she couldn't reel the interrupting words back into her mouth.

"I'll be right there, sweetheart." Rachael stood up, but Alex did not let go of her hand. It was his lifeline to hope. Without breaking the physical bond, Rachael lifted his hand cradling it between both of hers.

"If you still want to talk, we can go for a walk after dinner. There'll be fewer eyes and ears to probe our conversation." Rachael cocked her head toward the two in the pool.

"You're right. It would be better to wait."

Rachael walked away from him wondering about the fire in his fingers. The branding touch made it difficult for her to keep her thoughts straight. Could there be more than friendship? She had only felt this way once before in her life.

As the steaks sizzled on the grill, Rachael's desires rose with thoughts of possibility. She watched him stand and walk to the side of the pool. He was a good man. No matter what had happened in his past, Rachael's instincts told her that he was a rare man. But there had been no dancing eyes when he touched her only sadness. Alex needed a confidant. That was all.

Alex stood by the pool and watched his son play in the water with the closest thing he would ever know to a sister. Mark had never been so happy. This life they were trying to create for themselves was worth fighting for, but he was embarrassed by his show of weakness. He had never shared such emotional intimacy with Heather. She had never cared and he had never tried.

The kids chattered constantly at the dinner table. Alex had a hard time concentrating on the conversation. He tried not to be obvious, but he couldn't take his eyes off Rachael. She was so different from Heather. Had he ever really loved Heather? Sitting across the table from this woman made him doubt that. Mark suddenly grabbed his father's attention.

"Dad, guess what? I got an 'A' on my math test today."

"That's great. I'm so proud of you."

"That's not all. I got an invitation to a boy's birthday party. It's a sleepover. Can I go? Please, it's next Friday."

"We'll talk about it later; what about Snickers? Won't he miss you?"

"You'll take care of him. Won't you?" The joy in Mark's voice was infectious and caused everyone to laugh.

"Allie, will you and Mark clean up the kitchen? Rorie has a date and we're going for a walk."

"Sure, Mom." Allison and Mark looked at each other and rolled their eyes trying to conceal silly grins. They were still hoping, waiting to see if their attempt to help fate along on Easter Sunday by bringing their parents together would work. All three of them believed the match was so obvious that they couldn't understand why the adults didn't see it. Sometimes adults were so stubborn.

The silver moon was making its appearance in the young evening sky. Rachael and Alex walked in silence for several blocks, but Rachael's shudder brought a comment from him.

"Are you cold?"

Rachael turned around and looked behind them. "No, it's just that I have the feeling someone is watching us again. Maybe it's just some neighborhood kids."

Alex moved closer to her putting his arm around her shoulder. She was shivering even though the evening air was quiet warm. "Like this afternoon?" Alex asked her. "Come on, lets go back to the house."

"No, wait. I wanted to ask you something before I forget." Alex waited for her to bring up the subject of his still living wife. He was sure her female curiosity just couldn't leave it alone. "Yes?"

"Will you still let Mark come over after school? If you'll let him come over, I'll make sure he works on his homework and understands everything."

Now Alex was curious, "Why? You don't have to. He can go home, I mean back to his own house, you know."

"I know he can, but I hate to have him all alone after school. That's such an important time for kids. Besides, I like having him here." Rachael sighed and decided she might as well tell him the real reason she wanted the boy to come over. "Alex, Mark helps me focus on the present and future. Before he started coming over, I spent too much time in the past. He's brought a zest for life back into this house and into my life. Do you have any idea of what I am talking about?" She felt awkward in her explanation.

Alex wanted to ask her if it was only Mark who had given her a new zest for life, but he was afraid she might say yes. However, he knew exactly what she meant because he and Mark didn't want to lose the connection with this family either. Mark was a good excuse to spend time with them, with her.

"I'm sure Mark would love to come over after school. In fact, I was concerned about his going home alone after you said he didn't need tutoring anymore. I don't mind paying you for the time."

"Please, Alex. That would be insulting to our friendship and to Mark. Let's just say I need him as much as he needs me, so it's an even exchange."

Alex stopped walking and turned to face her. "I'm sorry. I didn't mean that the way it sounded. I only meant I'd rather have him here with you than home alone. You're more of a mother to him than his own mother ever was, and I don't think he's ready to spend a lot of time by himself yet. He had to spend so much time alone or with neighbors before I'm afraid that being alone would bring back to much of the past."

Rachael looked into his eyes and even in the darkness she could see them dancing. In a barely audible voice, she said, "Good, I'm glad that's settled."

Alex's body seemed to take control of his mind as his hand moved up Rachael's shoulder to her neck. When his hand started to caress the side of her face, he lowered his head until he felt her shallow breath on his chin. He expected her to pull away and gave her a moment to do so before he touched her lips, but she was already responding to his overture. Rachael could only reach his lips by standing on her tiptoes putting her slightly off balance which caused her to lean into his body for support. The strong masculine arms tightened around her slim waist nearly lifting her off her feet.

The heat of the kiss, filled with tender desperation, melted Rachael into his body. Emotionally emaciated, Rachael's body craved the lingering touch of his lips. Her arms naturally eased up around his neck until her fingers found their way to the soft ebony hair.

When Alex finally broke the embrace, he whispered in her ear, "Do you only need Mark?"

Rachael was breathless and shocked by the weakness in her knees. She didn't hear his question. "I'm sorry. What did you say?"

"Nothing. It was nothing. Let's go home. I still need to talk to you, but I don't want to get too far from the house."

Rachael wondered about his concern as they turned around, but after the feeling of being watched, she agreed they should head for home. She regretted not bringing Chance with them. She rarely walked without him because he always knew who was around.

Alex started rambling about a tragic tale of betrayal. Rachael thought it sounded more like a best selling novel than real life. He included everything right down to Heather's threat at the end of the trial. The reality check came when he told her the infamous Heather had escaped and could be headed for Tulsa.

"My God, Alex. What are you going to do?"

"I have to hope the police will catch her before she gets this far. If they don't, I have to wait for her. I don't want to live my life looking over my shoulder wondering when she will strike at Mark or me. Mark and I want our future to be here. We're comfortable here with you and the girls."

Rachael thought "comfortable" was a strange word used to describe her and the girls. She didn't find it complimentary at all. An old pair of pajamas can be comfortable, and they serve a purpose; but you don't really get excited about them.

"I am more concerned about Mark than myself. She's crazy enough to take him in order to get back at me."

"He can always stay with us when you're at the hospital. We can put him in the guest room if you need him to stay over. Have you had your security system hooked up yet?"

"They're supposed to do it next week, but I'll call them again tomorrow. I'm sure, under the circumstances, they'll take care of us right away."

"Be sure to have your telephone cable into the house buried, so she can't cut the telephone line because that would cut your security line. You might also consider putting in an extra panic button upstairs."

"Thanks. I'm going to have to tell Mark what has happened because he's going to have to be really careful. I don't want him to be shocked to see her, and I surely don't want him to go anywhere with her. I think I'll tell the principal what's going on tomorrow, so the school won't dismiss him to her if she should show up."

"How about if one of the girls or I take him back and forth to school or at least to the bus. That'd take some of the stress off of his walking alone."

"That'd be great. Let's ask him what he wants to do."

"You know school will be out in a couple of weeks. The girls and I are going to the beach for a week. They're each taking a friend along, but we still have room to take Mark with us. Has he ever been to the beach before?"

"When he was really little, we took a vacation to Florida; but I'm sure he doesn't remember it."

"If he goes with us, you won't have to worry about him while you're at work."

"Are you sure the girls won't mind having a boy at the beach with them? He might cramp their style. Besides, I'm sure all of this will be over by then."

"When the girls want to check out the boys, Mark can do something with me. I won't be going with them when they're on the search for hunks."

"I'm glad to hear that." A smile softened his stern mood, and Alex tightened his grip around her shoulders as they approached the front door of the house.

Rachael and Alex sat down on the couch with Mark. Mark looked from one to the other wondering what was going on.

"Is this our first family meeting? Don't the girls have to be here?"

Rachael started first, "We have good news for you. I wanted to tell you we're really proud of how well you've been doing in school, and we don't think you need a tutor any more." Both Rachael and

Alex were surprised by Mark's response to what they thought would be good news.

Mark sounded defensive as if he'd done something wrong. "The only reason I'm doing well is because Rachael helps me. If I don't come over here, I know I'll do terrible. I have to come over here."

Now it was Alex's turn to address his son, "You can still come over here whenever you want."

"Everyday?" The question was full of doubt.

Rachael put her arm around Mark's shoulder to ease his concern, "Mark, I still want you to come over after school if you want to. We'll still do your homework together."

"You'll be here?"

"If I can't be here, I'll let you know ahead of time. One of the girls will be here, or I'll pick you up at school and take you with me. Okay?"

"So you'll be more like my mom?"

The question shook both Alex and Rachael. She had no idea of what to say to the almost frightened young man, but now she began to understand why Alex had been so concerned about his son's going home alone.

Alex tried to get Rachael off the hot spot by saying, "You'll be more like good friends. Mark, we need to tell you something else, and you have to listen very carefully."

Tenderly, Alex tried to tell his son about his mother. Rachael's arm was still around his shoulders, and she could feel the shudders that made his little body tremble. Finally, the sobs could not be contained, and Mark cried openly in her arms. Rachael tried to comfort him by rocking him and caressing his hair.

Eventually the tears ran out, and Rachael could talk to him again. Now she really did feel like his mother because all the old maternal, protective instincts kicked in.

"Mark, your father and I love you, and we'll protect you. We need you to understand how careful you have to be when we aren't around."

A scared, teary eyed little boy looked up into Rachael's eyes, "Ya know, she never ever told me that she loved me."

Now it was Rachael's turn to get emotional, and she held him tightly trying to keep the tears at bay. Alex had also been torn by his son's revelation. He never knew how emotionally neglected Mark had been by both of them, and the guilt ate at his heart. Alex reached out and touched his son.

"Mark, I'm so sorry I didn't know. Why didn't you tell me after she left how sad you were?"

"It didn't matter anymore, Dad. You and I were together, and you did tell me you loved me. I knew you meant it. I don't want her to find us. The kids at school will tease me again."

"Hopefully, the police will find her right away, but until they do you have to be very careful. We'll tell only your teachers, so they can help keep an eye out for any strangers. No one else will know."

Rachael tried to ease his concerns, "In a couple of weeks school will be out, and you won't see most of the kids all summer. You're in a very big school district, and lots of kids have had bad things happen to them. When you get home in the afternoon, you can tell me if you're angry or scared. We'll work everything out together."

Mark sat up and looked at both of them; he tried to dry his eyes and then he asked Rachael, "Will Rorie and Allison hate me when they find out about my real mom?"

Rachael knew he was seriously worried the relationship might be in jeopardy, so she put his fears to rest. "Of course they won't hate you. By the way, would you like to go on vacation with us after school is out?"

"Really? Where are you going?" The question helped to cheer him up.

"We're going to Galveston to stay on the beach for a week."

"Can I bring Snickers?"

Rachael and Alex both laughed at the questions before Alex answered him. "No, I think Snickers will have to stay here with me. I'll need him to keep me company. Now we'd better get home. It's getting late."

"Can I sleep with you tonight, Dad?" The fear had clearly returned to his voice.

"Of course you can. I'd like that."

"Snickers, too. I don't want him to be alone."

Alex figured he owed his son special consideration under the circumstances. So he sincerely added, "Snickers, too."

CHAPTER ELEVEN

The sky was pleasantly overcast which blocked the sun's blinding glare. The four girls had been catering to Mark's every desire since the six travelers had left Tulsa, and he was sucking up the attention like a chocoholic devours a Hershey bar. All of them enjoyed watching him have so much fun after the stress of the last couple of weeks. No one had the slightest idea of what had happened to Heather. There hadn't been a single trace of her, and this lack of information concerning her whereabouts grew more unnerving everyday. Alex was sure, the longer it took them to find her, the more likely she was to show up on his doorstep.

Mark was constantly looking over his shoulder when he was outside. He never went any further than Rachael's backyard, and he always took both dogs with him. It broke Rachael's heart to see him so tense, and this stress had started showing its ugly head in his school work. Concentrating became harder and harder for him as the days went on, especially during tests. The teachers had been wonderful with him though by giving him extra time for completion and asking him questions to help keep him focused. Since the police had not wanted to broadcast Alex's whereabouts, there was nothing on the news, and not a single student found out about Mark's situation.

The poor boy had been exhausted when he got in the car for the long drive to Galveston. The lack of a peaceful night's sleep had taken its toll on everyone, but Mark had the hardest time. So finally, cuddled next to Rachael, he slept in peace for several hours while Rorie took the first shift driving. Rachael understood now why Alex had been so concerned about the boy when they'd moved to Tulsa. Rachael knew she was seeing only a fraction of the anxiety Mark had suffered in Chicago. At least here he was secure knowing there were people around him who wanted to love and protect him. In Chicago, he had felt all alone. He needed this respite more than any of them.

Rachael felt sorry for Alex because she knew he could have used the rest, too. Shortly after he found out about Heather's escape, a Tulsa police detective informed him that John had been shot to death in his office late one evening. They were pretty sure Heather had been the one to commit the murder. The office had been ransacked; and after the secretary pulled everything together including herself, she told the detective the only thing that seemed to be missing was the Zamora file.

Alex was hit by a cataclysm of guilt over John's death. He had intended on going back for John's funeral. It was the least he could do for the friend who had died for him. Alex suspected John had refused to give Heather the information she had demanded, so she shot him. The police, with Rachael's help, finally convinced Alex that Heather would be waiting for him to show up in Chicago. He had to face the possibility that Heather had killed John simply as a way of drawing Alex back to her territory.

After Alex made the decision to stay in Tulsa, everyone assumed Heather was on her way to find him. It was the obvious next move, which led to sleepless nights and endless images of Heather killing Rachael or kidnapping Mark playing over and over in his mind. Now, at least, he knew Mark was safely out of town for a week, and that was one less worry for him. So, while Rachael and the girls entertained Mark at the beach, Alex tried to concentrate on his patients rather than his wife. Just thinking about the fact that she was still married to him made the bile rise in his throat, but he couldn't stop feeling guilty every time he hoped the police would kill her rather than just catch her. It was obvious to him that she'd never agree to a divorce; however, wishing for her death at the hands of the police made him feel dirty. There had to be a way of getting a divorce legally, and the problem nagged at him. It didn't occur to Alex that his marital state hadn't seemed so important to him until he'd met Rachael and the girls. He missed the kids and the sense of family, but he especially thought about Rachael when he went home to an empty house.

The travelers' first mission upon arrival at the beach side condos had been to buy a big dragon floatie to play with in the water. Allison and Rorie surely didn't realize that buying the dragon was a tribute to their father, but Rachael saw the connection. Jack had always bought them one big floatation device whenever they went to the beach; it was a tradition. With care, it usually lasted the week and gallantly provided the girls with hours of laughter accompanied by intermittent loud screeching. Since Rachael's strong point was not entertaining the girls in the water, Jack had happily picked up the responsibility and spent hours playing in the waves with his darling daughters while Rachael watched from the shore.

This trip Rachael had some doubts about having so many kids to watch. Now, sitting on the beach watching them play in the water, she realized it was a blessing. The long green dragon neck decorated with blue and white stripes was easy to spot even when the waves blocked the girls from her view. Rachael wondered if her daughters had any memories creeping into their fun.

The rolling surf was like a balm for Rachael's healing heart. She was finally reaching the stage of grieving for Jack that allowed her to reminisce with joyful memories rather than sorrow, of course, having Mark and Alex around helped too. Her toes let the soft white sand sift through them as she watched the people walk by. Everything seemed to remind her of events gone by.

The siren behind Rachael startled her. Then the loud speaker blared as the local coast guard warned swimmers to stay away from the rocks. Every quarter of a mile a rock pier ran from the eight foot high sea wall out into the ocean. The water hitting the rocks caused dangerous undercurrents and deep holes to form. Rachael had noticed the deep holes that morning when the six of them walked along the beach during low tide. The holes seemed like harmless tide pools at the time; but hidden in the water, one could be deadly to a child.

Rachael smiled at the young father in the yellow swim trunks. His curly blond hair glistened in the sun as he helped his daughter build a sand castle. She'd had such gusto when they'd started ten minutes ago, but now her interest was waning. The hypnotic sound of the waves was pulling her attention back to the water.

Allison and her friend Lindsay were walking along the seawall. They must have wanted a little break from the tide. "Mom, we need some sunscreen."

"It's in the bag, Al," Rachael answered trying to look up, but her view was blocked by the sun. "Please tell your sister, Lissa, and Mark they need some too. The only lobster I want tonight is what I find on my plate." The three of them laughed as they simultaneously caught sight of the dragon flying across a wave upside down tossing Mark and Rorie through the air.

Within moments all four girls and Mark were riding the waves while Rachael sipped on her weak margarita. The sun had burned off the wispy clouds in the sky as well as the clouds in her heart. Rachael's mind started to drift, and she closed her eyes letting the sound of the rolling surf rock her tenderly.

Without warning, however, mist slowly began running in from the sea encircling Rachael. She realized she was alone on the beach but couldn't remember when everyone had left. As the gray mist rolled in from the ocean cutting her off from the sea wall, she felt the urge to panic swell up inside her. Then she noticed a tall dark form coming toward her. Rachael could barely contain the scream that wanted to push its way out of her throat. However, as the figure emerged from the fog, it slowly held out a hand. Rachael tried to resist but could not. The form was familiar; but she couldn't quite place his kind, soothing face. This was not the haunting shadow that had plagued her sleeping hours.

Rachael reached out touching the hand. The sensation pleased and stimulated her senses. She walked hand in hand with the tall unidentified man into the rolling water and disappeared into the mist.

"Mom, Mom! Wake up. We're getting hungry," Rorie softly whispered with a worried frown on her sun burnt face.

"Rorie, is that you? Where's your sister?" Rachael was disoriented coming out of the dream and took a few seconds to get her bearings.

"Mom, are you okay?"

"Yes, I'm sorry. I was dreaming."

"The nightmare? You haven't had that damn nightmare in weeks," Rorie stated in frustration.

"Rorie!" Rachael understood her daughter's frustration about the nightmare, but not the use of her language. Besides this dream was different.

"Really, Mom. I'm not nine years old any more. I can speak my mind, and it's yelling 'Damn! Damn! Damn!'"

"Well you can stop with the profanity because this wasn't the same. Actually, I don't know if it was better or worse, but at least I wasn't screaming on the beach. That would've been embarrassing."

"Yeah, mom. Try not to fall asleep out here. We'd have to pretend we didn't know you if you started yelling," Rorie finished with a smile.

"Be careful what you threaten, dear daughter; or I won't pay for your food."

As the six vacationers walked back to their condo, Rachael realized she had a new peaceful feeling inside. Whatever this dream had meant, it certainly didn't have the same effect on her as the nightmare did. After the nightmare, she was terrified, in a cold sweat and fearing sleep. This dream raised latent erotic feelings, and Rachael was strangely disappointed it had only been a dream. Even though she couldn't put a face to the man, Rachael had the strangest feeling of recognition. Somewhere before, she knew she had met him.

****

By the second day, Mark had named the dragon "Bob", and he was certainly doing his job of entertaining everyone. It was late afternoon when Rachael and her five charges put on their suits and headed for the sand and surf.

After sleeping in, Rachael had suggested all of them go down to the historical part of the island. Everybody bought crazy T-shirts and funky sunglasses. The old mansions were intriguing; and had the weather been cold or rainy, they might have opted for a tour. The roll of the surf, however, was beckoning; so after finding the beach shoes Rachael had insisted on, they headed for the water.

The beach was nearly deserted, which Rachael rather enjoyed. Since the weekend was over, all the locals were back at work. The flawless blue sky reached down to stroke the darker blue of the ocean. Rachael leaned back in her chair closing her eyes. The sound of the surf was broken occasionally by the cry of a sea gull or child's laughter.

Rachael began to wonder about yesterday's dream. Before going to bed the night before, she had logged it in her journal. It was an interesting contrast to the nightmares which had almost disappeared since she had started logging them and since Alex had entered her life. There didn't seem to be any consistent events leading up to the dreams, and she couldn't account for any concrete changes in her life that would cause them to stop. The girls, of course, credited Alex with the change in their mother's life.

The possibility that the stranger in her good dream might have been Alex had crossed Rachael's mind but had been quickly dismissed. The night before when she stood in front of the mirror wearing her red floor length satin nightgown, the word "comfortable" came to her lips. She was no fool. Why would a nice handsome man, who could have any woman in town, want a forty year old widow with two kids. He was still young enough to have more kids - she wasn't. If she let herself fall in love with this man, she and even the girls would most likely get hurt; and more importantly, she could end up losing his friendship and Mark's. *Besides,* Rachael had reminded herself, *you've had your love, now let him find his.* Rachael mentally took her feelings and locked them in a little black box, tucking it down inside of her heart where they should stay. She would count her blessings and be grateful she'd had a such a happy life.

After Rachael put her feelings away, she just wanted to enjoy the surroundings hoping that if she concentrated the mist would again roll in from the sea; and she wanted to recognize the sensuous stranger. Unfortunately, her auburn curls, caught in the sea breeze, were constantly tickling her face. There would be no drifting off to sleep today. Rachael had a good night's sleep and didn't need anymore rest.

For the first time since Jack's death, Rachael had the urge to read a good romance novel. The feeling surprised her because she didn't think she'd ever want to read about people falling in love again. Deciding that her desire to read again was a sign of recovery, Rachael promised to buy herself a new best seller the next time she went to town.

The father who had been on the beach yesterday returned with his small, pig-tailed daughter. He took her down to play in the water where, he believed, the waves had lost their slight undertow power. The little girl was enchanting with her big brown eyes filled with adoration for her father. When she walked out ankle deep, he was right next to her watching the waves push against her short thin legs. The ocean could be so unpredictable, and the father's concern was well placed.

Rachael caught herself reflecting about Rorie and Allison at that age. They had gone to the beach often when the girls were young, and every time she had worried about the possible dangers waiting just below the surface. They'd been fortunate during the years that the only maladies they had suffered were mild jellyfish stings and foot injuries. Over the years they had learned a cheap pair of water shoes protected their feet from the sharp points on seashells and meat tenderizer was a good antidote for jellyfish stings. After several painful sunburns, Rachael never let the girls leave the condo without a T-shirt in tow. Sunscreen just wasn't enough to withstand several hours in the sun. Even though she tried to be prepared, there was always the cloud of danger that hung over her. Rachael didn't know if it was just her motherly instinct to worry, but she respected the power and unpredictability of the ocean.

The sudden sound of the sirens brought Rachael back from her mental wandering. Immediately she let her eyes search for the disturbance. Two squad cars pulled up along the sea wall. Immediately the officers got out of the car and pursued the man Rachael saw running along the beach. He didn't have a chance of out running them in the sand; and within seconds, the loud speaker blared "Stop! Police."

The noise of the sirens had not disturbed the five fun lovers out riding the floating dragon as much as it had Rachael; however, at the sound of the loud speaker, they instinctively shot a glance at the pier. When they had heard the blaring sound before, it was a warning about the rock pier, so the girls just assumed someone had entered the danger zone again. They had not expected to see a tiny little girl being pulled under.

The sirens had caught the father off guard for a second; and when he reached down for his baby, she was gone. The instant heart wrenching fear caused him to panic. His cry for help instantly caught Rachael's attention because he was within a couple of feet of her. Most of the other people were watching the police chase down their suspect a few blocks away.

Rachael immediately started searching the surface of the water for the missing child. She caught sight of Rorie and Allison swimming toward the rocks. They knew better than to get too close; but then she saw their point of interest. The little girl bobbed up from the water. Her arms were waving in the air, and then she was gone from sight.

Rachael and the father had spotted her simultaneously and ran for the water. The girls were much stronger swimmers than Rachael, and they were closer to the girl. She was terrified for the little girl and for her own daughters. Who knew what was down there or how bad the current was; but the fear and panic were offset by the stronger urge to save a life, so she understood why her daughters swam toward the rocks of death.

What was only seconds seemed like hours. The father was trying to get out into the water, but his angle was wrong, and the waves were pushing against him. Rorie and Allison were making faster progress because they were able to move laterally with the surf. Rachael hoped and prayed the drowning girl would be thrown to the surface again so the girls would not have to dive for her.

The water was murky from being churned against the sand, and the rocks were slimy with sea growth. Rorie and Allison had no idea of what they would do when they got to the rocks. Their eyes met when they reached point of the last sighting. The girls knew Ali was the better diver because of her years on the school diving team, but Rorie was the stronger of the two, so they would have to work together in order to save the child and themselves from being crushed against the rocks.

"She's probably further out by now because the current moved her away from the shore," yelled Rorie.

"Yeah, we saw her twice, so she should be about there. Come on!" Allison started swimming to the spot. Both girls swam for the imaginary X on the water another ten feet out.

The child did not come up. Rorie and Allison knew Al would have to dive for her. She wouldn't be able to see a thing only feel on the bottom and along the rocks for the body of a child. Rorie admired her sister's courage to dive into the churning brown water not knowing what might be down there.

Allison popped out of the water gasping for air. Blood was running down her face. "Did she come up?"

"What happened to your face?" Rorie screamed at her sister.

"I hit the wall. The current pulls you in. Did you see her?"

"No! Al, you watch. I'll go down along the wall." *I must be crazy! Shut up and concentrate*! Rorie told herself just before the water covered her mouth. She took a deep breath and felt the water swallow her up.

Rorie used the slimy rocks to pull herself down. The current probably pulled the girl into the rocks. Suddenly her hand recoiled and she had to fight the urge to vomit. What she'd been searching for yet not wanting to find, was within her grasp. A human body was caught in the rocks. Was it the little girl? Rorie fought to control her fear and conserve her last seconds of oxygen. Reaching out, she located the body and realized a small foot was stuck in the rocks.

Up she went exhausted and out of air. "Al, I found her, but her foot is stuck in the rocks."

By now the father was within hearing distance but still too far to be of any help. Rachael had gotten the police to call an ambulance, and now they were all running down the pier. Lissa, Lindsay and Mark had joined Rachael. Mark was terrified the girls would be hurt. It was all Rachael could do to keep him back from the water.

"Mark, don't go out there. We have to wait. Lissa, you and Lindsay take Mark back to the condo."

"No. Rachael, please let me stay. I can't leave them. I know they wouldn't leave me." The tears of fear rose in his eyes and touched her heart. Mark really was part of their family.

"Okay, but please go back to the beach. We have to make room for the paramedics when they arrive, and I don't want to worry about you falling in. Understand?" She knelt down and looked into his eyes, "It's dangerous, and I don't want to lose you in the water. Okay?"

"I'll go. I'm so scared, Rachael."

She held him close for just a second and added, "So am I, Mark. Say a prayer for the girls while you wait."

"I will." Mark went to Lissa, and they headed off the pier. "Lissa, don't take your eyes off him. Got it?"

"We know, we'll watch him."

Rachael again turned her focus back to the murky quagmire of sea water just in time to see both of her daughters disappear.

Al took a deep breath to go under, but Rorie noticed the constant stream of blood running down her face and grabbed her by the arm. "I'll go again, you wait."

"No. If we go down together, Rorie we have a better chance. You show me where she is."

"Are you sure you're up to it?" Rorie's voice was full of concern for her sister.

Allison was already going under. Rorie grabbed her hand and led the way down the rock wall. When they found the lifeless body, Rorie held the body up so Al could try to free the trapped foot. The current kept throwing all of them up against the wall. Rorie doubted the child had a chance even if they got her free. Too long under water - too much current. Suddenly the foot was free and they were being pulled out to sea again.

Rorie and Allison held onto the limp body and each other using all the strength they could find in their legs to kick themselves to the surface. Allison reminded herself that she hated reading stories about heroes dying while trying to save a life, and she kicked harder.

All three bodies came to the surface another twenty feet down the pier. Police were climbing down the rocks as soon as the water had shown signs of giving up its claim. The girls handed up the small body of the little girl. They could tell her ankle was broken by the way it hung from her leg. There was blood running profusely from several laceration now that she was out of the water. And, of course, she was not breathing. Immediately the rescue team started mouth to mouth and CPR.

The panic stricken father was pulled from the water about the same time as his daughter. Rachael softly put her hand on his shoulder to catch his attention; and with her heart in her throat, she solemnly said to him, "I'm so sorry."

Tears filled his eyes as the poor man headed toward the police officer nearest his daughter and the working rescue team. Frantically, he announced he was the victim's father, and the officer moved aside to allow the man to be near his daughter.

By now Rorie and Allison had been hoisted out of the water. Running to hold her daughters, Rachael reached out her arms. Both of them were exhausted and covered with bumps and bruises. They were tightly entwined in each other's arms when Allison collapsed. The blood that had been washed away by the water now ran down Allison's face and into Rachael's hands.

"Rorie, get some help." Rorie was already speeding down the pier to find anyone who could offer assistance.

"It's going to be all right, honey, just rest until help comes." Rachael held her baby in her arms and rocked her back and forth as the tears streamed down her face. She forced the fear of death from her mind and prayed to God for the gift of life.

One of the paramedics from the second ambulance came immediately. She quickly worked through the throng assisting the first victim and followed Rorie toward the end of the pier where she could see two people on the rocks. Rorie tried to explain what had happened, but the paramedic could only catch about half of what was said.

When the medic reached Allison, she realized she hadn't really needed much explanation. The blood was still running though the girl's wet hair and down the side of her face into the mother's hand. Immediately a compress was applied to the wound and vital signs were checked.

"You're her mother?"

Clearing the throat to hold the tears in check, Rachael answered, "Yes."

"Her breathing is swallow, but the heart beat seems strong. Hold the compress firmly. I'm going to get help so we can get her loaded on a stretcher and into the ambulance." Looking at Rorie's disheveled condition the woman asked, "Are you hurt?"

"My arm hurts a little, but it's not bad."

"I want you in the ambulance too. You'll need to be checked out at the hospital."

Before the medic walked away, Rachael asked, "How's the little girl?"

"Not good. They were finally able to get a faint pulse but she still won't breath on her own. Actually it's a miracle your daughters even found her. They're lucky to be alive themselves. I've been down there looking for victims, and it's horrible." Moving as quickly as possible back towar the shore, the woman went for help.

By now Lissa and Lindsay couldn't hold Mark back. He was headed down the pier through the people toward his girls, his family. His ashen face portrayed his fear.

He whispered his question like he was afraid the sound might hurt her even more, and Rachael tried to soothe the desperate child's heart.

"We think she'll be all right, but we have to take both of the girls to the hospital."

When Mark hugged Rorie, he noticed her wince, "Are you okay? You look terrible."

"I'll be fine, but I'm afraid I may have broken my wrist."

"Rorie, that was the bravest thing I've ever seen." Pride replaced the fear on Mark's face.

"Thank's Mark. Let's talk at the hospital. Hold me on this side, away from my sore arm. It'll help me feel better."

"Can we go with you to the hospital?"

Rachael was still holding the unconscious Allison. Lissa and Lindsay had brought all of the towels out to cover her and Rorie. Allison had started to shiver, so Rachael tried rubbing her shoulders.

"I want you to meet us there. I have to ride in the ambulance with the girls; the three of you can follow us in the car." Mark was superglued to Rorie's side. She'd have had to pry him off. "On second thought, why don't you ride with us Mark. We'll make room for you, but you'll have to be very still and quiet."

"I will. I promise."

"Lissa, you and Lindsay go get the car and meet us at the hospital. You'll need to ask a police officer for directions."

"Is there anything else we can bring for you?"

"Yes, now that I think about it, I'm sure both of the girls would like dry clothes."

****

The waiting at the hospital had seemed endless for Mark and Rachael. Holding hands, they had paced the hall together and called Alex so that he wouldn't worry about them. Finally, the doctor confirmed the suspicions of a broken arm for Rorie. No one was surprised when she chose purple as the color for her cast; it was the color of almost everything in her bedroom. However, there was still no word about Allison's condition.

Even though not one of the kids had aired a complaint, Rachael suggested, "Why don't you guys go and get something to eat as soon as Rorie gets done. It could be a long wait. I know you must be starving."

Lindsay and Lissa looked at each other and then at Mark. Without uttering a single word to each other, they all started shaking their heads negatively.

Lissa was the first to speak, "We won't starve to death. When we leave, we all leave together."

Mark was asleep on Rachael's lap when the doctor finally came out to talk to her. She eased Mark over and stood up to meet the man coming toward her.

"Mrs. Carson, I'm sorry that it took so long. We checked her over completely though, and she'll be fine in a day or so. She has a concussion and an ostrich egg size lump on her head. We are fortunate that most of the swelling was outward rather than in which would have put added pressure on her brain. I do want to keep her at least over night so we can watch her."

Rachael sighed with relief, "When can I see her?"

"Now, she's still groggy, but awake and asking for you."

"Doctor, she'll want to know how the little girl is. Do you know?"

He laughed lightly, "She already asked. We still don't know if the girl will make it, but she seems to be fighting. The next twenty-four hours will tell us a lot."

Everyone got up and headed for Allison's room, but the doctor stopped them. "Sorry, guys, only your mother can go in. The rest of you can see your sister tomorrow." They all looked at each other and laughed. Did that doctor really think all five of them were Rachael's?

****

The rest of the week was spent quietly in the sun around the deck of the fresh water pool. Rorie and Allison had had enough of the ocean water and needed the rest. The others hovered around them like hummingbirds at a feeder. The girls had made the local news and were considered the heros of the year. Mark was so proud of them and told his father endless tales about the whole affair.

Rorie and Allison went back to the hospital to see Mary, the little girl whom they had pulled out of the water. She was going to live and was being flown to Atlanta for treatment. Mary's father hugged both of the girls when he saw them come through the door of the hospital room.

"I'll never be able to thank you enough for what you did for me and Mary. She's all I have in the world." The tears built up in his eyes and his voice cracked, but he continued, "you will always be in our thoughts and prayers. Mary never had the opportunity to know you. Would you be willing to send her a picture. I know it will help her understand what has happened and that her heros are real people."

By now everyone was crying tears of joy and appreciation. Rorie exchanged addresses with Mary's father and promised that they would always stay in touch. Allison walked over to poor little Mary who was still hooked up to an I-V, and a respirator was close by just in case she needed help breathing. The pretty little girl was ghostly pale and so still. Allison had to look intensely at her in order to tell if she was even breathing. Allie picked up the tiny bruised hand, held if lovingly in her own, and whispered softly to her.

"We have a special bond now. One that will last forever. Take care little friend."

The blue eyes fluttered open for only a moment, and a slight smile formed on the petite face.

CHAPTER TWELVE

The trip home had been especially uncomfortable for Allison, who felt her head was the size of Mt. Rushmore. There was always a special feeling of relief to finally get home. Rachael had done the ritual cleaning before they had left, so she knew the house would be nice and clean for them. She was the first one to go into the house with a load of luggage. Since Rorie and Allison were less than full strength, most of the unloading would be up to Rachael and Mark.

Rachael carried the big suitcase into her room and placed it on the bed. When she turned around, she noticed the carpet was covered with foot prints. It was strange. She remembered being the last one in her bedroom before leaving for Galveston. It was obvious someone had been in this room. Rachael shrugged off the silly notion. Alex had a key to the house so he could keep an eye on things and bring in the mail. It must have been his footprints she was seeing. She could see where one set went to the window, but another set, different from the first, had stopped in front of her dresser. Shivers went up her spine, but she tried to shake it off as an over active imagination.

"Mark, you need to call your dad and tell him we're home. Then we'll go to the vet and get Chance. I'm anxious to see him, how about you?"

"Yeah, I've missed him and Snickers, too."

"What would you think if we went to get some groceries, stopped and picked up both of the dogs, and then made dinner for your dad?"

"I like that plan." He was a good helper and seemed glad to be home. Rachael didn't think he realized that being home also meant waiting for his mother to show up.

Alex had told her just before they left Galveston that there was still no sign of Heather. The police said it was as though she had disappeared from the face of the earth, but Alex was sure she was out there. Ever since Rachael and the kids had left town, he had felt like someone was out there watching him, looking in his windows at home and sitting in the parking lot at the hospital. Snickers hadn't been much help at home. He either barked at everything or nothing; it just depended on his level of energy at any given moment. Alex had started letting the pup sleep in his bedroom though just to have him close by.

When Rachael opened the door Chance bolted into the house and headed up the steps to see the girls. He had greeted Mark and her at the vet's office, and now he had to search out the remaining two members of his family. Before Chance got up the stairs, his bark changed from its high pitched happy tones to fierce defensive growling. Allison yelled for Rachael. The dog's anger in the absence of visible danger made everyone uneasy. Even level headed Rorie got up and looked in her closet and under the bed.

Chance ran through each room like he had been possessed. The hair on his back was standing straight up like a bristle brush, and all of his white teeth showed beneath the curled lip. He was crazed with anger as he ran into Rachael's room stopping in front of her dresser.

"Oh, my God. Someone has been in here, in all of our rooms. It's okay, boy, you're right." Rachael rubbed his neck for a second, but Chance wouldn't be satisfied until he had searched the house several times over.

"What are you talking about, Mom?" Rorie asked with some doubt lingering in the question.

"When I came in, I noticed strange foot prints on the rug, but I assumed it was just my imagination. Chance, however, has confirmed my suspicions."

"Maybe it was Alex, he said he'd keep an eye on things."

"No, I don't think so. Chance knows his scent. This is a smell Chance abhors."

The girls knew how Rachael was about the floors in the house. She had gotten on their case several times about walking across her freshly vacuumed rug before company came or before going on vacation. They had learned to accept it as one of those traits which makes a person unique, and this was certainly a unique trait. If anyone had been in their house, the floors would certainly tell the tale.

The dog was still conducting his search when Alex arrived.

He hugged everyone, but saved a quick kiss for Rachael. Mark had been hoisted high in his father's arms and had his arms lovingly wrapped around Alex's neck, when Chance quickly came to find out who had entered the house. He gave Alex a friendly greeting and was off again searching for the source of the odor that was driving him crazy.

"He's acting strange. Does he always do this after you've been on vacation?"

Rachael and the kids quickly explained their suspicions. Alex hadn't noticed anything strange during his daily visits. The alarm was always set and the door was locked. His gut was screaming "Heather," but he didn't want to say anything in front of Mark. Alex wanted his son to be careful, not terrified.

"Mom, maybe we should call the police." Allison was always easier to scare than Rorie.

"Honey, what would we tell them? I don't think foot prints on the carpet and a barking dog are enough, especially since the alarm was set and working when we got home."

"I know, but Chance's sniffing is giving me the creeps."

"He'll settle down. Let's go eat dinner and tell Alex all about our week in Galveston." That was enough to take everyone's mind off the possible intrusion. The conversation immediately shifted gears.

Before the family was finished eating dinner, Chance insisted on going outside. Rachael stopped Rorie from opening the door just in time. Rachael caught sight of Mathew working on the bushes on the far side of the pool.

"Gee, Mom, Chance would love to chase Mathew around the yard for awhile. It would be great exercise for him."

"I know Chance would love it, but I don't think Mathew would ever come back to mow the yard. You know what that means, don't you?"

Allison knew, "Close that door. If Mathew doesn't mow; we do!"

"Rachael, do you think Mathew would be willing to help me put some boxes into the attic this weekend?"

"I'm sure he will if he has time. He needs the money for school."

"Are you sure he doesn't hate me? Our last meeting wasn't exactly friendly."

"He has kept a pretty low, polite profile since Easter. He just comes over, does what I ask him, and we have a little polite conversation. Just like it always was."

"He works for you because he has a crush on you, but will he work for me?"

Everybody at the table started giggling and Mark added, "Gee, Dad, maybe he has a crush on you, too." Out and out laughter rocked the room. Rorie and Allison had tears in theirs eyes.

"Stop, please stop!" Allison pleaded holding the side of her head with the bruise on it. "You're making my poor head ache."

The laughter felt good to everyone and continued for several more minutes until only smiles and watery eyes remained. It had helped dramatically to break the tension.

"You guys clean up the kitchen for us, please, while Alex and I go talk to Mathew. I need to pay him for this month's yard work anyway."

"Hey, Mrs. C., how was the beach? Dr. Zamora, how ya doin?"

"We had a wonderful time, Mathew. Thanks for asking. The yard looks great. I appreciate your taking care of it while we were gone."

"Sure, no problem. I enjoy working outside when the weather is warm, especially in this yard. I like all the great flowers and trees. My folks only have a small yard, so it doesn't take me very long to do theirs."

Mathew hadn't given Alex the evil jealous eye yet, so he decided he'd ask him for help. "Mathew, would you mind giving me a hand this weekend?"

Mathew was a little surprised, "Gee, sure, Doc. What do you need?"

The two decided on a time for moving the boxes, and Rachael offered to come along and help set up the kitchen for Alex. After living in the house for nearly two months, Alex was glad to finally have some help. Maybe he and Mark could start thinking of it as home.

The two left Mathew to finish his work and headed for the front of the house. There would be no walk tonight: neither of them wanted to get too far from the house or the kids. It was their fort, and Chance was the sentry.

"If things work out with Mathew, maybe he'll do my yard during the summer also. I've never taken care of a house or yard. My dad hired someone to do it when I was a kid because it had to be perfect, and Heather took care of the yard and house in Chicago by hiring anyone and everyone to do the work for her." The mentioning of her name stopped Alex in his tracks. He turned to look at Rachael, but she would not look directly into his eyes.

"Rachael, I'm so very sorry for putting you and the girls in danger. Please forgive me."

Now she looked up, "Alex, don't be silly. It certainly isn't your fault."

"But if we didn't spend so much time with you and the girls, you wouldn't be drawn into this mess."

"Alex," Rachael paused and put her hand on his arm, "You and Mark are worth it. We're friends, right? And good friends stick together."

Now Alex was serious and took her by the shoulders, and the shadows returned to his eyes. "I don't have many friends and one of them is dead."

"He was your lawyer and had information she wanted. We don't really know if she killed for revenge."

"Frankly, I don't want to find out if she's killing for revenge or just because of association."

"Did she kill the baby she took from the prison?"

"No, it was found at a gas station not far from John's office, but no one has seen the mother. They don't know if she's dead or on the run or still with Heather."

"At least Heather has some mercy."

"Promise me you won't take any chances." Alex was almost shaking her like she was a child. He felt helpless to protect them, and Rachael saw the frustration in his eyes.

"Alex, you can stop shaking me. I promise we'll be very careful. I would feel better though if...No. That's silly. Never mind"

He still hadn't let go of her arms, "What? What can we do?"

Rachael smiled into his eyes and softly said, "You can let go of my arms. I can't think straight when my brains are vibrating."

Now Alex realized how frantic he was acting, and it wouldn't solve anything. They had to plan their strategy.

"Okay, now can you think better?" Alex was smiling slightly at her. He couldn't resist her sense of humor. It always had a calming affect on him. "Do you have any ideas?"

"I assume the police are keeping a watch at your house just in case she shows up at the door."

"Yes, they tour the neighborhood regularly during the day and have someone posted all night. Now that we suspect someone has been in here, we should have them watch your place too."

"That would certainly make me feel better at night. I know the dog would let me know if anyone approached the house, but he wouldn't know if anyone was out about the streets. Have you told Debbie or anyone else at the hospital what's going on?"

"Yes, I told Debbie, and naturally, she insisted on telling security. She wants to post Heather's picture in the hospital lounges warning everyone to watch out for her. Damn her! Damn her!" Alex shook his head helplessly.

"Who? Debbie? She just wants to help, and it's her job to protect the hospital."

"Not Debbie, I mean Heather. This is just what Mark and I wanted to avoid. We didn't want everyone to know our dirty past. Putting Heather's picture up in the lounge is as good as putting it on the news. I know Debbie has to protect the hospital. One day last week, I was sure someone was watching me as I walked though the parking lot. Naturally, I guessed it was Heather. What if she followed me into the hospital? What if she shot an innocent person just because she wanted to hurt me? I'd have to leave again."

Rachael hadn't appreciated his level of desperation until he suggested moving on. She didn't want him to go. He and Mark had become part of their family even if their relationship was only platonic. "Alex, the girls and I don't want you to leave either. I really don't think the people here are as shallow as you may think."

Alex looked down at her with the worry pouring out of his eyes. "I just don't know what to expect."

Rachael took a small step closer to him and put her hand back on his arm. Looking up into his face, she said, "Alex fight for what you want. Don't give up. You might have to put up with some gossip and slanderous remarks, but the people who know you and respect you won't change their loyalty. Everyone has a skeleton or two in his closet; most of us, however, just don't have to watch those skeletons rattle through the hallways where we work."

"Well, I'd like to keep mine locked up like everybody else."

"Maybe its better this way. You won't have to worry about the past getting out anymore. It will be over and done with while the rest of us wonder when the closet door will be unlocked."

"I wonder if that is how someone came up with the term 'skeleton key'?"

Rachael was glad Alex could find some humor in all of this. "If people at the hospital are included in the hunt, maybe they'll see her threat against you as an affront to themselves."

"I don't know. I suppose it would be best to alert more people; the more eyes watching for her the better the chance of spotting her if she shows up there."

"I'll arrange my daily tutoring so if one of the girls can't be with Mark, I can. One of us will stay with him constantly until you get home from work."

"Thanks, I know he'll love that. He'll do almost anything to be with Allison and Rorie. I'll drop him off in the morning on my way to work. I don't want him left alone in the house at all."

"I'll be waiting for him. Tell him to bring Snickers along, and we'll all have breakfast together. I'll feed you too if you have time."

"Coffee would be great. I still haven't gotten the measuring right. My morning brew either looks like left over dish water, or it eats the spoon."

****

Rachael was gasping to catch her voice, but the iron grip was closing around her neck. This time the spiraling pit of darkness was being replaced by the depths of unconsciousness. Rachael knew no one could hear her screams of agony, so she fiercely grabbed at the strong hands which were forcing her back onto the bed. Her last lucid thought was to scratch the eyes of her attacker, but she couldn't see a face in the darkness or reach the eyes. Too quickly the pit of unconsciousness claimed its victim.

"Mother! Mother! My God wake up!" Rachael's thrashing arms struck Rorie in the shoulder nearly knocking her to the floor.

"Mother, wake up." This time, as Rorie's frightened voice pleaded, she shook her mother harshly.

"What's wrong, Rorie?"

"Al, she won't wake up. Call Alex. Hurry! I think she is choking to death."

The violent motion had subsided, and Rachael lay so still Rorie actually feared her mother was dead. There seemed to be no heartbeat or breathing. Rorie was nearly in a state of panic when Allie came back into the room.

"Is Alex coming?"

"Yeah, but he has to grab Mark first."

"Help me, we have to do something until he gets here." Allie knew immediately what Rorie intended as she tipped her mother's head back. "I'll start mouth-to-mouth. You check again for a pulse."

"My God, Rorie, she can't die."

"Shut up and concentrate."

"I found a heartbeat. Is she breathing?"

"Barely. Get the door, I heard a car."

Staring at her mother's nearly lifeless body, Allison's fear held her in place.

"Allison! Go!" Reality clicked for Allie, and she headed for the door just in time to turn off the alarm so Alex and Mark could enter.

"Where is she?"

"In her bedroom. Rorie's with her. Alex we can't get her to wake up."

"Please keep Mark with you."

By the time Alex ran through the bedroom door, Rachael had gradually started to come out of her dream state. The eyes fluttered open, and her trembling hands reached up to rub her aching throat. She glanced at Rorie, then at Alex, and finally at Allie and Mark standing in the door way.

In a raspy voice she asked, "Alex, what are you doing here? What happened?"

"Mother, you were screaming loudly, and I was so scared. I couldn't get you to wake up. I told Allie to call Alex. It's all I could think of to do."

Now Alex was at her bedside wanting to see his patient. "Let me take a look at her."

Rachael was embarrassed by the trouble she had caused and tried to get out of the physical and verbal examination. "Really, I'm all right."

"I still want to take a look at you. Allie called screaming to me that you were dying. I don't take house calls lightly; in fact, I don't even make house calls. So as long as I'm here, I'm going to examine you. Quite frankly, Mrs. Carson, you look and sound terrible."

Rorie looked at her mother with great concern, "You were dreaming again weren't you?" The accusation brought an affirmative nod of Rachael's head and the red glow of embarrassment to her cheeks.

"It was different though, wasn't it, mom?"

"Much worse. The man at the front door never attacked me before. In fact, I wasn't even at the door. It took place here in my bedroom." The terror in her eyes brought goose bumps to Rorie and Allison as they listened to their mother add, "I died in this dream."

"My God, Rachael, why didn't you ever tell me about this?"

After a moment she answered, "I guess I didn't want to introduce you to my skeleton."

Rorie and Allison shared questioning glances as Alex tried to do a basic check wanting to make sure Rachael was as okay as she claimed. The close proximity of his body made her feel uneasy. Maybe she was only a patient to him, but feeling his breath on her face and neck as he checked her throat nearly allowed that little black box hidden deep inside of her to spill her emotions all over the bed.

"Alex, really I'm fine. Stop hovering. All I need is a cup of tea to help me get back to sleep."

Allison was quick to offer, "Mom, I'll get it for you. Mark, how about some hot chocolate?"

"Yeah, sounds good. Ah, do you have any cookies?"

Allison smiled at him, "Yes, we have cookies too."

Walking over to the side of the bed, Mark purposefully stared at Rachael. Then he questioned his father, "Are you sure she's going to be fine?"

"Yes, I think so."

"Good, I was worried." Then he leaned over the bed, brushed a kiss on her cheek, and turned to hustle out the door toward the kitchen with the two girls.

Before reaching the kitchen, they heard Alex yell, "Forget the tea. I'll get us something a little stronger."

All three kids smiled at each other and shared a resounding "Yes!"

Alex returned to the bedroom with two brandy snifters and handed one to Rachael. She swirled the amber liquid watching it coat the sides of the snifter. The aroma had already started to soothe her raw nerves. Rachael set the glass down on the night stand and started to get up. She remembered, however, that she was wearing the scant red satin gown. She loved wearing the floor length fitted gown because it made her feel desirable - not comfortable, but it was not exactly the way she should prance around in front of a man even if the man claimed to be her doctor.

"Would you hand me my robe?"

"I really don't think you need to be getting up. I'll get you whatever you want."

"Ah, well, thanks. But I need to use the washroom."

Alex's cheeks flushed as he reached for the matching red robe and walked over to the bed. He held it up by the shoulders so Rachael could slide it on.

Rachael hesitated, *He's a doctor. This is no big deal for him. You are comfortable to him, remember, not sexy.* She flipped the covers back and stood up. The red satin barely hid the shapely figure beneath it. Alex tried not to stare, but his mind was possessed by the body in front of him. Rachael put her arms into the robe, fastened it securely around her trim waist, and walked toward the bathroom.

As Rachael walked away from him, Alex noticed the room he was standing in. He had been so concerned about his patient he hadn't even been aware of the beauty of the room. The room was huge with a grand black onyx bed. The headboard covered one whole wall with full length mirrors on each side while the matching dressers on the opposite side of the room balanced the ensemble. The white walls were not the stark hospital white but an elegant contrast to the onyx furniture. Wisps of teal and black were brushed through the white complementing the two tone teal carpet. The lighter color of teal was scalloped along the outside of the darker tone. It was the most striking combination Alex had ever seen. The back wall was all glass and gave a complete view of the gardens and sun room when the curtains were drawn. Lights had been recessed into the vaulted ceiling giving the illusion of extraordinary height. The best part of the room, in Alex's opinion, was the fireplace in the corner. It offered an easy masculine touch to the room; and from the way it was setting, it must be visible in the bathroom as well.

When Rachael returned, Alex was standing at the window with his back to her staring out at the stars wondering if there was any chance at all for the two of them to be more than friends. As he turned to face her, he was disappointed to see that she was pulling the covers up over the red satin.

Bringing a chair up beside the bed, Alex looked at Rachael, "Now tell me about these nightmares you've been having."

Rachael tried to abbreviate the past events, but Alex detected the gaps in her testimony and asked the necessary questions to fill in the holes.

"I'll prescribe something to help you sleep tomorrow. Since you don't dream every night, just take the medication after an episode." Rachael started to shake her head, but Alex continued, "It's only a mild sedative and will help you get back to sleep. I suggest, however, that you log the dream in your journal before taking it. You'll remember more writing immediately after you dream rather than waiting until morning."

Rachael nodded affirmatively and said, "Thanks, Alex for coming over. I must've scared the day lights out of the girls. I can still feel the fingers squeezing around my neck. It was terrifying. Why has the dream taken such a violent twist? Could I have died in my sleep?"

"I don't know why your dream changed, but I don't think you could've died from it. Your body's involuntary functions would kick in just like they did tonight. Where's your journal?"

"Here in my night stand." Rachael tried to reach for it, but Alex was closer. He opened the drawer and handed it to her.

"Here, you write down what you can remember about today and the dream while I freshen our drinks."

After several minutes, Alex returned with snifters in hand and informed Rachael that all three children were safely tucked into bed.

"If it's all right with you, Mark is going to sleep in the guest room. Rorie said she'd take him over to the house in the morning to get some clean clothes and Snickers."

"That's fine. I'm finished logging the day's events and the dream."

"May I see what you've written?"

Rachael had not expected to show anyone her journal, especially Alex. In addition to there being more details, she had purposely not told him about the sensuous dream she'd had on the beach; but there was no way to graciously get out of handing him the book.

"I suppose."

Alex didn't miss the reservation in her voice and wondered about what he'd find written in the diary of her dreams. Quickly he perused the pages gleaning the details that might shed some light on Rachael's subconscious. He raised an eyebrow and looked up at her.

"You left this dream on the beach out of your verbal account. Any particular reason why?"

"I didn't think it pertained to the nightmares. I only had it that one time."

"Then why did you log it?"

"Because I wanted to remember it."

Alex wanted to believe that she saw him as the man coming out of the mist to take her away, but he knew Rachael saw him only as a friend. Besides, he had too much emotional baggage to get involved with anyone right now; and no one with an ounce of sense wanted to be involved with a man who had a killer wife running amuck across the country.

"Do you see anything that might help me solve my mystery?"

"I get the strange feeling that your subconscious is trying to warn you about something."

"So do I, but I can't figure out what it is. I do feel, however, that the danger is getting closer. For months the dream was the same over and over. It changed when....." she stopped not wanting her idea to become audible, but the implication of her pause was as good as words.

"I know." Alex got up out of the chair and walked to the patio door. Chance who had been at Rachael's side the entire evening now lifted his head to follow Alex's movement toward the door. He jumped off the bed and went to stand beside his new friend. Alex let his hand lovingly rub the soft yellow ears. Chance responded by tilting his head to allow more area to be exposed for stroking.

He didn't want to look at her, "The dream changed when you met us." The words fell on her heart like rocks on a rose.

"No, Alex, I'm sure it's not that way at all."

"Rachael, yes it is. I can read. You wrote it yourself. It's my fault you and the girls are in danger."

Feeling desperate to save their relationship, Rachael became defensive. "I can tell you for sure the person in my dream isn't a woman because the arms are too long and too strong."

"Maybe it's me."

"No! No way. I'm sure it isn't you."

"You don't know who's in your dream. I think the person could be me symbolizing the danger I've put you in."

Now Rachael was out of bed pulling tightly on the belt ends so that her robe would stay closed as she stamped over to him. "It doesn't matter, Alex. We're in this together now; and if it's Heather, your pulling away won't make her disappear."

Chance was suddenly jumping at the door. He nearly knocked Rachael over has he pushed past her trying to force the door open. Alex turned his head just in time to see a shadow pass the gate.

"Someone's out there. Come on, boy. Call the police." The words were sailing back at Rachael. Left holding the door, she didn't have an opportunity to protest before they were gone.

It was impossible for Alex to keep up with the long legged Chance as he bolted around the side of the house, but the fierce barking was a guiding beacon in the darkness. Alex detected an interruption in Chance's call when a car engine started; and before he could call to the dog, he heard a second sound that echoed through the neighborhood. Chance's high pitched cry of pain pierced the darkness, and more guilt tumbled down on Alex's already heavy conscience. *The bastard has run over Chance. Our poor brave friend.* Alex ran faster in order to reach the side of the fallen ally and barely noticed a small sports car speed down the street.

From the back of the house, Rachael heard the cry that crushed her heart. "Don't panic! Get help."

"Allie!" Rachael screamed. "Allie!"

"Yeah, mom. What's wrong?"

"Chance was hit by a car. I'm afraid its bad. Call Dr. Carley. Tell him we'll meet him at the back door of the clinic. Oh, and tell your sister what happened and where we'll be. The police are on their way. Tell her to lock up the house."

"Done. You and Alex get the dog in the car - back seat. Hold him still. I'll drive."

Rachael raced through the front door just in time to see Alex pick Chance up off the pavement. He'd need help: Chance was heavy. Running down the street, she knew Alex would blame himself needlessly. Chance was just doing his job; protecting them.

As Rachael came up to Alex, it was not even possible for her to ask if Chance was dead, but the question must have been in her eyes because Alex answered it.

"He isn't dead yet, but we gotta get help."

Rachael softly touched the big, soft head and ran her fingers tenderly down his snout to the tip of his nose and was slightly relieved when she felt the faint breath escape from his nostrils.

"Help me hold him in the back seat. Allie is coming."

By the time the two of them could gingerly place Chance in the back seat, Allie was racing through the garage door. Rachael held his head talking softly to try and comfort him. Chance didn't move. She didn't know if that was good or bad.

"Is he stable? The doc is waiting for us. Rorie's up and waiting for the cops to arrive." She didn't wait for an answer, but started the car and pulled out of the drive. Someone in a small sports car watched at the end of the street as the Crown Victoria sped by.

Rachael felt, more than heard, the slightest whimper come from Chance as Allie turned the corner onto Yale Drive. "I'm here, boy. Hang on, please hang on." Then she turned to Alex and declared, "I'll kill the son-of-a-bitch who hurt my dog."

Alex heard the oath and reached for her hand, "I'll help."

Dr. Carley was holding the door open watching for his patient to arrive. When he saw Allie pull into the parking lot, he propped it open and headed for the car. Alex helped the vet lift Chance up off Rachael's lap and carry him into the operating room. Chance cried from the pain caused by the movement.

The two men delicately placed the dog on the table already prepared for surgery. Allie was washing up to assist. Rachael bent down so she was eye level with Chance which allowed her to talk to him while Dr. Carley quickly got an I-V started.

Rachael looked deeply into his big brown eyes, "I love you, boy. Dr. Carley will take good care of you. Please, God, please save my friend."

"He'll be going to sleep now, Rachael. There's nothing more you can do for him. Allie will stay and help me." The vet motioned for Alex to escort Rachael out of the room.

"Hey, doc?" Both men turned and looked at Allie. "Oh, sorry, I forgot both of you would answer. I was just going to tell you, Dr. Carley, that Alex is a doctor and may be able to help.

Dr. Carley, looking at Rachael, said, "Thanks, Allie, but I think he's needed elsewhere." Then Dr. Carley looked at Alex, "I'll yell if I need you, but Allie's a great assistant."

Alex took Rachael out of the room and closed the door. Her shoulders heaved as her body was overcome by the deluge of tears which had been dammed up inside of her. For several minutes Alex held her securely in his arms. He stroked the soft curls and couldn't help enjoying the essence of her closeness. Gradually the pleasure was replaced by remorse for the grief he'd caused her. This was all his fault.

"Rachael, I'm so sorry for everything. This is my war you and the girls have been dragged into. I was the one who opened the door and let Chance out."

Through the tears Rachael said, "He was doing what his instincts told him to do - protect his family. He is family, you know." Her words were mingled with the last lingering sobs.

"I know he's family. I understand that now." Alex tightened his grip on her shoulders. "If it's war Heather wants, then it's war she'll get. She'll not hurt me or mine again. Isn't that how the saying goes?"

Rachael knew she and the girls were part of his pledge, and she was glad he'd decided to stay and finish the fight. In spite of whatever might happen between the two of them, at least he and Mark would have a future in Tulsa if they wanted one.

"Alex, I need to check on Rorie. I hope the police are keeping an eye on the house."

"Good idea. We need to get a twenty-four hour watch on your house also."

"I think we're more likely to get a twenty-four hour watch if we're all living in the same house."

"I'm sure that isn't necessary. It wouldn't be right for us to move in with you."

"Alex, if you really think about it, the only time one or both of you aren't with us is when we're asleep."

Alex knew they spent a lot of time together; but now that he really considered the amount of time the two families were together, he realized Rachael was right. It had happened so gradually and naturally. Well maybe it wasn't so natural. The kids had helped to make sure the two adults were together whether they liked it or not.

"Let's talk about it tomorrow when we aren't so tired. It's been a long horrible night for all of us, and it isn't over yet."

The talking had helped Rachael keep her mind off Chance. Now that the conversation ended, however, she could think of nothing else. She was lost in a desert of time, and the minutes were endless grains of sand. The small, outer office hardly provided the room to work up a good pace; and the reading material consisted of the back of dog food bags and a few brochures about the woes of heart worm.

Rachael stood in front of the surgery door hoping her will would be enough to open it and show her what was happening on the other side. Then she tried sending Alex in to see if they needed any help, but he understood her intent and declined.

"I can't interrupt them. It wouldn't be professional, and it could do more damage if I unexpectedly opened the door. You know Allie will be out as soon as she can. Let's call Rorie again and make sure the police are watching the house."

"You can." A sound from behind the door caught her attention, and then she was looking straight at her exhausted daughter. Rachael put her arms around the red-eyed teenager and walked her over to sit down.

"He's was badly hurt, Mom. At this point, the doc has done all he can. We'll just have to wait and see."

"What's wrong with him?"

"Chance must have jumped to the side trying to get out of the way. He really shouldn't be alive at all. The car hit him in the side breaking his left leg and several ribs. One of the ribs punctured a lung. That's the worst part. If he doesn't develop pneumonia, he will probably live. We set the leg, but he may have a limp. Its hard to tell." The tears trickled down Allie's face, but she wiped them away.

"Can I see him?"

"Not yet. We'll keep him asleep at least until morning. It'll be easier to keep him still. He's going to need a lot of care for a while. I told Doc. Carley I'd work here until we can take the Chancester Boy home with us." Now the tears of fear and exhaustion could not be held in check. Rachael held her baby in her arms just the way Alex had held her earlier.

****

The police car had been parked in front of the house all night, but the three weary night owls had not seen it when they finally reached home. Sleep was all that was on their minds. This would be the first time in years Rachael had slept in her bedroom without Chance beside her. It was very lonely and her heart ached for the missing friend.

The first thing Alex did when they arrived home was to check on Mark. He was sound asleep in Rorie's bed with her sitting next to him reading a book.

"He didn't want to go to bed alone, and I couldn't sleep; so this was the arrangement we came up with."

"I can move him now."

"No, that's all right. I really don't mind if he stays here. I'll be able to sleep now that I know you're all home safe and sound. Did you see the police car outside?"

"No, we were too tired to look."

"Well, it's there. I've checked several times just to make sure."

"See you in the morning."

"Alex, will you and Mom be here?"

"Yes, I think we'll both stay home tomorrow." It seemed natural to talk about them all being home together. He wished the circumstances had been more out of desire than necessity.

Before going to bed, Alex called Debbie at home and explained what had happened. He asked her to call a staff meeting for the following morning so he could be the one to ask his colleagues for their help. When he gave Debbie Rachael's phone number as a place to be reached, there was a definite pause in the conversation before she acknowledged the information.

"Debbie, if you want to say something, just do it. You've always spoken your mind before."

"Oh, I will; but I'll wait until tomorrow when you are standing in front of me. Right now you sound a little short humored."

"Your intuition serves you well. Good-bye."

"Alex?"

"Yes, what is it?"

"Be careful."

"Thanks. We will."

CHAPTER THIRTEEN

The morning sun sneaking in the window could be blocked out by the teal shamed pillows, but the low base sounds that filtered into the bedroom could only be partially silenced. Rachael didn't want to acknowledge the morning; but once she realized the sounds she heard were male voices just outside her bedroom door in the foyer, it was impossible to ignore them.

Rachael threw back the covers and realized she was still wearing the gold and black silk sweatsuit she had worn to the clinic last night. Instinctively, she reached for the telephone and called Dr. Carley.

"Good morning, Doctor. How's Chance?"

"He's hanging in there, Rachael. He won't really be conscious until later this afternoon, but he seems to be resting fairly easily now. I'm going home for a while to get some sleep myself. The office will call me if there's any change in his condition."

"Allie will be in as soon as she wakes up, but she'll have Rorie with her and probably a police officer."

"I'm sorry. I didn't realize the situation was so serious for all of you. We didn't do much talking last night."

"Allie can fill you in later. Thanks for everything, Dr. Carley."

Rachael hung up the phone and headed for the bathroom. She wanted to at least comb her hair before going to see who was talking with Alex. Quickly, she threw off the wrinkled silk and donned a simple navy blue dress. It buttoned up the front, but Rachael just slipped it over her head letting the full skirt slide over her slim hips. Then she put on a hint of blush and light lipstick. Looking at herself in the full length mirror, she wished she could wake up looking like this, then maybe Alex wouldn't think of her as merely comfortable. *Oh, well. Maybe in my next life.*

Rachael opened the bedroom door and stepped into the vaulted foyer. The large arched window let the morning sun warm the inside of the house. Alex was standing in front of the door with his back to her. He must have been in a hurry to answer the door because he just had his pants on. Even though the two of them had spent several hours around the pool with the kids, Alex had always been fully dressed. Rachael enjoyed this view of him, especially when he turned around. His coal black hair was slightly messed, and it perfectly matched the soft black fur on his chest. Rachael mentally chastised herself for letting her mind wonder about other areas of body hair and had to actually pull her eyes away from his alluring anatomy when he spoke to her.

Alex felt uncomfortable under her gaze and wished he had taken the extra second to grab his shirt before running down the steps to keep the police from ringing the doorbell and waking everyone in the house. It was enough they had been talking right below his window, they didn't need everyone up.

"Good morning, Rachael. I'm sorry we woke you. This is Detective Archer; he's in charge of this case."

The short blond man was anatomically the exact opposite of Alex. Rachael was surprised to find herself making the physical comparison. She knew outside appearance did not dictate the deeper and more appreciated human characteristics. This man was probably a very competent detective. *First impressions are not always correct, look how wrong you were about Alex. Okay, I'll give him a chance.*

"Good morning, Ma'am."

Uck, Rachael hated the word "Ma'am". It made her feel old and comfortable. *Well, the man isn't off to a very good start.*

"Good morning. I'll make you a cup of coffee if you promise not to call me 'Ma'am' anymore."

"It's a deal." The detective followed Rachael into the kitchen, but Alex quickly went up the stairs. She was sure he had gone to get his shirt. She motioned for Archer to sit in the breakfast nook while she prepared the morning brew. Alex was back with them before Rachael could finish preparing the coffee pot.

"Dr. Zamora, we believe your wife committed a third murder before leaving Chicago."

"Jesus, no! Who? Who else did she have a grudge against?" Alex's mind was racing to consider the people who might have crossed Heather besides John and himself.

"The man's name was Stewart Chambers. He was found next to his car shot in the back of the head. It took a while to make a connection; but after the man's wife gave the detective a detailed account of the victim's past activities, the Chicago police were able to put together a possible motive."

"Let me guess. He was one of the jurors at her trial."

"Yeah, good guess. How'd ya know?"

"That last day in the courtroom, when the jury filed in, only one person would not back down from Heather's evil stare. He refused to be intimidated then, but she had the last word. Now he's dead."

"We are assuming that after last night, she's here. I think you, Sir, are her primary target not the children or Mrs. Carson."

Rachael didn't like the direction Detective Archer was taking. "We believe Heather may have been in our house sometime while we were in Galveston. That puts all of us in danger."

"I appreciate your concern, Mrs. Carson." His disrespectful slur on the word "Mrs." made Rachael want to take back her fresh ground coffee she had made for him. He deserved instant for that insult. The way he hung on the title made it clear that he believed Alex was keeping her bed warm at night and that Rachael didn't want him to leave. *But then what else should he think? Alex is staying here. People at the hospital will probably think the same thing about our arrangement.*

Alex caught the innuendo and was surprised Rachael didn't throw Archer out of the house. Alex had been in her house only one night; and already, people assumed the worst.

"Sir," Rachael slurred the title with as much disrespect as she could squeeze into one syllable. "Whoever hit my dog last night, assaulted me personally. That person was on my property stalking me and mine."

Rachael threw a quick glance to Alex showing she had appreciated his reference to family that included her and the girls the night before. A slight smile crossed his face as the meaning of her commitment to the new family sunk in. Alex was enjoying her verbal admonishment of the man and waited for her to continue.

"That presence here I take as a direct threat to all of us. Now, the way I see it is, you can do your job professionally with our cooperation and without your personal judgments as to our living arrangements, or we can request another detective be put in charge."

Now it was Alex's turn to verbally jump on this hot shot detective. "We are all here together to try and make your job easier. Is it not a better use of your manpower to watch one house rather that two? Isn't it better having two adults watching the children? Or do you prefer two households, two schedules, two careers to follow?"

"I'm sorry. I was out of line. One house is definitely better. Let's start again. Doctor, I know you'll have to go to the hospital. You can't stay locked up forever. Please let me know your daily agenda so arrangements can be made to have police protection with you. Mrs. Carson, will you be going to the hospital daily?"

"I'll have to clear it with the Chief of Staff and the parents, but I think I can take a couple of weeks off to stay home with the kids. I really don't think it's a good idea for any of my students to be coming to the house right now."

"You're right about that. The fewer people around here the better. The girls should never go anywhere without informing an officer."

"That'll work for a while because they're afraid now. I don't know how long we can keep them tied to the house."

"Hopefully, we'll get her right away. Would you show me around the house so I can see the doors and windows from inside. We need to get a good feel for the layout of the place."

The two men got up from the table to follow Rachael through the house. Rorie was on her way into the kitchen with a knee high, dark brown Snickers at her side. His long chocolate colored tail caught Rachael on the leg, and she reached down to give him the good morning pat he was waiting for.

"Can we go out the garage, Mom? Nature calls."

"I think so." Rachael turned to the detective, "Okay?"

"Yeah, sure. There are officers in the front of the house."

Rorie walked on with a desperate dog at her side while the others went on to examine the various entrances and windows of the house. Rachael could hear Rorie talking to Snickers as she put a leash around his neck, and then the expected doors chimes sounded signifying she had opened the door leading into the garage.

A scream of fright erupted through the house from the direction of the kitchen which caught everyone off guard. The detective was the first to head for the door with Rachael and Alex right after him. They had no idea of what could have terrified Rorie to let out such a heart stopping scream. The answer was far worse than any of them could have fathomed.

"Rorie, what's wrong? Rorie, answer me." Rachael was screaming for her daughter's attention, but there was no answer.

Archer went through the garage door first and stopped dead still. Blood covered the crown victoria Rachael had driven home only a few hours earlier. It was smeared over all of the windows and left running down the hood. Whoever had done this had easy access to the house in order to get all of this blood carried into the garage. It had taken more than one trip, especially for a woman.

"Jesus Christ, Archer, I thought your men were watching this place."

"We were. We were here before you got back. Someone did this after you got home."

"No shit! We figured that out all by ourselves."

Rachael tried to get Rorie to move back from the car, but her feet were glued to the concrete. Blood was dripping onto her shoes, and Snickers feet were covered in red. Rorie started to quiver just before the tears filled her eyes and her fist flew up with a paper clinched in it tightly.

"This is what's sick. This message was left for one of us. Here, read it."

Rachael took the blood stained note from her daughter's hand and opened it up so she could read it out loud. "The dog was easy. Who will be next?"

Archer tried to delicately reach out and take the paper from Rachael. "Let me take it for possible prints."

Rorie was shaking violently making it hard for her to speak clearly, "Mom, was it her? Where did she get the blood? Does it belong to Chance?"

"No, it isn't Chance's. I just called the vet, and he is still resting. Come on. Let's get you cleaned up and away from this."

Alex pried the leash out of her fingers and took the dog out through the garage door which was opening to let in a throng of dark blue uniforms. He was afraid if he didn't get out of there, he'd say something he'd regret about Archer's bumbling protection plan. They weren't even safe with the police right outside the door.

By the time Alex had cooled off a little and gone back into the house, all of the kids were sitting at the table with Rachael next to Rorie who was still trying to collect herself. Alex poured himself another cup of coffee and joined the family at the table.

Taking Rorie's hand he said, "Are you going to be all right, honey."

"Yeah, thanks. I've got to go with Allie to take care of Chance. That'll help me to get my head straight."

Alex looked at each of them and finally to Rachael. "We have to be so careful from now on. Don't take anything for granted. Watch everything and everyone. Don't go anywhere alone for any reason."

"Alex is right. We have to be smart, smarter than she is. Girls, remember what I've always told you?"

"Yeah, Mom. Don't panic. That's the rule. Think straight - be smarter than the other guy."

"Now we're in the ultimate fight. Some one wants to hurt us, and we have to be our own best protection."

"Your mother's right, girls. Mark, please don't go outside alone, okay?"

"Not me, Dad. After last night and this morning, not a chance."

"Good. The security company will be over this morning to check the system and try to find out how she got in. We will also change the code. Girls, when you're ready to go to the clinic, tell Detective Archer so he can send an officer with you."

Rorie was quick to snap, "A lot of good that'll do. It might keep her from walking in the front door, but that's all. What good are the cops if they can't stop her let alone catch her?"

"You're right, honey. That's why we have to be our own best protection."

"Let's get ready, Rorie. I want to make sure we're there when Chance wakes up."

The kids left Alex and Rachael sitting at the table. "It's going to be hard on them."

"Alex, it'll be hard on all of us, but we'll make it." He reached over and took her soft slender hand in his. Rachael smiled back at him and returned the caress.

"You know, Rachael, what happened this morning with Detective Archer is bound to happen again, especially at the hospital."

"I know. It wasn't really his fault. The fact that you and Mark are living here lends itself to that conclusion."

"I'm sorry. I hope we um....can..." Alex didn't know what to say that would make up for the rumors which would certainly malign her reputation.

"Alex, stop worrying. I'm a big girl. This wouldn't be the first time in my life people passed judgment on me or you for that matter. A few rumors can't hurt a strong friendship. We'll worry about our reputations after we get out of this mess."

"You make it sound so easy. Were you always the optimist in the family?"

"Yes, I guess I had to balance Jack who tended to be a little pessimistic. It was funny. When we went on vacation, he always felt lost, but I never did. He was the one who was lost, but I always had to go in and ask for the directions. I would get so frustrated with him."

"We never traveled much; but when we did, we flew. There wasn't enough time to drive."

"We always enjoyed the time in the car. I'm sure it has a lot to do with the fact that all of us are white knuckle flyers."

"You're what?"

"White knuckle flyers. We get nervous and keep our fists clenched, which makes our knuckles turn white."

"I guess I'd drive too then. Mark and I need to go over to the house and get some of our things, and I would like to clean up." Alex rubbed the shadow on his face indicating he'd really like to shave. He was definitely embarrassed by his disheveled appearance.

"Whatever you need to do is fine with me. I want to get some groceries in the house. After being gone on vacation, we're out of everything. Then I'll go to the clinic and see Chance. First, I'll wait for the security people to take care of the house. Will you and Mark be back by noon?"

"Probably, will you still be here?"

"I'll wait for you. That way I can show you the new code. Will you go to the hospital today?"

"No, I called Debbie last night and told her what happened. She's setting up a meeting for tomorrow so I can talk to the staff."

"Do you want me to go along?"

"No, I'd feel better if you were here with the kids."

"Alex, I hope you'll make yourself comfortable while you are here. I know Mark will be okay. If there's anything you need, please, just ask one of us."

"Thanks for everything." He gave her hand one last squeeze and went to get Mark.

Rachael found herself alone to think about the implications of having two new people living in the house with her and the girls. Mark would adapt easily. He already felt like this was home, but Alex would have a hard time adjusting to life with three women. Rachael knew he was a very private person because he had focused all of his energy into the operating room and not into relationships. It takes time to nurture friendships; they don't just happen. Alex had not given that time to anyone, including his wife and son. Now he was trying hard to change, but jumping into a household with three open and loving women might be too great an emotional shock for the socially constipated man.

CHAPTER FOURTEEN

Allison and Rorie sat in the small room where Chance was still sleeping on the table. Allie's chair was next to his head, so she could detect the slightest movement of his eyes indicating he was waking up.

"Ya know, Rorie, having Alex and Mark move in with us might help speed up a romantic relationship."

"It might. I like having Mark and Alex around. I can't believe the two of them are putting up such a fight about falling in love."

"Wow! My stoic sister is showing a romantic side."

"Not necessarily, Miss Matchmaker. I just think the two of them feel they are each destined to be forever alone; consequently, that belief can insure loneliness."

"So what do we do? Help them along?"

"Logically, if the chemistry between the two of them is strong enough, we shouldn't have to do anything but provide the opportunity for nature to take its course."

"My God, they have the opportunity. They're living under the same roof. Opportunity doesn't even have to knock on the door in this case."

"So lets give them some time. Alex and Mark have only been with us one night, and it wasn't exactly a romantic interlude."

Poor Chance had not only started coming out of his deep sleep, he was wide awake casting his gaze from one girl to the other. They had completely missed his waking, but the slight whimper brought them back to their immediate concern.

"Rorie, he's awake. Chancy, old boy, how do you feel?"

Chance whimpered again as if to answer the question and to tell them he was hurting.

"Yes, I know it hurts." Rorie came to stand by her good friend and gently touched the short white hairs around his snout.

"Rorie, I have to keep him as still as possible. Use that eye dropper to get some water into his mouth. I know he's really thirsty."

The girls loved and catered to their hurting friend for several minutes before thinking to call Dr. Carley and their mother. Chance wouldn't be moving at all for sometime to come. Someone was going to have to be with him all the time, or he might try to get up which could cause more damage to his lung. It would be easier for them to take care of him after they got him home, but in the meantime Rachael and the girls would take turns going to the clinic with a police guard, of course.

Dr. Carley predicted that if Chance made it through the next twenty-four hours, he'd probably make a full recovery. As long as Allie was around to clean the dressings every day and Chance's movements could be severely limited, Chance could go home in about a week. Rachael especially would feel better when her dog was home.

Having missed Alex at noon, Rachael didn't see him again until dinner time, and naturally he was completely groomed the way she was used to seeing him. She preferred the softer side he had revealed that morning.

Mark, as usual, was the one to break the stress that had been building all day. "Can we go swimming tonight? I worked hard today movin' all our stuff."

"Yes, you can go swimming. It'll be good for you and your father to have some fun. Go on now. I'll come out when I get finished in here. Rorie, when you send Allie home, tell her there is supper waiting for her."

"Okay, Mom. Do you want help with the dishes?"

"No, you go relieve your sister. I'll take care of these."

Everyone left Rachael alone in the kitchen. It was nice to be alone for a while even if it was to clean the kitchen. The only time of the year Rachael relished her time in the kitchen was during the Christmas Season when she and the girls made enough cookies and candy to challenge Fanny May. Now doing the dishes seemed welcome relief from the tension.

Rachael didn't hurry to interrupt Alex and Mark. She was sure they needed to find some privacy in this house or Alex would begin to feel claustrophobic. Through the large family room windows, she could see Mark sitting on Alex's lap out by the pool.

"Dad, I like living here with Rachael and the girls."

"Mark, I know you like it here and I'm glad; but we'll have to go home to our own house when this is all over."

"Dad, do you think you and Rachael might ever fall in love and get married?"

Alex couldn't see Rachael come out of the patio door, but she could see the two of them. Unfortunately, she could also hear Alex's response to his son's question.

"No, Mark, I don't think it's possible for us to ever get married. Rachael and I are good friends, and sometimes that's more important."

Rachael stopped in her tracks. She felt like an eaves dropper and wanted to get back into the house without being seen. Her own emotions were running wild inside of her. She had known they claimed to be just friends, but now she had to admit she had wanted more. Rachael never went around the corner of the house where she could be seen. Likewise, she never heard the rest of the conversation.

"Mark, I know this is hard for you to understand, but Rachael doesn't think of me like she would her husband. We have to get our own lives straightened out before we can try to win a woman's trust and love."

Mark jumped off of his father's lap and yelled, "My life is fine the way it is. I have my dad, two sisters, two dogs and a mother along with a great house and pool. What more is there for a kid?"

"I'm sorry, Mark but we don't always get what we want in life."

"No kidding, Dad. I feel like I've spent my time without a family, and now it's my turn."

"Maybe we'll find somebody later. First we have to take care of this business with Heather. It isn't fair to Rachael and the girls to inconvenience them like this. They didn't ask to be put in this situation with us. We're lucky they're willing to help us."

"Dad, they are helping us because they love us. Can't you see that?"

"I think they are helping us because they're good friends, and good friends help each other; they don't get married."

"Hey, you guys. Are you ready for some ice cream?"

Alex was sure it would be Rachael who came around the corner, but instead the two men were greeted by a tired Allison. Even though she was wearing a big grin, Alex could see the fatigue in her eyes.

"Gee, thanks, Allie. How's Chance?" Mark didn't like the way his conversation was going and Allie's ice cream offer was a way to end the talk with his dad.

"Mark, he's soooooo sore. We try to do everything for him and talk to him, but those big brown eyes tell everything he's feeling. Ya know, Alex, even though animals can't talk, the feelings and words are there. All you have to do is look into the eyes."

"You'll make a great vet Allie because you're willing to look into the eyes to find your conversation. If you think about it, people are the same way."

"What do you mean?"

"Sometimes we say something, but the eyes say another. Trust the eyes, Allie, they never lie. If I had learned that lesson sooner, maybe I would have seen the evil that was in Heather's heart and the pain of loneliness in Mark's."

"Yeah, you're right. It can be the same with love, you know."

"I suppose."

Mark had made it clear how he felt about this family and a union between the two adults. Now Allison was giving her opinion, and he hadn't even seen it coming. She had innocently dropped the line, and he sucked up the hook like a stupid fish looking for a free meal. Maybe he swallowed the hook on Easter Sunday, and the children were each taking turns slowly reeling him in and watching him squirm. The image brought a smile to his face as he looked back at her. She knew he understood the implication of her words.

"Reflections of the truth." Alex was sure he'd merely thought the words; but when Allie asked him what he'd said, he had to repeat himself.

"Reflections of the truth, the eyes are reflections of the truth."

"Wow, Alex, you'd better be careful. You are starting to sound like a romantic."

"Oh no. That's your department. I know your mother is the optimist, you are the romantic; but what is Rorie?"

"She's more like our dad was: very logical and objective. I guess she tends to be a little stoic too. What about you, Alex?"

"After the last couple of years, I don't even know what kind of personality I have, but I suppose I'm more like Rorie. I don't know if the science makes us that way; or if we go into science because it agrees with our personality. Where's your mother? Did you see her when you got home?"

"She was in her bedroom relaxing with a new novel when I got home. Why?"

"I was wondering if she'd have a brandy with me, or I could make her a cup of tea. My ability to work in the kitchen has progressed that far."

"I'm sure she'd love a little brandy. I'll swim with Mark for a while." Allie didn't tell Alex her mother was going to be sitting neck high in bubbles in the hot tub in her bathroom by the time he'd get there. He'd have to find that out for himself, and he would shortly. Allie quickly turned to Mark. She didn't want Alex to notice the sly smile on her face. If he did, he'd know she was up to something.

After pouring two snifters of brandy, Alex went to find Rachael. The bedroom door was open, but he didn't hear anything. He thought maybe Rachael had fallen asleep, so he didn't speak too loudly. "Rachael? Are you awake?"

"Alex, is that you?"

"Yes, would you like a brandy?"

Rachael was astonished at his asking. She was sure he didn't realize she was in the tub. "Actually, yes I would. Thank you."

Alex looked around the corner into the room, but there was no Rachael on the bed or on the lounge. "Rachael, where are you?"

"In here, I'm in the bathroom." There was no sound, so after a few seconds she added, "Alex, come in."

Alex hesitated and then pushed the door slowly open. It was so dark. How could she see to do anything let alone read? As the door came more fully open and he could see into the room, the flicker of the candle light caught his attention. Scenes like this were only in the movies.

Bubbles rose out of the tub like mountains of snow while the flickering candles hinted at a glorious sunset behind the peaks.

"Alex, come in. You can turn the lights on."

Why would he want to turn the lights on? Alex was transfixed as he stood staring at the most exquisite sight he'd ever seen.

Rachael's curls had been hastily clipped up, and now they were falling gracefully around her face while the bubbles nearly touched her chin. An arm rose up dripping white foam and reached out to him.

"Alex, will you hand me the snifter?"

"What?" Alex was still staring at the heavenly sight looking up at him.

"Really, Alex, haven't you ever seen a woman in a tub before?"

"Tub, yes, mountains of bubbles, no."

"It's no big deal. Pull up the stool and visit with me for a few minutes while I enjoy my brandy if I ever get it."

"Oh, yeah." He seemed slightly more at ease as he handed her the glass and reached to pull the stool over.

"I thought when you said you had a brandy for me, you knew I was in the tub."

"If I had known, I wouldn't have bothered you. Ali told me you were reading."

Rachael smiled realizing they had been set up. "I was when she was in here, but I told her I might take a bubble bath. I'm sure she's having a good chuckle about now."

"I'm sure she is." Still feeling out of place, Alex stumbled for conversation. "Tomorrow, I'll be at the hospital all day. I'll talk to the staff in the morning and then see my patients. Okay?"

"Sure, we'll have supper ready for you when you get home."

After a few uncomfortable moments for Alex, the two of them talked easily while sipping on the well-aged brandy. It was natural to talk about the kids and their comic episodes when the girls were growing up. His favorite story was about a ski trip to the Rockies.

"Allison was about seven years old that year. We had driven all night from Chicago to Winter Park, Colorado, and the change from near sea level to over ten thousand feet was a painful adjustment for all of us. The girls got up early the next morning to go to ski school with my sisters because I was tired from driving all night. Poor Allison could not handle the extra two thousand feet of altitude. By the time she got to the top of the mountain with her instructor, she was feeling terrible. She went up to her instructor and told him she had 'attitude' sickness. He said that he thought it was called 'altitude' sickness. She answered, 'I don't care what you call it, I've got it.' We've laughed about the slip of tongue ever since."

"I can understand why." Alex smiled at the mental image of poor Ali turning blue and claiming attitude sickness. "What did the guy do?"

"He was great about it. He had a safety ski patrol man come and take her down the mountain on a ski sled. She loved that part in-spite-of the headache caused from the altitude. She was fine the next day and had her lesson with the same instructor, who, according to her side of the story, was soooooo tall and handsome."

"Now that sounds like the romantic I've come to know."

"Isn't that the truth." They both laughed feeling relaxed and at ease with each other. Eventually the bubbles popped their way into oblivion and the water chilled, so Alex excused himself for the evening.

CHAPTER FIFTEEN

The anxiety Alex felt caused his stomach to turn. He was afraid his colleagues would resent the danger he had brought with him. Debbie was very eloquent in her portrayal of Alex's past trouble and why he needed their help. To his relief, the other doctors were not angry at him for bringing his troubles with him. They were curious about Alex's past, but he was part of the staff now, and they would not risk losing him or his talent by ignoring his need for support. Pictures of Heather would be posted throughout the hospital, and extra security would be hired and placed at all entrances. Alex thanked everyone for their support as they left the room.

"Debbie, I can't believe how understanding everyone was."

"You haven't been here long, but long enough for the others to respect you and your talent. Heather is the outsider threatening all of us because you are part of our team. I know it's hard for you to understand this, but we'd be foolish if we didn't do everything possible to keep you at the hospital. We all appreciate your talent."

"I'm grateful and relieved that my talent is valuable enough to help them overlook my troubles."

"There's more to it than just your talent. Believe it or not, we like you too. Our desire to keep you here is to keep the 'man' not just the 'doctor'."

"Rachael didn't say it the same way, but she also tried to convince me the people here would be understanding of our situation."

"I like Rachael. We think alike. In fact she has probably protected you from even more danger than you realize."

"What are you talking about?"

"The single women around here were ready to fight over your bones, but your obvious relationship with Rachael has kept them from having knock down drag out fights over you."

"You've got to be kidding. I never noticed anything."

"That's because you've been so occupied with Rachael you didn't notice anyone else. She's good for you, Alex. More than you even realize. I'll be glad when she starts coming back to the hospital. She is coming back, isn't she?"

"I think so. She hasn't indicated anything else."

"Come on into my office. I'd like to finish this conversation privately."

"What's up. You sound serious."

"I'm concerned about you and.."

"And what?"

"Sit down, Alex. Would you like a cup of coffee?"

"What is it? I've never known you to tap dance around an issue."

"Okay. Alex, I think you should be tested for HIV."

"Jesus Christ, Debbie. What are you saying?"

"Think about it. Heather may have had more than just one affair. Who knows how many or what kind of man or woman, for that matter, she may have been with."

"Debbie, that's disgusting. I can't imagine Heather being with a woman."

"You couldn't imagine her with anyone if I remember our original conversation correctly. So now that you know she has been with other men why not another woman? It's possible."

"So what?"

"Alex, I know you can't possibly be as naive as you sound. It's the responsible thing to do. You have no idea of when she started playing around; and unless you were celibate all of your married life, you were exposed to everything she was."

"Why are you dumping this on me now, why today? I have enough on my mind without worrying about sexually transmitted diseases my darling devoted wife may have passed to me."

"I bring it up today because you are living in Rachael's house."

"Not you too. I can't believe everyone is assuming we're sleeping together."

"No, I don't assume you're sleeping together; if I did, this would be a mute conversation. However, I do believe the potential may be there someday, if not with Rachael then with someone else."

Alex was silent. The thought of getting AIDS from Heather had never even crossed his mind. He was a doctor for God's sakes; and yet, he had never considered the possibility. Maybe he was socially naive.

"Why can't I wait until all of this is over?"

"Because you just can't. I know you may not be able to appreciate this, but a person can't always control himself in the heat of passion. When your body parts are screaming 'Yes! Yes!' its hard for your mind to say 'No, wait. You haven't had your test yet.'"

"In my wildest imaginations, I can't see Rachael and myself in that situation."

"Well then you had better take another look at the situation, because it's in your eyes, for both of you. I've seen you together and I've seen you look at each other when you didn't think anyone was watching. The smoldering flames are there, Alex, but you are trying to douse them with excuses from the past. Why do you think the other nurses have left you alone. Even they can see the obvious."

"You're wrong. We're good friends. That's all she wants and has made it very clear."

"Then she's as crazy as you are. She may be your last chance for a true loving relationship. Grab it, Alex. There are plenty of women around here who'd love to enjoy that gorgeous masculine body of yours, but I doubt if you would ever find a better match than Rachael. You can't deny that you'd never find a better mother for Mark."

"If I wasn't so angry about this, it'd be funny. I feel like everyone is pushing me into a relationship with Rachael except for Rachael herself. The three kids have made their feelings very clear, but I just don't see it happening. I don't know if I'll ever be able to trust a woman that way again."

"Alex, don't be so melodramatic. You can't base all future relationships on your experience with Heather. She was bad news from the beginning. I even told you that. Remember?"

"I remember. It's obvious I made a bad choice once, so how will I be able to trust myself not to do it again? I'm not ready for any of this, not now, maybe never."

"What about the test?"

"I'll think about it."

"Alex, that isn't good enough. Any doctor who starts to work here has to have a complete physical. That includes the HIV-AIDS testing, but I waved all that when you came in because I was more worried about your state of mind than your state of health. I remembered in med school you were the one who preached good health habits in-spite-of your evening brandy. Now, however, I can order it done if you don't want to take care of it yourself. Do it for yourself and for Mark. Do it for your patients and the hospital. I know you: you'll want to know for your own peace of mind."

"Peace of mind? You must be kidding. How will knowing something like that give me peace of mind?"

"Not knowing will eat you up. One other thing, as long as I'm on my soap box."

Alex shook his head rubbing his fingers through his hair in disgust and frustration. "Give me a break, Debbie. I can't take much more."

"Have you made a current will that appoints legal guardianship for Mark?"

Alex didn't use foul language as a normal practice. He'd always considered it an unintelligent form of conversation; but every time he had to deal with the effects of Heather's betrayal, he felt like a bumbling fool. The four letters words seemed to flow naturally which confirmed his belief that it took very little brain power to converse in gutter terminology.

"Shit, Debbie, do you stay up late at night thinking about how to make your doctors' lives miserable or does this just come naturally for you?"

"I'm glad you haven't lost your limited sense of humor, friend. I stay up worrying about a friend who is having trouble and may not be covering all of his bases."

"I'm sorry. You're right about the will. It's a good idea, and I hadn't even considered it. Do you know an attorney who can help me. I don't know anyone."

"That's no problem. We have an attorney, Tom Houston, for the hospital who would help you, and you can do it here in your office. I could also give you the name of someone else if you don't want to use Tom."

"Tom is fine and so is tomorrow if he is available. I'll call him."

The day couldn't get much worse. Alex brooded through each examination. The possibility of his being in one of these beds wasting away because of something Heather gave him ate at his gut like a vulture picks at a carcass. It would be her ideal way of wreaking revenge on him. He had to do it: take the test. As he made the decision, a sprig of fear sunk its root in his very soul.

CHAPTER SIXTEEN

Alex had said nothing when he arrived home. A mere grunt of a greeting was all he offered Rachael and Mark as he passed them and went upstairs to his room closing the door behind him. Allison had not missed the entrance.

"Gee, I wonder who puked in his lunch today?"

"Yeah, no kidding." Mark added to the observation.

"Allison!" Rachael chastised her daughter. Trying to make an excuse for Alex's behavior, she continued, "He had to tell the hospital staff what was going on and ask for their support and help. It isn't easy to hang your life in front of others wondering how they will pass judgment. Now help me finish supper, so you can eat before going to the clinic."

Eventually, Alex did join the others. He knew if he stayed upstairs too long, he'd really draw attention to his demeanor, and he didn't want to have to give any explanations. Besides he was so hungry he thought his stomach was beginning to digest his backbone, and the aroma of roast turkey was making his mouth water. It had been years since he'd had a home roasted turkey, and this wasn't even a holiday. After months of eating out or his own crummy cooking, the expectation of a delicious meal helped ease his bad mood.

With a meek smile, Alex looked into the family room where everyone congregated just before dinner was put onto the table. Mark was playing on the floor with Snickers and watching the Disney movie <u>Homeward Bound</u> for the thousandth time. It had been his favorite movie ever since he realized Chance was named after the dog in the story. He had even considered naming Snickers after the other dog,

Shadow; but his dark brown color and nutty antics didn't seem to match the dignity of the name.

Alex took great pleasure in the scene before him. This was the way family life was supposed to be: happy, comfortable, loving. He vowed to savor every minute of living here like it was a good meal: eventually it would have to end, but the memory and satisfaction could be taken away from the table.

"Good evening, everybody."

"Hi, Pop. How was your day?" The question was asked more as a term of endearment than as a prying question, and Alex received it as such.

"Not too bad, how about yours? What did you do to keep out of trouble?"

Mark went on to list a variety of activities, some done alone and others with someone else in the family. He'd had a wonderful day which was easily detected in his pleasant attitude. A stranger would never know Mark had virtually been locked in the house all day.

Rachael watched Alex walk into the room and over to his son. She was glad he finally came down to see Mark. Even though Mark seemed fine on the outside, the greeting he had received from his father earlier had bothered him. Having Alex give him some time now would help put Mark's mind at ease.

"Dinner will be ready in a couple of minutes. Would you like a glass of wine, a brandy, or do you want to jump to the hard stuff right away and just have two aspirin with a glass of water?"

Alex walked over to Rachael standing at the kitchen counter. "Does the bad day really show that much?"

"It's in your eyes. You've got a smile on for Mark, but the shadows are still in your eyes."

He waited for her to ask what had happened, but she didn't. Finally he tried to lighten his mood by asking, "Who had a bite out of the turkey already? No fair." A small effort at humor worked better to lift his feelings than taking a couple of aspirin to deaden the tension in his body. Rachael appreciated his remark, but didn't miss the constant rubbing of his neck.

"Allison had to go to the clinic, so I told her to eat. Rorie should be home by the time I get the rest of the meal on the table."

"It sure is convenient to have that clinic around the corner."

"Yeah, it is. I usually walk him over when he needs to go in. Would you cut the turkey?"

"Surely you jest. Me cut a turkey?"

"Well, you don't actually cut a turkey, you carve a turkey. With your soft operating touch, you shouldn't have any trouble. It'll taste the same whether you carve it one way or another."

"A glass of wine with dinner sounds nice if you'll have one too."

Alex did his best to join the small table conversation with dinner, but he was constantly distracted by the day's events. Tomorrow he would be putting together his will which would dictate Mark's future if he died. The only person he could think of to ask to be legal guardian was Rachael. There were no relatives who could take him, and he certainly wanted to make sure Mark didn't become a ward of the state. That would be the worst thing that could possibly happen to him, and it would be Alex's fault for not taking care of the necessary parental responsibilities. He'd have to talk to Rachael; he couldn't just let her find out by accident.

Mark started picking up the plates on the table and taking them to the sink. Alex watched him curiously and then gave the raised eyebrow look to Rachael. She understood the silent question and offered the explanation.

"Mark, I think your dad wants to know why you're clearing the table."

"Dad, you'll never guess. Rachael said that with the girls running back and forth to take care of Chance, she could use some help around the house. She is going to give me an allowance for everything I do."

"That's great, Mark. I think it's good for you to have responsibilities around here."

"I hope you don't mind, Alex. The conversation just happened today."

"No, it's good for him. I need to talk to you later."

"Sure. Do you want me to get the bubble bath ready?" The intimate suggestion brought a glimmer to his eye.

"No, that's not necessary; on the other hand, I kinda liked it."

The look of shock on Mark's face was missed by the joking adults, but his remark was not. "Dad, you and Rachael took a bubble bath?"

Alex was speechless; he had forgotten Mark was in the room. "Ah..Ah..No, of course not. We'd never do that."

Rachael was ready to give the same adamant speech, but now that she listened to Alex give it, she didn't think the words were simply for Mark's benefit. She wondered if he was trying to persuade himself or her that a dual bubble bath was out of the question. *It would do him good to be naked in front of someone else. Baring it all would go along way in solving his social constipation. The only time he really talks from his heart is when he has no choice, when he has to confess something or ask for help. Yeah, no question about it. It would be good for him, and I wouldn't mind either.* The last thought took Rachael's eye on a travel documentary up and down Alex's body, and there wasn't a guilty thought in her after the trip was over.

Alex never took his attention from Mark, so he didn't notice that Rachael had visually striped his clothes off piece by piece in order to savor the long lean legs and muscular buttocks which could only be partially appreciated in the tailored slacks he always wore. By the time Alex returned his look to Rachael, she was back from her visual journey and ready to help him.

"Mark, I was only joking with your father. I was hoping it would make him laugh a little and help him to relax."

"Oh, sure I get it." Mark turned without another question, but he was hoping some day it would be true.

After Mark left them alone, Rachael let the bursting giggles ring throughout the room. "Sorry about the bathtub remark. I don't know which was funnier Mark's reaction to the idea of us both covered in bubbles or your reaction to him."

Alex was laughing with her. It felt good to let some happiness into his gray mood. Rachael always seemed to make him feel better. She could bring a smile to his heart faster than anyone he had ever known. He would definitely try to find out what was in her eyes especially since she always seemed able to read his.

"Rachael, lets sit outside. I'd really like to enjoy the garden and the sunset tonight." Again Alex was rubbing his neck and his forehead.

"Sure, Alex." Rachael followed Alex to the door which he opened and then waited for her to exit. They walked to the patio chairs and sat with a full view of the rose garden.

"Rachael, Debbie suggested today that I have a will drawn up. I need to appoint legal guardianship for Mark, you know, just in case."

He didn't need to finish the statement. Rachael knew what 'just in case' meant. "It's a good idea for Mark's sake. Jack and I did it for the girls several different times over the years."

"I know it's the right thing to do. What I need to ask you is if you would be willing to be his guardian?"

Rachael leaned back in the chair and took a deep breath. She had not expected that at all. "Alex, I'm honored you would even ask me. Of course I would take care of him."

"Don't you need to think about it or something?"

"No, not at all. I love Mark like he's my own already. You know that."

"I just needed to hear you say it. Thank you. This means more to me, us, than you know." Again his hand went up to rub his temple. Rachael realized the obvious headache hammering inside his head had not eased. She got up and walked over behind him.

Alex was weary about her approach. When she reached up and started to massage his temples, the sigh escaped from his mouth before he could stop it.

"Relax, Alex. Let me help you get rid of the tension. This is just a simple neck rub."

In his eyes, there was nothing simple about it. The warm slim fingers worked miraculously turning small circles over and over against his temples. Slowly they traveled down his head toward the neck working the tired aching muscles. He hadn't even realized when she had worked her way up the back of his head running her fingers through his hair and over his scalp. The hypnotic motion of the fingers completely engrossed him. All negative thoughts slowly disappeared, leaving only the angelic vision of the creature standing behind him lovingly rubbing away the pain.

"Do you feel better?" Rachael spoke softly not wanting to startle him. The muscles in his neck didn't seem quite so taut any longer.

"Yes, much better. Where did you learn to do that. Were you some kind of exotic healer in another life or something?"

"No, nothing so dramatic. My mother taught me how by giving us back rubs when I was growing up. I remember seeing Daddy laying on the floor while Mom massaged his aching muscles. To give you the full treatment, you need to be lying down. You want to give it a try?"

"That's all right. Maybe some other time."

"Oh, come on Alex. What else are we going to do tonight? You've obviously had a rotten day, so take some time off and enjoy. Have you ever really learned how to enjoy life for yourself? I know you like watching Mark have fun, but I never see you let the walls of sobriety down and just enjoy something." She took his hand and pulled him to his feet. There was no resistance.

Alex appreciated her comments. She was right. Pure pleasure was something he didn't know how to have. For the first time in his life he was tasting bits and pieces, but the idea of having more tantalized his senses. *Why not? After the day I've had, why not? I could be dead tomorrow, so why the hell not?*

"I'm in your hands. What do you want me to do?"

"Really?" There was not just a question in her words, but also a sense of surprise.

"Yes, really. Are you backing down from your offer?"

"Absolutely not. I'm just pleasantly surprised you agreed. You won't be sorry. Are you totally in my hands?"

"I guess."

Rachael instructed Alex to take off his shirt while she went to get a blanket. "If you change your mind while I'm gone, I'll never forgive you."

"Then hurry up." The dancing eyes were finally back showing that the man did have a latent potential for fun.

"You would enjoy this more if you put on pajama bottoms or shorts."

"Don't push it."

"Okay, okay." Rachael hurried to get a blanket and some massage oil. She was disappointed when she got back because Alex was not in the room. The natural assumption was that he'd chickened out. The sound right behind her startled her and she turned around to see Alex, dressed only in his neatly pressed dress pants, standing behind her. The stiffly starched white shirt and shoes were missing.

"I figured if I was going to get the whole treatment then I might as well get all the pleasure I can from it, but I don't have any shorts or pajamas."

"That's fine. I'll take you like you are." Rachael warmed the oil, started some soothing classical music, and laid out the soft quilt motioning for Alex to lie down on his stomach. Straddling his buttocks, Rachael positioned herself over her patient and slowly dripped the warm oil down his back. Alex slightly flinched at the first drop having no idea of what to expect.

Rachael's fingers glided like dancers doing a waltz over the taut, well defined muscles. She was going to enjoy this as much as he, maybe more if he didn't relax.

Gradually his body succumbed to the power of the spell she seemed to be casting over him. It was truly the greatest pleasure he had ever experienced. Love making with Heather had never brought him such ecstasy. This was even better than the operating room after successful surgery. He was absolutely going to learn how to have fun in whatever amount of time he had left on this earth.

Rachael felt his pleasure as his body molded to her touch. Right now at this moment, he belonged only to her; and she reveled at the thought. *I'm going to get hurt falling in love with this man. He doesn't want me as a wife. Remember, he thinks I am merely comfortable. I hate that word.* Rachael had to fight the urge to kiss the smooth skin beneath her fingers. The magic of the moment was casting its spell over her as well.

Rachael had not noticed Mark come into the room and sit down on the sofa. He watched the two of them intensely for several minutes. Mark had never really seen two people in love except on television, but this sure seemed like the real thing. He thought about how badly he wanted to call Rachael "mom" and didn't realize that the word must have slipped out.

Rachael jumped when she heard Mark in the room. The trance had been broken causing both adults to look up when they heard him speak.

"Mark, what did you say?"

"Nothing, I was just wondering if Rachael would rub my back that way."

"Sure Mark." Rachael couldn't refuse him. It was special to have someone give you a massage; and although Mark didn't need the attention as much as his father did, the tenderness wouldn't hurt him either.

Alex hadn't moved except to raise his head enough to see Mark sitting on the couch. He wasn't ready for reality to take over, and he didn't want to interrupt the motion of Rachael's fingers. She had barely missed a stroke as she talked to Mark, and Alex was not going to be the one to stop the intimate interlude they were sharing. The sensuous movement of the fingers made it clear to him that she was enjoying this time together as much as he was.

"Later, Mark," were the only words that Alex uttered before putting his head back on the blanket.

Mark left the room with a smile on his face and hoping his father would not regain total consciousness before he showered because he'd certainly realize how silly he looked with his back all greasy and his hair sticking up. Boy if he looked in the mirror when he went upstairs, he'd never let Rachael do that to him again. Mark knew his father didn't like being messed up.

Rachael and Alex were so absorbed in each other's presence neither of them sensed the eyes that were stealing part of their intimacy. The eyes from outside the window were watching and filling with rage. They would pay, both of them would pay.

****

The peaceful sleep that had been induced by Rachael's dancing fingers lasted until the early morning hours. Alex started tossing in the twin bed which was barely big enough to offer any comfort when he was lying still let alone when restlessness set in. Dream images of Rachael in her red satin, running seductive fingers over his body, caused him to wake feeling lonely and frustrated. With the blankets on the floor and the sheets around his waist, Alex finally got up to go downstairs where he hope to find some mental relief from both of the women who haunted him whether he was awake or sleeping.

Alex carefully closed the door behind him so Mark would not be disturbed. As he approached the top of the stairs, he noticed a light was on in the kitchen. Someone was up because he knew it had been dark when he had gone up to bed. Could it possibly be Heather, not likely since the alarm would have sounded. Ever so quietly Alex snuck around the staircase to get a view of who was in the house.

There was no mistaking the culprit. The red satin was a dead give away. Alex watched her move gracefully around the room. *So she was having trouble sleeping too. Maybe she had another nightmare. Maybe she can't sleep because she's thinking about me. After her little seduction of me last night, she doesn't deserve a peaceful night's sleep either.* He couldn't tear his eyes from the sleek body that was moving lithely around the room. He wanted her so badly his body ached mentally and physically. Never had anyone seduced him so completely and without even taking off her clothes or his for that matter.

Heather, now that was a seductive crock: *She never possessed me the way this woman does. Maybe Heather was right putting some of the blame on me for her crime. I never really loved her; shit, I didn't even know what passionate love was until I met this alluring woman in red.*

And, of course now that I finally understand what I've been missing, I can't have it or touch it.

Rachael nearly jumped out of her skin when she turned around and saw Alex standing in the doorway. "Oh! Shit, Alex. Don't sneak up on me that way. What are you doing up in the middle of the night?"

"I could ask you the same thing, but the answer is obvious isn't it? Neither of us could sleep." Rachael didn't like the sarcastic tone of his voice. It made her uncomfortable, but not as uncomfortable as his gaze browsing over her figure.

Alex let his eyes purposely move slowly up and down the sexy curves of the night gown taking special pleasure in watching her squirm. He had caught her staring at him several times when she didn't think he noticed. It was his turn to enjoy the scenery.

"Really, Alex, you're acting like a school boy. With all of the naked bodies you see, what's one more?"

"Yeah, you're right. So take it off." He moved in toward her like a big cat ready to pounce unsuspecting prey.

Rachael found herself backing up but stopped by the counter behind her. "What? You're kidding. Come on, Alex. You're scaring me."

He took small steps in her direction wanting to prolong the episode in which he finally had some control. "Take it off, Rachael, or I'll do it myself."

"Alex, this isn't you. Let me get you a brandy."

"I don't want a brandy, I want you." He put his burning hand on her neck and ran it down to the top of her gown. With one stroke of his hand the red satin had been ripped from her body and dropped on the floor.

His hand continued its roaming down her side savoring the curve of her breast. "You want this as much as I do, Rachael. I may

-202-

not have seen it in your eyes last night, but the desire was definitely in your fingers."

Rachael searched Alex's eyes looking for the love she had wanted to be there, but there was no love only frustration and anger. That didn't change the fact that she wanted him to touch her, wanted his body to satisfy her own hidden desires.

All of her senses were reacting to the hands that were exploring her body, and she leaned forward to kiss the bare chest in front of her. *I'm going to regret this in the morning, but right now I don't give a damn.* Alex picked her up in his arms and walked out of the room leaving only the small mound of torn red satin as testimony that anyone had been there.

Alex dropped Rachael on her bed and leaned over her. A hint of recognition hit Rachael. *No, its impossible. It can't be him.* The episode of her last nightmare was replaying itself right before her eyes. The angry man looming over her now WAS Alex. The arms were reaching down to touch her, to caress her body, but fear possessed her now.

"Alex, no, we can't do this."

"It's too late, Rachael. I'm going to have one thing before I die, and it's you." He lowered himself onto her body and smothered her fighting figure with kisses. As her desires pushed out the fear, Rachael's body began to respond to Alex's touch until he suddenly stopped. He left her laying naked on the bed and simply walked away.

Rachael's fierce anger at being awkwardly left in the middle of passion subsided as other thoughts surfaced. She couldn't get the image of her nightmare out of her mind. Was Alex the man who had tried to kill her in the dream? He had left her bedroom before finishing what he had started, but the words he had uttered as he left the room hung like heavy thunder clouds.

"Rachael, I don't know who to be more afraid of: you or Heather."

Why on earth would he be afraid of her. She had only tried to help him and Mark. She had given them her home and friendship. She'd never asked him for anything.

"The arrogant bastard doesn't even know how to make love to me." She said softly as her own tears of frustration spilled onto her cheeks. This was the first time she had cried for a man since Jack had died.

****

Alex's anger festered the rest of the night. He never went back to sleep only waited for the first hint of sunrise so he could leave for the hospital.

"Good Morning, Dr. Zamora. You're leaving for the hospital early today. Does Detective Archer know?"

Alex was ready to snap someone's head off, and this poor officer was the lucky recipient. "No, I didn't tell him. I didn't tell anyone. If I die, then all of this will be over. Hallelujah!"

The uniformed officer backed away from the angry man and headed for the squad car. He'd have to make arrangements for someone to get to the hospital early to stand watch. "Detective Archer, Zamora just left for work."

"Shit, I thought he knew he had to tell me his schedule."

"He was really angry at something."

"Thanks, I'll take care of it."

A blue uniform was waiting for Alex to pull up in the parking lot. It surprised him that anyone in the department could react so fast because Rachael's house was less than ten minutes from the hospital. Oh well, he was going to have a tail all day whether he liked it or not.

The first thing on his agenda was to make notes for his will. After last night, he wondered if Rachael would still be Mark's legal guardian.

It would probably irritate her like crazy, but he was going to assume she'd still do it for Mark, of course. After all, he'd be dead; and she wouldn't have to deal with him anymore.

Alex was so absorbed in his own thoughts of dying that he didn't notice his office door was open until he tried to put the key in the lock. Slowly he pushed it open not thinking to call the officer who had stopped at end of the hallway to watch the people coming and going. Alex was ready to face Heather. He was sick of her, sick of hiding, sick of living with a woman he couldn't have. At least he had the satisfaction of knowing that when his body was telling him "Yes! Yes!", he could control himself and stop. The cold shower had washed away the desire but not the frustration or anger.

"Come on, Heather. Give it your best shot." There was no sound in the room. Alex walked cautiously toward his desk, and then he saw the message that had been left for him. Some kind of dead animal, with a note nailed to its head, had been left in a pool of blood. "You're a fool to play with her. You will pay. Both of you will pay."

Alex crumpled the paper in his fist and threw it on the ground before going to yell for the officer. Detective Archer was at the office door within ten minutes reprimanding Alex for having gone into the room alone where Heather could have been waiting to shoot him.

"I want to know how the hell she got in here." Alex's anger was like a whip lashing at anyone within reach, and the next person to walk into the room was the next victim of his wrath.

"Debbie, no one saw her. What kind of security do you have here that someone whose picture is all over the place can just waltz in with a dead animal over her back, break into my office, and leave without being seen? This is ridiculous!"

"Alex, we don't know that no one saw her. We haven't even asked yet."

Alex just stared out of the window running his fingers through his hair. His mind immediately conjured up images of Rachael rubbing his neck. If it wasn't Heather who was mentally haunting him, it was Rachael. All this time he thought she had been his friend, a true confidant, but she had cast her own spell over him. No matter how hard he tried to fight it, he couldn't deny his desire to be with her.

"Women, I'll never get it right. I'm hopeless, and so are relationships."

****

"Look at what's coming down the walk." Several of the bellmen watched as Rachael walked toward the entrance of the DoubleTree Hotel. She was wearing a simple white sleeveless dress with a scooped neckline. The elegant tan legs and arms gave the perfect contrast to the dress. No necklace, only white earrings served as an accent. Rachael entered the lobby where a short white haired man asked if he could help her. The name tag on his lapel had "Bob" engraved on it.

"Are you by any chance the bellman who was a friend to a young man named Mark."

"I sure am, Ma'am. Do you know the youngster? How's he doing?"

"He's fine, and he really liked you."

"Please tell him to stop by some time. I miss him."

"I'll bring him by myself." Rachael gave the sweet man a warm smile as she went by.

"Bob, you old fox, who was that? Do you know her?" The bellmen watched as Rachael headed for the restaurant where she was going to meet Debbie for lunch. The invitation had surprised her, but then it would be nice to get out of the house. Mark stayed with Rorie while Allison went to the clinic to take care of the healing Chance.

Debbie was already waiting at a table. "Hello, Rachael, it's good to see you. You will be coming back to work when all of this is over, won't you?"

"Of course. I miss my students and the hospital. Right now, however, I have no choice but to stay home with Mark."

"I understand. Did Alex call you this morning after he got to work?"

"No, why? What happened? I'm sure there's something on your mind to have called me, especially since you didn't want to meet at the hospital."

"I didn't want Alex to see us talking. He'd assume we were talking about him."

"Would he have been right?"

"Of course, who else would we talk about? Actually, I'm worried about him."

Rachael didn't know Debbie very well. She liked her, but she didn't know how far Debbie could be trusted when it came to talking about Alex. After all, Debbie was his long time friend. She would be his ally before she would be Rachael's. In fact, maybe she was here on his behalf to find out how Rachael would treat him after last night. He deserved to be thrown out on his tight, arrogant doctor's ass.

"Debbie, I don't know what I can tell you about him. Tell me what happened and why he should have called me this morning."

"There was another message from Heather."

"Oh no, what'd it say?"

Debbie described the scene as she remembered it and Alex's animosity about the whole affair. "There was more to his remarks than just anger about Heather. His remarks were about 'women' plural, not singular."

"Oh?" Rachael tried to play innocent, so Debbie would give her more information.

"Rachael, I know you are aware of my long time friendship with Alex. He likes his world to be nice and neat, everything in its place. That includes people too."

"Boy that's for sure. I don't think I've ever known such a prude." The two women had a good laugh and ordered a glass of red wine. It was nice to poke fun at the man whom they both cared for in-spite-of himself.

"He couldn't help it. That's all he saw at home. His father lived for the operating room, and his mother accepted whatever tid bit of attention she got and went on with her life as the proper doctor's wife doing volunteer work in the community and raising their son alone."

When the waiter brought the wine, Debbie instructed, "Please bring the bottle. I'm done with work for the afternoon. I hope you can indulge a little." Rachael gave an affirmative nod of her head, and Debbie continued filling in some of the gaps for her. "When Alex married Heather, he assumed he'd live the same life his father did. Getting excited about life was done by saving someone in the operating room not by really living it. He never walked in the park, went to the theater, or even went to his son's ball games. Heather, on the other hand, was willing to live her own life as she saw fit; but it was just not the life Alex's mother had led. It certainly was not the life Alex had foreseen."

"No wonder he has such a hard time living with three women who insist on drawing him into conversation and enjoy laughing at and with each other."

"I don't ever remember a time when Alex lived for anything but the satisfaction of surgery, so I'm sure living under your roof has given him a very different perspective of what a home can be."

"Poor Mark. Did you know Alex asked me to be listed in his will as Mark's guardian?"

"I kind of expected it. Yesterday, we talked about his need to draw up a will for that purpose, and I assumed he would ask you."

"Did you really? I was surprised that he not only asked me, but that he even thought of making a will. Now some of his actions make sense."

Debbie was curious, "What actions?" She wanted to know if Alex had told her the rest.

"It's hard to describe. He was different last night: angry, perplexed. We had, I guess you could say, a difference of opinion."

"The note said, 'You shouldn't play with her.' Do you know what that means?"

Rachael could feel her face begin to flush, and Debbie acknowledged the reaction by looking out of the window giving Rachael a minute to collect her thoughts and come up with some explanation.

"Well, maybe."

"Really, this is none of my business, but," Debbie looked directly into Rachael's eyes and added, "There's nothing I'd rather see than Alex being truly happy, and I think you are the only one who can give him that."

"I hear a 'yes but' coming after that lovely thought. What's your reservation?"

"I can't believe that after my talk with Alex yesterday he went home and had, well, had, played around with you."

"Debbie, what are you talking about? I gave him a back rub, and he kissed me. That's all. Then we argued. He was so mad, and he talked about dying. I was frightened of him; and, in the end quite frustrated."

"Good. I'm glad nothing else happened."

"What are you talking about? If you know anything that'll keep me from throwing his prudish butt out of my house, tell me."

"Are you sure you want to know? I'm sure Alex will always resent what I said to him."

"I don't know how things can get worse for us. At this point we have no future together, not even a friendship that can be left intact after last night."

"That bad?"

"You wouldn't have even recognize him as the same Alex you've just described. So tell me what you know."

"Remember, you asked. Not only did I suggest he make out a will, I told him if he didn't voluntarily have an AIDS test then I'd order one for him."

Rachael had never known such a weight of regret. She had been angry at him for leaving her, and now she was grateful. "My God, Debbie. That had never even crossed my mind. No wonder he didn't... well he just didn't."

Now Debbie smiled, "I'm glad he didn't."

"Fear must've been eating a hole in him. No wonder he's so angry at everyone. Of course, he feels he's alone in all of this with no one to understand his frustration."

"That's our Alex. He's going to an outside source for the test. I really don't blame him for not wanting it done at the hospital. We generally do the test as part of a normal physical; but with his exposure, the chances of it being positive are increased. If it's positive, he'll have to quit his practice. You do understand that don't you?"

"Yes, he'll move on with Mark and try to set up some kind of life elsewhere. He wouldn't be able to stand living here with all of us knowing, no matter how much we wanted to help."

"You're probably right about that. Our dear, sweet Alex doesn't want anybody inside that wall of self preservation. On the other hand, since he has asked you to be Mark's legal guardian, maybe we can convince him to stay."

"How did he learn to be so desperately private?"

"Who knows, but you and I are the only ones who have had a glimpse inside of the man. Even Heather had no appreciation of his true character."

"How long before he gets the results?"

"It could be four days or it could be fourteen. It just depends on how busy the lab is. If he puts a rush on it, all the red flags go up, and anonymity goes out the window especially with him in the medical field. The results would be back at the hospital before Alex."

"Will you tell me the results? I know he'll tell you; will you tell me?"

"That depends. Do you love him, Rachael?"

Rachael had not expected that question. She hadn't even decided for herself yet. "Wow! Alex told me you get straight to the point. Honestly, I don't know for sure. I think so, but with everything that's going on, it's hard to get the emotions straight. You have to admit this is a strange situation."

"That's for sure. Well, at least you're thinking about it."

"The kids are ready for us to walk down the aisle."

"It sounds like they're the only ones, besides myself, of course, who can see the writing on the wall. Alex is in love with you."

"That's news to me. You didn't see him last night."

"He stopped didn't he? Do you know what it takes for a man to stop in the middle of his...a...passion?"

"No, not exactly, but then maybe that's why I heard the shower running shortly after he went up the stairs." Both of them shared a giggle as the wine worked its magic helping each of the women to shed their inhibitions.

"Thanks, Debbie. What you've told me does a lot to explain what happened last night. I also know someone was watching us. We'll have to do better at this game, or we'll always be hiding from someone who wants to terrorize us."

"Good luck on that. The police are asking all the night shift employees who and what they saw, but so far nothing."

"Do you suppose they're looking for the wrong person?"

"What do you mean?"

"Her pictures are up everywhere. The police comb the neighborhood for her every night. And nothing. What if they're looking for the wrong person? Maybe she doesn't look the same."

"You're right. She could use a number of ways to disguise herself."

"She could be different every day. Why not a nurse's uniform at the hospital or a police uniform around our house?"

"Only Alex or maybe Mark would have a remote chance of recognizing her."

"You take care of informing the hospital security, and I'll talk to Detective Archer."

"Who's going to talk to Alex?" Both of the women cringed at the thought of even trying to broach the subject with the surly bear they had last encountered."

The two women exited the revolving door. "Thanks for everything, Debbie. It's been wonderful getting out of the house. And you'll never know how much I've enjoyed our little talk together."

"Let's do it again soon, and when we have good things to talk about."

"Yes. I'd like that."

The same men who had enjoyed Rachael's entrance watched the exit with no less appreciation. This time, however, she saw the reflection of their gawking in the windshield of her car, and it felt so good to feel sexy. *Comfortable, Alex Zamora? Eat your heart out. You ain't seen nothin' yet. A new plan, we need a new plan.*

****

"Alex, good evening. I'm glad you're home." Rachael walked up to Alex with a smile on her face. The shadows in his eyes were back, and he was distant. It was going to be hard to break through the wall.

The angry edge was still on his voice, "Do you want me to leave? I'll understand, after last night it might be best."

"No, Alex, I don't want you to leave. You don't have to say anything either. We're both under unusual pressure, but nothing terrible happened last night. I gave you a back rub, and you were right. I was partially to blame for what happened afterwards. Alex, would it really have been so bad to make love together?"

"Yes, Rachael. It would have been wrong. So wrong."

With all the love she could send from her eyes, she answered, "I'm sorry you feel that way. Will you be coming down for supper."

"No."

Rachael was floundering for some way to get him to talk. He was pulling away from her, and she couldn't stop it. He only seemed to open up when he was angry. So, maybe, that was the key.

"Alex, I heard what happened at the hospital today. We need to talk about it."

"Not now, later."

Rachael and the kids tried to enjoy dinner, but it was obvious something was wrong. Alex's chair was empty, yet they all knew he was upstairs. Rachael tried to keep a smile on her face and the conversation going.

"So, Allie, how was Chance today. I didn't get to see him. Mark, will you go with me after supper for a while to see our poor sick friend?"

"Yeah, Rachael, I'd like to go out with you. How long until Chancy gets to come home?"

"He's getting stronger everyday, Mark. Doctor Carley said he could come home in a day or so. With all of us to take care of him, it'll be easier on us if he's home so we don't have to run back and forth to the clinic."

"I'm sure he'll be happier to be at home with his family. Let's clean up the kitchen, Mark. I think today is a good day for you to get your allowance."

"That's great. Why didn't Dad come down for dinner?"

"I think he was really tired tonight. We'll save him some supper for later."

Rachael and the others didn't see Alex standing in the doorway. He'd been there long enough to hear Rachael cover for him and appreciated it. Maybe someday he'd be able to tell her what he really wanted her to know about his feelings.

"If you two wait for me to eat, I'll go with you to see old Chancy."

"That's great, Dad. Rachael's going to pay me my allowance today. I'll buy you an ice cream cone after we get done at the clinic."

"Sure. I'd like that."

"Guess what else happened? Rachael saw Bob today, and he said he missed me, so Rachael said she'd take me to visit him."

"Bob who?"

"You remember, Bob the bellman at the hotel."

"Oh yes, I remember. Now will you give Rachael and me a minute to talk." Alex turned a sheepish face toward her.

"I'll behave myself from now on. Will you let us stay?"

Rachael was surprised by his statement and this was reflected in her answer, "Alex, I never even considered asking you to leave. Did you really think I would?"

"Yes. I know that at least for a moment last night, you thought I was the man who had tried to kill you in your dream. Don't deny it."

This was not the way she had wanted the conversation to go, and she couldn't deny what he had said. "I'm sorry, but it scared me the way you were hovering over me."

"I know I frightened you. I regret the whole episode."

"I know. You've made that perfectly clear." Now was as good a time as any to make her point. He had brought up the topic, so she might as well take the opportunity to push the issue. "After all I'm over forty and simply comfortable." She spit the word at his feet.

"Why would you want an old woman when you could have a fresh young thing to make your body happy?"

Alex grabbed her by the upper arm pulling her up close until he could feel her heart beating through his shirt. "Is that what you think of me? Do you think I've been out chasing young skirts instead of coming home to you and the kids?" Before the words were out, he realized how silly they sounded. Rachael couldn't mistake the bewilderment in his voice.

"That's just my point, Alex. You don't need to come home to me and the kids. There's no obligation here. I never tried to make you feel that there was. You're still a young man, why would you want to be shackled with an old woman who can't have any more children."

"I don't want anyone: young or old, and I certainly don't need anymore children. I'm having enough trouble being a good father to the one I have. It sounds to me like you're angry because I didn't finish what I set out for last night."

"Of course not." Rachael tried to pull out of his iron grip but could not.

"Then what in the hell are we yelling about?" He couldn't hide the desire in his eyes from her when he looked into her face. Then he reminded himself, *look at the eyes, its in the eyes.* Alex found what he was looking for in the deep pools of aqua staring up at him, but he didn't know if he should be happy or sad at the love that was reflected.

"Alex, why won't you let me into that inner world of yours?"

"Rachael, I can't play word games with you."

"You said 'before coming home to me and the kids.' Do you really think about coming home to me and the kids?"

"I don't know what I think. Please, don't ask me for anything."

"Fine, I won't ask. You won't give. Let's finish this game of chase with your dear wife and move on with our own lives."

"There's nothing I'd like more."

"Great!" she snapped at him. "First of all, please let go of my arm. I hate it when you shake me." Alex didn't know if he wanted to let her go, but he had no choice.

"Next, I think we should send the kids somewhere for safe keeping."

"What?"

"If we're going to try to force Heather to play her game, then I'd feel better if the kids were out of the picture."

"So, Miss Know It All, what do you suggest." The sarcasm she remembered from the night before was in his voice again, and she didn't like it.

"Damn it, Alex. Do you want to do this or would you rather play along with her until she hurts one of the kids?"

"No." Now a meeker sounding Alex added, "Do you have someplace in mind?"

"Yes, I called my mother today to ask if we could send them to her until this was over."

"Did you buy the tickets too? Without asking?"

"No, I only called for prices and times." Now Rachael was yelling at him. "Stop feeling so sorry for yourself and think about what you said at the clinic a few nights ago. Remember 'no one's going to hurt me and mine'? What's really bothering you?" Now Rachael was standing in front of him with her hands on her hips.

"Come on, Alex. Tell me what's really going on. You aren't angry at me, you're just taking it out on me and the kids. Why are you so afraid to tell me."

"You really want to know? Fine I'll tell you! I had an AIDS test done today. There I said it; are you happy with yourself for getting me to spill my guts at your feet? Does it make you feel all powerful?"

Rachael tried to choke out the words, but she could only give a negative nod of her head. She wanted to reach out and touch him, but he pulled his arm out of her reach. "No, don't touch me. Never!"

Even though Alex went with them to the clinic, he never said a word to Rachael. The trip to the local ice cream shop didn't even make Mark happy, and it certainly did nothing to lighten the mood between Rachael and Alex. The cloud of animosity hanging over Mark's two favorite people was wreaking havoc on his small realm of happiness. When they got home, Alex took Mark up to bed.

"Why are you and Rachael fighting?"

"I don't really know, Mark. Sometimes it's hard to explain why adults disagree."

"Will you make up?"

"I don't know, but I hope so."

"Please try."

"Mark, I know how much you love Rachael, and I know she and the girls love you very much. That makes me happy because I love you too. I'm worried about you and Rorie and Allison. Rachael and I think it might be a good idea for the three of you to go and stay with

Rachael's parents for a while. Wouldn't it be great to have a grandma and grandpa for a few days?"

"Yeah, I guess. But I don't want to leave you. If we aren't here, you and Rachael won't have to live together. You'll go back to the other house and be all alone."

"Mark, that other house is our home. I know you understand that. When this is all over, we will go back to our home; and you will visit Rachael and the girls whenever you want." Mark didn't want to accept this as the final word, but now was not the time to push. He and the girls would make a new plan while they were gone.

Alex went back downstairs to find Rachael. He'd have to face her again tonight. All of the lights were out in the family room, so he knocked on the bedroom door.

"Come in."

Alex walked into the bedroom and found Rachael sitting up in bed with a book in her hand and a brandy on the night stand.

"May I talk to you for just a minute?"

"Sure, do you want to get yourself a brandy first?"

"No, I'll be quick. I agree we should send the kids away as soon as possible. When are the flights? I'll pay for the tickets."

"They can be on a flight out before noon tomorrow, but I haven't told the girls yet."

"Really? I thought you had everything taken care of."

"Stop it, Alex. I had only tried to get information I thought you might want. I never talked to anyone about this until I saw you tonight."

"You talked to someone today."

"I talked to Archer because he told me about the bloody message left in your office."

"You saw Bob the bellman; you must have been at the DoubleTree. Did you meet Archer there? I didn't think he was your type."

"Don't be ridiculous. Of course, I didn't see Archer there. He was here at the house with his entourage in blue."

"You talked to Debbie didn't you."

Rachael looked into his eyes and answered, "Yes, Alex. Debbie and I had lunch today."

He wouldn't hold the eye contact because it let her into his soul, and she knew too much already. "Why did you make me tell you about the test if you already knew?"

"I wanted you to be the one to tell me. Silly me, I had hoped you would let me be your friend through all of this. Debbie and I are concerned about you."

"You should go away with the kids."

"No!" The answer was loud and final.

"I don't want you getting hurt. This is my war not yours."

"You don't want me to get hurt, or you just don't want me around?"

The words cut on both sides, but he got up and walked over to the bed. There was no more red satin, and he regretted the shredding that replayed itself in his mind. A plain cotton night shirt had replaced the seductive gown.

"Do you feel safer in cotton?"

Rachael felt uneasy under his gaze. "No, but it isn't as expensive to replace."

The remark couldn't help but bring a smile to his face as hard as he tried to fight it. "You have the baffling ability to make me laugh especially when I don't want to. I'm sorry about the night gown. I liked it too."

"You have the strangest way of showing it."

"Yes, that was rather unique wasn't it?"

"Should I go out and stock up?"

"Maybe, I like the satin better than the flannel."

"Then you agree, I don't need to go with the kids?"

"I fell for that didn't I? You and your daughters can lay a verbal trap with more finesse than anyone I've ever encountered. The choice is yours."

"The message said 'both of you.' If I leave, she may hunt us down just to make her point, or hold out until we get back. We couldn't stay away forever."

"I suppose you're right. Good night."

Alex left the room in a slightly better mood than he had been in all day. At least the two of them were on speaking terms. He was still not convinced that sending the kids away was necessary, especially since it had been Rachael's idea. Maybe he'd have felt stronger about it if he had suggested it himself. They'd talk about it again in the morning with the girls. They might have their own doubts about leaving. It was bad enough dealing with one woman without having three of them ganging up on him. *Come to think of it, I'd have a better chance of controlling my life if at least two of these women were out of town; however, they do give life more color. Heather might have been pretty on the outside, but she was pale in comparison to these three women.* Alex finished the climb up the staircase with a smile on his face.

The distant roar of thunder caught Rachael's attention as she was turning off the light. Weather reports hadn't been at the top of her priority list, so she turned on the radio to see what was happening. Oklahoma thunderstorms were serious business, and nobody took Mother Nature for granted when she started rumbling.

Much to Rachael's chagrin, the severe warnings were posted for the Tulsa area until after midnight. With a tired sigh, she sat up and turned the light back on. The only way to really know what was happening was to stay awake and keep the radio on. The storm kit was packed and neatly stored in the hallway closet for when the tornadoes were threatening. It was impossible to hear the tornado sirens when she was sleeping especially with her constant companion at the vet, so she would have to stay up and wait for the worst to pass.

It wasn't long before Mother Nature was terrorizing the night's peace; and when the lightning strikes became dangerous, it was time to get everybody downstairs. The radio announcer plotted the direction of the oncoming storm. It was only a matter of minutes now until the hail and high winds accompanying the storm would be crashing in on them.

"Alex, are you awake?"

"Yes, how could I sleep with all the noise outside."

"I think it would be a good idea for you and Mark to come downstairs. You can put him in my bed. I'll get the girls. Please hurry."

Alex had experienced severe storms in the Chicago area, but they were nothing like this one. It sounded like he was on the inside of a base drum. The vibrations shook the house, shook the bed, and shook his brain. There was no doubt in his mind that when Rachael said hurry, he was going to be right behind her with Mark in his arms.

With all of the noise and light, no one could go back to sleep. Mark thought the fireworks show in May was very unusual and unique even though none of the rest of them seemed to be sharing his excitement. Rachael tried to distract everyone by suggesting they all go into the kitchen for a snack. Before they could get out of the bedroom, a flash of lightening and crack of thunder made even Mark jump with fear. The lights were instantly gone, and darkness surrounded them.

"Mom, I'll get the storm kit out of the closet."

"Good, Allie, be sure to turn the radio on right away. Rorie go open a window in the game room and one in the garage, just a little."

"Yeah, I know."

"Rachael, where are you going?"

"I have to go out and pull the flowers on the patio up by the house and get the hanging baskets off the trees."

"I'll help. Besides I don't want you outside alone. Mark stick with Allison."

"Sure, Dad."

Alex and Rachael hurried out the patio door toward the trees in the back. The wind was picking up speed and throwing the neighbor's garbage cans across the backyard. Rachael handed Alex two plants and grabbed two for herself.

"We'll put these in the sun room. Let's push the table up close to the house and put the bigger plants under it." Rachael was yelling as loud as she could, but Alex still had trouble hearing her over the roar of the thunder.

"Okay. It seems odd that no police officers are around to lend a hand."

"What?"

"No police. Where are they?"

"Probably didn't want to get wet. I've got to go around front to get the basket of roses off the mail box and bring in the big planter. Open the garage door for me."

"No way. We open the door together and go out together."

When they got back inside and dried off, Alex again questioned the absence of police officers.

"Alex, with a storm like this, they're probably needed else where. It's amazing how much damage the high winds and hail can cause: power lines are down, traffic lights are out, there are a ton of accidents. It's a mess."

Everyone was still in the family room waiting to see how much havoc the storm would cause. The spectacular light display was intriguing and Mark went up to the window for a fuller view of the show.

Before everyone could say get away from the window, the lightening flashed, and Mark was screaming at the top of his lungs.

"AHHHHH!!!!!! Somebody's out there! Somebody's looking at us."

Alex immediately ran to the window, but it was so dark again that he couldn't see anything. He crossed to the patio door and went out into the storm, but there was still no way of telling if someone had been at the window.

Mark was clinging to Rachael like vines to a fence. "I know someone was looking in the window at us. When the lightening flashed, I saw it: big and scary. Was it her, my mother?"

"I don't know who it was, Mark." Rachael wrapped her arms tightly around the shaking boy.

Alex came in from the rain. He was dripping wet and had leaves in his hair. "What a wicked night. I couldn't see anything. Mark, can you describe what you saw?"

"Honestly, Dad, it was hard to tell. It didn't look like mom."

"Are you sure it was a person?"

"That much I am sure of. It was on two legs, not four."

Rachael had opened the blinds so that the lightening would give them some light, but now she closed everything up again. The flashlights would have to be enough. Alex was still trying to comfort Mark and get what information he could.

"Do you think it could have been a policeman?"

"I suppose, but it didn't look right. The hat was so big. Out to here." Mark made a big circle around his head with his arm trying to show his father the size of the hat. "And it kinda hung down in the front and covered the face, so I couldn't tell. The person just seemed awfully big to be mom."

Rorie was the first to add her fear to the boiling pot. "I sure wish Chance was here. He would've known if someone was out there. Nobody can get close to the house when he's here."

"Mom, when will the lights come back on?" Allison was taking her turn now to add just a little more panic to the situation. "What's that noise? Before Rachael could say anything, Allison answered her own question "Oh, no! It's the tornado siren."

"The guy on the radio says it's coming this way, Mom. We need to get out of this room."

"Girls, relax. Remember the first rule: don't panic."

"Right, Mom. Remind us later." The girls were gone before Rachael could say another word.

"Let's go, guys. We need to get away from the windows." Rachael led Alex and Mark into the "fraidy closet" and closed the door. Allison and Rorie were already sitting on the floor with the radio repeating the warning.

"What did you call this closet?" Alex was trying to ease the obvious tension by making small talk, and he hoped Rachael would play along and let one of the girls answer.

Finally, Rorie decided to satisfy Alex's query, "Most houses have a special place, or closet where people hide during bad storms."

"Why?" The conversation was enough to distract Mark from his earlier ordeal.

"There are lots of bad storms here, Mark. Since most houses don't have basements like you did in Chicago, there has to be somewhere else for the people to go and be fairly safe."

"'Fraidy closet' is sure a weird name."

"Yeah, it's kind of funny, but when you hide in the closet, you are afraid, right?"

"I guess so."

"That's where the name comes from, 'fraidy closet' kind of like 'fraidy cat.'"

"Now I get it."

"I think the worst of the storm is past us. The weather tracker has confirmed that we should only have rain showers for the rest of the night."

"Can we get out of the closet now, Rachael?"

"You sure can, Mark. How 'bout a snack before you go back to bed?"

"Sure, that sounds great. I'm not tired right now anyway."

Rachael took the three kids to the kitchen to find something to eat while Alex tried to telephone Detective Archer or one of his men. When he returned to the kitchen, he held two brandy snifters in his hands.

"I thought you might enjoy this while the kids have their snack."

"Thanks, I'd love it. Did you get a hold of Archer?"

"He's on his way over. He did confirm that most of his men had to be sent on other emergencies, but he left one car here to guard the house."

"During the bad storms, crime usually drops because the bad guys don't want to be out in this kind of weather either, but there are a million other emergencies the police have to attend to."

"That's what Archer said too, and it does make sense. What he wants to know is why his blue shirts weren't around when we were outside."

Within twenty minutes Archer was at the front door. A parade of flashing lights lined the street, and officers were streaming all over the street. Alex hadn't expected such a grand response to his call.

"Archer, what's going on? You brought a lot of officers with you just to look for someone who was standing in the rain."

"Doctor, is there someplace where we can talk without the children hearing us?"

"Sure, we can go into the study. Rachael and the kids are in the kitchen." The two men walked into the study and closed the door behind them. Alex knew something was wrong. Archer was being so secretive and police like.

"What's wrong? Did you find her?"

"We found the police car. Both of the officers have been shot to death."

"Son-of-a-bitch, I can't believe she could do it."

"Strange things can happen to people. Sometimes anger can smolder like a sleeping volcano until the day it decides to erupt. Then nothing can stop it. The violence can feed off the violence until there is nothing left, or as in this case until we catch her."

"I'm sorry about your men."

"Thanks. They were good men and good officers."

"It's too bad it had to come to this."

"Yes it is. What did Mark tell you about the person he saw outside the window?"

Alex filled the detective in on the details Mark had given him. The two men discussed the murders and strategy for a long time. Rachael knew something was wrong, but she couldn't go in and ask without alarming the kids. Finally, Rachael saw Alex escorting Archer to the front door. After the door closed, Rachael heard a deep sigh.

Alex came into the room and picked up the brandy snifter he had left on the counter, "Well girls, you need to pack your bags."

"What? Where're we going?"

"The three of you are going to see Grandma and Grandpa for a week or so."

"Mom, you're getting rid of us?"

"No, Honey, we are trying to protect you. Alex and I want to force Heather to make her move, but we want you safely out of harm's way."

Alex knew Rachael had questions about his visit with Archer, and he was glad her intuition told her to wait until they were alone. He had to help convince the kids to go away for the sake of safety. Things were getting too dangerous.

"Please, guys. It's hard for us to do what needs to be done if we have to worry about you."

"What about Chance?"

"And Snickers?"

"I think it would be best if we have Snickers boarded at the clinic with Chance until this is over. He'll be safe there, and Chance will enjoy his company. I'll go over during the day to see both of them."

"Mark, girls, are you okay with this? Do you understand why we need to know you are safe?"

"Yes, Alex, we don't like it, but we understand. Rorie and I will take good care of Mark for you."

"Thanks, girls. I know you will."

CHAPTER
SEVENTEEN

Alex walked into the physical therapy room and saw Tony Broadmore on the walker. His recovery was coming along nicely now and so was his school work. The muscle tone was beginning to return to his upper body as he worked out, but it would still be a while before his legs were what they should be.

"Hey, Doc. It's good to see you. I saw Mrs. Carson this afternoon. Man, she was gone for a long time. I was afraid I'd have to finish all that school work alone."

"Tony, it's good to see you up and around. Another week or so and you'll be going home."

"Really?"

"It's about time; don't you think?"

"Wow, that'll be great. How about therapy and school?"

"You'll have regular sessions here until you are running down the field."

"Think so?"

"I don't see why you won't make a full recovery if you work at it."

"I don't think Mrs. Carson will let me get away with anything less."

"She can be pretty persistent can't she?"

"Yeah, but if it wasn't for her, I'd still be in that bed."

"You're probably right. As far as your school work goes, you can set up times to see Mrs. Carson. I'm sure she plans on getting you caught up before school starts in the fall."

"That's what she said. Ya know, you two think a lot alike."

Alex laughed at the boy's statement. He had no idea of what he was talking about. "See you tomorrow, Tony. I have to go and see someone who's really sick."

Tony laughed and waved at Alex as he walked out of the room. Alex hadn't expected Rachael to show up at the hospital today. He had the uncanny feeling that she and Debbie were hiding in some dark closet sharing tales about him. The mental image set him out on the mission of locating these two meddling women.

Rachael and Debbie were standing at the window in Debbie's large corner office when one of the beepers went off. They both reached for the little black box that was safely tucked into a pocket. Before Debbie could acknowledge it was her beeper going off, Rachael's sounded.

"It's Alex. He must have heard I was here and doesn't want us trading secrets."

Debbie smiled, "It's good for him to wonder what we're saying about him. His sweet little inner world is opening up, and he's uncomfortable with that."

"I know. He'll never be able to appreciate the goodness in others if he doesn't learn how to let people, like us, naturally, into his life."

"Another minute or two and he'll be knocking on that door."

It was only a matter of seconds before the door was hastily opened without a knock. "So, what are you two doing?"

Debbie was the first to comment. She appreciated the fact that the relationship between these two people was ambiguous to say the least. She would have to help Rachael break down the private walls of Alex Zamora, or he would miss having a meaningful relationship with anyone, and she would lose her famous doctor and hospital ally.

"You were faster than we expected. What were you worried about? Did you think we might be talking about you or something?"

"The thought never crossed my mind. I just wanted to know if the kids got off on time."

"They're on their way safe and sound to be spoiled and pampered by grandma and grandpa."

"Mark will enjoy being with the girls, but is there anything to do out in the sticks of civilization?"

"Of course there is. The Black Hills are full of entertainment. Everything from Mt. Rushmore to fishing. Don't worry the girls love going to the hills, and they'll show Mark the time of his life. My sister lives in a beautiful house five miles west of town. She and her husband have five acres of prime Black Hills beauty. Rorie and Allison think they have a piece of Heaven when they go out there. The deer come into the yard to feed at night, and the stars are so close you think you could pick diamonds off a blanket of black velvet."

Alex had enough sappy description of life at grandma's. "Rachael," he snapped, "Do you always have to be so disgustingly optimistic?"

"It's a reasonable balance to your bad attitude. Don't you agree?"

"Why didn't you go back home after you took the kids to the airport?"

"I didn't want to be there alone."

"Why not? The police are keeping a closer watch than ever."

"Oh sure. And that's supposed to make me feel safe."

"What about Snickers? He'd keep you company."

"The kids and I left early in order to take him to the clinic. Mark wanted to make sure he'd be safe there, and the girls wanted to say good-bye to Chance. I needed to see my students anyway. Whenever you are ready to leave, you can find me in your office."

"Are you sure Jack was killed accidently? Maybe he ran into that car on purpose just to get away from an optimistic manipulating wife." Alex hated himself for saying the words, but damn she brought out the worst in him. He left the room before he could hear her response or suffer the consequences of the malicious remark.

"He didn't mean that, Rachael."

"I'm not so sure." The tears hung on the long black eyelashes. "It's hard to live like this. I never know what he's going to be like. One minute he's fine and the next... Well, you saw what he's like. Do you still think he's in love with me?"

"More than ever."

"Well, I can't live with a man like that. Never knowing what to expect from him. I was happier before I met him."

"Were you really happier alone?"

"Not the last two years, but before that I certainly was happier."

"Are you saying Jack was a saint to live with?"

"No, of course not. His first mission every morning was to see what new geometric pattern he could spit on the bathroom mirror. It used to drive me crazy."

"And you never argued, right?"

"We didn't argue often; but, like most married people, we did disagree from time to time. It was usually about money. I thought our partnership worked well: he earned most of the money, and I spent most of it; but he didn't appreciate the balance of the arrangement."

"I suppose not; most men don't. I bet he was always more agreeable after you were intimate."

"Naturally, aren't most men."

"Exactly my point. I think Alex's head is about to pop off, if you know what I mean."

"Not a chance, he doesn't deserve any sexual gratification; and frankly, he doesn't want anything like that from me."

"Oh, yes he does. He just won't admit it because he's afraid he might not be healthy."

"You mean he's afraid he might give me the HIV virus?" Rachael watched Debbie shake her head affirmatively. "I don't know, Debbie. He's pushing so hard to keep me at a distance."

"We both know why. He doesn't know what's going to happen to him. Between the AIDS test and a murderous wife, he's a wreck. Just play along for awhile and see what happens."

"That much I can do. I want this whole episode over as soon as possible. Actually, I think I was better off before I met the socially impotent Dr. Zamora. Now I am going to see the rest of my students and try to forget about how rotten he has been today."

The afternoon wore on, and Rachael was glad to have the students to distract her. As she headed to Alex's office, where she could update some student files, she realized it felt good to be back at the hospital. If for no other reason, she was grateful to Alex for getting her involved at St. Thomas.

Alex threw the door of his office open and barked the words, "I'm ready to go."

"Fine, I'm ready. Do you want to go out and get something to eat before we go home? I'm tired of cooking."

"No."

His lack of manners was fanning Rachael's flames of anger left over from his earlier remark in Debbie's office. She was absolutely not going to put up with this adolescent attitude. Slow and deliberate, Rachael walked over and closed the door. She turned around to face the man who supposedly loved her. *He wouldn't know love if it bit him on his socially impotent butt.*

"Alex, to be perfectly blunt, you have a major case of attitude sickness. Now I don't really care what you think of me, but we're in this together. When we get home, you can lock yourself in your room for all I care; but if you expect me to feign lover's bliss when we are in public then you had better do the same."

"What are you talking about?"

"Have you even thought about a plan, or are you just going to mope around with your head shoved up in a dark dank place?"

"I don't need to plan; you do enough planning for both of us."

"You're feeling sorry for yourself again, and you're taking it out on me."

Alex turned away from her because he knew she was right. Well, she was partially right. He was feeling sorry for himself and had made only one plan: to wipe out the love he had seen in her eyes the night before. He had to push her away. He wanted her to have more than the short future he had to offer.

With his back still to her, he made an attempt at peace. "I'll work on my attitude. Do you have any ideas?"

"Not really. However, both of the messages suggested there was some kind of lover's relationship between us. So if we're going to make her play by our rules, then we have to force the issue. That means, my dear, when there are other eyes around, you have to at least be civil, and nice wouldn't hurt."

"Then let's eat out. I'm sure I can count on you to tell me when I'm not playing the proper role."

Rachael opened the office door and walked out into the hallway locking the door after Alex had followed her out. She linked her arm around his, and they headed for the elevator with a forced smile on each face.

Alex followed Rachael home so they could take just one car out to dinner. The last time they had been out together was before Rachael and the kids had gone to Galveston. It would be good for them to be alone because they would have to talk to each other or not at all.

The police were now plain clothes men pretending to do something constructive around the neighborhood. Once it was television cable people, then it was a water problem, and some were supposed to be gardeners. Alex headed for one of the men as Rachael pulled into the garage and checked the alarm on the house.

"Alex, Mathew is here. I need to talk to him for just a minute. Do you mind?"

"No, I want to talk to the officer trimming that tree."

"How do you know he's a policeman?"

"Because he hasn't cut a single twig yet. Look around his feet....nothing."

Rachael walked around the house to see how Mathew was doing. Friday was his normal day to clean the pool area; and as she had expected, he was working hard washing down the blue and white tile.

"Mrs. C. How are you today? I was surprised to not find anyone at home."

"I went to the hospital after I took the kids to the airport."

"The kids are off on another vacation?"

"I guess you could call it that. The three of them went to see grandma and grandpa for a few days."

"Three?"

"Yes, Mark went along with them."

"So you and the doctor can be all alone now."

Rachael didn't like the tone of his voice or the fact he even thought it was any of his business. If he had a crush on her, it was time for it to be over. She would rather do her own yard work than have his opinionated crap thrown at her every time Alex's name came up.

"Yes, we wanted some time together. We are old enough, don't you agree?"

Mathew looked down into the water before he answered, "Consenting adults. Does the Doctor still want me to help him tomorrow?"

"I don't think so. With the children gone, we will probably make other plans." She put extra emphasis on "other" hoping Mathew would understand her interests were not in him but in Alex, which was most definitely true. She wanted to make it perfectly clear to the boy there would never be anything between them.

"In fact, Mathew, after you finish up this evening, I probably won't need you any more."

Mathew knew he had over stepped his bounds and was being fired. His anger flared as he jumped out of the pool and walked dripping wet to stand before her. Before he could say anything, Rachael tried to defuse the situation.

"I'm sure you need the time for your studies, right? After all, you are going to be a senior next year. You need to get more experience under your belt in your field of study. By the way what are you studying, Mathew?"

"I am studying electrical engineering if you really care to know. I really can't believe that after all I've done for you, you would just fire me."

"You've done a lot for us, and I've paid you well for your services. Now I think it would be a good idea for the girls and I to take over the work again, at least, for the summer. It's good exercise for all of us, and I'm feeling so much better now."

"I'm sure I can figure out why." He watched Rachael turn and walk away from him. The only woman he'd ever loved had just thrown him out for the first man to show up on her doorstep.

With his last remark, Rachael decided it was time to get out of the way before one of them said something regretful. She was anxious to be away from the young man who obviously wanted more from her than she was willing to give.

While Rachael was talking to Mathew, Alex wanted to find out if anymore information had been collected. The officer stopped playing the tree trimming game and walked to meet him.

"Hello, Dr. Zamora."

"Good evening. Have you found out anything yet?"

"Detective Archer believes the blood that was used on the car was stolen from an ambulance during the night. A report was filed at the station that one of the trucks had been robbed of several units of blood plasma. We don't know for sure if it was her, but it's the only missing blood we've heard about. Ya know, blood isn't something that is stolen very often."

"I'm sure it isn't, and it isn't worth a lot unless you're the one dying."

"That's what we figured. There isn't much of a resale market for it on the street, if you know what I mean."

"What about today's episode?"

"No finger prints on the paper, a standard toy crayon was used for the writing. Nothing to trace."

"Did anyone at the hospital see anything?"

"No, Sir, but we have started looking for any type of disguise that might be used; we're doing a closer check of ID's. Anyone on the street is checked and rechecked."

"Good idea about the disguise. Who suggested it?"

"Oh, ah, Mrs. Carson and the Detective talked about it yesterday afternoon."

"I see." Alex wanted to be angry that Rachael was discussing strategy with Archer rather than with him, but then he hadn't exactly been cooperating. She had asked him if he had a plan; obviously, she had been doing more serious thinking about trapping Heather than he had. *I have to shake this self pity routine and help get Heather out of my life...our lives. I may not want Rachael to be in love with me, but at least I would like her to respect me.*

Alex opened the door for the woman standing next to him. He was concerned about the distraught look on her face. She was upset about something; and since lately he had been the most routine cause of her distress, he didn't even want to ask what was wrong.

Rachael slid quickly into the car seat and waited for Alex to close the door. *At least he knows how to be a gentleman. It must be something his mother taught him to do instinctively because I doubt he really wants to treat me so well.* Alex walked around to the driver's side of the car and got in. Rachael could still smell the remnants of his cologne. No matter how angry she was at him or anyone else, she couldn't ignore the power he had over her physically. What she really hated was having to tell him she had fired his handy man for tomorrow without even asking him. She knew he'd accuse her of making decisions for him again.

"Do I have to be nice in the car too?"

"It would be good practice."

Alex couldn't help the smile that crept into his black mood. She had done it again: made him smile. He wanted to look at her, to enjoy the auburn curls as they glistened in the sun, to imagine the softness of her skin under his fingers. *I wish, Rachael, more than anything that I could just enjoy the little time that we'll have together. Nice, she deserves more than nice. I want more than nice. As long as we have to play at being in love, I might as well enjoy it. Hopefully, she'll assume I'm merely acting. I hope I can remember I am ONLY acting.*

Rachael decided it was time for Alex to see more of Tulsa, so she took him downtown to McGills for a wonderful dinner. It was a crowded place; but if they sat in the front, no one would be able to get in or out without walking into their line of vision. The food was some of the best in town, and the ambiance of the place made everyone feel relaxed. Having dinner in the softly lit atmosphere would help Alex get his attitude straightened out. It was slightly romantic but not overly done, and he definitely needed all of the help he could get.

"Good evening, ma'am. May I get you anything from the bar?"

"Yes please. I would like a glass of champagne."

Alex order a Rob Roy and then turned his attention back to Rachael. "Are you celebrating the fact that I haven't said anything nasty in almost an hour?"

Rachael was pleasantly surprised by his attempt at humor. She didn't want to say anything to spoil the attitude check he had made. "No, I just really like to drink champagne. It's my favorite just like you enjoy your brandy at night."

"I see. Your suggestion to Archer to look for someone disguised was a good one. I hadn't even thought about that, but you're right. I'm sure Heather wouldn't just walk into the hospital for everyone to notice."

"Thank you. It really is the only explanation for not being able to find her." Rachael sipped on her champagne wondering when would be the best time to spill the bad news about Mathew. Maybe another drink would help him to mellow out.

Rachael nearly choked on his next words. "So is Mathew still coming over to help me move boxes?"

"Well, not exactly."

"What does that mean?"

"Before you pass judgment on me, let me explain the whole story. Agree?"

"Maybe."

"When Mathew found out the kids were gone, and we were staying together, that same jealous streak we saw on Easter flared its ugly head. I decided, that's right without asking you, I decided to make sure he understood there would never be anything between him and me." Rachael stopped and waited for Alex to angrily jump into her explanation.

"Yes, what else happened?"

"Well, I kind of didn't deny what he suspected. Then he made the derogatory comment about 'consenting adults.' It wasn't the words as much as the way he said it." Rachael waited again for Alex to verbally jump on her.

"So how did you fire him?"

"I tried to be tactful; but any way you look at it, he knows he was fired and he knows why. So, aren't you going to get mad at me for doing something without consulting you first?"

"Not in this case. I would have fired him after the Easter scene. I know you didn't see it, but he felt like I was intruding on his territory."

"I guess you were right. I just didn't want to believe it. Well, it looks like the girls and I get to start doing our own yard work again. They are going to love that."

"Mark and I will help. The fresh air and exercise will be good for us." Rachael looked surprised at his offer. For the first time in days he sounded like the man she had fallen in love with. Maybe he was planning on staying around after all of this was over.

"That'd be great. Now about your place, you and I can go over in the morning and do some of the work. Getting your place in shape would give us something to do while the kids are gone, otherwise we might get into trouble."

"That's true. You know what they say about idle fingers."

The rest of the evening was very pleasant. They watched people go in and out of the restaurant wondering if anyone had on a disguise or what a woman would look like in blond hair, a nose job or other variations of plastic surgery. Many of the possibilities were hopelessly funny causing the two of them to giggle until tears filled their eyes.

Alex hated to leave, but they had been there for hours. Not even one slightly suspicious person had entered the place, so Alex paid the bill and escorted Rachael to the car. The warm beautiful evening felt so good. It was the type of night when love is born. The stars were so bright he had the notion of plucking one out of the sky to place on Rachael's finger. The moonlight reflected off thousands of large magnolia leaves which provided backdrops to large white blossoms. Alex could detect a slightly sweet fragrance lingering in the air. He didn't know if it was from the magnolias or from the dozens of other early summer flowers that surrounded them as they walked to the car.

"Alex, I think I'll sleep in Allison's room. I don't want to be downstairs alone."

"Why? You were downstairs alone before." He wondered about her reasoning. He would have to be so careful. Playing the role of lovers in public would be hard to turn off when they closed the door of privacy.

"It wasn't so dangerous before. Besides, if somebody breaks in and comes up the stairs, he or she will get you first."

"Now I understand your logic. I don't care where you sleep as long as it's not with me."

"Hey, I never thought of that. There are twin beds in your room."

"Don't even consider it! Remember, you promised my room was all mine." Alex was laughing at her and wondering if she was being truly honest about her fear.

Rachael had never been serious about using that twin bed, but she was sure she didn't want to sleep downstairs. A fear had been gripping her all evening, and even though she had enjoyed the dinner and conversation, she couldn't rid herself of the apprehension. It was always hard to explain a woman's intuition to a man, especially one who based everything on logic.

Everything appeared normal as the car pulled into the garage. Rachael noticed the extra cars parked at the end of the cul-de-sac which she presumed were unmarked police cars. A tall dark haired man walking a German Shepherd was two houses down from hers; no one on the street owned a German Shepherd. Another person posing as a neighbor was watering the grass, but every yard on the street had an automatic sprinkler system. The people she saw outside were not her neighbors; they were policemen who were doing a much better job of creating a picture of neighborly bliss since the death of their fellow officers. Now they saw themselves as victims and took the apprehension of the murderer as a personal vendetta. Rachael felt bad about the loss of the two officers; however, she did feel better knowing everyone finally understood how dangerous Heather really was.

Alex unlocked the utility room door and went in to turn off the alarm. Rachael, coming in behind him, noticed things were not the way she had left them in the morning.

"Alex, stop!"

"What's wrong?" He looked around the room but could see nothing out of place.

"Someone's been in here."

"You're kidding. The place is spotless."

"No it isn't; look at the floor."

Looking down at the high gloss red wood finish, he could see nothing. "There's nothing on the floor."

"Sure, come over here and look down the hall."

"Okay, what?"

"Don't you see the dirt prints that go across the wood? Only the tips of the shoes show, and look there are tiny pieces of grass here."

When he stood just at the right angel, the glare of the kitchen light shifted and revealed the three maybe four prints of someone's shoe. Alex was harder to convince than that. With the alarm system and the officers outside, how could someone get in.

"Really, Rachael, how do you know it wasn't you or the kids?"

"The last thing I did this morning was mop this floor. You know how I am about my floors."

She wasn't kidding about that. Alex had never imagined anyone could be so obsessive about a floor. *Come to think of it, she is a little nuts about the whole house. It's always clean when I walk in the door. The carpets always look freshly vacuumed. If anyone knows someone has been on her floor, it would be Rachael.*

"Rachael, before we get Archer over here, lets check the rest of the house."

"What if she's still in here?"

"I don't think the door chimes and alarm would have gone off normally. Somehow she must be able to get around it."

Rachael looked across the family room floor, but she couldn't detect anything. "The kids were in here while I finished the cleaning, so I can't tell if anyone else walked on the floor."

"What was the last room that you cleaned?"

"My room, none of us were in my room before we left."

Alex and Rachael headed for the master suite. As they entered the room, it was not necessary to look for foot prints. The violation was perfectly clear; the room was in shambles. Shredded lingerie was strewn across the floor and on the furniture in a rainbow of pink, blue and purple lace. Rachael's eyes followed the trail of vandalism until they come to rest on her pillow. Alex followed her gaze and understood the silent terror portrayed on her face. A pair of scissors was stabbed threw a piece of white paper and into the pillow. Alex walked over to Rachael and put his arm around her. The inner tremors of fear were starting to surface, and he was afraid she would collapse.

"Holy Mother of God! Rachael, I need to call the police in."

There were no words only an affirmative shake of her head, so he lead her over to the lounge and eased her down. Then he went to signal an officer to come in. Within minutes police were all over the house looking for clues, but the only real violation had been in Rachael's room.

Rachael finally asked the million dollar question, "Alex, how does she get in?"

"I honestly don't know. Frankly, I didn't think Heather had that much brain capacity to plot anything so intelligent. The first murder she had helped to plot was a farce."

"Maybe she didn't do the planning. After all, she kept her real life a secret from you for nine years. She must have had some mental ability."

"I never thought about it that way. Let's call the security system tomorrow and have them do another check for any possible tampering."

"I suppose. I don't know if I'll ever feel safe here again." Now the tears fell and the shoulders dropped. Alex tried to offer comfort, but there was little he could do. *How did she know this room wasn't safe tonight? She knew at the restaurant when she suggested sleeping upstairs. Weird.*

"Rachael, you knew. How?"

Looking up at him with a tear streaked face, she asked, "What are you talking about?"

"You said that you didn't want to sleep downstairs. How did you know?"

"Just a bad feeling. I get them sometimes."

"Are they always right?"

"Usually."

"Well for Heaven's sake please tell me the next time you have one, especially if I'm supposed to get on an airplane."

Rachael tried to smile at him for giving her intuition some credit. "Now, I have to replace more than just my night gown."

"I'll take you tomorrow. Now let me get you something to help you sleep." Archer's men were all over her bedroom. What the intruder had not violated, they had. Alex could feel her eyes watching with agony as they turned the room, her sanctuary, upside down; but he knew they'd find exactly what they had found before: no prints, no clues.

"Rachael, come upstairs with me. I want to get you out of here." Alex led her up to Allison's room.

The room, full of tropical red, orange and green, was host to a throng of yellow and orange butterflies. The beautiful creatures had been painted on the walls and hung from the ceiling and light fixtures. Even the quilt on the giant waterbed was covered with the vibrant flying colors. Alex had never been in either of the girls rooms, and now he wished he hadn't waited so long to check out the unique decorating. He shouldn't be surprised considering the way the rest of the house looked.

"I'll find something of Allie's to wear and go to bed. Will you get rid of the police as soon as you can?"

"As quickly as I can, then I'll bring you a cup of tea and a mild sedative." There was no reaction to his comment. He knew from her languid speech and movement that she was having trouble dealing with what happened. He was too, for that matter.

"Archer, you have to find out how she got in."

"We're trying, but there's no sign in any part of the house of forced entry. None of the officers saw a thing. Believe me, we are as baffled as you are."

"Do you by any chance have a police dog we could keep here in the house? I don't know if Rachael will stay here without some other protection. Obviously, the alarm system can be bypassed and so can your men. We need something else if we are going to stay here."

"I understand. I'm sure we can get you a dog for a couple of days. I could also station someone inside the house."

"Ah, well, I really think Rachael would prefer having the dog. No offense, but you know how she is about her dog. She puts a lot more faith in them than she does in the rest of us."

"You're right about that. I'll have Ginger brought over in the morning. She's best suited for the job."

"Thanks, are you guys about done here now? I'm worried about Rachael, and I'd like to get back upstairs."

"I think we're finished. What a mess and not a single thing to go on. Frustrating, you know what I mean."

"From my point of view, frustrating isn't the adjective I had in mind."

After the last officer left the house, Alex locked the door and set the alarm for all the good it would do. He didn't know if he felt safe in this house anymore either. Rachael had placed such stock in Chance and the alarm system, now both had been rendered helpless. He made a cup of tea and headed for his room to get something to help Rachael sleep. He had made it a habit to keep mild medications on hand because it always seemed that something was needed for one ailment or another, and he hated going into the office for such little things.

Rachael was in bed, but her eyes were wide open. She was going to have a hard time relaxing and falling asleep tonight and for a long time to come.

"Here's a cup of tea and something to help you sleep. Let me prop the pillows up so you can drink this."

"Thank you." Rachael took the cup of tea but not the tiny white pill. "Is everyone out of the house?"

"Yes, Archer is going to bring a guard dog over tomorrow. He said her name is Ginger."

"Alex, I'm surprised you'd do something like that without asking first."

He started to defend himself and then saw the slight impish gleam in her eye. "You're not as bad off as I thought if you can give me a hard time."

"I'm upset, but I'm not incapacitated. The dog's a good idea. I can't believe I didn't think of it."

"You aren't the only one, my dear, who can make plans."

"Why didn't you bring yourself a brandy to enjoy?"

"I had enough at dinner, and I want to be able to hear anything that might go on downstairs."

"I was thinking the same thing, so you can keep your little pill for someone who needs it. Pull up some pillows and sit down beside me. I really don't want to be alone yet."

"Are you sure?"

"Yes, you won't drown. Allie has had this bed for years, and it has never killed anybody....ah, sorry, bad choice of words considering the circumstances."

Alex took two of the shammed pillows off the floor and propped them against the head board. Then he gingerly waded onto the waterbed. Grace was not his strong suit as he fumbled for balance on the precarious bed. He finally settled in next to Rachael so she could enjoy her tea without spilling it.

"What did the note say?"

"Nothing significant. There were no prints on it and no other clues in the room."

"I didn't think there would be. Now what did it say? I can always ask Archer."

Alex hesitated again; but he was sure if he didn't tell her, she would find out in the morning anyway. "It said you'd be next." The silent seconds seemed like hours as the fear vibrated through her body.

"I see," was all she said before changing the topic. "Are we going to work at your house tomorrow? I think the work will be good for me: keep my mind occupied, you know what I mean?"

"The work would be good for both of us and my house could certainly use the attention."

"You know, I have never been in your house. What's it like?"

Rachael rested her partially full cup on her lap and her head on Alex's chest. Without realizing it he had put his arm around her and started talking about the house on the other side of the main street dividing their subdivisions.

Alex felt himself begin to relax as his body absorbed the warmth of the waterbed. He had never been on one before but now understood its attraction to so many people. After several minutes of giving Rachael a mental tour of his house, he realized at some point she had fallen asleep. Rather than breaking the spell of the moment, he took the cup out of her hand setting it on the headboard, then reached up to turn off the light. He slid down a little further into the bed planning to enjoy this rare opportunity to hold the woman he loved without giving her any false hope of a future together. Eventually, he drifted off to sleep with Rachael in his arms. The only thing that was missing was the red satin.

CHAPTER
EIGHTEEN

"Com'on, Sleepy head. It's time to get up" Alex walked into Allison's room with a steaming hot cup of coffee.

Rachael was still sound asleep. She had barely moved all night. Sometime about sunrise Alex had gotten out of bed and gone downstairs. He had several things to take care of before Rachael got up.

The heavy sleep still had Rachael in a haze, "Alex?"

"Yes, it's me."

"Where are we?"

"Where do you think we are?"

"I had the strangest feeling I was on the beach with...with I'm not really sure, but I thought it was you."

"You were dreaming the good dream? That seems odd after last night. What happened?"

"I was sunning on the beach when the mist started to roll in. It was just like the other one except this time when I looked for the man's face, I saw you."

"Are you saying I'm the man of your dreams?" The question was followed by a large smile of satisfaction. He had known she was dreaming part of the night. Calling his name was a dead give away, and her hands had not been lacking in seductive caresses. If she only knew, she would certainly not look so innocent now.

"I guess, in a matter of speaking, you are. What time is it?"

"It's almost ten, and we have things to do."

"I can't believe I slept so late especially after last night." Rachael took a few moments to get her bearings. She barely even remember coming into Allison's room or getting into bed, and she certainly had no idea Alex had been in bed with her all night.

"Last night? The last thing I remember is you bringing me up here." She waited a second pondering the events of the night. "Then you came back with a cup of hot tea and sat on the bed with me."

"Yup. That's what happened. I started a boring description of my house; and before I knew it, you were snoring in my arms." Alex smiled at her. He was enjoying the feeling of being in complete control of the situation for a change.

"I was not. I don't snore."

"I beg your pardon. You most certainly do." Teasing her would, hopefully, keep her from wondering why she had slept so easily.

"Alex?"

"Yes?" He could tell by the sound of her voice she had guessed the truth.

"I can't believe you put something in my tea."

"Me? Never. I couldn't trick you like that."

"I can't believe it either, you scoundrel. But you had the pill in your hand. How did you get it in the tea?"

"I put it there before I came into the room. The one you saw was the one I knew you'd refuse to take. See, I'm learning the way you think."

"I'm going to have to watch you more closely."

Rachael crawled out of the waterbed after Alex opened the window shade and left the room. The sun burst in the window declaring another glorious summer day. The aroma of the coffee setting on the dresser caught her attention, and she picked up the cup. Alex had obviously been watching her make coffee and had learned the steps because the hot steamy brew was delicious.

With the mug in hand, Rachael went down the flight of stairs toward her bedroom. A hot bath with lots of bubbles would feel so good; but as she approached the doorway of her room, all of the fear from the night before raced into her memory. She had to go in and face the destruction.

The room, to her pleasant surprise, was spotless; not a shred of lace was anywhere, no scissors in the pillow and no note. The furniture had been wiped down and the carpet freshly vacuumed. The shades were open allowing the sun to sterilize all evil from the night before. At first she was confused, wondering if it had all been another bad dream; but the bedspread was missing. Then she realized it must have been Alex who'd cleaned everything up while she was still asleep. The bedspread was the only thing he could not fix. His concern for her well being helped to heal some of the pain caused by the intruder. Quickly, she decided a bath would take too long, and turned on the shower.

Alex had showered and shaved early in the morning after cleaning up the destruction in Rachael's room. He had planned on cleaning it for her before going back up stairs with the cup of tea. He knew she needed a good night's sleep, but he also wanted her to sleep late. Facing the room in the morning would have been like having an instant replay of the night before. If nothing else, he wanted to spare her that pain. During the cleaning process, he noticed many of the labels in her lingerie were from Victoria's Secret, which gave him the idea for the second part of his plan.

Rachael entered the kitchen to find Alex sitting at the table paging through the morning paper. "Alex, thank you."

The dancing eyes she loved looked up to greet her. "It was nothing. After all the cleaning and cooking you've done for us, it was the least I could do. I didn't want you to have to face it again."

By now Rachael was standing beside him. "I don't know if I could have." She bent down to kiss him on the cheek. "Thank you again."

Alex couldn't hold the intimate eye contact, so he looked out the window before he answered her. "You're welcome. Now have a quick bite so we can go."

"Are we going to your place?"

"No, silly, we're going shopping. I can't believe I'm offering to do this, so hurry up before I change my mind."

"Are we shopping for something special?"

"You're joking, right? You need to replace your ...a...personal items."

"You mean my bras and panties?"

"I mean your lingerie."

"Anything else on your shopping list?"

"Yes, as a matter-of-fact. I'm buying satin. Red satin."

Rachael sat down to eat the bagel and cream cheese that had been put out for her. His attitude was so different this morning. Why? Looking at the handsome man sitting next to her, she wondered if more had happened last night than she could remember. *No, not Alex. No way. He would never take advantage of a sleeping woman. It just isn't in his character. Still, I wonder.*

"Alex, last night you were sitting in bed holding me when I fell asleep. How long did you stay there?"

"Does it matter?"

"Not really. I had hoped that you stayed all night."

"I stayed long enough to know I prefer satin gowns to faded T-shirts with puppy dogs on the front."

They both shared the humor and the smile that followed the remark. This time he couldn't pull away from her wonderful aqua eyes, and he knew she would see the emotions he wanted to hide.

The look in his eyes gave Rachael the courage to go one step further. "That's right, you don't like things that are old, just things that are comfortable."

"What are you talking about? You used that line once before and I didn't understand it."

As matter-of-factly as possible, Rachael started her explanation. "One night when we were walking, you told me you and Mark liked it here because it was comfortable."

It was too late to force her out of his life. Rachael was in and hanging on to the treads of his soul. "So what was wrong with that?"

"I didn't like being compared to a pair of old slippers."

"I still don't understand what was so insulting that you have let it fester like an open wound. Most people cherish their comfortable old slippers."

"Alex, a woman doesn't appreciate being described as merely comfortable. Besides, when you go out you wear your shinny new leather."

"Yes, but the first thing I look for when I get home is something comfortable. I used the word to tell you how Mark and I felt being in your home not how I felt about you. You are anything but comfortable."

She liked to lead the conversation, but this was not where she wanted to go. "I don't think I like that any better."

"The other night when I, well, you remember, did I give you the impression then that you were merely comfortable?"

"Come to think of it, no. But that's what I thought when you left me."

"Don't strain your brain, Rachael. You know how I feel and why I left."

"There are ways, Alex, to ...a...enjoy each other." Rachael knew she was really pushing his rare good humor now.

"You know as well as I do that condoms don't always work, and by the time you find out, it's to late. This is not negotiable. I will not talk about it anymore today."

"How about tonight?"

"No, Mrs. Carson; however, if you are good today, maybe I'll buy you some red satin. Now, I'm in charge today so get used to it." Alex tried to sound curt, but the dancing eyes told her he was not angry just serious.

"Yes, Sir." Rachael didn't want to push any further. The humorous side of Alex was so much nicer to be with, and she didn't know when Oscar the Grouch would rear his grumpy old self again.

"Alex, will Archer bring the dog over before we leave?"

He looked at his watch before answering. "Any minute now we will be introduced to our new protector."

"You know, Chance isn't going to like having a woman take over his job."

"In this house? I'd think he was used to it. By the way, when I talked to Archer this morning, he wondered if you wanted an officer to stay in the house while we were away."

"I don't know, Mr. In Charge Today. What do you think?"

"Good answer. You do learn new rules quickly." The warm smile that lingered on her face was life giving sunshine to his love starved person. "I told him that if the dog did her job, it wouldn't be necessary."

"I agree. Of course, if they did their job outside right, we wouldn't need the dog. Speaking of jobs, I had better tell the security people to come and check out the system."

"Excuse, me, my dear. I am in charge, remember."

"Sorry, it was a momentary slip."

"I'll forgive you, but remember three strikes and you're out. I already called them. The top man himself will be here about three this afternoon. I wanted to make sure we had time to get our shopping done, before getting back to meet him. I want to be here, so he can explain to me exactly how this system works, and how someone keeps getting around it."

"I'm impressed. You're good at being in charge. I like it."

"Don't try to patronize me, young lady or should I say old lady?"

"Careful, if you want me in satin, you better be good."

"Touché. I'll be good. You'll be good. My God, do you think we can stand each other?" The jesting was good medicine for the stress they had been under, and they were disappointed when it was interrupted by Archer.

Rachael took the time to show Ginger around the house. She was a beautiful German Shepherd, and Rachael immediately bonded with her. She talked to the dog like it was an old friend who understood every word that was being uttered for her benefit.

"I see what you mean, doctor, about Mrs. Carson and her dog. You'd swear by the way they look at each other that every word was passed through the eyes."

"You know what they say, Archer, 'the truth is in the eyes.'"

"I don't know who said it, but he was right. I can always tell when someone is lying to me by the look in his eyes."

When Rachael finished the tour of the house, she showed Ginger to a water dish and locked the place up before joining Alex and Archer outside. "I swear, Mrs. Carson, no one will get into this house."

"Thanks, I'd appreciate that," was all Rachael said as she opened the car door and got in. Several other possible remarks passed through her mind like "don't die trying" or "I won't hold my breath;" but she knew he was as frustrated as she and Alex.

Alex started up the car and backed down the driveway. Rachael was curious about where he was taking her since he hadn't ask where she wanted to go, and she didn't know if he had any idea of where the mall was. *Who cares. He is in charge today, so let's just see where he wants to go. I'm tired of worrying about everything. I haven't been able to sit back and let someone else make the decisions in a long time.*

Alex knew exactly where he was going. Before waking Rachael a little after ten, he had called the Victoria's Secret store and asked for its location. He had even arranged for one of the clerks to be waiting for them. Special instructions had been given for sizes and payment. Alex was excited about this buying trip. He wanted to dish out a little of Rachael's own medicine and see how she liked it.

Alex parked the car and came around to open the door for Rachael. It was clear to him she enjoyed being treated like a lady, and he had no problem with it because in his mind she was that and more. He just couldn't tell her. As he opened the car door, he held out his hand for her. She was surprised by the offer.

"We're supposed to be in love, aren't we?"

"Yes."

"Then please, my dear, let's get it in gear and act like it." The dancing eyes were intoxicating. She could never resist his pleasant side. *He has something on his mind. I can tell he is trying to play some kind of game with me.*

"Of course, darling. Whatever you say."

"That's better." Alex led her into the first floor of the Woodland Hills Shopping Mall. Rachael was very familiar with it because she and the girls had spent many happy hours there browsing and buying in the various stores. She was surprised that he seemed to know his way around. Within moments, however, she began to read his game plan. Rachael tried to walk past Victoria's Secret. She and the girls loved this store, but it isn't where she wanted to take Alex. Buying underwear was something she might do with the girls along, but she certainly didn't want Alex standing next to her while she picked out her bras and panties.

"Here, dear, isn't this where you shop for personal items?"

"This isn't the only place, sweetheart." There was special sarcasm on "sweetheart."

"Oh, but this is where I want to go." Alex pulled her into the store and asked for Lori, who was obviously expecting them.

"Congratulations, Ma'am, on your wedding. I'm sure we can get you everything you need."

Rachael was stunned. Wedding? He was playing a game with her to teach her a lesson. She didn't know whether to hate him or love his ingenuity for having caught her completely off guard. The later would certainly be more fun.

"I'm sure my bride wants everything you have in red."

"Oh, absolutely, and blue and purple and green."

"Satin, she especially likes satin."

"No, dear, you like satin, but I really prefer silk."

Alex was afraid for only a second that she might beat him at his own game. After all, she had more practice at this than he did. Then a brilliant retort flashed into his head. "My dear, I'll buy you anything you're willing to model for me."

Now it was Rachael's turn to hesitate. She didn't think she could really model the things she was sure Alex was going pick out. Then again, why not? She watched the grin on his face widen as he believed she would back off. She didn't know if she had the guts to call his bluff. He would make her go through with it. On the other hand, he didn't have to buy her anything.

"That's okay, dear. I know my size; I really don't need to try anything on."

"Oh, honey, please for me."

The clerk had started to suspect something was fishy. Their sappy talk was more than she had experienced: and she believed, after working for five years in an intimate apparel shop, nothing could surprise her.

"Excuse me, Doctor, why don't I give you two a few minutes to...a...look around."

"Alex, damn you, what are you trying to do?"

"I'm just playing along. Besides if Heather does see us in here, she'll go nuts. I never bought her lingerie."

"I won't model underwear in front of the world."

"Let's compromise then. You model the night gowns for me here and the undies at home."

"I'll buy my own and not model anything."

"You forget the rules of the day, my dear, and the purpose of our being seen in public. You have to model a few things for me, and I deserve to see what I am replacing. Please, darling, for me."

"Alex, you've made your point. You don't like baring all emotionally, and I don't like baring all physically."

"You may understand, but I still think I would like to see what I'm buying."

"Well, darling, you can think about it all night."

"I plan on it. Lori, my bride..."

"Your bride? I'm impressed. You want to play the role, dear. Then I'll play. Every item I model for you adds another thousand dollars to my engagement ring."

Rachael saw Alex choke on his smile. Hopefully, he would not agree, but she wondered how far he would carry the game. It was time for one of them to call a truce before they started fighting again. Rachael smiled and forced a little laugh, "Alex, I was kidding about the ring. You're right about us being here. If Heather sees us here she'll go nuts. And it isn't like I don't need the stuff. Lori, did you find anything in red satin or silk? I really do like silk."

Alex hadn't even heard the last words. He was still thinking about a ring. It would be the ultimate insult to Heather if she was watching. What else would he spend his money on? He had saved and saved for all those years, and for what purpose: to be murdered or die of AIDS. Not only would he buy a ring, but he needed to add an addendum to the new will that he had just drawn up.

"I'm sorry, Rachael, I didn't hear you. Anything you want is fine as long as you agree to at least one red gown."

Lori brought several night gowns and matching robes of satin and lace for Rachael to try on. "Here's a more private fitting area for you. If there's anything else I can get for you, just let me know."

"Thank you, Lori. I will." Rachael went into the fitting room where the items had been hung and closed the door.

"I'll be right here, darling when you're ready to model for me. Lori, you have the list of the items I gave you on the phone?"

"Yes, Sir."

"Please get the things together. I'll browse around and see if there's anything else I want to add. Please feel free to make suggestions. I've never done this before."

"Of course, Sir. It would be my pleasure."

Rachael opened the door of the dressing room and walked out to show Alex what he had been waiting for. The red satin shimmered in the light. Knowing he would insist, she took the robe off revealing a beautifully tailored negligee. A shear red mesh formed the front and back yoke of the gown which hung to the floor. A slit on the right went all the way to her thigh.

"That'll do for me," Alex said giving a confirming nod of his head. "Do you like it, Dear?"

"It"s beautiful, Alex." Rachael noticed Lori with several other items in her hands. She motioned toward the girl and asked, "Alex, what's she doing?"

"Rachael, this is the first time in my life I've had a legitimate reason to do something so irrational and impulsive, so please let me enjoy myself."

She walked back into the dressing room thinking about what he'd said. She was sure he was telling her the truth. This was so out of character for the Alex she knew. Debbie would be absolutely flabbergasted to see him buying bras and panties. Maybe this was part of the therapy that would help her crash down the walls which kept him a prisoner from society.

Rachael modeled several other items for him. It didn't take him long to understand why she liked silk the best. Lori brought him a couple of negligees that had such a sensuous texture to them. He looked at her saying one word, "Silk?"

He got a one word answer, "Silk."

"We'll take it."

Rachael joined him once again, but this time she had her own clothes back on. "I'm sure Lori thinks she's died and gone to Heaven. Most clerks only dream about customers like you."

"I suppose, but it's been worth it because I've learned a lot about women's intimate clothing and had fun too."

"Yes, I'm sure you did. I could hear the two of you talking and laughing."

"Are you jealous, darling?"

Rachael answered the dancing eyes with a smile before adding, "Absolutely. By the way, did you happen to look at any of the price tags on that stuff?"

"Didn't look. Didn't care. I charged it. Is there anything else you would like before I sign my life away?"

"This isn't necessary, Alex, I'll never be able to wear everything you're buying."

"Yes, it's necessary because I want to do it. Now, if you're ready, my dear, we'll be on our way. We'll pick this stuff up on our way back to the car. I have another stop to make."

"Where are we going?"

"You'll see," was all he said as he offered her his arm. "I really do hope Heather's watching this because I'm having a wonderful time. We never did anything like this together. I want to do this again when the kids get back. I know Mark would have a great time. He's never been on an outrageous shopping trip."

Rachael had no idea of where he was leading her, but he obviously had a specific destination already in mind. Lori had told him where the best jewelry store in the mall was. At Alex's request, she had even called ahead and told the manager to be waiting for them. He may not have ever gone on a shopping spree of his own; but having listened to the other doctors, he knew service was better if a specific clerk or manager was waiting to help.

As soon as Alex went up the escalator, Rachael knew he was headed for the jewelers. She hated herself for putting the idea in his head. Playing along with nighties was one thing, but diamonds were out of the question.

"Alex, please don't. I can't let you buy any jewelry."

"Oh com'on, Rachael. Let's have some fun. We don't have to buy a ring, but we can try some on. Only a fool would buy a diamond without checking around first."

That sounded sane to her. At least, he hadn't lost all of his senses. It had been many years since she'd even looked at the good stuff. About the time they entered the store, the goose bumps streamed up her arms and neck. She grabbed onto Alex's arm moving in closer to him.

"Alex."

"I know. I feel it too. She or somebody is watching. Try to act normal. And happy." Alex led her to the counter and asked for Mr. Temple.

"Good Morning, you must be Dr. Zamora. Mr. Temple is waiting for you. He'll be right out."

Rachael looked at him in wonder. "You are constantly amazing me."

"Oh, I have talents you haven't even seen yet."

"Of that I'm sure. I can't wait."

Alex blushed at her sexual insinuation. "Rachael get your mind out of the gutter, please; we're in public."

"It a...wasn't in the gutter; it was in.."

"I know exactly where it was, and we have more pressing issues to discuss right now."

"I know. I thought you wanted me to play the part of the bride-to-be for the benefit of whoever is watching."

"I do but not with the sexual implications."

At first Rachael thought he didn't like her remarks because he was embarrassed by them; but when he looked at her, she realized it was because there was no hope of consummating them.

"Dr. Zamora, I'm Mr. Temple. How can I help you today?"

"This is going to sound very strange, but please hear me out and, please, pretend you're showing us the items in the case."

"I don't understand, Sir."

"I know you don't because I haven't explained anything yet, but our lives depend on your helping us. We're being followed, but we don't know by whom."

"Let me call security right away." Temple made an attempt to walk away.

Alex tried to keep his voice down and pretended to look at the diamonds in the case. "No, don't do that. They'd never get her."

"I thought you said you didn't know who it is?" Now Temple started to wonder what kind of game these two were playing.

"We don't know for sure, but we do suspect someone specific. Just wait a minute. I'm going to write down a phone number for Police Detective Archer. He's in charge of this case. As nonchalantly as possible excuse yourself and send someone else to help us. Give the Detective this message. It's short: if I write down too much, she'll know something's wrong."

Temple was having a hard time believing the man. He hadn't been robbed in a long time, but it was always the weird people who seemed to lend themselves to that outcome. He would have expected anything from these two, but the mention of Detective Archer gave them some credibility.

"So what's the message?"

"Tell him who you are and that you are calling for Rachael and Alex. Then read this. 'We're being followed; come right away. We'll wait here.' And don't start looking out the door. This person's no fool, and she's extremely dangerous."

Temple still had his doubts, but he'd play along by at least making the call. The first call he'd make, however, would be to the central police station to see if a Detective Archer really existed. "Carol, please go out and keep an eye on those two. I'm calling the police. For Heaven's sake, don't show them any of the good stuff."

"Police Department. May I help you?"

"Do you have a Detective Archer there?"

"Well, he works here, but he isn't here right now. He's out on a case."

"Could you please tell me if he's working with a Dr. Zamore?"

"Who the hell is this?" The officer demanded. This case was too important and too confidential for someone to just call in with random questions. Archer would have his ass if he gave out any information especially to some reporter.

After Temple gave the officer the message from Alex, he got a curt response letting him know how wrong he had been about Rachael and Alex. "Holy shit, Man. Tell them Archer will be there in five minutes."

Temple put the phone down and leaned back in his chair for a moment. He wasn't quite ready to face the man he'd suspected of robbery especially since that man had probably already felt the insult of suspicion.

"Sir, may I help you with something while Mr. Temple's on the phone?"

"Yes, we'd like to look at diamond engagement rings."

"Certainly. There are some very nice ones in this window."

"Don't you have anything bigger than that?"

"Well, yes, but those stones are not mounted. You pick the stone first and then the mounting."

"I see. Then may we look at the stones." The girl was starting to fidget. Alex knew something was wrong.

"I think I should wait for Mr. Temple. He likes to be the one to show the larger diamonds."

"Mr. Temple didn't believe me. Did he even call the police like I asked?"

"Oh yes. He said he was calling the police department."

Alex was furious. The affront to him and Rachael was despicable. Alex's face turned red as he leaned over the counter. "You tell that son-of-a-bitch to call Victoria's Secret and see how much I spent there. Then, I hope he has a hell of a nice day!"

Alex took Rachael by the arm, and they walked out of the store. Temple saw them leave and knew he should've tried to stop them, but Carol, anxious to deliver the message word for word, caught him. He picked up the phone just to satisfy his curiosity. Within a flash the phone was smashed down on the counter. Carol smiled when she heard, "Only a jerk would spend that much on underwear!"

Alex took Rachael into the next jewelry store they came to. He was still incensed by the indignity of being suspected of thievery.

"Alex, wait. Take a deep breath and think about what you're going to do."

"Let's look for just a minute. I need to collect my thoughts. I don't know if Archer will even get the message, so we have to assume that we're on our own."

"As long as we stay in the mall with people around, she can't do anything. Let's give Archer ten or fifteen minutes to get here. I hate to run if we have the slightest chance of getting her."

"I agree. So lets buy some expensive jewelry. I want that asshole Temple to regret the day he suspected me of being a burglar."

Within seconds a clerk came over to help them. Alex would not make the same mistake twice and simply played the part of the man in love, not the man wanting help to save his life.

"Yes, I want to buy the biggest diamond you have for my fiance."

"How exciting for you, Ma'am. Please step over here." Alex knew nothing about buying diamonds and didn't like feeling as if he was at the mercy of one clerk's sales pitch. After looking at several stones and discussing color and cleavage until he was totally confused, he admitted he would have to compare prices and quality. The truth was that after five minutes, he realized he couldn't concentrate on what the clerk was telling them.

"We'd like to see some of your other pieces though. Why don't you give us about ten minutes to look around and then we'll tell you what we want to purchase." Alex put a little too much emphasis on purchase, but only Rachael knew why.

"Are you sure that's enough time, Sir?"

"That's all we have."

"Rachael, if you see anything you like, please tell me; or I will pick something out myself."

"Alex, are you sure about this?"

"Yes, the bigger the better. I want Temple to wallow in his mistake."

"He was only trying to protect his store."

"He was a sniveling little weasel."

"Alex, I've never seen you act so irrationally. It becomes you. The red face, bad language, even revenge. Wow! I'm impressed."

Now he smiled at her as the humor made his anger dissipate. She could always do it: make him laugh at himself. "I see your point. Now do you prefer rubies or emeralds?"

"I have always wanted a diamond pendent with matching earrings."

"When I buy you diamonds, I want to know what I am getting is the right cut and color for the money. We'll shop again after I get more information. Today, however, you have to pick something that's in the case."

"Really, Alex, there are plenty of diamonds in the case that look fine to me."

"I will pick out the diamonds another time. Now help me find something for the girls."

"You pick out what you want. You have excellent taste. Surprise me like you did in Victoria's Secret even though I won't know what the surprise is until we get home."

"That's a great idea. I'd love to." Alex walked around the cases several times with Rachael and the clerk talking about different stones and cuts. Rachael constantly stole looks through the mall entrance to see if she could detect anyone standing around.

The feeling of being watched had ended when they'd left the other store. It was going on fifteen minutes, and Rachael was beginning to believe Archer had never gotten the message. What she didn't know was that several plain clothed officers were watching her and everyone else in the place.

"Okay, I've made up my mind. First of all, do you take American Express?"

"Absolutely, Sir."

Alex pointed to several items in the various cases. He was truly enjoying himself. Rachael was curious as to what he'd picked out, but the majority of her pleasure was watching him shop. He was the epitome of the kid in the candy shop. After the items were each wrapped and placed in a bag, Alex signed the charge receipt. Rachael tried to peak over his should, but he wouldn't let her. He knew she would complain about the money, and he just didn't want to hear her fuss about it.

"Before we leave, would you do me one last favor?"

"Of course, Sir, anything you need." Rachael thought it was a pretty stupid question considering this girl had just sold more in twenty minutes than she probably did in a month. Rachael had the mental image of a woman running naked down the street, but figured that wouldn't be Alex's request.

"I would like you to call this man and tell him how much I just spent in your store because you were so nice to us."

"It would be my pleasure, Sir. Have a nice day."

Temple was still sitting in his office when the phone rang. Carol watched him place the phone down again and shake his head. "Jesus, Mary and Joseph! It's always the weird ones who screw up my day."

Alex and Rachael stopped in to pick up their earlier purchases. It took both of them to carry all the bags. Alex had carefully placed all of the jewelry in his inside jacket pockets or in Rachael's purse. He wanted to make sure they were safe. As they walked out of the mall entrance, Archer met them.

"Jesus, Archer, you sure took your sweet time getting here."

"What are you talking about? We've had the entrances sealed off for the last fifteen minutes and dozens of plain clothes in the mall."

"Really, we didn't see anyone."

"That was the idea."

Rachael and Alex felt sheepish about their assumption that Archer had not shown up. Alex was the one who offered a verbal explanation. "I'm sorry. We didn't know if Temple had even called in the message. He was such an..."

"Irritating man." Rachael jumped in.

"No, he was an asshole, Rachael. He wouldn't help his own mother if the axe murderer was chasing her down the street. Did you find anyone?"

"No, nothing. She had probably seen enough to fire her fury and left before you could spot her."

"Archer, who's at the house?" Rachael asked worriedly.

"What, at the house? Two officers are there watching the place."

"Alex, let's go; I'm worried about Ginger."

"Mrs. Carson, Ginger is, for all practical purposes, an officer of the department. She knows her job."

"I'm still worried about her."

Alex knew enough about Rachael's intuition not to delay by trying to understand her reasoning. "Let's go." He hurried to the car with Rachael on his heels.

It was a twelve minute drive home when the traffic was good and all the lights favorable; but with Archer leading the way, a good five minutes were chopped off the time. Rachael was the first one to the door after they pulled into the driveway.

"Ginger, Ginger, where are you?" There was no dog. There was no Ginger anywhere in the house. The only thing they found was the message scrawled in red lipstick on the bathroom mirror. It said,

"Rachael, you are making this too easy for me." Consternation filled her body again as she stood in the middle of her bathroom. Alex was the next one to arrive on the scene. When he saw Rachael standing there, he knew Heather had been in the house again.

"Archer! Get in here."

Archer rounded the corner within seconds. He had been searching the upstairs for Ginger, but there wasn't a trace of anything. "What? Did you find the dog?"

"No. Another message. How in the hell does she keep getting in?"

"I have no fucking idea, no fucking idea. It's like she's a ghost coming and going whenever she wants."

Alex was fuming, "She may be a demon, Archer, but there's a reason to explain her comings and goings. I think it's about time we find out, don't you? I'll call that security guy and tell him to get his carcass over here because no one is leaving until we get some answers. Rachael, let's get you out of here."

Her feet were stuck in concrete, but the determination not to be beaten by this crazy woman gradually brought Rachael back to her senses. "I think it's safe to assume I have taken over the honorable position of being her primary target. Don't you, Archer."

"Yes, Mrs. Carson. You may have been the real target all the time. I never gave credence to all the possibilities in the beginning."

Alex was quick to jump on the admission. "So, in other words, if you had taken us seriously from the start, we might not be in so deep now."

"Who knows at this point. We still haven't even found anyone who can say it's your wife."

"Archer, the woman is not my wife. Don't refer to her in that way again. It might say that on paper, but I find it insulting to be linked to her in any way other than 'ex'. Is that clear? Now, what if we moved Rachael out of the house?"

"No, Alex. I won't let her chase me out of my own home. Besides, I don't want to start all over. This is where the ultimate show down will be, in this room."

Archer's doubting nature showed for the last time, "How do you know that? It could happen anywhere. If we move you to a more controlled environment..."

"She'd wait until I gave up and came home. Think about it. This is the only room in the house that's been violated."

"No, she did the car and the office."

Rachael shook her head, "No, it will be here in this room."

"Com'on, Mrs. Carson, how do you know? Woman's intuition or something?"

Rachael didn't say a word, but Alex did. "Archer, don't be a jerk. I trust her intuition more than all of your officers at this point. At least, so far, she's the only one who's been right about anything."

"All right, you stay here, but I want a minimum of three officers in here at all times, and SHE is never alone." He looked at Rachael to make sure she understood his statement was a command not a request. The frustration was evident in everyone's tone. Alex still couldn't believe the woman he'd been married to for nine years had enough smarts to get by all the police and the security. Alex took Rachael out to the patio while the police, once again, started combing through the house. Something had to be there.

"Rachael, tell me what you know about your system. Somehow she's getting past it. Now, Heather's no brain surgeon, hah, neither am I for that matter."

Rachael smiled at him. "See, you can make me smile too when I'm upset."

"I learned from the best. Now, like I was going to say, there has to be some rather simple way for her to bypass the system."

"Let's see. Only the downstairs is wired since most burglars don't scale walls; there are no motion detectors because we used to have a cat. Maybe we should have the motions detectors put in."

"That might help. What else?"

"Well, if any of the doors or windows are opened while the system is armed, the siren goes off and the monitoring company gets a signal."

"How's it hooked up to send the signal?"

"It goes through the telephone wires which are buried underground so no one can cut them. If they were cut, the company would detect the interruption and call us or send out the police."

"What else? How about if a window is broken rather than opened?"

"Oh my God, Alex. I never thought of that. But the system would not detect a broken window. Do you really think?"

"I don't know, but we'll find out." Alex went off to tell Archer what to look for. Rachael was left sitting in the sun trying to put together the pieces of the puzzle. There must be something they'd missed. The violence had made a steady progression from simple and relatively harmless stalking to murder. It won't get better until they catch her. "Paper, I need some paper and my journal. I know something isn't right." In spite of her effort, Rachael could not find any clues in her memory of events; nevertheless, she hung on to the notes she'd made. Something would come to her. It was hard to concentrate with all of the motion around the windows. Each one was being checked two or three times. She was almost ready to give up hope that anything would be found when Alex yelled for her.

"Rachael, we found it." Instantly, she dropped the pen and ran to the sun room entrance where Alex's voice had come from.

"What, which window?" It had to be a window. That's all they had been looking at for the last hour.

The window in the sun room had been cut out so it could be easily removed. A tacky glue had been put on the edges to hold it precariously in place. The plants on either side of the pane concealed it from view and offered extra support to keep it from falling out. After the pane was removed, it was easy to get inside the rest of the house via Rachael's bedroom.

"Archer, double check all of the windows. This may not be the only one."

"It's already being done. Just to be on the safe side, I still don't want, Mrs. Carson to be left alone. Agreed?" He looked directly at her and waited for a response.

"I agree, but please give the bathroom area a good check because there I insist on some privacy."

"It will be secured." Rachael hated all that haughty police talk. Archer was feeling pretty confident right now, but there was still a long way to go. He certainly was taking a lot of credit since it had been she and Alex who'd figured out what to look for.

"Archer, do you have any idea what happened to Ginger?"

"No, there were no traces of her. Any suggestions?"

He turned away from her before hearing an answer. There were several things to take care of, and he really didn't care if she had any ideas or not. He never had put much stock in woman's intuition or feelings. The facts of a case told him everything he needed to know. If he had the facts, everything fell into place. Putting too much stock, or any faith in a woman's intuition, made his police work look weak.

Archer, you ass. At some point I'll have my chance to tell you what I think about your arrogant chauvinism. Alex caught her eye and smiled. He knew exactly what she wanted to do and waited with great anticipation for the day when she'd put the man in his place.

Rachael was glad when the last officer left her house, except for the three who had drawn the night watch. She wouldn't have much privacy until this was all over, but it really did seem safer with them in the house. Alex ordered some pizza for everyone and took Rachael a glass of wine. They sat on the patio staring into the garden for several minutes. It had been an exhausting day. The security guy finally showed up to do a check on the system. He had agreed that everything was in tact, and it must have been the window which allowed entrance.

"The security man was a lot of help, wasn't he?"

"I wonder if all of them are so inept when it comes to detecting a trespass to their system. You'd think there would only be so many things to look for, and they'd target those possibilities."

"I know. He kept trying to suggest it was our imagination. He kept insisting that his system had never been violated."

"I guess you never know how good your system is or the company unless someone breaks into your house. I do remember him saying when he installed it that if a person wants into a house bad enough, he'll find a way."

"Well, I'll give him credit, he was right about something. I have some work I want to do tonight, Rachael. Do you mind if I sit here?"

"Of course not. Would you like some help."

"No, I have to make some notes about a couple of my cases. I'm still a doctor, ya know. I've brought all of your purchases in and put them in your room. The jewelry we bought is in my room. Do you have any place where we can hide it?"

"I forgot about that. I sure don't want it setting around with so many people in and out of the house. Let me think about it." Rachael realized they had to be careful of what they said because ears were everywhere now that officers were staying in the house. There would be no more intimacy between them, but then there hadn't been much to begin with.

Rachael looked at the man sitting next to her. The wonderful dancing eyes had once again been replaced by the deep shadows signifying heavy thoughts. She wished she could read his mind. On the other hand, she could ask.

"Alex, what are you thinking about?"

"Why do you ask?"

"You look serious. What's up?"

"I was thinking about one of my patients." He didn't offer anymore information because he didn't think she would care.

"Yes, so what's wrong?"

He looked at her in earnest hoping her question was from legitimate concern and not the desire to just make small talk. "I'm supposed to operate next week, but I'm afraid my concentration might be impaired by everything that's happening here."

"I take it this is more than just a routine operation if there can be such a thing."

Again the surprise. Heather never wanted him to talk about his work. She found it gruesome and disgusting. "Yes, it's very delicate, and even though all surgeries are unique, this one's going to be more difficult."

"So what are the specifics in layman's terms?"

"My patient is a thirteen year old girl with a tumor on her left ovary. It's unusually large and wrapped around the blood vessels. If I leave any of it, it will grow back. If I cut to much, she may never be able to have children."

"That would be hard for a young woman to face. So much of our self image is based on whether or not we can have children. Even if we choose not to, the option's still there. She can't wait a little longer?"

"That's part of the problem; the parents waited until school was out thinking it would be better to deal with the recovery during the summer, but in reality it just allowed the tumor time to grow seriously large."

"What if you stayed at the hospital the night before, would that help your concentration?"

"I doubt it. I'd worry about you all night."

"What if I stayed there too?"

"Would you do that?"

"Of course. This little girl's life shouldn't be screwed up because of us. I'll even stay in your office rather than insisting on a private room with you."

"Oh, thanks a lot. I'm sure we could request a room with a king size bed and a view."

"Okay, then it's settled. Any other cases you need help with?"

"Thank you for understanding how important this is."

"Alex, I work there too, remember? Those kids are like my own."

He knew she was genuine in her concern which made him even more convinced that his next step was the right one. "Did you and Jack build this house?"

"Wow! That was a complete change of direction. No, it was partially finished. I was able to make a few changes, but not many. I did, however, pick out the colors and fixtures."

"Who did the decorating?"

"I did all of it. This house is mine, an extension of myself. I used to clean it everyday while the girls and Jack just got out of the way."

"Rachael, you still clean everyday, and we still get out of the way."

"Yeah, it's just so natural now, like brushing my teeth."

"Is there anything you would change if you could?"

"Sure, a few things like the girl's bath and the guest bath need to be bigger. You can barely turn around in them."

"I can vouch for that. Anything else."

"Nothing major. More closets would be nice and a bigger utility room."

"What if you could build a new house from the bottom up? What would you do differently?"

"Only one major change besides the ones I already mentioned. I've always wanted a full circular staircase that opened up onto a landing where I could set up my office. I want a vaulted ceiling and big windows which overlook the garden."

"Now let me add one more element to that, and think about it before you go nuts because I am serious. What if Mark was living with you?"

"Damn you, Alex. You set me up; played me like a grand piano, and I fell for it. I'm going to have to be more careful. Your innocent conversation and leading questions can be dangerous."

"Yes, my dear. How does it feel? I am still waiting for an answer."

Rachael had to think for a minute. "Well, if Mark's with me, then you're not. Right?"

"Brilliant. But you're stalling."

"Not really, I'm thinking. The girls and I are living on healthy but limited means now. If Mark was with us, we would do the guest room and bath over as his. I wouldn't move to another house."

"Now tell me what you'd do for living arrangements if I was staying with you while I was sick."

"Alex, can't we wait until we know for sure before we start making those kinds of plans?"

"I would rather know what my plans are before the results come. It makes a difference to me. What would be the best living arrangement as opposed to the most logical?"

Reluctantly, Rachael started to calculate the possibilities. "Well, I come up with three options. First, we all live together as a family under one roof. Unconditional love, through 'sick and thin'."

"Oh, Rachael, that was a terrible use of English for a teacher."

"Yes, but you get my point. The second option, would be for you and Mark to be with us, but you could have separate living quarters so when the illness got bad, you could have some privacy."

"And be left alone? At one time that's what I would have chosen, but thanks to you and the girls, I no longer wish to make that choice."

"Then I guess your third option is to live here with us. We'll give Mark the guest room and turn the game room into a suite for you."

"You must think I'm going brain dead already. All three of those options are identical; you just worded it differently three times."

Without intending to, that's exactly what she'd done. "Hah. I guess I did."

"Don't sound so innocent."

"Really, I didn't do it on purpose. How long have you guys been here? Almost two months. It seems like a lifetime."

"Thanks. Is that anything like comfortable?"

"In a way, I suppose it is. I just can't imagine living without the two of you. Our lives have become so..."

"Tangled?"

"I was looking for something with more positive connotation."

"It doesn't matter how you wrap the thought, Rachael, it means the same."

"You brought the topic up, you must have had some thoughts. How do you suggest we handle the living arrangements?"

"I don't know yet, but I wanted to hear your side before I made a final decision."

"Alex, are you really working on hospital files?"

"Why?"

"I was wondering why you have a pad of paper but no file."

"Besides making a decision about the surgery, I am making a list of things I have to do Monday. With all of the confusion around here, I have trouble remembering to do the necessary things at work. It can be very embarrassing."

"What do you have to do?" Rachael was sure he had something up his sleeve. Alex was so predictable. He'd never forget anything work related. This mess might be having some impact on his thinking, but she doubted he was being completely honest.

"Com'on, Alex, what's really on your mind? You were a crazy man shopping today, and now you are making lists of things to do. It's all out of character. We're living together, talking about a future together, however long it might be; but for all we know, we may die together tonight. So, for Heaven's sake, tell me what's on your mind."

She was right. They could play the word games, but at some point the games had to stop. "Rachael, I am going to have some changes made to my will. I want to make you the executrix of my estate as well as Mark's guardian. I am setting up trust funds for Mark and each of the girls."

"Why, Alex? You know I'll take care of Mark."

"I know, and that's why I want to make sure you know how much I appreciate it."

"I'll accept that Mark should have a trust fund, but the girls already have one from their father."

"Now they'll each have one more. It's my money, and I want to do this."

"Will you and Mark stay with us?" Alex could tell the question was straight from her heart, but he wasn't sure how he should answer it.

"For Mark's sake, I would like to. It would be okay for awhile, but the end is hard."

"Alex, you're assuming the worst. Do you know something you haven't told me?"

"No, it's just that if I cover the worst possible scenario, anything else will be easy to deal with."

"I see. In that case, Mark should be with you as long as possible, and you shouldn't be alone. We'll make the necessary arrangements."

"Will it bother you to live with a man you're not married to?"

"Jesus, Alex, why do you have to ask me this now?"

"Because I want to know now. The test results could be back as early as Monday, and I want to know what to do."

"What are you going to do with the other house?"

"It's bigger than this one; we could move in there. I don't really like that idea. I'd rather stay here or build a brand new house for all of us. Don't worry, I have plenty of money to build and pay for anything you want."

"I don't know what to say. What do you want?"

"I want you to answer my earlier question."

"You want me to spill all my feelings out on the table for you to sift through and pick out the ones you like." Rachael wasn't sure if she could tell him the truth. She knew he had seen the love in her eyes, but she doubted if he had recognized what he saw. She might have only one chance to be honest. The walls were down now; but if he got up and walked away before this was resolved, there may never be another opportunity. He was worth it. She mentally reached down inside of herself for the little black box that had all of her emotions locked safely away.

Rachael took a deep breath deciding to bare her soul. "I love you. I have loved you, Alex, ever since Easter Sunday when you so graciously played along with our children's plan. I love you in spite of your murderous wife, in spite of the HIV, and in spite of your arrogant, love starved self."

He hadn't expected quite that much honesty and just stared at her. What could he say?

"To answer your question about living together, I think you know the answer. We're living together now, and we aren't married."

"The conditions are special, but eventually, things will return to some resemblance of normalcy. Then what?"

"The kids will get teased at school. Rorie and Allison are old enough to take it, but Mark might be more sensitive. On the other hand, they all want us to be together so badly, maybe it won't matter."

"Will it matter to you?"

Alex could feel her touch his heart, and he knew the answer to the question. He reached out to take her hand, "Rachael, I'm asking so much of you and the girls. Please think about what you're committing to."

"The commitment was made. We both tried to fight it, but it was made for us."

"If you agree, I think it would be best if we got married as soon as I can arrange for a divorce."

"Wow! You'd better think about what you're saying. This isn't a business arrangement. If the only reason you're saying this is for Mark's protection, then it's the wrong reason."

"Rachael, I cannot offer you a full marriage. You know that, but it would make the transfer of guardianship and property easier."

Rachael pulled her hand away from his. "Stop. I don't want to hear how practical it would be. Tell me how you feel. What's in your heart, Alex?"

"Do you know how bad it will be when the end comes? I can't offer you more than I already have."

"Why do men always think sex is so important to a relationship. I swear you all have your brains stuck in your zippers. Intimacy is only one part of the union and not necessarily the most important part. Alex, I want all of you: your heart, your soul, your mind. The sex part is the icing on the cake not the meat and potatoes. I have lived all of my life on a diet, so why should this be any different."

"That's not enough for me."

"Why did you ask how I felt if all you wanted was a business contact. You offered that much before suggesting marriage and before I bared my soul. I don't want your money or a different house; put it all in a trust for Mark. I'll be sure he gets it. Shit, no wonder Heather went ballistic on you." At that point, there was nothing left to say. She had striped herself emotionally naked in front of him, and he had thrown it back at her. Rachael stood up and headed for the house.

Alex wanted to say something, anything that would mend the rift he had caused; but he couldn't give her what she wanted. He jerked his head up when the door slammed. The officer who had been sitting by the door looked at him curiously. The poor guy would have been much better off if he had kept his mouth shut.

"Women can really be a pain, huh, Doc?"

"Oh, eat shit and die!" Alex stormed past him slamming the door again for his own satisfaction.

Angry eyes had been watching the two of them through binoculars for several minutes. The rage hit a crescendo when Alex reached out for Rachael's hand and the binoculars were thrown against the wall. Had the killer waited for only a brief moment, the fight that ended the hand holding would have certainly eased the raging volcano which was near eruption.

Since Rachael's bedroom was her only sanctuary, that's where she headed. It was ironic that she felt this would be the place of the final battle, and yet it was the only place the men would let her be alone. The bags of new lingerie, which were setting on her bed, she moved to the closet. The room was messy from being mauled by the police, so she set her mind and body to cleaning. It was the mental respite she needed from everything, especially Alex.

After several hours, Alex had to go and check on her or one of the policemen would. Even though she was mad at him, he felt Rachael would rather have him look in on her than a stranger. He knocked lightly on the door, but there was no answer. Quietly he turned the knob and looked around the corner. Rachael had fallen asleep with a book in her hands. Alex picked up the book and covered her with a blanket. *I do love you, Rachael; I just can't tell you. It wouldn't be fair.* He leaned over to kiss her lightly on the cheek before leaving the room.

Alex and the officers checked and rechecked the doors and windows to make sure everything was securely locked for the night. Even though the window had been replaced, Alex was still skeptical about the vulnerability of the house and specifically Rachael.

When he went to her room this time, he had a pillow and blanket with him. Slowly he walked into the room so as not to wake her. The lounge would be his bed for the night. Earlier in the evening, the officers had flipped a coin to see who got the bedroom duty with Rachael, but Alex had quickly put a stop to their over eager desire to spend the night watching her. If anyone was going to sleep in Rachael's bedroom, it was going to be him. As he tried to get comfortable, he watched Rachael sleeping and realized it had been jealousy that brought him in here. He hadn't recognized the green monster at first, but that's what caused him to jump on Peter, the officer who had suggested the flip of the coin. All three of them volunteered for the duty, but Alex was the one with the last say.

For several hours Alex pondered over the disastrous conversation he'd had with Rachael. His good intentions had gone all wrong, and now she was further away then ever. Maybe Debbie could help him convince her to accept the proposal even if it wasn't romantically perfect. It would serve both of those meddling females if he turned the cards on them playing them against each other instead of against him.

Alex must have dropped off to sleep because he didn't notice Rachael starting to toss and turn. It was the heart stopping scream which brought him to his feet and Rachael's bedside. Her arms were reaching up and trying to strike at something. The nightmare was ravaging her again.

"Rachael, wake up. Rachael!" Alex grabbed her by the shoulders, but her thrashing arms broke his grip.

"Let go of her, or I'll shoot!"

"What?" Alex couldn't believe his ears, but when he turned around there was Peter with his revolver drawn and pointed at him.

"Put your arms up! Hurry up you guys. He was trying to kill her."

"Jesus Christ, Peter, she's only dreaming."

"Yeah, right. That's why you had your hands around her neck."

"You wake her up then."

"I'll check her when the others get here; she looks dead to me, you son-of-a-bitch. You sure had us fooled. We all thought you two were in love."

"We are, you ass."

Rachael still had not moved. The deathlike dream trance still held onto her subconscious. Alex remembered it had taken her several minutes to come out of the dream state before. If he could keep this jerk from shooting him for a few more minutes, Rachael would bring herself out of it.

"Peter, what's going on in here?"

"Quick, check her. This bastard tried to kill her."

One of the other officers went to check Rachael whose shallow breathing was barely detectable. "She's breathing. Mrs. Carson, are you okay? Go call an ambulance." The third officer left the room.

There was no answer and no movement. "What was he doing to her?"

"Choking her. When I came in he had his hands around her throat."

"I was trying to wake her up!"

"Shut up or I'll shoot you just for the pleasure of it."

A deep moan from Rachael finally caught their attention. Alex was relieved that she was finally starting to come around and would help to clear him. Alex put his arms down and watched with the men as the eyes fluttered open.

"Mrs. Carson, are you okay?"

"Alex what's going on?"

Before Alex could answer her, Peter jumped in, "I heard you scream and came in here to find him standing over you with his hands around your neck."

"Rachael, you were dreaming. Tell them before they shoot me."

Rachael rubbed her throat which was the psychosomatic response to the dream. "I was dreaming again, wasn't I?"

"Yes, can you tell me about it?"

That was enough to make the men put their guns away and Peter feel like a fool. "I think I'll cancel the ambulance."

"Yeah, you better tell Archer too because he'll have been notified that a call came from this location. Jesus, Peter, can't you tell the difference between a nightmare and the real thing."

"Better safe than sorry," was all that Peter said as he left the room, but he did feel just a little asinine.

Now Alex could sit down beside Rachael and make sure she was fine. "Can I get you anything?"

"No. I just want a minute to collect myself. Did Peter really think you were trying to kill me?"

"Oh, yes. There was no doubt in my mind that he was very serious. Now what about the dream. Was it me?"

"No, it wasn't you. I still don't know who or why, but it wasn't you."

"How do you know?"

"There is something different. Hand me my journal. I need to log this with the rest."

Alex bent over to get the book out of the night stand. "You didn't log the dream from last night, did you?"

"No, I don't remember much. I was drugged thanks to you."

"Yes, you were and I enjoyed it."

Rachael could feel her cheeks get red under his gaze. "How much could I have done in my sleep?"

"I'll never tell. Now would you like to change? You never did get undressed."

"I suppose."

"Would you like a cup of tea or a brandy?"

"A cup of tea sounds best, thanks." Alex turned to leave the room and heard her add, "Alex, just tea this time, please."

"Of course." He smiled to himself as he went toward the kitchen. Then he wondered if she would really trust him to bring her just tea.

Rachael put the journal down and looked through one of the bags until she found a new night gown. It was purple silk and had a matching robe which she also pulled out. For a moment, she thought about digging for the red satin, but he didn't deserve that not after being such a turkey earlier. *In fact, he deserved the scare Peter gave him.* She smiled at herself as she donned the new, elegant gown. This one was her favorite. Then she took off the day's make-up and brushed her hair.

Alex was back with her cup of tea before she had finished her bedtime ritual, and he enjoyed catching the finishing touches. The purple was exquisite on her. It covered her shoulders but left no doubt about the fullness of the breasts. His eyes roamed downward not able to miss the spot where the tuft of womanly hair pushed out slightly on the silk. He would definitely have to rethink about which gown was his favorite. On the other hand, he was beginning to think he was safer with her in cotton because as his eyes grazed on her body, his own desires began to rise. *Dear God, am I destined to live a life of frustrated desire followed by cold showers.* Alex wasn't sure if he could walk away from her without the extent of his desires being obvious, so he just stood there.

"Here's your tea." Alex set the cup on the night stand and the returned to the bathroom door.

"Thank you, so do you like your purchase?" Rachael knew his eyes had made a slow journey up and down her body, and she was glad he seemed to appreciate the view.

"Yes, I do."

"You were sleeping in here? Why?"

"It's dangerous for you to be in here alone all night; so when the guys started to flip a coin to determine who would win the midnight watch with you, I told them I was the only one who was going to be in this room all night." Alex was still standing by the bathroom door waiting for his desires to become less obvious, but Rachael had stopped right in front of him. Her soft alluring fragrance nearly driving him out of control.

"I see. Are you going to stay the rest of the night?"

"It's either me or one of them; take your pick."

"I pick you, but it's silly for you to try to sleep in that chair. Really, Alex, the bed is plenty big enough for both of us to get a good night's sleep and not even touch each other."

"Sure, Rachael. I think I'd rather sleep with a she-wolf. It would be less dangerous."

"If that's the way you feel then get out. Peter..."

"What are you doing?"

"Getting someone who will be more agreeable."

"Not dressed like that, you won't."

"You turned me down, so what I do is none of your business."

"Rachael, no one is going to see you dressed that way but me. Do you understand me?"

"I understand you are being very possessive of something that's not yours."

"Well, I paid for it, so it's mine." At that point, Alex reached up, took the purple silk in one hand and with a single motion, it was off her body and in his hand.

"Get out! You have no right to treat me this way. I should have worn the red satin."

Alex exited the room with the purple silk hanging from his hand leaving Rachael naked and miserably alone. *I'll replace my silk gown myself, tomorrow! I am not going to cry. The son-of-a-bitch doesn't deserve it.* But the tears came anyway.

Alex stomped down the hallway into the kitchen and threw the torn silk into the trash. Peter was on his way to see what Rachael wanted and couldn't miss the fury on Alex's face.

Their eyes met, and Peter reacted first. "I know, eat shit and die."

"Sorry about that. It's just that she can be so irritating. I'm going to spend a fortune in sleep wear and never have any of the pleasure. I guess you get the midnight watch."

"Does she bite?"

"Only me. You should be safe enough." Alex filled a brandy snifter and headed for his own room to lick his wounds.

"Hey, Pete?"

"Yeah, Sam?"

"Do you still think they're in love?"

"Oh, yeah. For sure. They just don't know it yet."

"Maybe they know it but won't admit it to each other. Pride can be a hell of a thing."

"Good night, Sam."

****

The next morning it was so cold at breakfast that even the rain forest would have frozen. The Titanic would have sunk again in the iceberg infested waters surrounding Alex and Rachael. Both of them chomped down the cereal trying to ignore the other. Rachael was the one to finally break down and force a very limited conversation.

"I'm going to church. Do you want to come, or should I take an officer with me?"

"Why do you have to go?"

"Because I need to go. To get some direction in my life, some strength. I need to be in touch with God."

"Why can't you pray at home?"

"It's not the same. You don't have to go. Make your own peace with God!" Rachael put her dishes away and left the room.

"Fine!" Alex yelled at her.

An hour later, Rachael walked into the kitchen dressed in a pretty hot pink suit. The short jacket was adorned by a silk scarf and gold pin. Her intent was to collect an officer as an escort for the morning. She was surprised to find Alex dressed and waiting for her at the door. He was afraid that if he hadn't been right there she'd have left him.

"Well I guess things are back to normal. We're fighting and play acting for the public. Are you ready, my dear?"

"I suppose I have no choice." Rachael reached up to take his arm. He walked her around to the passenger side of the car, opened the door and waited for her to get in.

Both Rachael and Alex were consumed with frustration, which led to a silent ride to church. Stubborn pride would not let either of them break the vow of silence. They walked into the church arm in arm, but emotionally they were miles apart.

"Rachael, Alex, it's so good to see you. It's been a few weeks."

"Oh, hi, Rev. Dan. The kids and I were at the beach on vacation for a while. How have you been?"

"I'm fine, thanks. Where are the children today? They're usually with you?"

"They went to Rachael's parents for a visit."

"I see. It's good for you two to have some time alone."

"Yes, we've enjoyed ourselves; haven't we, Rachael."

Rachael wanted to kick him in the shin. Rev. Dan didn't know anything about their situation. He had seen them nearly every Sunday since Easter sitting in the center of the fourth or fifth pew. Everybody who saw them assumed if they weren't a family already, they soon would be.

It was uncanny how the sermon seemed to be directed at them. Rachael was sure Rev. Dan was staring right at her as he talked about the dangers of pride, and how it could destroy relationships. "Throw down your pride and pick up the love of God; it can heal the aching heart."

As Alex walked out of the sanctuary, he said, "So, do you feel better?"

"I don't know. It seemed like he was staring at me the whole time. I don't know if I should feel guilty or forgiven."

"You? I thought he was staring at me."

"I suppose he was staring at both of us."

After they got in the car, Rachael put him on the spot. "Alex, what are you going to do with us if your test results are negative and you don't need a guardian for Mark? Please, don't answer until you're sure of what you are saying."

There was no answer.

"I understand. Things would be different. You don't need a business contract then."

"Yes, things would be different. You wouldn't feel sorry for me or the need to step in on Mark's behalf."

"I told you last night I fell in love with you before all this trouble started, so things wouldn't be all that different for me. You, however, wouldn't need me anymore. I guess I have a decision to make. Should I settle for the money, or do I hold out for the sex?"

"Damn, you, Heather." *Oh shit! I can't believe I said that. Maybe she didn't hear it.* Fat chance. Rachael was frozen by the insult. If he had slapped her, it wouldn't have stung half as much. Alex couldn't even look at her.

"Rachael, I'm so sorry. I didn't mean that."

"If our relationship is so bad you can't keep the two of us straight, it's better we find out now. Don't worry, I'll take care of Mark for you."

"Stop it! You're making me crazy. You know I love you. Why do you have to make me say it?"

"You may be in love, but you're scared to death of it. You're afraid your love will never be a perfect love. Well, there's no such thing. Every couple has problems to overcome. Some people are paraplegics; they still have a good life. Some have chronic illnesses, but still make happiness. Happiness is a state of mind you choose, not a gift someone gives you or owes you. You have to grow your own green grass, Alex, because it's never greener on the other side of the hill. It's easier for you to make excuses to stay out of a relationship than to fight for it."

"You don't know what you are talking about."

"You're like a turtle, Alex. You use that macho hard shell of arrogance to protect your soft underside of feelings. You're afraid to expose the heart and flesh of your inner self because you may get hurt again. Well, that's all part of the game. It takes feelings to have a good honest relationship; and if all you're going to give is the hard outer shell, then that's all you are going to get in return. I'll keep a contract with you to love and care for your son, but it will not be tied to a marriage. We'll stay in my house making due with the space we have there."

"Do you realize it could be years before you have a life back?"

"I'm not giving you my life, only a place to stay so you can be cared for and have your son around. You will be a boarder, and when the time comes we'll hire a nurse for you. I'll go on with my life, Alex."

"What in the hell does that mean?"

"I'll work, I'll go on vacation with all of the kids, and I'll date when I feel like it. You don't want to make a commitment to the family, so you won't be treated as part of the family."

"Now you've gone too far. That's not the way it was before."

"That's the way it is now. You want all of the good stuff without the bad. It just doesn't work that way. You take all or nothing."

Alex didn't say another word. There was nothing left to say. Part of what she had said was right. His desire to keep away from any physical bond in order to protect Rachael had also cut them off from the most valuable part of any union: the emotions. She had pretty much set the ultimatum: all or nothing.

Rachael headed for her bedroom when they got home. There were no more angry words or tears. It was time for her to take her own advice. Maybe the grass would never be green with Alex, but she would make her happiness with or without him; he would suffer the loss, not her. *He may stay here physically, but emotionally he has already left. I will not grieve for him. I will not.*

"Peter, are you my guardian for the day?"

"At least for now, Mrs. Carson."

"I need to run to the grocery store. Would you mind going with me?"

"Why don't you just make a list, and one of us will go for you. It would be safer that way."

"I'll stay home if you or Sam goes for me and if you stop at the mall to pick up a package for me."

"I have the funny feeling I was just set up?"

"Not really. I'm perfectly willing to go myself, but I was pretty sure you would offer to do it in order to keep me at home."

"Just write down what you need."

"Here's the list, the money, and the instructions for the package. It's already been paid for. Just ask for Lori when you go into the store."

"Mrs. Carson, who are you cooking for? I didn't know you were having people over."

"Pete, the steaks are for you guys. As long as you're giving up a Sunday to take care of us, the least we can do is give you a good meal."

"Really, that's not necessary. We eat lots of fast food on these stake outs. It's normal."

"It's my house and Sunday. The kids are gone, so you guys have to play the part of family. So get going. Can I go out by the pool?"

"Yeah, sure, there are plenty of guys outside to watch you."

"I'm counting on it, Peter. Now if you'll excuse me for a moment, I'm going to change."

He watched her as she closed the door of her bedroom wondering about her intent for the afternoon. He wasn't sure what their conversation meant, but he was glad he was on her side. *Dr. Zamora doesn't stand a chance; my money's on the woman.*

Rachael picked out a black and red one piece bathing suit with a low back and deep plunging V in the front. She pulled her hair up leaving a few curls hanging around her face and neck. Small gold earrings picked up the gold glitter that sparkled in the suit. It was going to be a beautiful day by the pool, and she planned to enjoy it with a cool drink and a good book.

Alex, in the mean time, took off his suit and replaced it with neatly pressed black pants and a stiff white shirt. He picked up the new medical journal and headed for the kitchen hoping Rachael had locked herself in her bedroom for the day.

Unfortunately, as he proceeded into the kitchen and glanced out the window, her movement on the patio caught his eye. Alex watched her smooth, glistening, lightly tanned body as she spread out the beach towel on the lounge. It dawned on him that her description of him had been right. The protective covering of long pants and starched shirt was part of his hard tortoise shell. He didn't even have shorts or swimming trunks. There was never a need. It wasn't necessary when most of his life had been spent in an operating room, and that had become like a hard shell too.

"Sam, where'd Pete go?"

"He went to the grocery store for Mrs. Carson."

"What'd she want?"

"He said she wanted steaks for dinner and a package from the mall."

"Sam, I'm going out for a while. I'll get one of the other guys to go along." Alex walked out the utility room door before Sam could agree or disagree. He got into his car and drove away.

CHAPTER NINETEEN

Alex was not sure where Debbie lived, so he called her from the mall. "Debbie, I need some help. Can I come over?"

"Of course. What's wrong?"

"I'll tell you later. By the way, where's a reputable place to buy diamonds?"

"I'll find someone." Debbie gave Alex the directions with an additional request to hurry.

Alex picked up several shopping bags and headed for the car. He was going to show Rachael he could shed the tortoise shell, at least part of it anyway, and Debbie was going to help him.

Within a few minutes, Alex pulled up in front of a beautiful white house not far from Rachael's. Debbie was standing between two white pillars waiting for him.

"Debbie, this is a wonderful porch."

"Stop with the small talk and tell me what's going on."

Alex walked up the six steps to stand on the huge porch which went across the front of the house and along each side to the back. "Last night I asked Rachael to marry me."

"That's wonderful. She's crazy about you."

"She may be crazy about me, but she said no."

"Why? I know she loves you."

"Well, I kind of told her marriage made it easier to transfer money and guardianship."

"Jesus, Alex, you are socially impotent."

"Is that what she said about me?"

"Yeah, I thought she was exaggerating at the time. How could you insult her that way."

"Oh, that isn't even the good part."

"It get's worse?"

"I really don't want to talk about it."

"No, you never do. Just hide in that shell of yours."

"Are you on my side or hers?"

"Neither and both, if that can make any sense."

"In a perverse womanly way, it does. Now are you going to help me or not?"

"How bad is it? Is there anything left to fix? Do you want to marry her?"

"Yes, I do."

"Why?"

"Damn it! You called her didn't you?"

"No I didn't. Should I have? If you only want to marry her for the sake of Mark, then don't do it. She'll take care of him. You can take care of all the legal papers before...Alex, did you get the results of that test already?"

"No. I was hoping to make some decisions ahead of time before my emotions got in the way."

"I'd say they're already in the way. Now tell me how bad it is."

"I ripped her silk nightgown off last night."

"Another one?"

"She told you about that? Oh well, it still gets worse. This morning when we were arguing, I accidently called her Heather "

"Did she throw you out?"

"No, she went home, put on a disgustingly sexy swimsuit and is parading around the backyard in front of the police."

"Sounds like you're little jealous."

"I am not. She's a grown woman. How can she do something like that?"

"Is it a string bikini? She has the figure. Why not? It's not like she was walking around the mall."

"It's a black and red one piece with little gold flecks."

"Alex, a one piece, in her own backyard? You're turning green, my friend. I'm impressed. I didn't know you had it in you."

"Are you going to help me or not? I'd like to call the hospital attorney. Do you think he'd help me on a Sunday?"

"Let's call him and find out. If nothing else, he'll give us the name of someone who will."

Alex followed Debbie into the house toward the office. She handed him the phone and then dialed the number.

"Hello, Tom? This is Alex Zamora."

"Alex, what's up?"

"I'm sorry to bother you on Sunday afternoon, but I really need your help."

"I'll try. Do you want to come over here?"

"Let me tell you what I need first. Is there some legal way for me to arrange an annulment from my first marriage? I tried to get my wife to sign divorce papers while she was in prison, but she wouldn't do it. Do I have any options at all?"

"I'm not sure, but let me check into it. I'll try to let you know tomorrow. Anything else?"

"I want to make some additions to my will. I have everything written down for you."

"Why the urgency?"

"As soon as I can get the legal stuff taken care of, I'm getting married?"

"Congratulations. To Rachael, I presume?"

"Yes, but please don't say anything to her. I want it to be a surprise."

Debbie added, "Oh, it's going to be a surprise, all right."

Alex threw her a frown. "Sh."

"Sure, Alex. I understand. If I can get anything today about the annulment, I'll call you at home. Are you at Rachael's?"

"Yeah, thanks, Tom. I really appreciate this. Good-bye." Alex hung up the phone.

"When are you going to tell Rachael that you are still going to marry her?"

"Probably as I am dragging her to the alter."

"You still haven't told me why."

"Because I love her, damn it! Because I love her."

"Did you tell her that?"

"She doesn't believe me. She said I treat her like a comfortable old slipper or something silly like that."

"Do you?"

"I don't know. She makes me so crazy."

"That's good. You've always been so...so"

"So stiff."

"Yeah, I guess that's it. She's good for you, Alex. So what were you doing at the mall?"

"Buying shorts, swimming trunks, casual shirts and shoes."

"Radical move, Alex. Can you handle it?"

"I'm going to try. Do you have any other advice?"

"Well, yes. Stop ripping off her night gowns unless you're planning to do something with the opportunity."

"I can't do anything. Not until that damn test gets back."

"Kiss her, Alex. Let her know how you feel. You have to make her want you to stay. Are you still going to try to get married before the results come in?"

"That was my original plan. I thought it would show her I wasn't afraid to make the commitment to her and the kids. Now she believes it's only because I need her; and if the test comes back negative, I can go on to shorter skirts or something like that."

"And is she right?"

"Of course not. I want to spend my last days with her whether its one or one thousand."

"Have you told her that?"

"No. Which reminds me. I need to know about diamonds."

"Com'on, my neighbor's a dealer. He can tell you whatever you want to know. We're going to meet him at his shop."

"Can I trust him?"

"I've known him for many years. He's a good, fair man. Every piece of fine jewelry I have bought over the years, I've bought from Leroy."

Leroy spent almost three hours showing Alex how to shop for fine gems. It was a great education. He realized he'd made some good choices the day before and some bad. Leroy told him to take the bad ones back. Before they said good-bye, Alex had picked out several wonderful pieces including a diamond pendant, matching earrings and a diamond ring for Rachael, which would be ready Monday afternoon.

On the way back to Debbie's house, Alex had to plan some strategy. "What can I do tonight that will soften her up?"

"Get out of those stiff clothes. Relax and, for Heaven's sake, don't talk about what happened today."

"Shouldn't I apologize?"

"Don't even bring it up. With you two, it's likely to end up in a fight. Try to laugh, talk about the kids, and stop ripping her clothes off!"

"Okay, that part's easy enough. Although it is becoming my trademark."

"Alex is making a joke. You're progressing, my friend. Did you replace the purple silk?"

"Well, kind of. When I went into Victoria's Secret, I found out someone had just bought all of the purple silk in her size. I think it was Rachael. That gown was her favorite. So I bought all of the gowns in her size that matched the robes we bought yesterday."

"You're both crazy."

"Maybe that's her way of admitting she's going to keep me around for awhile."

"I think it's her way of showing you how stubborn she can be. By the way, don't let the green monster show. Jealousy is a very unbecoming trait, and most women hate it in a man."

"Thanks for everything, Debbie. Wish me luck, and don't call her."

"You're going to need luck and the help of God himself."

****

Alex was met by some angry police officers when he walked in the door. "I thought you were going to take an escort with you."

"I forgot, Sam."

"Sure, Doc. And I was born yesterday."

"Really, Sam? Happy birthday. Now excuse me." Alex headed up the stairs to change. He was going to show her he had something besides a tortoise shell to wear. Within minutes, he was down the stairs and headed for the back door. It was nearing dinner time, so he wasn't surprised to find Rachael at the grill. *Remember, act like nothing's wrong.*

"Hello, do you need any help with dinner?"

Rachael was stunned to look up and see him in blue shorts and a matching tank top. There was no way to hide her reaction. He had really taken her seriously. "You look better. How do you feel?"

"Cooler. Naked, actually."

"You'll get used to it. I'm grilling steaks for the guys, do you want to help me cut up a salad?"

"Sure? What did you do this afternoon besides sit by the pool?"

"I worried about you like everybody else."

"Seriously?"

"Sam was really mad when he found out you'd left. The longer you were gone the more frantic they became. Were you at the mall all afternoon?"

"I needed some time to think about what you'd said and to shop. I tried to replace the purple silk, but someone had already bought all of your size."

"Gee, that's funny. Isn't it?"

"It wasn't you by any chance, was it?"

"It was my favorite."

"Well, I bought all of the red just in case."

Rachael couldn't hold back the laughter. What he had done was so outrageously funny and out of character. When Peter came into the kitchen, both of them were holding their sides laughing uncontrollably. The tears were streaming down Rachael's face, and she caught herself on the counter to keep from falling over.

After catching her breath, she finally tried to talk to him. "Alex, do you know how silly we are. Lori must be having the best laugh of her life."

"So am I."

Peter still had no idea what was so funny. "Are you two going to share the humor?"

"There isn't much to share, Peter. We're both crazy." Rachael admitted which brought another onslaught of giggles.

"Debbie thinks so too." Alex was trying to gain some self control. "I stopped by her house on my way home."

"I know. When I got so worried about where you were, I called her. She told me that you were just pulling into her driveway."

"She didn't tell me you two had talked."

"We didn't exactly talk. I asked 'have you seen?' She answered 'he's in my drive, gotta go,' before I could finish my question. Did she give you any good advice?"

"She told me to stop ripping your clothes off." Again they were sharing amusement that escaped Peter. He watched as they reveled in shared pleasure. "Hey? what have you been drinking all afternoon?"

"Tea, only tea."

"How about something with me now?"

"I'd like that. There's a bottle of champagne just waiting to be opened."

Alex and Rachael finished feeding the officers who were watching over them. When they were done cleaning the kitchen, they took their last glass of champagne and went into Rachael's room. It had become their private den, since it was the only place the officers didn't follow them.

"While we're still on speaking terms, lets call the kids. I hate to call them if we're fighting."

"Rachael, I don't want to fight any more."

"I don't either; but I have the funny feeling that as long as we are living under one roof, we're going to have some huffy disagreements."

"Huffy disagreements are entertaining, especially making up. Fighting is too hard to fix when it's over."

"I agree. No fighting." She held her glass out to toast the covenant.

The kids were fine with Grandma and Grandpa. "I sure do miss them, Alex. We have to get this settled. What day do you need me to stay at the hospital?"

"The surgery is set for early Wednesday morning, so we'll stay over Tuesday night. Is that okay?"

"Yes. I'm going to see Chance and Snickers tomorrow morning for a while, so I won't be in until about noon. I miss my dog, and the two of them are so homesick. Now, what color do you want me to wear tonight?"

"Let's do red tonight. Maybe I'll have more restraint if the gown is my favorite."

After getting ready for bed, Rachael offered to show Alex the pictures she had gotten back from Galveston. They talked and laughed for hours about the funny antics the kids had done on vacation. The children were always a safe topic of conversation.

"Do you have other pictures of the girls handy. I'd like to see what they were like when they were little."

"Sure, some of my picture albums are in the cabinet by the window."

Alex pulled out the three large books of family pictures and returned to the bed. Rachael opened the first book and started pointing out the circumstances around the best ones. The years were mapped out by holidays, birthdays, and various vacations. He was truly impressed and a little jealous by the amount of time and fun the four of them must have shared. He watched the girls grow through dance recitals and soccer, cheerleading and band, and even a variety of boyfriends and school dances.

The pictures taken after Jack's death had not been mounted in the book yet. It was easy to notice the change because he disappeared from the family stories and a sadness filled Rachael's voice.

"The four of you were lucky to have the life you did. It's obvious you all loved each other very much."

"I know I was lucky. Jack was a good husband and father. Look, I hadn't realized it before, but this is the last picture I have with him and the girls. He was just getting ready to leave on his bike, and Allie and I were taking Rorie to soccer practice."

Alex didn't want to hear "and that was the last time that we saw him," so he tried to move the conversation on. "Look at the neat old blue Mustang that's parked down the street. It's a classic." He pointed to an old car in the picture.

"I wonder who it belonged to. I don't remember anybody having a car like that. It's pretty." Rachael appreciated his attempt to lighten the mood. It was still hard for her to reminisce without becoming melancholy.

"Are you going to put Galveston in an album?"

"Yes. And I had doubles made for Mark. I'll let him and the girls do books for us. The girls do a better job of labeling the pictures than I do."

"It's late, Rachael, we'd better get some rest."

"Are you or Pete sleeping in here?"

"It's up to you."

"If you'll sleep on the bed, then I'll take you. If you plan on sleeping on the lounge, then go upstairs. I wouldn't want you operating on my child if you had spent all night in a chair."

"I agree. I'll sleep here." Alex left the room to go change his clothes and lock up the house. By the time he had returned, Rachael's robe was on the chair, and she was asleep on the far edge of the king size bed.

He laid awake for a long time listening to the soft rhythm of her breathing. They had spent a nice evening together without fighting or his destroying another night gown. There was no talk about the future, their feelings, or the past. They had talked only about the kids. Alex wondered if that was enough to build a relationship on.

Rachael had missed the extra warmth that Chance's body had given her during the night, so Alex's body heat was like a magnet to her. Gradually during the course of the night, she moved closer to him. By first light they were wrapped in the comfort of each others arms. Rachael's hair caught Alex in the face when she moved her body slightly closer to him.

The hair tickling his nose caused him to open his eyes. He had his arm draped over Rachael's waist and tried to slowly move it off her and up to his nose. If he didn't get the hair brushed off his face, he was going to sneeze before he had a chance to enjoy the warmth of the woman next to him.

Rachael stirred as he moved his hand, and that was it. Before he could move his hand the short distance, her hair caught him one more time on the tip of his nose, and he let out a sneeze that could have raised the hen house. Rachael sat up instantly looking at him in amazement.

"Alex, I thought you wanted to stay on your own side of the bed. You cheated!"

"Not me, my dear. You're the one on my side."

Rachael flushed as she realized she was definitely the intruder. "I'm sorry. I guess I got cold."

"It's okay with me. I wasn't complaining. In fact, if it hadn't been for your hair in my face, I would've enjoyed you much longer." Alex didn't want to push his good fortune, so he threw back the covers to leave. It was dangerous for them to be so close. He couldn't control his body and that always led to an argument.

Rachael was disappointed he was leaving and watched his long lean legs move away from her under the covers When he threw back the blankets, she was surprised to see he'd slept only in his briefs. Rachael had never seen him quite so naked before, and what a sight to behold. If she'd been warm before, her blood was boiling now. *Stop it! Don't be a fool. Don't let him strip you emotionally again.* Mentally Rachael had packed her emotions back into the little black box for safe keeping and hid it deep inside of her after the fight yesterday morning. She promised herself then she would not open the box for him again.

Alex didn't have to turn around to know she was staring at him. He could feel her burning desires as she looked up and down his tall frame. Without looking back at her, he reached down to pick up his own robe at the foot of the bed. He still couldn't honestly rationalize why he'd slept only in his underwear. Except for the fact that this was how he had always slept even as a kid, he knew he could have worn pants or shorts. Last night, however, it seemed ridiculous to go to bed with pants on. He'd buy some pajamas today and take another cold shower this morning.

"I'll see you at the hospital later?" Rachael was irritated at the sound of her own voice. It reminded her of a teenager's comment after a night with a lover. *Will I see you again?* How disgusting!

"Yes, I have some errands to run around lunch time, so I may not see you until after I finish my rounds. You can wait in my office for me if you want." Finally he had enough control of his body to turn around and look at her.

Her hair was disheveled and the red satin was slightly askew as she kneeled on the huge bed waiting for his response. He had never seen anything look so beautiful, and Debbie's words came back to him. *Kiss her. Make her want you again. What the hell, I could be dead tonight.*

Alex walked back to the bed and pulled her to his chest. Before she could offer any protest, he bent his head forward and kissed her tenderly on the lips. One hand fell to her hips and caressed her lower curves and finally pulled her firmly against his barely covered body.

Rachael couldn't stop her arms from reaching up to his chest. Her desire to run her fingers through the furry covering and up to the glorious black hair on his head obsessed her. As her fingers roamed over his upper body, the kiss intensified. One strong arm held her against his all too firm body while the other traveled up toward her breast.

Regretfully, Alex broke the kiss. They stared into the each others' eyes reading the desires that were shared.

"We have to stop."

"I know." Rachael watched him leave the room before going to take her own cold shower.

****

"Rachael, I didn't expect to find you in here." Rachael looked up from the file she had been working on.

"Hi, Debbie. Alex told me to use his desk if I had some paper work to do. He even cleaned out a couple of drawers for me. I guess he didn't want me to just sit in the cafeteria to wait for him."

"I thought he must be back from lunch since his door was open."

"I saw him in the parking lot with Tom before I came in. He said it would probably be around three when he got back. Do you know what he's up to?" Rachael watched Debbie move across the room and intentionally divert eye contact.

"I know, Rachael, but I can't tell you."

"At least that's better than saying you have no idea. I understand. It's hard to be on both sides. If I need to know, he'll tell me."

Debbie looked curiously at her. There was a melancholy sound to the voice that caused her to worry. "How did things go last night?"

"Okay, he didn't tear any more of my night gowns if that's what you're referring to."

"That's good, isn't it."

"I don't know anymore. What I do understand is why he fights with me."

"Please enlighten me."

"Fighting helps to keep the distance between us. I think he's more afraid of the closeness, and maybe I am too."

"What happened?"

"This morning when he got out of bed..."

"Wait! Start with how he got into bed first, please."

"It was no big deal. I fell asleep before he crawled in. It was either Alex or one of the officers to guard me, so I picked Alex as long as he would use the bed so he could get a good night's sleep. That's all!"

Debbie nodded her head waiting for the rest of the story. "You two could be a soap opera."

"Do you want me to continue or not? By the time he woke up, I was wrapped around him like...like..."

"His lover?"

"I guess. Anyway, when he got out of bed all he had on was his briefs. I was dumbfounded. I had no idea that an almost naked man had been holding me all night."

"You sound disappointed that you weren't able to take advantage of him."

"If I had known, I don't know, maybe at the moment, I would have. Anyway he got up but came back to the bed and kissed me before leaving the room."

Debbie was trying to keep her cool, but inside she was cheering, *Atta boy, Alex!*

"We both ended up taking cold showers. I can't live like this. It's like I'm blindfolded and on a roller coaster. I never know what's coming."

"Is that so bad?"

"It could be tolerable, but what's worse is I'm afraid I've proven myself wrong this morning, at least in Alex's eyes."

"What do you mean?"

"When we argued about getting married the other day, I told him that sex was not the most important part of a relationship. I tried to make him understand we could live without it. I think this morning was his way of showing me I was wrong."

"Are you?"

"I don't know. The act of sexual intercourse is not what makes a marriage. Without the friendship, the emotional bond, there's only sex, no love making. A union based only on sex never lasts, you know that."

"Yes, but is the emotional bond without the intimacy enough?"

"Debbie, there are other ways to satisfy the body."

"Yes, have you told him that?"

"He doesn't believe me."

"Did you show him?"

"Debbie! Of course not!"

"Don't be so shy with me. Jesus, we're grown women, Rachael. All I know is that when he got here this morning, he was happier than I've seen him in days."

"Did he get the test results back?"

"That, I honestly don't know. Rachael, the results could be negative."

"I don't think it matters at this point. I don't see much hope for the two of us one way or another."

"Rachael, do you know why Alex left yesterday afternoon?"

"Just to get away?"

"He was so jealous he couldn't stand himself. If he hadn't left, he would have dragged you in from the pool and put some clothes on you. To hear him talk, it sounded like you were running around the yard in a G string."

"You're kidding? I didn't even know he saw me out by the pool. What was he jealous of? I didn't do anything."

"The thought of any other guy even looking at you without his being able to say 'don't touch; that's mine' made him nuts."

Rachael and Debbie heard the sound of someone running down the hallway. Suddenly Alex ran into the room. "Rachael, I'm glad you're here!"

"What's wrong? What happened?"

As he pulled off his suit coat and threw some papers on his desk he answered, "I was paged, the Anderson girl is bleeding internally. I've got to operate now. Please wait for me here. Peter will be here to stay with you until I'm done." That was all he said before going out the door.

"Well, I guess my fate is sealed. I'm staying here for now." Rachael and Debbie were both staring at the papers Alex had thrown on the desk. The law office logo was at the top of the page, but the rest of the writing was too small to read at a distance.

"Debbie, you know what he's up to don't you?"

"I told you already I did."

"Well, then take those papers and lock them in your office. When he comes back, he'll assume I read them if they're still here."

"Would he be right?"

"I don't know, and he can read me like he has radar these days. Just take them, and then I don't have to worry about it."

"I'll put them in the small safe in my office. If he gets done before I leave, he can come get them."

"Thanks. I'm going to finish my work and check on my students again as long as I'm here. The Anderson girl, is she the one he was supposed to do on Wednesday?"

"I think so, why."

"He was worried about her and his ability to concentrate."

"When Alex walks into the operating room, nothing can disturb his concentration, nothing. That's what makes him a world class doctor, and why I have a dozen calls a day for him from all over the country."

"I had no idea he was that good."

"Yeah, he's that good, and I only hope we can keep him when this is all over."

"Debbie, is that why you are pushing for us to get married? Do you really think I could keep him here for you?"

"Originally, yes. I was being selfish. The hospital needed his talent, and I needed him as an ally to give me credibility. With his reputation, he could make my job easier. Please don't misunderstand, I know Alex would never be a rubber stamp; but we do share similar medical philosophies. Now I just hope he will stay because he wants to. He deserves some happiness. In spite of the negative traits you may see in him, he really is a good man. See you tomorrow."

Rachael was left alone to contemplate the words Debbie had left with her. She knew Alex was a good man. Even when he was angry, he wasn't so bad. She tried to concentrate on the students she was going to see, but her curiosity kept taking her back to the legal papers Alex had thrown on his desk. It was a good thing Debbie had taken them. *If he ever asks again to marry me, I won't let him get away.* That was the last thought on Rachael's mind before she was interrupted. At the sound of the knock, Rachael looked up from the desk and offered the invitation to enter. She was pretty sure it was going to be the mild tempered Peter. These guys had to be very dedicated to their jobs to give up so much time.

"Mrs. Carson, how are you tonight?"

"Hello, Pete. I'm fine. I bet your wife is really tired of your being out at night."

"No, she understands. That's the nature of the beast, if you know what I mean. In this business, spouses are either candidates for sainthood, or you aren't married very long. There really isn't anything in between."

"It's great you have someone at home waiting for you. I have to check on a couple of students. Do you want to come? Then I'll take you down to the cafeteria for a gourmet supper. Alex will probably be quite a while."

"Just lead the way."

Rachael was reading a medical journal when Alex finally came into the room. He looked exhausted but relieved it was over. The sweat stains were clearly visible on the greens he still wore.

"How is she, Alex?"

"I think she'll be all right. I had to remove the ovary, so having children may be difficult if not impossible."

"And her parents?"

"Full of guilt for deciding to wait so long. I told them everybody makes the best call they can at any given moment. It's always easy to see in hind sight what would be right or wrong."

"Do you want to wait for a while and check on her again?"

"I'd like to wait for an hour or so. Do you mind? You can go home with Peter."

"No, I'll wait with you. What happened to cause the internal bleeding?"

"The tumor basically just got too big for her little body."

"Let's go to the cafeteria. You can get something to eat while I get a soda."

"Actually, I hate that food. Will you have a brandy with me here, and I'll have a sandwich at home." Before she could say yes or no, he reached into his bottom drawer and took out two small brandy snifters and a bottle of Hennessy Cognac.

"Wow, Alex, the good stuff."

"If I take the bottle out of this drawer, I want the good stuff. Pete, how 'bout you?"

"Thanks, Sir, but no thanks. Nothing on duty."

"I understand." Alex handed Rachael the small crystal glass and sat down in the leather chair at his desk.

Rachael got up and went around behind him. "Relax for a minute, Alex. Let me rub your neck." Her long limber fingers worked wonders on his sore aching muscles. As she rubbed his upper shoulders, neck, and up into his hairline, Alex looked across his desk. The papers were gone.

"Rachael, the papers I put on my desk when I came in, where are they?"

"I had Debbie put them in her wall safe."

Now he turned the chair around to look at her through perplexed eyes. "Why? They weren't that important."

"I didn't know what they were. All I saw was the legal logo on the top and decided what was on them was none of my business."

"So why didn't you just put them in the drawer."

"Because I was afraid my curiosity would get the best of me, and I would look at them."

"I see. So you hid them more from yourself than anyone else?"

"I guess you could see it that way. I didn't want you to think that I had been snooping in your stuff. If I just put them away, I was afraid you'd automatically assume I had read them whether I did or not."

Peter was still sitting across the room listening very intently to the conversation. It would have been impossible to ignore them, so he might as well enjoy it.

"Peter, would you give us a couple of minutes. We'll be ready to get out of here in about forty-five minutes. I'll bring Rachael to the cafeteria before I go back to the recovery room to check on my patient. Can we meet you there?"

"Sure, Doctor." Disappointed about missing the good stuff, Peter left closing the door behind him.

"Rachael, I have no secrets from you, and I don't want to have any. You can read anything of mine you want. The legal papers were divorce papers and amendments to my will, and there's one copy for you."

Rachael had nothing to say. She just looked into his eyes and finally reached out to run her hand along the side of his face. He loved the feel of her hand on his flesh and closed his eyes for a second to savor the tenderness before pulling her down onto his lap.

"Rachael, listen to me." She shook her head affirmatively. "Promise?"

"I promise."

"I love you. More than I ever thought it possible to love another human being, I love you." She took a breath to confirm his love, but he stopped her. "You promised. I love the way you rub my neck when I'm exhausted, I love the way you worry about my patients, I love the way you love Mark, and the way you make me so angry. With you, I feel alive. Please marry me; good or bad, please think about it."

"Can I talk now?"

"Now," he smiled at her, but was worried about her reaction.

There were no words to express her feelings the way she could with actions, so she reached her hands up around his neck and pulled his head down to meet her lips. The long sensuous kiss left no doubt in his mind about her feelings.

"Is that a yes?"

"Maybe. Let me think about it for a few days."

He knew she was kidding by the smile of her face. "No way. If you tell me now, I'll give you a present."

"All right then, just to put your mind at ease the answer is 'yes.'" With that Alex lifted her up off his lap so he could reach into his pocket. He pulled out a little black box and tried to give it to her. Rachael knew it was a ring, but she still didn't take it out of his hand. Finally Alex opened the box himself, took out the ring, and placed it in her hand.

"My God, Alex, it's beautiful. Where on earth did you find it."

"I'll not give away my secrets, Ma'am. Will you put it on or shall I return it?"

Rachael slid the marvelous diamond onto her finger. It was a perfect fit. "This wasn't necessary."

"Yes, for me it was necessary. Thank you for accepting. Now let's get out of here. I'll take you to wait with Peter until I am done. It'll take me about fifteen minutes."

"I'll be fine."

Alex was even less than the fifteen minutes. He was in a hurry to get home. "Peter, you go and get your car. I'm around in the doctor's parking garage. We'll wait for you there." Alex put his arm around Rachael as they headed for the outside door. He was exhausted and happy.

Alex pushed the door open so Rachael could walk out first. "Are Sam and the other guy still at home waiting for us? What's his name? It's some kind of animal."

"It's not an animal; his name is Noah. Why?"

"That's it. I knew it had something to do with animals. He's so quiet all of the time." Alex reached out to take Rachael's arm after letting the door close, but he froze in his step as the pistol marked a spot in his back.

"Well, Alex, my dear. Are you cheating on me already?" The words were hissed at Alex and Rachael.

"Heather, it's about time you decided to show yourself." Alex didn't know how much he could say to her without getting his head blown off.

"So this is my replacement? Did he tell you, sweetie, that he's married?"

Rachael was afraid to answer her. *Where in the hell is Peter?* was all she could think about.

Without taking the gun away from Alex's backbone, Heather nearly pushed Rachael off her feet. "Answer me, bitch. Did he tell you?"

"Yes, he told me."

"Turn around. I want a closer look at you."

Rachael slowly turned around to face the woman who had been terrifying her and the whole family for several weeks. Her gut desire was to reach over and pull all of the hair out of Heather's head. The two of them met eye to eye and Rachael would not drop her glare any more than Heather would, but Heather had the gun. The evil that looked back at Rachael made her skin crawl. There was no longer a human being in that body, only wickedness.

"Heather, we're not married anymore." That certainly got her attention.

"What in the hell are you talking about. I didn't sign any of those papers John brought over."

"I took care of it today. Annulment papers were signed by a judge this afternoon. As far as the law and I are concerned, you and I were never married."

"At this point, Alex, who gives a fuck. You were never worth dying for anyway. But then I'm going to find out just how far this little pussy will go for you."

"Heather, how did you become so vile?"

She spit the word back at him. "Vile? You ain't seen nothing in life until you spend some time in prison. It's truly an education. Survival of the meanest, if you get my drift."

Then she looked again at Rachael. "Wow! Honey, that's some rock on your hand."

"Alex, dear, you surprise me. Have you done it yet? You know the sex: slam, bam, thank you ma'am?" Heather backed up a couple of steps and instructed Alex to turn around. "Now move four steps away from her."

He had no choice but to do as she demanded. He was surprised by the woman wielding the gun at him. She was nothing like the person he had been married to. The beautiful blond hair had been cut short, left without style and dirty. There were no rosy cheeks or red lips like he remembered. Her skin was pale and gray circles surrounded her eyes.

"I'm really doing you a favor, bitch. He's a terrible lover. You'll want to kill yourself by the time he's done with you." Alex wanted to grab her and virtually ring her neck, but she sensed his desire and waved the gun in his face again. "Do you want to go first? I told you I'd get even with you one day. You watched me lose my lover; now I get to watch you lose yours."

Rachael's gaze had never wavered. Alex was sure her bravado would pique Heather's anger. He hoped by keeping Heather's attention, she wouldn't notice Rachael's glare. *Where in the hell is Peter, or the other security that's supposed to be watching out for us?* During the day, this was a busy place, but after the supper hour, most of the doctors had left the parking garage for the day. Any cars still here belonged to the doctors who'd be spending the night. Alex didn't want to admit the absence of the guard probably meant Heather had been out here long enough to kill him. She seemed fairly confident they wouldn't be bothered by anyone. He was on his own to try and save them.

"Let's play a game shall we. Do you like to play games, bitch? Alex isn't very good at them. He always has his head stuck in somebody's carcass."

Alex was desperate for something, anything that would save them from Heather's wrath. Without moving his head or body, his eyes started gleaning the area for whatever might be useful. He was standing too far away from Rachael to pull her out of the way and too far from Heather to grab the gun without giving her time to shoot. The adrenalin was pumping through his body causing his stomach to do flip flops each time Heather flinched. His hands were so damp with his own fear he doubted he could even hang onto that tire iron. The tire iron! It was hanging from a hook on the wall and within easy reach for him. That was his only option as he heard Heather's voice slither through the air.

"Here are the rules. You do what I say; and, of course, I win. This is how it works. I hold the gun to your head and slowly pull the trigger. We see how long you can stand there eye to eye with me before you blink which means you lose, and I pull the trigger. How long can you last, bitch."

The barrel of the gun was pointed right in the middle of Rachael's forehead. It was a simultaneous motion when Alex reached for the tire iron and heaved it at Heather. His action caused Rachael to blink, and the tire iron hit Heather's chest as she finished the squeeze of the trigger.

Rachael dropped to the ground with her hand on her shoulder. Alex didn't even see her as he jumped on Heather to keep her from waving the pistol in his direction. He tried to wrench the weapon out of her grip, but couldn't do it. They wrestled for control, but she was so strong. He couldn't direct the aim away from..."BANG!"

Rachael had heard the gun shot but was afraid to roll over. If Alex was dead, then Heather was sure to be coming her direction. She had to think. The kids, all three of them needed her to live. Control, she had to control the fear. Wait...Wait...Now! Rachael swung the bowling ball size purse she had been carrying with all of her strength at the person standing over her.

Alex, in his own state of exhaustion, caught the full force of the bag in the chest almost knocking him over. "Rachael! It's me. She's dead."

"Alex, thank God. I was so afraid she'd shot you."

"Shit, if it wasn't her trying to kill me, it could've been you. What do you carry in that saddle bag anyway, bricks? I don't think I'll ever breath the same again." He reached down and pulled her up into his arms holding her close to his chest.

"See, you even make jokes now at the most inopportune time. Is she dead?"

"Yes, she wouldn't let go. The shot caught her in the chest."

Alex and Rachael heard the foot steps running toward them. "Doctor, are you okay? What happened?"

"Peter, where were you?"

"My car has four slashed tires. I had to run through the whole garage looking for you. I found Dick, the officer on duty tonight, with a king size lump on his head; but he'll be fine. Is that her, Doctor?"

"Yes, Pete. It looks like the worst is over. Rachael was shot in the shoulder. We need to get her inside so I can take a good look at her though."

"Mrs. Carson, you okay?" Peter's concern was genuine as he questioned her. "You get her inside, Doc. I'll take care of things out here. I already called for assistance on Dick's radio, and Archer will be here in a few minutes. I'll tell him you're inside since he'll need a statement from you."

"Sure. Tell him we're in the emergency room."

As the shock of the episode started to wear off, the pain set in. Rachael grimaced every time she took a step, and the blood was starting to soak through her jacket. Her breathing became more shallow until she finally stopped walking.

Alex looked down to see a paste white face staring painfully up at him. "Alex, I..." Rachael fainted in his arms. He should have carried her to begin with or at least slowed his pace. Alex was pretty sure it was only a flesh wound, but it'd still hurt like hell. When he entered the ER, several staff people offered to help.

The smelling salts brought Rachael around quickly. Alex helped her get her jacket and blouse off. "It's not bad Rachael. I'm going to clean the wound, bandage it, and give you some pain killers. Then I'm going to take you home and tuck you into bed."

"It's over, Alex."

"Almost, Archer will be running in here any minute for our statements, and I want you dressed before he gets here so sit still." Alex, with the help of two hovering nurses, cleaned up the wound. Alex sent a nurse to his office to get one of his clean shirts he always kept on hand.

"Rachael, here's a shirt for you."

"Thanks, is Archer here yet? I'd really like to get this over. I'm exhausted. Alex, did you call Debbie. We should tell her what happened."

"I'll do it right now, and I see Archer coming down the hall."

"Mrs. Carson, how are you doing? Peter told me you were hurt."

"It's nothing, just a flesh wound. I'll be fine. Did you see the body?"

"Yes, you're both lucky to be alive. She was determined to kill both of you."

"Yeah, that was certainly clear to us."

"Did she say anything? Give you any information at all?"

"What do you mean?"

"Like where she's been all this time, and why she killed the officers, and where's my dog?"

"Sorry, Detective. We weren't exactly in the position to do an interview."

Alex returned to the conversation after talking to Debbie. "She's glad it's all over. Now what do you need to know, Archer? The woman tried to kill us. She's the only one who had the motive."

"I suppose you're right. Just tell me what happened tonight point by point."

It took almost a half hour longer for Archer to get the information he wanted before letting them go home. "Well, I guess it's over for you two. I'll need to talk to you again though."

"I'm sure all of your men will be glad to get home for the night. Have you told them yet?"

"Peter went to the house to get Sam and Noah. They have to fill out their own paper work before they can go home, but at least they'll get there eventually."

"How about the guy who got hit on the head?"

"He was already released from the ER. Now you two should get going. I'm sure you'll be glad to have your privacy back."

Alex didn't wait another second to get Rachael out of there. The pain killers would have her asleep in no time, and he really wanted to get her home. Thank God it was a short drive.

Rachael was pretty groggy by the time they got home, so Alex took her straight to her bedroom and got her undressed. Since he was doing the dressing, he chose the red satin and then gently tucked her into bed.

Alex went to the kitchen to satisfy his hunger. Something Archer had implied about the whole affair was beginning to bother him. The lack of information tying Heather to all of the terrifying things over the last few weeks all culminated in the strange feeling Alex had that tonight was the first time Heather had seen Rachael. She never did call Rachael by name, only by some derogatory label. *It had to have been her. Who else wanted to kill them? Stop letting your mind wander. You've been looking over your shoulder for so long you're perpetuating the fear.*

Alex went back upstairs to his own room for the night. He had no right to assume the spot next to Rachael was open now that this mess was over. Maybe that was why he felt rather solemn; maybe he didn't really want all of this to end because it took away their reason for being tied together. Rachael's agreement to marry him was not exactly made under duress, but then again it was not made under the most desirable circumstances.

****

Alex was up at the first hint of sun. Sleep had eluded him most of the night. The scene with Heather had replayed itself continuously like an old record with a scratch on it. She was so different, so malignant. He may have neglected her some over the years, but there was no way he had caused such a destructive change in her. No matter how hard Alex tried to convince himself that he was not at fault, the guilt did not cease.

Rachael was still sound asleep when he went in to check her shoulder. "Rachael." He didn't want to startle her, so he spoke softly at first. It finally took a good firm, "Rachael!" to bring her out of the deep sleep.

"Alex? What's wrong?"

"Nothing's wrong. I just couldn't get you to wake up."

"Was I dreaming again?"

"I don't think so. Were you?" He thought it was odd that she couldn't tell if she'd been dreaming or not.

After a moment she answered, "No, I don't think so. I was so tired." When she tried to move the reality of the night before came painfully back to her. She winced at the discomfort and tried to pull herself up with her good arm. "Did you by any chance bring me a cup of coffee?"

"Yes, ma'am. It's on the dresser with some breakfast and a pain killer. First, I want to see your shoulder."

Rachael hadn't realized until then that she was wearing the red satin Alex liked best. She knew she had not dressed herself last night and looked at him with questioning eyes. Only one arm was through the gown, so she would have to take the whole thing off for him to do his check.

"You did this on purpose, didn't you?"

"Did what?" Alex was truly innocent. He had no ulterior motive last night; however, this morning he was pleased with his choice of garments.

"Don't play the fool with me, doctor, only you would've picked the satin."

"I am guilty of the red satin, but not of premeditated planning, although I wish I could take so much credit."

Rachael tried to get out of bed, but Alex stopped her. "Where are you going?"

"Alex, unless you are going to rip this off of me, I have to get up and put on a robe. Then you can check all you want."

"Let me help you." He pulled the blankets back and gave her an extra lift to stand up. "Most of your strength will be back to normal by tomorrow, so just rest today and enjoy the peace and quiet."

From the bathroom he heard, "Alex, I really don't like taking the pain pills. They make me so dizzy and weak." It took a few minutes to work the gown up and over her head, but persistence won out. The red robe she pulled off the hanger was much easier to get on.

"Do I have to take them?"

Alex watched her walk back into the room. He didn't enjoy the robe nearly as much as the night gown, but it would have to do. "One more won't hurt you. The less you move around for a day or so the better off you'll be. By tomorrow the healing process will have had a good start, and you'll feel much better. Now get back in bed."

Rachael crawled back onto the big bed and waited for the handsome doctor to examine her. His hands were gentle and warm. She had hoped he'd be a little less professional, but his only concern now was for her welfare. Little did she know that while his hands seemed to be doing their job, his eyes were enjoying the view.

"Alex?"

"Yes?"

Rachael looked at the ring on her finger and then up into his eyes. "Is it all over?"

He wasn't sure about the question. It sounded simple enough, but there was more emotion to the words than the simple meaning indicated. "Is what over?"

"Heather's dead. That much I know is done. She cannot hurt us anymore. We can bring the kids home?"

"Yes, I called your mother this morning and asked her to make the arrangements. She said she wasn't ready for them to leave, but she understood how much we missed them."

"That sounds like her. She never wants them to leave. What else did you tell her?"

"I didn't tell her or the children anything except that Heather had been shot. Did you want me to tell them more?"

"No. I'm glad you didn't tell them I was hurt. It would have caused to much worry for nothing."

"What else is on your mind? I can tell you're beating around the bush. Just tell me."

With the deep breath, Rachael forged on with the burning question. "Now that Heather's dead, do you want your ring back? We don't have to play act anymore."

Alex was slightly stunned that she even asked and insulted as well. He pulled her robe up over her shoulder and tucked the blankets in around her before bringing the breakfast tray over to her. "Here, your coffee will get cold if you don't drink it."

Alex sat down on the bed beside her so he could look into her eyes. "I know sometimes it's been hard to know where the acting stopped and real feelings picked up; but just in case you couldn't tell, I was not acting last night when I asked you to marry me. I love you. I love you enough to let you out of the relationship if you are having doubts."

"Alex, I just wanted to know for sure. You didn't sleep here last night, so I was afraid you were having your own doubts about the future."

"There are doubts; that's for sure. None of my doubts, however, are about my feelings for you. I didn't sleep with you because that spot isn't officially mine yet."

"So when will it be yours?"

"As soon as you can arrange it. Okay?"

"Did you really have your marriage to Heather annulled?"

"Yes. That's what you would've read about on the legal papers you had Debbie hide from you. I told Tom I didn't care how he did it, but I had to be free from her immediately."

"How about Sunday?"

"Let's wait for the test results to come back before we set a time or tell the kids."

"Why? Do you think that will make a difference."

"Yes, I do. If the results happen to be negative, we're going to have one hell of a party." Alex leaned over to kiss his bride to be and then got up off the bed. "I have to get to the hospital. Do you promise to rest?"

"Yes, have you called about the Anderson girl?"

"She's doing fine, but I want to see her myself. Then I have to meet Archer and give him a positive ID on Heather. I'll try to be home early, so I can make dinner for us."

"Now that's a scary thought. I'll probably need more of those pain killers."

"Be nice or I'll make hotdogs." He left the room feeling better than he had in years.

Alex was literally burying his past and could look forward to the future even though it may be bittersweet. Rachael, bless her heart, was willing to risk sharing with him a life that could be filled with pain and sorrow. He vowed to live and love every minute he had left. All of those years he had his head buried in the operating room would now come full circle, and he would make up for the fun and family he'd missed. After all, it was dying that made living and loving so special. Now he understood he could live ten years or ten days and not be sorry because he had learned how to enjoy every second of the life God gave him.

Rachael ate the breakfast Alex had brought her but didn't take the pain pill. She didn't want to vegetate in bed all day. The house was empty and belonged to her again, so she was going to enjoy it. The pain was not so bad that she couldn't walk to the patio and enjoy the hummingbirds at the feeder. With all of the commotion the last week, she had not had the time to see if any of the tiny, graceful creatures were around. The peace and the sun would do more for her than any pill.

It was early afternoon before Alex had finished his work at the hospital. He needed to stop at the medical clinic on his way to the police station. The report he had been waiting for would be in a sealed envelope and ready for pick up at one o'clock today. The anxiety and fear centered around this one test was greater than all of the fear Alex experienced waiting for Heather to kill him. Heather he could fight, but this disease had no rival; it always won.

Alex put the envelope in his coat pocket. He didn't have the courage to look right now. Archer was waiting for him to help tie up the loose ends around the shooting last night. Reading the results would have to wait until he had some privacy to deal with it.

"Alex, I'm glad to see you. How's Mrs. Carson this afternoon?"

"She's doing better. Of course, she won't take the pain pills I gave her. God, she can be so stubborn."

"Really? I hadn't notice." Archer, glad to see someone else the victim of her stubbornness, tried not to let his smile seem to obvious.

"Let's get the positive ID out of the way, and then I have some questions for you." As usual, Archer couldn't wait to start the interrogation. He went over everything Rachael and Alex had told him the night before. It all made perfect sense to Alex, but Archer kept pushing. So, by the time they had returned to Archer's desk, Alex was frustrated with him.

"Ya know, Doctor, something just doesn't add up."

"You mean you have a gut feeling?"

"You know I put my faith in the facts not gut feelings; but when the facts aren't in the right spot, my gut does act up. There are too many questions left unanswered. Too many discrepancies."

"Can you be more specific?"

"First, how did we keep missing her all this time? She wasn't wearing any disguise when we found her, so had she ever worn one? We checked and double checked everyone around the house and the hospital. Two, if she killed the two guards at your place, why didn't she kill the one at the hospital last night? Three, the gun that killed the two police officers is not the same one she was carrying when she tried to kill you. Bad guys don't usually change weapons unless there's a good reason. And last, Mrs. Carson was sure that whatever was going to happen, was going to take place in her bedroom."

"I thought you didn't believe in her intuition."

"Not usually, but in this case she was right often enough to give me some doubt."

"So what are you saying, Archer?"

"I'm not saying anything. I'm asking, can you think of anything Mrs. Carson has told you about herself that indicates any past violence, any reason someone may want her dead?"

"No, nothing except that her husband was killed in a hit and run a couple of years ago."

"Com'on. There must be a file. Let's see what's in it." Archer went to a file cabinet and opened the appropriate drawer. "C...Carson...here it is. Hum.....".

Alex waited for Archer to peruse the information on the page. "He was hit by a blue car. Does she know anyone with a blue car?"

"Not that I know of. Mark and I have spent a lot of time with Rachael and the girls in the last couple of months, and I've never seen a blue car around."

"What about the girls? Do you recall either of them saying anything about some old boyfriend who wanted revenge?"

"Oh, shit. There was a blue car." As Alex's mind had raced through the pictures trying to retrace the lives of each daughter, he remembered the car. "In one of Rachael's photo albums there was a picture of an old blue Mustang."

"What makes you think it's important?"

"The picture was taken just before her husband left for his last bike ride. The car was parked down the street."

"So have you seen the Mustang?"

"No."

"Cars can be painted, ya know. Anyone around driving a Mustang."

"Oh, my God." Alex was standing, pacing the room. He made the nervous gesture of running his fingers through his hair. "The kid who did all of Rachael's yard work drives a red Mustang."

"I know who you're talking about. We all knew he did the yard work, so he had easy access to the house. No one stopped him from coming and going as he pleased. Anything else about him special?"

"Oh, yeah! He was terribly jealous of me. If looks could kill, I'd be history. And the dog, Chance. Rachael's dog went nuts with rage every time the guy came to the door. Shit! How could I have been so stupid? I read her journal, but never put it all together."

"What? What journal?"

"Rachael has been having reoccurring nightmares ever since her husband's death. The man at her front door terrifies her, but he never gets in. It was Chance. In her subconscious, the dog always kept the bad guy out just like he always kept Mathew out."

"Chance was hit by a car, right?"

"Yeah, a small sports car. We just assumed it was Heather. Now, oh, Jesus, we have to call her. There's no dog to keep the bad guy out, and she's home alone."

Immediately, Archer reached for the phone and dialed. "The line's dead. Let's go." Archer was on his feet racing out the door with Alex on his heels. "Taylor, get me as much back-up as you can muster at the Carson house. Now!" The man sitting listlessly at a corner desk jumped at Archer's command.

****

After some time soaking up the healing power of the sun, Rachael prepared her hot tub with plenty of bubbles and scented candles. Her shoulder was throbbing continuously and bed sounded better every minute. She washed her body as quickly as she could, and with careful maneuvering over her arm, she eventually let the red satin gown glide down her silky skin. By noon she had crawled back into bed and fallen into a restless sleep.

There was no noise to wake her, no door chimes, no phone ring, only the feeling of being watched. Rachael got out of bed and paced the room. She did not understand her fear. The doors were locked, the alarm was set and Heather was dead. What more could she ask for? Still the hair on the back of her neck was on end. The fear. Like in her dreams. The fear. Something was wrong. She'd been dealing with the nightmares for months, and yet what happened last night did nothing to put the dream to rest. That part of her life was not over yet.

Rachael walked over to the table where she kept her journal and pulled it out. With pen in hand, she crawled back into bed and began to read. The clues were there. Then she got up to get out the family album. The last pictures of Jack had reminded her of something. Quickly she flipped through the pages, but there was nothing until she found the one of the blue car. Rachael had completely forgotten the blue car that had so often been parked in her driveway; but the day of the accident, it was parked half way down the street. She knew the car belonged to Mathew, but why had he parked so far away. *Remember! What happened that day. Was he even here?*

Rachael got up and walked the length of the room again. Something must have happened that was blocked out by the accident. Little by little the pieces fell together. She and Mathew had been studying in the morning while Jack and the girls were gone to the store. Mathew made a clumsy attempt to profess some deep feeling for her, and she had answered it with "I'm happily married, Mathew. A nice girl your own age will come along." That was all there was to it, or so it seemed. There was never any proof Mathew had done anything wrong. After all, he did come over and help her keep up the house. Now she wondered why. Guilt? Or was he hoping to endear himself to her?

The dream? How did the dream play into this? It changed when Alex came and Mathew made it very clear he was jealous. As Rachael had become closer to Mark and Alex, the dream intensified along with Mathew's anger. In the beginning, the evil stranger stayed at the door. Why? Now he was coming into her bedroom to kill her. His smooth glistening chest was always over her; the chest she had seen before. "It's Mathew's chest. When I was close to him the day Alex came over, I saw the same chest that hovers over me in the dream. Mathew had easy accessibility to the house when we were gone and even when the police were here. Nobody would have expected him."

Rachael reached for the phone, but there was no dial tone; the line was dead. She had to trip the alarm system; but before she could get out of the bed, Mathew walked into the room dressed only in his jeans.

Rachael nearly jumped out of her skin. "Mathew! You scared the day lights out of me. How did you get in here? The alarm is set."

"It still is set as far as the company is concerned. It was a simple bypass, Rachael." She didn't like the dirty way her name slid off his tongue. "I learned the technique in class and perfected it while you were gone on vacation."

"So, you were the one in the house all along. But the window, we thought you came in through the window."

"That was only a diversion. When you found the broken window seal, I knew my time of getting in and out of the house was limited. Eventually, that stupid guy from the alarm company would have seen the slices in the cable."

"Why did you kill the guards?"

"They found me coming around the house that night. Most of the time I could come and go as I wanted to. The fools were used to seeing me during the day, so it was no big deal, but that night things were pretty intense. When they decided to call you for confirmation of my work, it was easier to get rid of them than try to explain."

"You killed Jack, didn't you?"

"You finally figured that out, too. I really had you fooled. If it wasn't for that damn doctor friend of yours, we could've gotten serious eventually."

"Mathew, you know I never gave you any hope of a relationship between us. You didn't even come into the house."

"I didn't come in because of that man eating dog. I should've killed him a long time ago." The anger was starting to fester in his eyes again. "He's dead, isn't he?"

She didn't know whether to lie or not. "It was you who killed my dog?" She tried to manifest her own anger in tears to buy some time. "What about Ginger, the other dog? What did you do to her?"

"Really, Rachael. You should've learned your lesson the first time." He pulled a small pistol out of his faded denim jeans and pointed it at her. "A single quick pop between the eyes was all it took. She dropped like a rock."

Rachael felt sick to her stomach. The poor innocent dog was dead because of her. "What did you do with her?"

"Jesus, Rachael, you don't cook much do you?"

"What are you talking about?"

"Well, I couldn't exactly walk out the front door with her now could I. She's in your freezer in the garage."

Rachael put her hand over her mouth in an attempt to keep her stomach down. He repulsed her as he walked closer. Time. She needed time. "Didn't you wonder why all of the police were around?"

"Stop stalling me, Rachael. That whole deal with the doctor's wife played right into my plans. With all of you blaming her, I could keep on ticking, if you get my drift."

His smooth glistening chest was hovering over her now, and she tried to roll off the bed, but the soreness in her shoulder impeded her movement. Mathew grabbed her arm and forced her back down on the bed. As he yanked both arms over her head, the scream of pain could not be stopped. Blood from the opened wound trickled down her neck.

"What's this, Rachael? Is the doctor being a little rough these days? Or did his little wife get jealous last night?"

Rachael offered no answers. It was obvious that he already knew what had happened. He had been watching everything. "How do you know?"

"I watched, followed, listened. It was easy. Besides, my grandparents live just a few houses down; and with binoculars, I can see everything in your back yard right down to how many ice cubes are in your tea."

"You son-of-a-bitch."

"Now that's not nice talk from a lady. But then you aren't a lady are you? You can sleep around with your doctor, but you wouldn't give me the time of day." He bellowed at her. "Well, fuck you, Rachael Carson. My, my, that sounds like a good idea."

Rachael tried again to get away from him, but the pain in her upper body sucked all of the strength out of her. He was towering over her now just like in the nightmares. Slowly he lowered his face until his breath mixed with her own. Instead of forcing his lips on hers, he leaned over and licked the blood off her shoulder. Rachael's stomach heaved at his touch.

"Not a good reaction, Rachael. You have to show more appreciation than that. You aren't going to spoil my fun. This has been a long time coming, and I plan to enjoy it while dear Alex and his police buddy talk about business downtown."

Rachael was consumed with desperation. She was on her own and at his mercy as he pulled her up off the bed. He took a thin piece of cord out of his pocket, wrapped it around her wrists and then tied it up to the ceiling fan. He pulled her up so she was standing precariously on her toes.

"Now don't wiggle, Rachael. That ceiling fan isn't very strong, and it will crash down on your head." The blood from her opened wound was now running down her waist. "Now let's see if we can't clean you up a little bit." He reached up to the bloody shoulder, grabbed her gown and ripped it open to the waist exposing her left breast. The blood soaked bandage was yanked off her skin and dropped to the floor.

"There that's better; the fresh air will be good for it. Now, let me clean it for you." Again with his tongue, he licked up her waist and around the open sore. "It isn't a very creative opening, is it? Let's see if we can do better than that."

Rachael had closed her eyes to try and block out the disgusting closeness of his body, but his suggestion caused an immediate reaction. "That got you to open those eyes. Keep them open." He demanded.

"I'm sure you'll want to watch this." Mathew pulled a small knife out of his pocket.

"Mathew, what do you want from me?"

"Just respect, my dear." He opened the knife and ran his finger over the blade. "You were so easy to predict; right down to sending the kids away. Let's see, I bet you sent them to your mother. I wanted to get you all alone, and here we are. Really, I thought you'd be smarter, but then you never did respect my talents. I was always the dummy in your eyes. Well, what do you think now? Your smart Jack and smart Alex are not here to save you. You're just going to have to let smart little me have a turn at you."

Rachael decided letting her anger flare was the only way to save what little self respect she could summon, considering the position she was in. "Why did you have to kill Jack? He never hurt you."

"My wrath wasn't for him; it was for you. You were the one I wanted to punish. Jack was so surprised. He knew it was me in the car. I even waved at him just before I hit the accelerator."

Images of Jack filled Rachael's aching mind. It was her fault he was dead.

"Now, you will get to wait for your wonderful doctor to show up so I can punish you again."

"No, Mathew. You have me to work your will on, leave Alex out of this. We were together because his wife was stalking us. That's all. We were only friends."

"Rachael, Rachael, now you're lying to me. Remember, I've watched you when you didn't think anyone was watching. I've seen you on the patio holding hands. I've seen you at the mall buying panties and bras. It was so sweet. Did you buy this that day?" He sliced the satin with the knife to demonstrate it's ability. "I'm sorry, but the rock on your hand is a little to convincing for just play acting."

"Really, Mathew, we were trying to make Heather angry so she would make a mistake."

"Wrong again, Rachael. You wanted me to make the mistake. You wanted to make Me angry, but I didn't make any mistakes, did I? Heather was just a convenient cover for me." Mathew was still so close to her she could feel the heat coming off his body. He lifted the little knife up to her face. "Cute, isn't it. Kind of like a scalpel. I've been practicing on grapefruit. I guessed that would be about the right size." He lifted his hand to cup the exposed breast. Rachael tried to pull away from his touch, but there was nowhere to go. Any movement pulled on the unsteady ceiling fan.

"Oooh, feels like I was right." He fondled her breast waiting for her to flinch under the touch. He could tell by the repulsed look on her face she hated being touched. That was enough to encourage him.

Rachael was trying to think of anything that might give her more time before he started wielding the knife again, but there wasn't much left to talk about.

"I think a pretty 'M' is just what you need etched into that nice ripe breast of yours. It will remind you of who had the most power in your life every time you look in the mirror."

Again she pulled herself slightly away, but falling paint chips and plaster from the ceiling reminded her of the spinning fan just inches from her head.

He grabbed her by the nipple nearly squeezing it off. "Now, Rachael, you don't want to move. I have no idea how good I am on human flesh. You don't want me to slip. You can scream. Yeah, I'd like that. Com'on now. Give me a good scream."

Rachael didn't make a sound. She held his hateful glare with every bite of animosity she could send through her eyes. She wouldn't give him the satisfaction of hearing her yell. Mathew poked her nipple drawing blood, but she held herself in check.

"So you think you're tough? We'll see how long you can hold that tongue of yours." He firmly grasped her skin in his hand and ever so slowly began carving his initial in her flesh.

Rachael clinched her teeth together to stop the screams of pain from escaping. *I will not! No! No! You son-of-a-bitch.* She could feel the blood dripping onto her toes and still there was no sound.

Mathew stopped his carving and looked into her face. "I give you credit, my dear. I didn't think you were quite so stubborn. However, you can't hold your breath forever. Let's see if this will help to motivate you."

She had to take a breath and slowly tried to inhale. Control. She had to maintain control; but when Mathew lifted up what was left of her gown and began running his fingers back and forth through her pubic hairs touching her most private area, control was replaced by tears of humiliation. She would have rather had him continue the carving.

"Tears? Really, Rachael. I expected something a little more feisty from you."

"You God Damn Son-Of-A-Bitch! You'll pay for this. Alex will kill you for this."

"Now that's better. He'll probably try, but I'll be waiting for him. Actually, I'm looking forward to his finally showing up. Now let me clean the blood off of you so I can finish my inscription." Again he licked the blood off her skin and then raised the knife to finish his work.

Rachael did react to the crashing of the front door. Alex came around the corner of her bedroom before Mathew could retrieve his pistol out of his belt. The two men faced off with the small knife between them. This time she wanted to dish out the winning blow.

To satisfy her own anger, Rachael yelled, "Mathew!" When he turned to face her, she used all the strength she could channel through her leg kicking him in the groin. Mathew dropped to the floor giving Alex the necessary seconds to grab the knife and the gun.

Archer and several other officers came into the room just in time to see the heave - ho kick and Mathew's eyes nearly pop out of his head. It was obvious that Mrs. Carson had some torture of her own to dish out.

The ceiling fan didn't come completely off the ceiling, but another second and it would be wrapped around Rachael's neck. Alex used the knife to cut her free. "Well, that's another of my favorite night gowns shot to hell."

She smiled up at him as he picked her up and carried her off to the bathroom. Archer could deal with Mathew while Alex took care of his bride-to-be. "Are you okay?"

"I am now. How did you know?"

"Archer and I figured it out at the station. When I called and got no ring, I knew you were in trouble. Did he...hurt you any where else?"

"No. This is bad enough. He wanted to carve an 'M' in me for posterity. Thank God, he didn't get a chance to finish. I don't know if I could have lasted much longer. Will I have a scar there?"

Alex had been cleaning up both wounds and trying to assess the damage. "Not much. If anything, it will look like an 'A' for Alex."

"That's not funny. But it's better than an 'M' for Mathew."

"I certainly agree. I'll pull the bandage tight, and you shouldn't see much of a mark at all. I'll have to look real close, and nobody else will have reason to look. Right?"

"Absolutely, Doctor."

"Now let's get you out of this room while Archer goes over it again. You know how he is."

"Mathew killed Jack."

"We know. He'll get what he deserves now. It's over this time, Rachael. Really over."

"Do we still get married on Sunday?"

"Yes, Sunday it is."

"Do we have a party?"

"That I don't know. I picked up the results but haven't had the courage to look at them yet."

"Are you going to?"

Alex took the envelope out of his pocket and handed it to Rachael. "This is more terrifying for me than waiting for Heather to show up."

"I understand. You know I love you no matter what the result is."

"That's the only thing that makes this tolerable. Open it."

Rachael took out the paper reading it to herself then she handed it to Alex. "Oh, Rachael, I can't believe it. Negative. It's negative.

Alex scooped Rachael up in his arms and twirled her around the room. "We're going to have a hell of a party: tonight, Sunday, and for the rest of our lives."

****

Rachael and Alex waited arm in arm for the plane to arrive. They were anxious to see the kids' reaction to the upcoming marriage.

"Do you think they'll be surprised, Alex?"

"I'm sure they'll think it's about time we got our act together. They've been waiting for this since Easter Sunday."

"Mark will be surprised his bedroom set is already moved over to his new room."

"Yes, and I'll be glad to give up my twin bed. Do you think Allison and Rorie will be upset about moving?"

"Not after they see what you're building for them. There they are."

The greetings were warm and loving. Mark had a big hug and kiss for Rachael, which made her feel especially good.

"How are the dogs. I miss Snickers."

"They're both at home waiting to see you. Chance is up walking around already. He was so glad to leave the clinic."

Alex's arm was wrapped around Rachael which did not go undetected by any of the three kids. They wanted to ask what was going on, but were afraid to push what they remembered as an ambiguous relationship. Alex turned around to see why the questions had stopped coming. Rorie, Allison, and Mark were all smiling and looking at their parents walking in front of them.

"So what do you three want to do on Sunday? Any plans? We were thinking a picnic would be nice."

"Dad, I'd really like to go swimming in our pool and play with my dog. Grandma has me picnicked out."

"Well how about a wedding then?"

It took a second or two for the meaning of the question to register in their minds before the excitement exploded.

"Really, Dad? You two are getting married?"

"If you agree."

"We agree! We agree!"

"Then Sunday it is." The five family members strolled out of the airport looking forward to what the future had to offer.